VOLUMN **4** WATCHER

HELLRAISERS & HEARTBREAKERS

WATCHER
OF THE
DAMNED

BY R.H. SNOW

Rosa De Oro. A Texas Publishing Company.

DEDICATED TO THE TREASURES OF MY HEART:

God my Father, David my Love, Roxanne my Heart, Danny my Soul
— and Texas, my Texas!
We Will Be Free!

Dear Reader,

Is survival or the treatment of the people around us more important? Many argue that is what makes us human, yet both have played that role in the history of our species.

Hellraisers & Heartbreakers is the fourth in the Watcher of the Damned series, encapsulating the struggles of human life after the biological apocalypse. Post-apocalyptic source material, like graphic novels, video games, shows, and other books, have inspired the series, which deals with mutlifaceted divisions along biological, societal, moral, and religious lines. Though some have argued that the cultural fascination with mutants and the apocalypse is indicative of an overall fear of globalization, the fear is not that we could become an animal with lesser humanity; rather, that we already are.

Thank you for picking up the book, and enjoy.

Arthur DeVitalis

Table of Contents

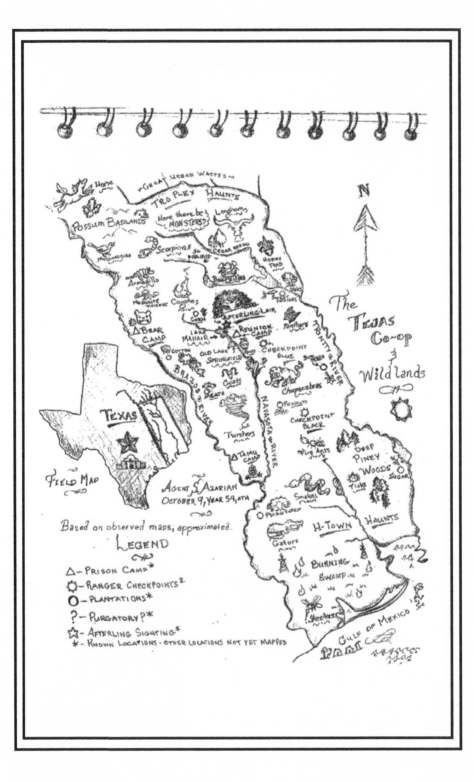

I

Rose's nightmare started the way it always did:

Jarrod was making love to her in the Garden, under the flowering blue clematis vine; the starry flowers dangled down from the skylight to brush her bare arm. For once it seemed as if Jarrod actually loved her, almost. His leonine face loomed above her; her legs tightly wound around his hips, heels dug into his thighs, she gazed into his blue-gray eyes and reached up to stroke the curly, golden-brown hairs on his broad chest.

He thrust, and she was filled with ecstasy; he thrust again, and she was filled with Child—

Then he thrust again, and she was filled with pain as his manhood transformed into a knife. The Garden became a small, white-walled room, and their bed became an operating table. The dangling flowered vine was now an IV, and her arms were strapped down so she couldn't pull it out. She tried to scream but couldn't, and he plunged his knife into her over and over again. Blood everywhere, the Baby came out in pieces with every thrust, one little leg, then another—

Now Jarrod was reaching in with his rubber-gloved hand to pull out the rest of the Baby, her perfect tiny mouth open, moving silently; the hope of a thousand Asura, the treasure of her mother's heart—

A wail of agony welled up from inside her and spilled out of her soul.

Sparks... then ripples spread across a patch of wall on the opposite side of the room, pixelating and disrupting the porcelain tiles. Soft light pierced the gloom and the rest of the dream faded. Against the light, a man in a black oilskin hat and too-large, long black coat coalesced before a glimmering portal.

His clothes belonged to the Watcher, but his face and form belonged to someone else entirely—medium tall, with an athletic, lean build; ruddy complexion, aquiline features, and straight ash-brown hair that brushed the rose-print shawl tucked under his collar. A blocky, chiseled jawline with a short beard framed a thin mouth. Only the deep-set brown eyes seemed familiar.

"You are safe now." It was the Watcher's voice, matter-of-fact and dry, yet oddly reassuring. "You are with me." His hands, long-fingered and slender, seemed almost sensitive; they fiddled with his WeSpeex Ring.

He seemed more real than her dream but detached from his surroundings. Making no move towards her, the young man stood near the portal. Jarrod suddenly vanished, banished from the room along with his instruments of torture. Only the afterimage of the Child lingered, suspended in mid-air, decaying to a nebulous shadow.

Suddenly self-conscious, Rose tried to cover herself with the white sheet, but it crumbled to papery shreds in her hands. Distressed at the Watcher's intrusion into her nightmare, she swept her hip-length hair to the front, draping curled ebony tresses across her body to hide her bloody nakedness.

"Why are you here?" she asked, afraid of his answer.

"Because I am."

His brusque declaration was jarring. Tucking her trembling legs beneath her, she peered at him, unsure of his intent. "But why do you come?"

"Because I do." From across the hazy room, he looked down at her. "Think of me as your Guardian Angel—your Watcher from on High."

Rose glanced at him suspiciously. "You don't look like an angel..."

A thin smile slipped across his lips. "That can be arranged." A white glow spread behind him, unfurling into a pair of massive, feathered wings—

Rose awoke with a jolt to find herself still in the saddle. High overhead, the waning moon glinted through a gloomy spiderweb of twiggy ash branches, and far below her, she heard the soft crush of horse's hooves brushing between clumps of fescue grass. Longings for home and memories of love mingled with terror of abuse, created a glitch in her reality. *I'm not in Tesoro anymore; but where am I?* Disoriented, she reached down to feel the Watcher's plated arm wrapped around her waist.

Oh, yes, I'm escaping death. It all came rushing back in a tumble of confused images: an invisible flying machine, faceless armored men, and the horrible hum of the Super-Heating Internal Volatility Activator—the SHIVA device. Her mind trailed her journey back through the fearsome Texas WildLands to retrace the events leading to that encounter, and a sinking dread gripped Rose. Waking life wasn't much better than the nightmare. Jarrod's rejection, Angelina's abortion, and Rose's banishment from Tesoro lurched through the fog of sleep once more, haunting Rose with the memory of her brother's gruesome death from the SHIVA heat ray—

Then shame at her broken Taboo with this Devil and guilt over their subsequent missed conception threatened to overwhelm her. *It's all too much...*

She thought back on all her pregnancies and all the heartaches she had experienced when they were miscarried—or in Angelina's case, forcibly aborted. Jarrod had never comforted her when she lost their children—like all the other Church Fathers, Jarrod would only say that Rose's "Projects" were "failures." She had always felt defective, broken...

But the Watcher had been fierce that day, if not comforting, declaring her to be faultless in the loss of their own Project. Amazed at his passion, she shook her head. *The Watcher even called our Project a Child.* It seemed so strange to her that any man—whether they be Deva or Devil—would care so much about a Project, or call it by the forbidden name—a pregnancy. That moment of unabashed paternalism made her care about the Watcher, more than she liked to admit.

His horse descending a shallow slope, the Watcher's arm tightened around Rose's waist. He leaned back in the saddle, loosing the reins. Rose glanced down and saw an ungainly, hunchbacked beast the size of a large dog bounding alongside Oro's legs. Wickedly recurved claws dug into the sandy loam beneath its prehensile paws as a twisting, rope-like tail thrashed behind the lithe, hairless body. At first, she recoiled in fear at the dark silhouette running alongside Oro; but he glanced up at her, and the moonlight revealed round ears perked forward and a blunt underslung snout split into a goofy grin. Fear gave way to recognition—*Oh, Oskar! You've grown so much in such a short time*—and she gave a wan smile back to the chupacabra cub.

As the Watcher's big Palomino stepped sure-footed down into the grassy ravine, Rose felt the Watcher pull her in securely close to his bulky body, and dismay gave way to a relieved resignation:

I'm not with Jarrod now; I'm with Saul...

Unlike the civilized Governor of Tesoro, the Watcher was brutal, a mutated poet-barbarian in cowboy garb. Her fingers brushed the tops of his knuckles, almost accidentally, seeking some kind of acknowledgement.

Strange emotion assailed her, a simultaneous repulsion and perverse attraction for this mute Devilman, her learned bigotry challenged by his intelligence and bravado. The Watcher's fearless protectiveness brought comfort, but his inhuman appearance and primitive brutality provoked an uncanny apprehension. *But this Devil's a Deva,* Rose reasoned, calling him by the name all her kind gave to the holy men of Tesoro; *therefore, God wills it*. Still, she felt confused by this Deva-turned-Devilman...

There was a lot to be confused about.

Trying to hide her distress, she wondered if the Watcher noticed she was upset; her heart was still racing from the angst of her nightmare, and she could feel cold sweat on her brow. Her time of uncleanness was almost gone, having tapered off after four heavy days, but there was still a discomfort that came with the trappings of that monthly event. Rose shifted in the saddle, uncomfortable inside and out.

If the Watcher noticed her agony, he gave no sign. Peeking back over her shoulder at his red, cracked visage, she saw his eyes focused on the trail ahead, seemingly ignoring her. For a brief moment, in the aftershadow of her dream, she hoped he would break down the wall of pride she had erected between them, and ask—*"Are you frightened? What is wrong?"*—but he kept his eyes fixed on the trail and that moment passed.

He doesn't care a whit, you twit. Something was dangerously close to breaking within her, but she beat it back with the relentless cudgel of independence. *Asura must save themselves.* So she was taught, so it must be. She doubted this Devil could be that Angel anyway; *well, maybe a Fallen Angel.* Humiliated by her own longing for comfort from the Watcher, she faded back into sleep...

As she drifted off, he pulled the rose-print shawl from under his coat collar and tucked it in around her shoulders. From this side of her consciousness, Rose heard him humming to himself, satisfied.

✦

On the far side of another consciousness, another dreamer dreamed.

When she looked out over the lake, she sometimes wished she were fishing on the far side, under that tree, alone. There was something pure about fishing, even if one never caught a fish; it would just be her under the tree and sky, with a pole in her hand and the water lapping around her feet...

The sun was high in the sky this day, warm on her soft, bare arms, and the summer cicadas were singing. At the end of the pier, in the sun, her little brother was threading another worm on the hook—she felt sorry for the worms, so she used a piece of grass on the end of the line and made it wiggle, plopping it across the surface. She tried to show him how it's done, just skipping the hook across the surface, even letting it sink a little bit, then pulling up just in time. Billy Dale just laughed at her, orange

creamsicle smeared all over his nine-year-old sassy face, t-shirt, and raggedy jeans
—"I've got a worm, I don't have to work at it."

"You a mess, boy."

He laughed in that annoying little-brother way, and she loved him for it.

Dipping her bare toes off the end of the pier, she could just almost reach the
water. She checked under the pier, her straight, sandy-blonde hair hanging down almost
to the water—nope no snakes—and dragged her toe across the water, leaving ripples.
The water was warm and the mosquitoes weren't biting—so why not jump in?

She heard her father calling her name from across the street—"Destiny! Mr.
Dou's grilling burgers, and if you want one, you better hurry!"

Oh Billy Dale, I've got a bite... it's really bobbing...

The bobber went "ker-snuk," loudly, again—

And she woke up.

It wasn't a bobber. It was Jip McMasters, and he was snoring, stopping
breathing, then snorting back to life again. The air smelled foul, even for a
LifeAfter lakeside shack. She wrinkled her nose. Lying there, still, she was
trying to not jiggle Jip—as long as he was drunk and asleep, she didn't
have to meet his needs for the last scheduled five minutes of his winnings.

She closed her eyes, trying to get the dream back, but it had drifted
away; still, she was glad to see Billy Dale again—even if it was just in a
dream.

She wondered how long it had been since she put her feet down in the
Lake water. Decades? Not since the gators got so bad; but even before
then, she just didn't want to see the bodies washing up in the inlet. She
stopped wading in the Lake that day she walked along the shore and a
bloated hand floated up out of the sand, all by itself, and brushed against
her peeling leg.

It had been forever ago.

Dreams like this brought back the feeling of hopelessness. There were
days she felt like she just couldn't go any further. It had been so long,
nothing was going to change. *Why get up? Why go on living?*

She would have laid there longer, but she needed to go to the
bathroom.

Welp, this is how we make it through from day to day—we'd just lay down and
die, but we have to get up to pee, and then the whole cycle starts over again.

She rolled out of bed in one smooth, silent motion, and let her feet
touch the ground softy so she wouldn't wake Jip. The big macho was
rolled to one side, his mouth open, drooling; the tan scales of his naked

back testified to the stab wounds and scars he had tallied up from all his fights over the years. He was a good fighter but a bad drunk, and he was drunk a lot...

He started to shift, and she stood quickly, pulling her skirt away from him so he couldn't roll on it as she left. The floor was planks of rough wood; she carefully picked up her bare feet so she wouldn't get a splinter, then stealthily padded out the door and down to the outhouse. From the gate, she could hear the guards banging a tire iron against a cut-up propane tank-turned-bell. Eight gongs—time to get back to Sam, or all hell would break loose.

It was eight o'clock in the morning, and it seemed all the world was hungover. An occasional groan oozed out of an open window from one of myriad shacks that lined the shoreline of the Lake, but no occupants were outside in the mud lanes. The mud wasn't so bad today—it had been dry for a spell, and the puddles were almost gone. An enterprising soul had put up some cedar logs to border the rutted roads between shacks, and a couple of Hombres from Boss Balogun's Work Crew had thrown raked leaves into the road just to keep it from being so muddy and hopeless looking. Those little touches kept the locals of LowTown happy —it made Purgatory look like a real town.

But still, it was Purgatory, a haven for hard-drinking, hard-headed Hellraisers and Heartbreakers from all over the Tejas Co-op. What started off as a Fishing Camp turned into a Hunting camp, turned into a permanent habitation; a group of like-minded regulars and visiting VIPs with an eye for trouble. The local constabulary kept tabs and made sure everyone paid tabs. Those who didn't could do a stint as a Public Servant to pay off fines.

It's how she ended up as a Hostess, one of only five in this camp. She had been one now for nineteen years, having run away from LandLord Johnson one night in a fit of rage over his treatment of her; she was captured by a local, who brought her here and then promptly lost her in a game of pool. In desperation, she tried to gamble for her own freedom in a game of Texas Hold'em, but she lost—and kept losing. By the time word was sent back to her LandLord, she was already in so much debt, no one could afford the fines, and he let the Camp have her in exchange for a cancellation of the debt.

Some days I think I should have stayed back on the plantation.

Walking the path from Jip's LowTown shack to the Main Drag,

Destiny made sure to stay in the middle of the ruts so she wouldn't slip down into the cold puddles. It was early for a Purgatory morning, and all its hungover inhabitants were still asleep. As she wandered up the dirt road, she skirted the Industrial District. In the misty morning, she watched a lone Foreman opening up the bays and preparing the workroom floors for the coming day. Various containers of recovered oil stood ready to refine through filtration barrels, and scavenged building materials were separated into piles for cleaning. She was glad Survivors were making progress, but she wasn't sure she wanted their pay... she wrinkled her nose at the thought of using drugs and liquor, but Stuff and Shine was the expected pay for Boss Waitie's laborers at Purgatory.

Making her way up from the LowTown lakeside, she could see the fence completely encircling the camp. It was nice to know the gators and cougars wouldn't be making their way into town, but she also needed to watch out for the strung-out two-legged critters that might attack her on her way back to Sam's Cabin. The Main Drag opened into a central wash here, widening out into the section of Purgatory known as the Municipality. What had once been a primitive campground and open pasture now centered the great LifeAfter public works of Survivors under the inspired direction of Boss Winston. These included the Campground, the Commons, a public wellhead complete with working windmill, a cinderblock Jail with its municipal offices downstairs, and a spacious metal pavilion. Down the sandy path past the Jail was the Park—a fenced-off inlet of the Lake with a refurbished dock. Adjacent to it was the Dump— a twenty-some-odd acre mountain range of rotting trash at the edge of town, held at bay by a ramshackle wooden fence. But the true pride of Purgatory was Destiny's current objective: the Purgatory Porta-Johnnie Public-Sanitation Project.

Grateful for a haven, she ducked into one of the outhouses.

The old Porta-Johnnies, re-engineered as real working outhouses, were a great source of civic pride. She was glad to have them—it such a welcome relief to not get splinters, like old wooden out-house seats would give, and the plastic let the light shine through. She finished up her business, then headed back to Sam's for her morning break—*gotta get cleaned up and ready for the next round of winners.*

Coming out, she wiped her hands on the skirt of her dress—a faded, flowing red cotton affair, full, almost reaching the ground. It still looked pretty good, but she would change out today. Fortunately, it was a slow day today—no major events were scheduled, so she could expect a little down time, maybe even time to just do laundry and think.

Heading to HighTown, she shuffled her bare feet through the dry leaves. The Bosses forbid the Hostesses to wear shoes—it stopped them from running away. Bare feet didn't get far in the WildLands. *Not even socks, for crying out loud*—it was one of the reasons she wore the skirts; she could tuck her feet up under the folds in the winter to keep them warm.

The other reason she wore the skirts was to remind herself she was still a woman.

As a Marginal Hembra, she was low on the T-scale compared to most, but it still bothered that her breasts had become so much smaller. She was glad she hadn't become too muscular and big, but she still missed the feeling of her own curves—they had captured a man's attention long ago in another life, and after that man married her, those curves fed her children. Now, thanks to the TransMutation Virus, all that was a half-century dead—the husband, the children, the breasts—and she was just a skinny little Hembra in a frilly dress and a crocheted shawl, walking back to the whorehouse to start another day.

Stopping by the public water troughs, she washed her hands and splashed her face and neck to wash away the smell of Jip McMasters. It was a chilly morning, and she made certain to avoid wetting the cuffs of her bell-shaped sleeves.

A sputtering from a nearby trough interrupted her reverie: it was Boss Zhu coughing, plunging his head under the cold water, then pulling it back out. He blinked, then immediately set about straightening his dingy collar and making himself more presentable.

"Oh, hey, Destiny—I didn't see you there." He rolled his sleeves back down to cover his IV port. A big Hombre, Jack Zhu was the Boss of HighTown, the most prestigious area of Purgatory. He was almost handsome, with twinkling black eyes and copper scales covering his muscular body; unfortunately, he had a constant need to shoot up on the Stuff, sometimes even in the middle of a session. "So, I'm up next?"

"Hi, Jack—you have your standing appointment tonight, 10PM to 8AM next morning—do you need to change it?"

"No, I... I just need to see you. I just want to talk."

She sighed. *He said that the last time, too.* No one ever just "talked" to her, even when they said they wanted to talk. *"Talk" is just another word for "bang,"* she thought sourly.

"I'm sorry Jack. I've gotta get back—you know I'm not allowed to talk off the clock. Ask Sam." Boss Zhu was powerful at Purgatory, but even he had to wait his turn, like everyone else in town. He was privileged in that he got to make a permanent appointment. Other Survivors had to gamble to win a spot.

"Okay, I wrote a poem for you." He scratched at his port, jittery. His eyes were darting, watching for Sam. He handed her a small scrap of paper. On it was written in pencil:

Roses are red
Violets are blue
You are the one
I want to 'do'

She tried to look impressed. "Aww, Jack, that's sweet. Later...".

He grinned. "You know it babe."

She turned away, wandering towards the biggest cabin in HighTown, right next to the main drag. Up the road she ambled, taking her time to just be alone in the chilly morning breeze. The Cabins were original to the Camp, a large cluster of four-room log houses now known as HighTown, along the one-way looped Main Drag.

Across the Drag, she saw the festive rag banners and tin-punched lanterns of Pair'O'Dice Pier swaying gently in the early morning breeze; the barns, trailers, and garages of the expanded LifeBefore lakeside settlement had been turned into a gated haven for high-stakes gambling, dining, and drinking. Barns-turned-Hotels, upscale scavenging boutiques and eateries jostled cheek-to-jowl with drug dens, porn palaces, and pubs, all vying for the patronage of LandLords and their entourages of ne'er-do-wells rolling in for Market Mayhem Weekend. Beyond them, down to a fenced bay on the lakeshore lay the crown jewel of Boss Chartreaux's prized district: the twin party pontoons that gave the district its name—Pair'O'Dice Pier.

But even outside Pair'O'Dice, games of one-to-one-competition were scattered everywhere, on card tables and stumps—checkers, chess, backgammon, acey-deucy, cribbage, marbles, and every card game known to man—

There, in between the roads, a greenway with trees and open spaces provided ample room for rolling crap games and poker tournaments. Occasionally, games of mumblety-peg would break out, usually followed by knife fights. Almost any kind of drug, vice, drink, game, or competition you could think of, on almost any given day of the week, you could find it at Purgatory.

But the greatest draw for most visitors was Friday Night Fights during Purgatory's monthly Market Mayhem Weekend. Those souls who thought themselves tough enough would show up for a round or two in a no-holds-barred free-for-all tournament, with a sudden death option for those so inclined. Those who didn't think themselves tough could make a bet. It was a great way to make a buck—or go in debt to Purgatory. Depending on how much in goods or flesh you bet, you could end up a big winner or you could end up a Public Servant. And if you didn't like that option, you could end up thrown in the Lake with the gators.

God, how I hate gators. Destiny shuddered, putting distance between herself and lakeshore. Her destination was close to the gates with two big machos guarding the entrance to Purgatory, high palisaded walls surrounding the town. Another Guard was stationed at the top of the wall; he was pointing, and talking to a traveller outside the gate—

Well, that's different. We usually don't get visitors this early in the day...

The lookout called down to the others, "Incoming! Open the Gates—visitors coming through!"

Creaking forward, the massive gates swung outward, pulled by chains in the hands of the guards. The gate framed the figures of two trail-worn Hombres; one lean and medium tall, with black scales and a blue-plaid poncho, the other shorter, athletic, with bronzed scales and a strong jaw, clad in an olive-drab army jacket. Their cowboy hats bore the dust from the road.

Destiny held her breath—*The Director?* Him she knew—*but who was that man with him?* She ducked behind the thick trunk of a spreading oak in the greenway. It was an automatic response. Everyone knew that lawmen occasionally came looking for runaways, or criminals—or a good time. They were always welcomed when they came, and it was always welcomed when they left. Lately, though, the law hadn't been leaving; some regulars had begun to murmur that the lawdogs had overstayed their welcome.

But the Director... He was Big Time. *Sam's gonna wanna know about him.*

She peeked around the trunk of the tree again. They were striding down the road, heading for the camping ground. The Hombres walked by the tree, and the younger man looked down at her as they walked by... his eyes were startlingly beautiful, brown streaked with green and gray.

The men tipped their hats, and kept walking.

She felt suddenly bashful and turned to run up the street; the two guards, Sampson and Jorge met her at the door of the cabin. Jorge jerked his rough-hided head towards the door, rolling his eyes, warning Destiny —*yup, Sam's mad*—and she gave a slight nod of thanks back.

"Where have you been?" Sam hissed when the door opened, dragging her inside. "I sent Lazarus to escort you back, and you were already gone —what gives?"

"I'm sorry Sam, I just couldn't wait any longer. You know how mean Jip is when he's drunk. I got out of there before the bells might wake him up."

"Well Lazarus is beating the bushes for you now—I'll have to send Herman after him, and that leaves me one man down at the door." The tall Hembra pulled off her black leather beret and smoothed the steel-blue scales of her forehead—she was trying to ward off a stress headache.

"You know you can't walk alone out here! Someone will kill you or run off with you—come on, think! We've got to stick together on this and not break protocol. Right now, we have a way to help one another and maybe even someone else before it's all said and done—if you don't mess it up for us."

"Yeah. I'm sorry Sam. I just couldn't stand it any longer."

Sam closed the door. "Girl, you've got to get your act together. You're just going through the motions anymore. What's gotten into you lately?" She pursed her full lips, her dark, up-tilted eyes angry. Tall and broad in the shoulders, narrow in the waist, Sam still had an incredible cat-like grace about her, long-boned and lean. Dressed in worn black road leathers she had scavenged from a motorcycle shop, Sam exuded a fierceness that had served her well in LifeAfter, keeping her on top of the food chain. Her own ability to fight and intimidate was keeping her and her girls alive and protected at Purgatory.

Destiny sat down. "I dunno—I just keep thinking about my kids. I can't stop lately—I keep dreaming about them, and about my family. I saw my little brother in a dream last night, and everything was so wonderful. I just want to go to sleep and never wake up again..."

Sam slapped Destiny's face. The staccato strike reverberated through the worn lace curtains and chipped china cups that decorated the genteely-worn great room. Shocked, Destiny raised a slender hand to her cheek.

"I didn't fight my way down I-45 from Sunny South TroPlex after all hell broke loose just so my recruits can decide to die." Sam was livid. "You don't think I miss my babies? You don't think I still dream about them at night? I was going to be a Gramma for the first time—you don't think I can still hear my daughter crying for her own dead baby? Their suffering is burned into my soul."

"I'm sorry, Sam—I'm just tired of the pain never ending, that's all. I don't think it's ever going to go away. It's been fifty-four years, but I just can't..." she hung her head. "I just want it to end."

"Well, I lost my children, too, you don't see me crying about how I want to die, do you? That's a waste of the life God gave you—"

"That's funny you say that, Sam, with all those tears in your eyes." Destiny looked up to see Kendra standing there, her simple t-shirt and jeans skimming the subtle curves of her androgynous body. Beaded ivory skin glistening in the morning sun, she was lighting a cigarette stuffed with dried green buds.

"It's too damn early for weed, you little heathen—put that out." Sam snatched it out of Kendra's hands. "Y'all are making me crazy."

Kendra smirked and leaned her sinuous arms against a wooden chair. "It's not like I need to be level right now, you old Church-Lady—ain't nothin' gonna happen today that didn't happen yesterday or the day before. Besides, I'll just score another one from my next client."

"You need to stay vigilant, Kendra. This is no party." Sam crushed out the hand-rolled cigarette and put it in a little metal box on the table. "Weird things are going down all over Purgatory, and I need you to stay alert—you can self-medicate later."

Destiny rubbed her cheek. "Kendra, Sam's right, there's strange things happening; so, you best keep your wits about you." She turned to Sam. "The Director's here, and he's got someone new with him, a fella I've never seen before..."

Kendra dropped her air of nonchalance.

Sam gave her a pointed look. "The Director, huh? Kendra, wake up the rest of the girls—Destiny, go get cleaned up, and get the safe room ready." She pulled the blinds down.

"The Director doesn't arrive without bringing a storm."

———◆———

Dominic and Evangelo both sat in the whorehouse parlor, the shades pulled down low. They had respectfully removed their hats in the presence of the ladies, as was their custom, and made polite talk while waiting for Sam to enter.

It smells like sin and desperation in here, the Ranger thought with a barely contained scowl. The Director had explained the situation—an established Hostess Club, it was now a cover for another kind of human trafficking operation, one in the Cause of Freedom. But it still didn't make it any less distasteful to Evangelo...

"Would you care for some more hot chicoffee?" The lean Hembra held out a ceramic pot filled with the chicory-dandelion coffee substitute, polite but distant. Her blue baseball cap, white t-shirt and jeans gave her a tomboy look, black eyes questioning and cynical. The satiny golden-ivory scales of her bare arms shimmered in the morning sun.

The Director graciously accepted: "I do believe I'll take another half-cup if you don't mind."

The ivory Hembra poured the chicoffee into Dominic's waiting cup, and offered some to Evangelo. He held the white cup out for her to serve.

"Would you like some sugar?" The Ranger looked up to see the slender Hembra he had met on the way into town; she was coming from the kitchen now, a china bowl of sugar cane in her hands. For some reason, she made him nervous.

Maybe it was because she was wearing a dress—a tomato red one— and he hadn't ever seen a Hembra wearing a dress. Like most Survivors, she wore a head covering—hers was a cap crocheted from shredded, mostly red jersey rags, giving the appearance of a mop of red hair, with a big fuzzy pompom on top for a "bun." She was not overly masculine, but she had a slightly angular quality about her, common to low-t Hembras; a little shorter than Evangelo, she was slender and willowy, and carried herself with a grace that made him feel like a clumsy bull in the delicate parlor. Her skin was a rare, velvety pink color, evenly covered in tiny spots of the lichen planus variety of skin affliction, making her appear as if she was covered in a peachy. polka-dot crushed velvet.

She held out the bowl and blinked her soft gray eyes at him. He couldn't help but notice they were flecked with gold, and had a darker gray starburst in the center. He had never seen eyes like that. *Pretty...*

"Sir, did you want some sugar?" He jerked awake from his pondering.

"Oh, I'm sorry M-ma'am. Please excuse me, I'm just tired... yes, I would like some s-sugar please." She handed a chunk of cane to him, and he stirred his chicoffee with it. He stared intensely down into his cup.

A stunning Hembra dressed in black leather entered the room, and both the Director and the Ranger stood to greet her. She extended her hand to the Director, and he greeted her warmly:

"Sam, as always, it is a pleasure to see you again."

"Thank you, Director. What sort of adventure do you bring this time —and who is this quiet man?" She turned her dark eyes to Evangelo.

"Agent Ellison, this is Captain Evangelo of the Rangers."

Evangelo stood to shake her hand. "I've heard much good about you and the work you are doing on behalf of the Cause..."

"You don't look like a Ranger." Sam said pointedly. "Where's your white hat and white shirt?"

Taken aback, the Evangelo blinked: "I'm sorry to disappoint Ma'am, but I am traveling incognito."

"Well, we already have enough Rangers here, and they just won't leave." Sam said it firmly but politely. "They're obnoxious, demanding free drinks from the bars and unscheduled sessions with the girls."

"They are not true Rangers, or they would not exploit your ladies. It is against the Code of the Rangers to do so, and I'll see to it personally that they do not bother you again." Evangelo replied coolly, his jaw clenching. He flipped back the leather flap to reveal the badge on the wide lapel of his brown coat. "I'm here to investigate Ranger corruption, Ma'am, so I would appreciate any information you might give me."

Kendra and Destiny stood against the wall, looking as if they had seen a unicorn. A door opened, and another two pairs of amazed eyes peeked out from the ladies' bedroom to watch the Ranger; he heard feminine whispers and one "shush"...

Sam looked surprised. "An actual good Ranger—the kind that people used to talk about? I'm shocked."

Evangelo's eyes turned a clear, cold gray. "It wounds me that you are shocked to see a good Ranger. I give you my word you will not be troubled by these bad characters anymore when I am done."

Sam smiled again, a genuine smile of relief. "I don't know what their purpose is here, but the Rangers have been hanging around the periphery of town, lingering by the gates."

"Do you have an estimate on how many might be here?" Evangelo asked.

"Nine of them; they take shifts near the gate or down by the Jail, and sleep at Boss Chartreaux's house... they seem to be looking for someone."

"How long?" Dominic asked.

"The last two weeks or so," Sam proffered.

The Director nodded to the Ranger "I didn't notice any on our way in —this is probably a bad sign. Are there any outside now, Agent Sampson?"

Sam nodded to her security guard, Sampson; pulling the curtain aside slightly, he peered through a gap between the shade and the window frame. The tall Macho grunted and counted in a gruff voice—"Three, scattered among the trees in the greenway. All eyes on us." He fingered the handle of his shotgun absentmindedly; his partner Jorge went to stand by the back door.

Just beyond the tree line, three Survivors hung back, white standing out against the greenery, blue bandanas wrapped around each neck. Evangelo leaned over to follow Sampson's gaze. "It's Rangers Danforth, Leroy, and Gupta of the Checkpoint Brown detachment—why are they here? And those matching bandanas... strange." He pulled back away from the window. "They're not part of any official Ranger investigations at Purgatory—I would know, I handle logistics and personnel at Checkpoint Black. Given the timeframe, they could be involved with Chief Emmanuel, or sent by Shaney; but there's no way to know which one without an encounter..." He frowned.

The Director smiled and straightened his cuffs. "Ah well, now is just as good a time as any for an encounter—perhaps the Rangers will afford us a good reason as to why they are here." Dominic sipped his cup once more before setting it down. "Our backstory will be pursuit of a female runaway, an old account on a slender Hembra with pink skin; if inquisitive Rangers ask you why we are here, tell them that we heard one was here and came to investigate."

He took a deep sip from his cup and savored it.

"Meanwhile, Agent Ellison, please send word to our field operatives that the time has come to muster recruits and rally them to their designated locations outside Purgatory, so as to not attract scrutiny. In twenty-four hours, unit leaders return to Purgatory, smuggling recruits in their wagons; meet at the Camp Ground Commons under the guise of attending Purgatory's monthly Market Mayhem Weekend. There, covered by the gathering crowds, we may discreetly interview new recruits, rally more, then supply them with the bounty that the fine merchants of

Purgatory offer. At my signal, leaders will depart Purgatory in small groups and gather their troops to the next location, to be revealed at that time."

He handed Sam a small, round object plus a slip of paper, and leaned forward to whisper confidentially: "Please pass this to Agent Mansour with my regards. This beacon is to be used only in case of emergency—in the unlikely event we do not return, you will need to pass a message to our new Agent. He has a high value Package I would like you to help him secure."

"A Package, huh? Must be something special..." Intrigued, Sam studied the beacon. "And a new Agent too? It's been a while since we got any new blood on board."

"That new blood is the Watcher of Reunion."

"That explains why our WildLand Express Teams reported him missing from the Gate at the Reunion Archway..." Skeptical, her dark eyes scanned the Director's enigmatic face. "Are you certain the Watcher's the man for this job?"

Dominic appeared hurt at her question. "Have I ever been wrong?"

At his injured expression, Sam relented. "I'm sorry, Director Santos; I'm just trying to keep the Team safe. You know the Watcher is more than just the most dangerous prisoner in the Tejas Co-op; he's the reason we could never breach the Reunion Gate. If not for him, we could have overthrown Judge Leona and freed the Prisoners of Reunion Camp long ago—"

Evangelo edged forward, eager to defend the rough Survivor he now considered his friend: "I will vouch for his character. Despite my misgivings at his sordid past, the Watcher has proved to be a Man of Honor."

Sam's eyes flashed in challenge: "Did this Man of Honor assassinate the Judge?"

Answering her challenge, the Director demurred. "Not he, but another did; still he is tied to it all, as you will learn soon enough." A subtle revolutionary fire suffused Dominic as he leaned forward in the delicate wicker chair. "Men change. Agent Azarian is no longer a slave to his addiction; the Stuff no longer has him in its thrall, and he no longer has any bonds of affection to chain him to Reunion Camp. Agent Azarian has been set free by the Truth, and I have recruited him to the Cause."

"The Cause..." Sam said it with the weary reverence reserved for those who strive to overcome overwhelming odds. "I know you've been after the Watcher a long time—and I've expressed my reservations about him repeatedly. But I'll trust your judgement; if the Watcher's committed to Freedom, then I'll welcome him." The Director tilted his head in acknowledgment of her reluctant trust. "And whatever your Package may be, you know you can count on our Team to keep it safe." An unabashed pride infused her voice—she glanced at Kendra, and the sleek Hembra nodded back, business-like.

"I believe you will find he passes even your most stringent requirements." The Director helped himself to another piece of sugar cane. "The Watcher's one of the best."

"You mean... one of the B.E.S.T.? Are you certain?" At the mention of the name, a glint of recognition crept in, along with a healthy dose of skepticism: "How could he be one of the B.E.S.T. and no one else have snatched him away?"

"You're assuming he wasn't." Dominic smiled. "Why do you think Leona kept him in chains all these years?"

Sam blinked, surprised.

"And now, he's ours." The Director held up his cup, and Kendra indulged him yet another helping of the precious coffee substitute. He sipped once more, then leaned back, appreciating the bitter bouquet. "Agent Azarian has been briefed regarding our Unit here; use Encryption Level Six, follow the instructions, and give the passphrase, Fenix Creciente. The Agent will answer back with the passphrase, 'We Will Be Free'. Share this with no one else, and destroy these instructions once you have memorized them—the Agent will fill you in on what needs to be done next."

Unpinning his Badge with its leather cover, the Director passed it to Sam: "Should you need to make contact, Agent Azarian will identify himself with a deputy's badge; behind it will be hidden the leather representation of the Cause's new incarnation—the LoneStar Revolution." He flipped over the badge cover to reveal Evangelo's hand-tooled emblem; the Phoenix born of fire, wreathed in broken chain, all embossed upon an encircled five-pointed star with the words We Will Be Free—TEXAS.

"The Revolution..." Fervent, Sam ran her fingers across the leather emblem before handing it back to Dominic. "It's beautiful, Director."

"Thank you, Agent Ellison. It is Captain Evangelo's leather work—I am glad you approve!"

A tap at the back window—two soft raps in rapid succession, repeated twice. Covering the back door, Jorge looked to Sam, and she nodded. A sinewy Hombre tougher than shoe leather, Jorge pushed the window open just a crack, and a folded slip of paper fell to the floor. He passed it to the Director.

"Thank you, Agent Mercedes." Dominic read it then passed it back to Sam. "Agent Mansour awaits us near the gate; he sends word that there are an additional two Rangers sitting in the woods just outside the fence. We are to not acknowledge him, but he is there for backup just in case we need it, and to listen to the conversations of the guards and Rangers after we pass through. Perhaps he will get some insight into our observers." The Director stood. "Come, Captain, let us go greet your friends—they appear to be eager to say hello."

Hat in his hands, Evangelo thanked the Hostesses. "Thank you for the chicoffee and sugar. It was quite nice to have it in such pleasant company." He bowed his head slightly.

Entranced by the little Ranger's gallant demeanor, the slender Hembra in the red dress pressed another piece of the sweet cane into his hand. "Have an extra sugar, Sugar... I mean, sir—" Nervous, she smiled brightly, and her sharp features softened.

"Oh!" He blinked. "I mean, thank you, M-ma'am." He fumbled with the sugar, nearly dropping it before managing to place it in his pocket. He looked at her eyes again, just for a brief moment, then turned away.

Replacing their hats, Dominic and Evangelo strode out the door.

Icy stares from hard men followed them down the street as the Director and the Captain headed towards the Gate; as they passed, Evangelo folded back the leather cover on his badge, allowing it to shine in the morning sun, but none of the Rangers returned the favor, or acknowledged his rank. Wary, the Director and the Ranger continued down the road, watching their watchers with open challenge.

As they approached the Gate, one of the guards called down, "Leaving so soon?"

"Our work here is done—for now," the Director affirmed. He did not look toward the compact, coppery Macho hammering away at a hinge in the Gate, two rapid taps, followed by two more; a pattern.

You must be Agent Mansour. Evangelo grunted.

The Director whispered low to the Ranger—"Lazarus..."

The Ranger turned back to look at the watchers on the greenway: he could feel their contempt for him, and he returned it. Out of the corner of his eye, he caught the motion of a curtain being pulled back in Sam's parlor window, and a flash of a pale, delicate face peering out from behind the curtain.

"Do you have nothing to say to your Captain?" The little Ranger spoke clearly, his hand lingering near his silver revolver. "Or did you not expect me here?"

Silence answered him as the corrupted Rangers pulled back into the shadows of the trees...

He spoke again, loudly, so all could hear him. "We'll be back." No one dared answer him.

The Gate swung open, and the two Survivors walked through it and into the waiting WildLands.

                                 •———◆———•

Sunrise found the Watcher running behind schedule.

What was meant to be a straight ride to the East through the dark of night had become a comedy of errors directed by Murphy's Law. The free-running Chupacabra had spooked Shadow at first, prompting the Watcher to stop and calm the horse, and chastise Oskar; then a strap came loose on the supply bag, resulting in the kitchen gear falling to the ground in a loud, clattering heap. After calming horses and repacking gear, he had to escort the Afterling to a perfect place to attend her needs—sheltered, but not dangerous, where she declared it was too cold to attend her needs but she still took ten minutes to do so. Finally, when everyone and everything was all loaded back up, they spent forty-five minutes riding southeast only to realize they were headed the wrong way, thanks to him designating the wrong destination point on the map.   He corrected his destination and re-routed, but by that time, it was already an hour and a half later than he had planned.

The Chupacabra cub was another complication for the trail. The Watcher found himself constantly looking for him in the dark, but only because Oskar had never run free before. *Impressive*, the little beast was keeping up with the horses. Even as young as Oskar was, he was already able to run long distances without tiring; the Watcher was fascinated with the fearsome animal, as well as a being a little apprehensive of him.

Fortunately, the Watcher's chupacabra-training sessions with Evangelo had been a very productive—with just another day at the cabin, he could have learned all the commands Evangelo had been teaching Oskar...

The Watcher was frustrated with the turn of events, and all the missed opportunities for trail prep; he also missed the comfortable cabin with its books and pillows. Rose's attempt to hack Chief Emmanuel's Ring—and her subsequent revelation of her location data to Jarrod—had cost them much, and she knew it. Quiet for most of the trip, she knew better than to push her luck with idle chatter, and she contented herself to snuggle against the Watcher's back, silent as she rode behind him on the pillion.

She knows how to get out of trouble, the Watcher grumbled—*be warm and cuddly, and pretend to sleep.* He was all too happy to let her do that, and he spent his time watching the trail and gazing at the bright stars overhead, with her arms wrapped tightly around his waist up under his coat.

That's fine—I'll deal with you later.

It was then Rose actually fell asleep, sliding off the pillion, her arms coming loose from around his waist. She nearly tumbled to the ground, but the Watcher caught her arm, and pulled her back up just in time. He stopped the horse again, transferred her back to her usual position in front of him in Oro's saddle, then started down the trail once more, Oskar loping beside them.

That was how morning found them: Rose asleep in the Watcher's arms, him still riding, trying to reach the safe house. Taking care to avoid open areas—in case another aircraft might be surveilling the area—the Watcher chose to take the most obscured path under a canopy of bare autumn branches. The trail was heavily wooded, and the sun's rays had just begun to weave through the thick branches of the oak trees that dotted the way. A lone sunbeam hit Rose's face; still sleeping, she stirred, then held out a hand.

"We need all your pumpkins..." She murmured. " ...so round..."

Pumpkins? Who dreams of pumpkins?

"Don't be afraid. They float..." she murmured matter-of-factly again, then rolled her head to the other side to rest her cheek against his arm.

The Watcher tried to remember the last dream he ever dreamed while sleeping, over twenty-three years ago... he dreamed he was in a department store, just like LifeBefore, but the sales girls kept decaying when he asked them a question about where to find boots.

This sounded like a much better dream.

He briefly considered inserting himself into this dream, as he had earlier, just to see what Rose would do with the pumpkins. But combining the Ring's Neural-net Xirxes Chat Exploit with the Auto-Speex function to hack her dream demanded concentration, and the Watcher couldn't devote that much mental real estate to the task when they were so deep in unknown territory. Under these dangerous circumstances, he wouldn't have inserted himself into her last dream, either—but his investigation into his sleeping fugitive demanded answers, and her recurring nightmare held them...

The Watcher shuddered. Beyond the horror of Rose's traumatic dream encounter with her ex-lover, Jarrod, the Watcher was unnerved by his own appearance. It had been a sobering experience to see himself as he once was, and to hear himself speaking naturally in the virtual reality of the dream insertion. Unmutated and unmuted, it was remarkable how much he had taken for granted in the world of LifeBefore. His sleek athletic body, with his smooth, tanned skin and glib tongue had given way to a monstrous physique with an itching, armored hide and tongue-tied silence. He almost wished he hadn't seen himself that way, so he wouldn't miss it... but he had wanted Rose to see him, just once, as human—

even if she isn't.

He glanced down at the slumbering little clone-woman in his arms, and wondered if all her sisters slept with such a remarkable abandon. Anytime, anywhere, Rose seemed to be able to sleep; even now, she was sprawled, limp in his arms, curly head bobbing in time to his horse's hooves. He wished he could snooze at all, even for a brief moment, with such complete oblivion.

He let Rose sleep in the filtered mid-morning light as they continued on the trail towards the safe house. As they made their way, his heavy-gloved fingers fiddled idly with his Badge, its Eight-Pointed Star of the System obscuring the embossed leather of the Five-Pointed Star of the Revolution behind it. *La Revolucion hiding beneath the trappings of The System...*

The Watcher pondered his next steps. *If I'm ever going to make a break for it, now is my chance...*

Everything the Watcher needed to execute his first plan was completely in place.

He had the Afterling, he had horses, he had supplies, he had weapons. Everything the Watcher could need to start a life together with Rose in the WildLands, he now had it...

The only thing he didn't have was a conviction that escaping with Rose was now the best course of action. Before meeting the Ranger and the Director, he had it all planned out—find a nice house in a secluded area, build a fence, make a garden, go hunting, and have lots of "quality time" alone with a little woman... *To be honest, that still sounds pretty good.*

But now, it would seem cowardly to run away with Rose. It wasn't so much that the Watcher wanted to do the right thing—it was more about pride. He had promised Rose to fight for the Asura, and to avenge her Angelina—and while keeping promises had never been his strong suit, fighting and avenging were among his best strengths. *Only a coward would run from such a great opportunity to bust some heads.*

Running away with the Afterling was no longer an option for Rose's chosen Champion of the Asura.

He grimaced. *So much for Freedom;* his own long-awaited personal Freedom—to do anything he wanted, go anywhere he wanted—had been subverted by his own inner White Knight, who promised to fight for the Freedom of some little clone-princesses he'd never met.

Fine. In that case, I've got forty-eight hours to pursue my own Freedom, with my own little clone-princess. He grunted to himself in approval at the prospect of his own Freedom, and kept his eyes sweeping the trail ahead. When they got to the safe house, he decided the first order of Freedom would be quality time. But before that Freedom could be enjoyed, the trail demanded breakfast.

A small meadow opened to their west, filled with Late Goldenrod and Pink Muhly Grass. This was as good a place as any to allow them to prepare for the work ahead. He jiggled the Afterling, then inserted the WeSpeex Ring's stone into Rose's now-ringless neural port to "speak" to her through her embedded neural implants:

#Morning comes—time to wake up. We'll take a break here, then reconnoitre the safe house nearby.

She stretched and yawned, raising her hands in a languorous sweep; he slid out of the saddle, then helped her dismount so she could attend needs once again. He found a suitable spot for her then waited patiently, securing the horses so they could graze and have their own breakfast.

Now to secure the Afterling. Upon her return from the clump of bushes, he set about to inspect his Troop. He removed her deerskin cloak and laid it across Shadow's saddle. It was the first time he'd had the opportunity to see his scavenged leather gear turned-armor on her in a clear light, and he was impressed with how well it had all worked out. Without her measurements, he had to estimate, but every strap was adjustable and that made the fit a lot easier. He turned her around and checked all the adjustment points in back, loosening and tightening each buckle along the way.

"But what about your own armor?" the Afterling protested.

#*I grow my own armor. If you want to check it, I'll arrange it.*

"Oh! I hadn't thought about it that way... " She mused about organic body armor. "That's very practical *and* tactical."

The Watcher made a quick the armor fit assessment on Rose:

Neck—good: The wide belt-collar protected her slender neck, and the circular bib of the leather gorget covered her sternum in front, draped over her shoulders and hung down between her shoulder blades in back. The duty harness assembly was layered over the top of the gorget, the shoulder straps of her up-armored apron securing the leather bib underneath.

Shoulders—good: The 12-gauge bandoleers were heavy, but the buckles allowed him to shorten for fit, and the rib cross-belt allowed maximum support.

Ribs—tighten: He didn't want it slipping if he had to extract her; the adjustment belt was fitted under her breasts, allowing for chest expansion so she could breathe easily. He could still slip two fingers under it. *Good.*

Waist—tighten: Same as above... he needed to punch another hole in the belt—*I thought twenty inches would be small enough...* The grab-strap and handle were sturdy and well attached.

Skirt—good: the short leather skirt encircled her hips and split in back, protecting the lower abdomen and buttocks; metal plates in the pockets could add protection if needed, *but more weight would mean less agility...* and she relied on agility to keep herself alive. *Maybe in a firefight, more armor would be good*—but otherwise, no. A box of 5.56mm ammo went into one pocket on the short leather skirt, and a small first aid kit into another pocket. He stuffed paracord, a pocketknife, and some peanuts into the remaining pockets—after all, he might get hungry.

He checked all fittings for security, then swept aside her bangs to check the scar on her forehead, healing into a slender, pink streak. *She still needs a helmet.*

The armor didn't look too bad—it accented her small waist, and veiled her vulnerable neck and upper chest beneath the high-collared leather gorget's bib. The overall effect reminded him of a leathered-out steampunk Alice in Wonderland, bandoleers full of ammo replacing ruffles on the pinafore. He cracked a smile. *Perfect.*

Now to review weapons and logistics...

Setting aside the Mariner Shotgun, he replaced it with the AR-15 for mid-range engagement, and kept the Remington V3 Tac-13 for closer work. Loading the Remington with alternating 12-gauge rounds of double-aught buckshot and slugs, the Watcher got prepared for whatever might come at them. The Bowie Knife stayed because—*the Bowie Knife always stays.*

#*If we engage, I'll not be able to communicate with you verbally, so pay attention to hand signals. If I jerk twice in rapid succession, look at me for further instructions, and don't resist if I pull you or carry you— rapid movement should be expected.*

She nodded. A mixture of excitement and apprehension expressed itself in her rapid breathing and eager half-smile, and for some reason, the Watcher found her expression extraordinarily attractive. He studied her: *You just can't resist trouble, can you?*

How could he deal with Rose effectively? The Watcher had always been a solitary warrior, emulating Musashi's style of leadership. He wasn't as experienced in Command situations... What strategy could he use that he had already learned? His mind dwelt on Miyamoto Musashi's approach to leadership:

> *"The warrior is different in that studying the Way of strategy is based on overcoming men."*

In this case, leadership strategy meant overcoming Rose's... what? *Doubt? Fear? Prejudice?* That's what it was—prejudice.

Rose's prejudgement of the Watcher as "less than human"—a Damned Devil—meant he had to overcome her prejudice against him as not worthy of being in Leadership. His eavesdropping on her through AutoSpeex had gained him valuable, if unwelcome, insight into her puzzling behavior. Rose followed Jarrod simply because he looked like an alpha human male—a Deva. And now the Watcher knew: Rose didn't follow his lead because the Watcher didn't look Human to her—he was big, twisted, rough, and red, *just a Big Ol' Ugly Devil...*

Rose treated the Watcher as she treated Oskar; with kindness and occasional indulgence, to be given a treat when rewarded, trained for responses, thrown a stick for play, and ignored when she thought better—all because he didn't look like a Deva.

This needs to change. the Watcher grunted: he had to overcome her prejudices against him—but how? Pondering this, he set about securing their next item of business: breakfast. His muscles ached, demanding calories...

Rummaging through the supplies bag, the Watcher pulled out the jar of Amrita. It would not last too long out on the trail, and it looked tasty to him now. *Time to finish it off.* He sat Rose down on a fallen log, then handed her a spoon and opened the jar for her. Linking with her Neural Port, he sat next to her and messaged her through the Ring:

#Breakfast is served—bon appetite.

Rose made a face. "I'm sorry—I shan't. I'll eat something else later..."

He lowered his own spoon and turned towards Rose so she could see he meant business.

#I didn't ask. You'll die without this, so eat it.

"No."

He politely took the jar out of her hands, then removed the spoon from her fingers, and set both items neatly down on the log beside her. Then he removed his coat, his vest and rolled up his sleeves. He reached out to link with Rose:

#All right, let's go.

"Go where?"

#Go 'round and 'round. I was given a job by your Father—I was asked to keep you alive. You didn't challenge me for the job then, and you accepted me taking the job, in front of witnesses. So I took the job, and you had no complaints.

She shifted on the log uncomfortably, looking from side to side.

#But now we're alone, and every time I try to do my job, you openly challenge the way I do it. So, I'm going to give you the same chance I give everyone else who wants to challenge me—if you think you are better than me at keeping both of us alive, then prove it. You want this job? Fight me for it.

He took off his hat.

"But I don't want to fight—I just want to eat what I want. Why does either one of us have to tell the other one what to do?"

#That's part of the whole "keeping you alive" job—you can't survive without the Amrita and its B-12. You want to be a vegan? Fine.

If it wasn't part of keeping you alive, I'd leave you alone about it... but you've got no other source for B-12 right now, and you're hurting yourself.

He straightened his collar and bent down to look in her eyes.

#If you don't like the way I'm doing my job, take my job and do it yourself... but you're going to have to take the job from me, because I'm not going to just roll over and give it to you. It's MY job.

He pointed at the Amrita.

#So, I'm going to do my job, and you're going eat this Amrita—or you're going to fight me. What'll it be?

She looked up into his eyes and smiled, then without warning twined both her arms around his neck.

What is she doing? His eyes opened wide, and his heart began to hammer wildly—she pressed her lips to his ear and whispered:

"Fight."

She kicked his shin, hard—then leapt back away, laughing.

The Watcher sucked in a deep breath and cursed silently. *So that's the way it is...*

Looking up, he heard Oskar whine, confused at the sight of them fighting, and Rose looked at Oskar.

Bingo.

The Watcher stopped all action and gave Rose a disapproving look. He pointed at Rose, then at the little Chupacabra, who whined again, softly, then looked down the trail.

Rose's face fell. "Oh, I'm sorry—Oskar, it's okay, we were just playing." She turned to reassure the hairless mutant.

Just playing? There's no time to play, there's no time for any of this crap...

A swift, soft boot landed on her backside, pushing Rose face first into a pile of dried oak leaves. She looked behind her to see the Watcher standing over her, a dark expression on his face.

"Shhh Oskar, it will all be okay." Rose turned towards the Chupacabra as if to reach out to him—then threw a handful of dried leaves and dirt in the Watcher's face.

He felt an overwhelming itch crawling over him in a vicious wave— *leaf mould, ah gah—*

He sneezed. And sneezed again. *You little Jezebe—*a paroxysm of sneezing overwhelmed him; he became dimly aware of the Afterling laughing at him from somewhere above him. *What the actual hell is wrong* *with me? Why do I keep letting her get away with this? I've never been whupped like this...*

Still violently sneezing, the Watcher stumbled over to the horses, where he blindly groped until his hands found the canteen. He poured the water over his face, then untucked his work shirt to wipe his eyes and nose with the tail of it. Something soft hit him in the head. He reached down to pick it up—it was a sweet yellow pear, just now ripening—

Another pear came sailing through the air, and he caught it. He looked up and saw the Afterling in a pear tree, rising up from a nest of blazing red leaves and golden fruit.

She was wearing his Hat.

Nonchalantly, Rose plucked another fragrant pear and bit it, then threw it at the Watcher. It rolled to his feet; the bruised skin of the fruit displayed the perfect arc of her sharp, perfect teeth.

"You are helpless, Deva..." Rose called down from a tree branch, mirthful; "and I am holding your precious black Hat hostage. Surrender, and I won't fill it full of moldy leaves and ragweed." She pelted him with pears.

The world turned red.

The Watcher tried to remember his anger management classes, but it sounded like static in his memory. The recent struggle with his addiction assaulted him through the static—*it's morning, when the craving hits the hardest...*

The Sun peeked over the tree line, and the golden rays burnished the Afterling's laughing eyes and wild hair with light, and she became a ripe golden pear just out of reach. "Don't be mad, Deva—you told me to fight and I did," she quipped, waving his oilskin hat from the twiggy branches of her tree.

His thick red fingers gripped the battered silver buckle of his tooled leather belt, and he felt his knuckles turning white. He pointed up at Rose, and beckoned her with a gnarled crimson claw. *Come here, now...* She blanched, but maintained an air of bravado.

"Oh, Saul..." She said it with a honeyed voice, murmuring his name as he had always hoped she would say it; he still advanced, heavy feet stomping through the deep dried leaves. *I'm not Oskar—I won't roll over for you.*

The Afterling wheedled: "Don't be angry—you know it's funny."

I'm not laughing. Wicked snarl splitting his face, the Watcher took a step towards the tree as Rose scooted higher into the fragile branches. A high-pitched growl filled the air, growing louder—but it was not his own.

Oskar was standing in the middle of the trail, pointing towards the direction of the distant safe house; the cub's white, wiry hackles were raised, round ears laid back. Abruptly, Oskar leapt into a tree and ran silent along a wide branch, cat-like towards the clearing ahead.

The Watcher grimaced at Rose, pointed down the trail, then put a finger to his own lips—*something feels wrong*. Rose mirrored his motion, suddenly serious. He looked down the lane; he still heard, saw nothing, but Oskar laid his blunt ears back again and growled softly.

He tried to get the Chupacabra's attention with a hand sign—one open hand sweeping up from the waist, then swiping inward to the chest. *Come here*. Oskar, eyes on the clearing, was too far forward to notice the signs. *No way to speak to him—unless…*

The Watcher opened his Xirxes Chat Room to check—Oskar was still logged in to the chat through Chief Emmanuel's hacked Ring, now installed on the hapless cub's tail. Dominic had expressly blocked voice files on the Chat server due to a security exploit—so how to get the Chupacabra to hear a command from the silent Watcher? He scratched his head and whipped through their shared settings… he opened up a tab.

It's worth a shot.

Hacking in to Oskar's Ring through their shared HeadsUp display, the Watcher quickly toggled on the cub's internal setting for Text-2-Talk; he flipped through the pre-set voices and chose Big Tex #1. A pre-packaged digital male voice called to the cub:

#WATCHER: Oskar—come here.

The beast paused, and looked up, confused at the strange-sounding digital voice; an undeniably deep, male voice boomed out with a warm, artificial twang. The sound of the Watcher's digital voice had no direction—it existed only in the Chupacabra's brain. The Watcher tried again, clapping his hands softly this time.

#WATCHER: Oskar—come here.

Oskar turned to look at the Watcher, his small black eyes curious, questioning, the stiff vibrissae of his wrinkled brows quivering. The Watcher made the "come here" gesture again, and spoke to the animal once more via the Ring.

#WATCHER: Good boy, Oskar. Come here.

Once more, the Watcher gestured, and the Chupacabra tilted his head, then came back. *Excellent.* The Watcher gave the signal for heel—bringing his fist up to his chest, then lowering it to circle by his leg. Oskar returned to the Watcher's side.

Rose effused from the pear tree in a whisper: "Good boy, Oskar! What did you see?"

The Watcher pointed to Rose, and beckoned with his finger once again, grumbling. *A wild animal responds better to commands than you do...* he grunted. *That's fixin' to change.*

"Truce?" she whispered.

He growled and slapped the trunk of the tree, and its vermilion leaves quivered.

Duly warned, she hugged the quaking pear tree and tried once more, making her eyes big and shiny: "Truce, please? I'm sorry, but you did ask if I wanted to fight... I was just doing what I thought you wanted me to do. I thought you wanted to spar, and I do know how much you love to spar!"

He shook his head, tight-lipped. Oskar growled again. The Watcher scanned the trees but saw only forest.

"Truce? Please? I'll even say you won if you want me to!"

I don't need you to say I won, you little minx, I'll do it fair and square. Huffing, the Watcher grimaced then pointed at the ground at his feet.

"A truce it is then! Oh, thank you, Deva!" Rose slid down through the thin branches of the tree, landing lightly among leaves to sidle up next to him, handing him his hat as if nothing had happened. He slapped on his hat, then grasped her wrist, scowling wickedly:

Game over.

Incensed, the Watcher hauled her over to the fallen log. *I'll show you a truce...*

A gurgling bark split the air as Oskar lunged forward again. Wiry backridge standing straight up, the little Chupacabra leapt down the trail once more, spitting and snarling toward an unknown danger. Releasing his Afterling trickster, the Watcher bounded after Oskar, grabbing his collar to wrestle the cub back to safety with Rose and the horses.

First, we deal with this threat—then I'll deal with you.

The Watcher tethered Oskar, securing him with a short length of chain to one side of the horses. Nervous, the Chupacabra hassled, then climbed up the trunk to hang upside down from a low branch; the Watcher patted his head and gave him the signal to stay, arm sweeping up, then pushing away from his chest. *Stay.*

Now for the Afterling. He threaded a sinewy hand through the grab-strap on the back of her belt and shook it to get her attention.

#*Stop messing with the Bull, or you're going to get horned.*

"But we don't have any Bulls..."

Aggravated, the Watcher growled.

No, ME—I'm the Bull, and you keep waving red flags at me, trying to rile me up. Just because I told you I'd never hurt you doesn't mean you can do whatever you want without consequence. Stop deliberately provoking me to anger.

"But I wasn't trying to make you angry—I was just playing." Crestfallen, she backed away, confused by his sullen rebuke and her own disappointment at it. "I just wanted to have a little fun with you. I only..."

#*If I want fun, I'll tell you I want fun. If I give you an order, I want you to follow an order. Because you aren't following orders, you aren't going any further away from me than the end of my arm.*

"But that will make it harder for me to scout properly—"

#*If you don't like it, follow orders.*

Time to find out what was lurking in the clearing near the safe house.

#*Can you see anything up ahead, Rose?*

She shook her head. "I can only see movement. I can't make out shapes—the trees are too thick." Peering through the early morning shadows down the trail, she tried to count: "I can see four, maybe five big things, darting shapes? From the trees down to the ground, then moving more slowly back up again... I could scout ahead and see if I can get a closer look if you like."

#*No. I don't want you going up ahead alone.*

"Oh, don't be fussy. I am trained to be an excellent scout. Besides," she leaned back to look at him, smiling brightly, "if you give me a gun, I can dispatch anything you deem a threat." She smiled, deliberately sweet. "Please."

#*Absolutely not. We will go as a team; you will scout, and I will provide cover.*

One hand on Rose, the other holding the Remington, the Watcher led into the woods, off-path. The Watcher's new moccasins made stealthy creeping easier—the rounded soles were less likely to snap twigs. He felt a surge of gratitude to Evangelo for his gift of the moccasins and vowed to repay him somehow. Waxy oak leaf litter was thick here, and dark twisting branches formed a criss-crossed canopy overhead; the slanting rays of the morning sun knifed through the trees to spotlight dark patches between wide oak trunks. He chose a low-slung oak and lifted the Afterling onto a branch, then pulled himself up into the tree. Here, they should be out of harm's way.

The Watcher coupled their ports to speak to Rose:

#Climb out as far as possible on a branch that will support us both, one that will allow you to overlook the clearing. Scout, and tell me what you see.

She nodded and chose a branch, crept down it a ways, then backtracked and chose another one, thicker, with a higher angle. This she followed about halfway out, until at last she could look out over the clearing. Lying on the branch to spread out his weight behind her, the Watcher held on to her grab-strap as she perched lightly on the branch, surefooted.

A decrepit, corrugated metal shack, maybe twenty-four feet by eighteen feet, was half-obscured by twiggy, bare bushes. Sagging timbers and cracked windows hinted at abandonment, but a glimpse of a high, comfy bed and an overstuffed chair beckoned beneath a metal five-pointed star, and a small wood stove waited inside, much like the one found in the previous safe house at Mystery Outpost.

At the thought of forty-eight hours of private, secure comfort in a warm cabin the Watcher blushed; there beneath a downy plaid quilt was the perfect place to lay down the rules of engagement with Rose. He made plans for the comfy bed and turned his attentions back to the reason for his plans.

Rose seemed intensely agitated by something below in the heavy brush, and he could feel her tension and excitement as she observed, head following a motion unseen to him. "Oh Deva, it's wonderful!" Rose whispered, "I had never even hoped to see these in the wild!"

See what? Skip the wonderful and tell me what it is...

"This is absolutely stunning! Oh, take a holovid, please, and put this in my Life-List notes, time and date stamped—an autumn denning of five Feathered Serpents, large, in adult plumage. They may be going through a fall molt.... "

Wait... *Feathered Serpents?* He tugged on her grab-strap, twice. She turned to him and he held out his hand to message her:

#What do you mean "Feathered Serpents?" There's no such thing except in drunken rumors and Ancient MesoAmerican Religions. Explain.

She looked surprised—"Oh, they are real! The Asura are trained to look for them, in the wild, along with other rare creatures such as Horny Toads, Melanistic Jaguars, and Soft-Shelled Turtles. Now, if I told you it was an Ivory-Billed Woodpecker, well then you'd have a right to be skeptical. But these are verifiable..."

#*Tell me what they do. What are the threats?*

"Oh... I thought you'd know. Well, I shan't leave out any necessary details; they have short, back-curving, non-venomous fangs, a venomous cartilaginous tail spine, and beautiful feathers along the back ridge, with the smaller breeding males exhibiting a ruff and crest of brilliant feathers. Of course, they have spreading ribs which allow them to glide, like all flying snakes—"

The Watcher's face became ashen.

#*What the hell do you mean "flying snakes?"*

"Well, technically they don't really fly—they just glide. They have to climb up the tree and then swoop down out of the branches to land on their prey, their glorious feathers trailing behind them like living rainbows." She appeared entranced by the thought of gliding, rainbow-flavored death.

#*But there are no flying snakes in Texas, those are old-world tropical reptiles...*

"But there ARE flying snakes in Texas—they're right here. Look, one's climbing that tree—" Rose pointed.

Next to the clearing he saw a sinuous shape ascending an oak, moving upwards in rapid, hypnotic motion—

A snake the size of a full-grown green anaconda—perhaps fifteen feet long—was rippling up the trunk of the tree, sporting a ridge of fantastic emerald feathers trailing along its back, ruby eyes glittering against olive green scales—*Quetzalcoatl come to life, the Feathered Serpent of the Aztecs*—the Watcher felt a wave of nausea sweep over him as the reptile turned towards them, raising its gigantic head to flick its tongue out.

"Oh Deva! Just look at how majestic—"

Whipping his Remington from the quick-grab holster behind him, he blasted it in the head, and the snake's cranium split open like a melon.

"But I wanted to watch it for just a moment..." Rose's voice trailed off.

The snake slid to the ground, coiling and uncoiling; a gleaming white spine perhaps a foot long, reminiscent to a stingray's spine, jabbed out of the tail as it writhed. He aimed into the elm to their left, shot again, and another green reptilian fell wriggling to the ground.

Something was sailing through the air towards them—flat, long, with narrow green feathers fluttering out behind it...

He raised the Remington to fire. Awestruck at the sight of the gargantuan reptile's rippling plumage, Rose gasped and bumped back against the Watcher's arm—

Missed!

The Feathered Serpent landed on the branch behind them, branch groaning beneath the weight of the huge creature. Prostrate, the Watcher turned to see a feathered head the size of a dinner plate sliding along, tongue licking the air, ten feet away. Sindee belched fire as the Watcher fired at the bobbing head. He didn't miss this time; the snake's crested head splattered, spraying bloody droplets everywhere, spangling the feathers with gore. The spiny barb unsheathed as the tail contracted, whipping through the air—

The snake's tail spine slashed the neck of another Feathered Serpent as it glided through the air, landing on the branch behind the first. Still lying down, gripping the bark with his legs and one hand threaded though Rose's grab-strap, the Watcher unloaded a slug into the snake's widening jaws. Gleaming double rows of teeth shattered as the Remington's last chambered 12-gauge slug tore through them, disrupting their perfect symmetry. The tail spine stabbed the tree branch as the beautiful abomination fell twisting to the moldering leaf litter below.

The air vibrated ahead of the Watcher, to his right—

Gripping his legs tightly around the stout oak limb, he yanked Rose off the branch as another enormous Feathered Serpent ripped past where she had perched only a split-second earlier. Off balance, the Watcher's body swung underneath the branch. Bushmaster dangling from its sling, Remington in one hand and Rose in the other, they were swinging some thirty feet above the forest floor.

Missing its mark, the Feathered Serpent overshot the branch and glided gracefully to earth, down the trail. The Watcher and Rose heard Oskar growl shrilly.

"It's heading towards the horses and Oskar!" Rose squealed.

Upside down, the Watcher held Rose's grab-belt with his left hand and the Remington with his right. The weapon was out of ammo, and there was no way to quickly perform a one-handed reload—*time for the Bushmaster.* Swinging from the branch by his powerful legs, he clipped the

Remington into his belt holster, and reached for the rifle—

Rose snatched the dangling AR-15 off the Watcher's quick-connect swivel.

HEY—

Glossy scales slithered through waxy leaves, whispering against the trail, echoing the hiss of the serpent. Oro and Shadow whickered and jumped at the end of their tethers, whites of their eyes showing their terror. Oskar lunged to the end of his chain, claw flailing, fangs foaming as the snake raised its head to strike—

Hands clammy with a cold fear, Rose breathed out and squeezed the trigger in a smooth, slow motion.

Blood spurted from the perfectly placed shot, a crimson fountain beneath the serpent's feathered plume just behind the snake's left eye. It suddenly coiled into a wiggling, rolling mass as the horses shrieked, panicked. Obscenely beautiful in death, the Feathered Serpent thrashed just feet beyond the reach of Oskar's straining leash...

"Oskar—no! Stay—" voice trailing away, fear finally overtook Rose and the rifle dropped from her cataplectic fingers to bounce into the leafy duff below.

Awe temporarily replaced the Watcher's aggravation: *that was one hell of a shot.* He was all at once glad she was good marksman and angry she had disobeyed his order.

Still hanging from the branch, the Watcher clambered sloth-like towards the trunk, gripping Rose's belt. Now limp, Rose was a lot less trouble... the Watcher eased down to the next branch, and propped himself into the crotch of the tree, draping a limp but recovering Rose up across the branch beside him. He kept one hand on the back of her grab-belt so she wouldn't slip off the branch, and put his other hand on his Remington, scanning the surrounding trees for any more gliding, glittering death vipers. Minutes passed and no new reptiles presented themselves; that was good, because Rose was attempting to gain control of herself again, pushing up to climb back on the branch again—

If I wasn't so busy fighting Ancient Aztec GodBeasts, I would lay down my Law on you right now.

Still pushing down on her grab-belt, the Watcher toyed with his weapon, scanning for movement.

Rose gave a small grunt and pushed up. "I'm good—you can let me up now..."

Holding her down, hand spread across the small of her back, he let a long, low growl escape his lips, expressing his displeasure without words.

"Oh, this is ridiculous—I just saved Oskar and the Horses! I did it for you..." Tears welled in her eyes, looking up at him as she tried to push up off the branch. The Watcher threw a leg over her and reloaded his Remington as a wriggling emerald creature slid through the leaves below them.

The Watcher fired off a slug into a smaller, gorgeously green-gold feathered snake, flicking a forked tongue at the growing pile of blasted serpents at the base of the tree. Blood spattered as the slug tore through the sinuous muscles rippling beneath the gleaming scales. Torn by the shot, the serpent twisted and stabbed with its tail spine.

Patient, he waited until he was at last satisfied there were no more feathered monsters lurking in the shadows. *How many more of these things are out there?* Time to find out and wipe them out...

Holding tight to the grab handle, he pulled Rose in close and slid down the trunk. Eyes up, and steering clear of the mound of Serpents, he retrieved the AR-15, no worse for wear, then looked to their animals tied at the end of the lane. They all seemed well, but he needed to check. Rose seemed to be fully functional, and the Watcher let her walk beside him.

They moved low and fast, wary of any additional surprises that might be lurking in the trees. Rose, apparently aware of the Watcher's irritation at her, kept her eyes open and her mouth shut... for now.

Reaching the horses and Oskar, the Watcher pointed for her to check the Chupacabra while he inspected the horses. Oro was sweating, and Shadow rolled his eyes, but Oskar was just glad of the company, twirling his hairless pink tail around Rose's arm and yowling as if he wanted to talk.

"Oh, did you miss me?" Rose squeezed Oskar. "Don't worry sweet baby... when we settle in, we can have cuddly-wuddly time." The Chupacabra's fleshy muzzle showed a happy row of jagged teeth as he burped and grinned, still clinging to his branch with razor-clawed, prehensile paws. Rose stroked his single curl between his ears.

Cuddly-wuddly... It aggravated the Watcher to hear her talk that way to the odious little beast. *She never offers the Snake Killer cuddly-wuddly time.* Not that he needed any such thing, he grumped to himself. All things apropos, he secured the animals, then inspected the surrounding area once more. Nothing seen, he turned his attention to the Afterling, joining hands with her—

#Don't ever touch my weapons again without asking. Make up for it by helping me find these horrors. Can you see through walls?

"Well, I'm not sure it's really seeing, but it's more like detection, or like feeling light. Sometimes I can detect through thin walls, only warm things, and if the weather is cool, I can detect better."

#I need you to detect these snakes now—we are approaching the safe house, and if you detect any heat or motion, even if it's faint, tell me.

"Will do!" She seemed to be glad to be busy and not have to deal with interpersonal dramas.

They entered the clearing, creeping slowly through the heavy brush. The morning sun was heating up nicely now, and the little clearing around the shack, with the sunlight reflecting off the unpainted metal of the ancient outbuilding, made a warm place for snakes and other cold-blooded creatures to gather. The wooden door to the shack was closed, and the windows boarded, but a heavy, musky odor belied the snakes. He could feel them—an uneasy, unnatural presence.

"Well, that's odd—there appears to be a heat source inside the house; some kind of very large object." Rose wrinkled her nose at the smell. The Watcher was getting a bad feeling about this...

They flanked the house, checking the sides from a cautious distance of twenty feet; as they turned the corner at the back of the house, he was overpowered by acrid musk, the unmistakable eye-watering stench of snake wafting up from a clump of thorny bushes by the back wall. Circling with her behind him, he saw it—a large burrow, perhaps four feet in diameter, tunneling under the back wall of the shack.

"Oh, that's where the heat source is located! It's much brighter when I look down this hole—"

Her keen observation was interrupted by the Watcher picking her up, tucking her under his arm, then stealthily beating a hasty retreat back down the lane towards the Horses.

There's not enough kerosene left in the world to burn this thing fast enough... Even though the morning air was still cool, the Watcher could feel himself break into a sweat at the thought of a den of possibly dozens of giant, feathered, flying snakes wriggling out to lance them with massive stingers. His absolute horror at this development did not go unnoticed by the Afterling.

"Are you afraid of snakes?" Rose asked sympathetically, bouncing beneath his arm. He held out a slightly sweaty hand.

#I am not afraid of snakes. I hate snakes.

"Oh! Perhaps we should leave... this may not be a good place for you to be if you have a phobia of snakes."

#Hate is not a phobia—hate is a well-earned and completely rational feeling, and the last thing I need to do is leave. I just need to think for a moment.

"Would you like to talk about it?"

#No, I don't want to talk about it, I want to do something about it, but I don't have a flamethrower.

He glowered as he mourned his lack of flammable liquids.

"Silly, why would you need a flamethrower? That would just burn the shack down... anyway, you shouldn't just kill them. Perhaps we could train one to be a pet, like Oskar."

The Watcher shuddered at the thought. The only way he'd ever train an abomination like that would be with a SHIVA device—*with the setting on high...*

Suddenly the Watcher's eyes lit up with an unseemly joy. He bounded to the Horses, Rose still clutched under his left arm. Lifting her into Oro's saddle, he pulled out the weapons bag. Rose became suspicious.

"Why are you so happy all the sudden?"

He pulled out the silver SHIVA weapons. Two were small hand-held affairs, cleverly disguised as a power drill and a cake mixer, to allow them to be smuggled into LifeBefore Texas during the Sino-Straya War. The other a longer device in the guise of a large reciprocating saw; he took the large energy weapon, turning it over in his hands to inspect it...

Rose turned a paler shade of gold.

"Oh, Deva I'm sorry, I'm sorry I took the weapon from you. I'm sorry I dropped it—please..." Her lips trembled, real fear this time.

He shook his head, then jerked a thumb at his own back, and held up four fingers—

"Oh—Bodyguard Carry Number Four—Piggyback, right? But why?"

He growled and motioned again, backing up to Oro so she could climb on easily; not wishing to bring down the wrath of SHIVA, Rose complied and climbed up, Piggyback, putting her arms around his thick neck to hold on tight. As she hooked the toes of her pink cowboy boots into the pockets of his long trench coat, using them as stirrups, he reached over his shoulder to message Rose:

#I won't ever use a SHIVA device on you. I don't need a weapon to

show you I'm in charge. But I do need your heat detection powers. You're coming with me to help me deal with my feelings about snakes. We're going to their burrow, and you'll tell me what you see.

"Well, dealing with feelings is certainly healthier than just burning everything to the ground. You know, everything has its place in God's creation." Her cheery Morale Officer voice masked her fear; Rose seemed relieved that the Watcher was not ready to use SHIVA devices on her yet. "If we are going to try to capture a Feathered Serpent as a specimen, then a young one would be best..."

Not quite what I have in mind. The Watcher rubbed Oskar's head and gave the signal for the stay command; then he made his way quietly back down the trail and around to the burrow, with his Afterling guide clinging to his broad back. He lined himself up with the hole, some fifty feet from the entrance to the snake pit.

"How do you intend to capture one? Shall I make a noise to lure one out?" Rose inquired of the Watcher. He emphatically shook his head, then pulled the SHIVA rifle and the Remington out from under his coat, one in each massive hand...

Placing the wristband on his arm, he pushed the brass sliding toggle on the right side of the SHIVA weapon all the way towards the muzzle of the device and opened the brass collet aperture wider to cast a medium choke pattern. He then pointed the muzzle of the weapon down the hole.

"Deva, that might not be a good idea..."

He squeezed the handle of the stock and kept holding it. The musky smell wafting out of the snake pit became heated, and the sound of hissing became louder...

Five seconds passed, then a pop, and the sizzling sound of bursting snake carcasses filled the air. One, then two, then more—like popcorn, only louder, and meatier. He released the trigger momentarily to avoid overheating the SHIVA device.

Rose gasped—"Something is coming up out of the hole!"

Sing, Sindee, sing... the Remington sang out a blast just as the Watcher saw the glint of the Serpent's metallic feathers, then another shot, and the remains of the giant snake stopped mid-slither to slide back down into the hole. He resumed squeezing the trigger of the SHIVA device...

An unholy glee seized the Watcher for the next twelve minutes as this pattern repeated itself; the sound of exploding snakes interspersed with the roar of his gun, a symphony of glorious reptilian carnage to his ears, interrupted only by rapid reloading of his Remington.

Rose threw up twice, discreetly, hanging off the Watcher's back; he did not notice.

Now the crackle of fats and skin was heard as the charred snakes finally burst into flames. Not content to leave them to their fate, the Watcher shot a few more rounds into burrow, until a fireball belched from the hole; they could smell wood and snake flesh burning. Sick, Rose paused from her heaving to observe: "I think the floor of the shack is catching fire..." The Watcher grimaced wickedly, his scar twitching with each burst of flame.

Let it burn.

The flames roared up, catching the interior of the house ablaze; then the metal roof started to fall in. He stopped shooting long enough to realize that he was probably wasting ammunition at this point.

Good. Snakes are well worth the ammo spent.

The Watcher stepped back, enjoying the warmth of the flames. Rose, still clinging to his back, buried her bare face and gloved hands in the heavy leather of his coat collar to protect them from firebrands as they floated down. The Watcher had no such intention to hide from the devastation of his Serpent War; the heavy plated skin of his face rippled red and gold, lit with an inner fire, fed by outer conflagration around him.

Rose whispered: "Something rises..."

A twisting column of fire rose from the ruins as the final Feathered Serpent writhed up from the ashes, towering twelve feet skyward. Fire wreathed each feather in glowing scarlet and liquid bronze; showers of sparks cascaded as the billows of light and energy surged upward. Higher the Serpent climbed, expanding, rising free of the burrow in the superheated updraft—then the glorious monster spontaneously combusted, disintegrating into thousands of molten stars.

A scream of metal echoed, and the burning back wall of the shack toppled onto the burrow, burying the snake den in a serpentine pyre of wood and metal. Fiery clouds ascended from the collapse, carrying the ashes of the Feathered Serpents upward into Heaven.

Mesmerized, Rose murmured through the smoke: "I don't believe we'll be staying at the safe house tonight."

A shudder of satisfaction shivered down the Watcher's spine, and Rose felt it ripple through her hands—frightening, fascinating, she could feel the energy of his uncontrollable Elemental Spirit. Savage, the Watcher

bared his teeth in triumph.
Some things just need killing.

———————◆———◆———◆———————

The safe house was burning to the ground—and any safety left in their world was burning with it. Having rid their present surroundings of the horrors known as Feathered Serpents, the Watcher prepared to depart from the resultant enormous bonfire, which would soon beckon any enemy looking to find them.

Stopping to document the Feathered Serpents with his Ring, the Watcher made several Holo-graphs; then pulling his Bowie Knife, he approached the tail of the smaller snake, cut in half by his slug. Even a half-hour past their demise, he was concerned about reflexive biting or spinal envenomation, and he approached both ends cautiously. Planting his boot on the tail of the creature, he carefully plucked several handfuls of sparkling green feathers from the genetically modified terrors, then scalped the glimmering crimson and gold crest off the male. Perhaps the feathers could be used as barter...

As they passed the pear tree, he stopped to stuff Rose's apron pockets full of the pears she had earlier pelted his way, exploiting the Afterling's cheeky escapade to gain the previously unreachable fruits. All the while deep in thought, the Watcher was planning their flight to some as-of-yet-undisclosed location—and Rose was pleading her case as to why the Watcher should be merciful unto her, a sinner:

"I only grabbed the Bushmaster because the snake was going to attack Oskar. I would do the same thing for you—remember, I killed that Lady Devil, Judge whats-her-face—"

#And I'm eternally grateful. I too was going to shoot the snake, but when I reached for the Bushmaster, it was gone—someone took it. That someone was you. So, we are going to come to an understanding, since you are not understanding.

Reaching the horses, he secured all gear, and prepared the horses to leave. He pulled Rose's deer hide cloak over her head, jerking the hood up to hide her in case they were spotted on the trail. Rose gawped. "What choice did I have? I had no way to know that you could hang upside down, hold on to me, and still make the shot!"

#Well, maybe I wouldn't have made the shot—maybe I would have

missed, like I missed that earlier one. We'll never know. What we do know is you missed your shot at following the Rules. You didn't follow me, you didn't trust me, and you didn't tell me.

Rose was confused. "But you don't follow anyone else's rules..."

One hand still linked to the Afterling, he reached under Oro's belly to tighten the cinch strap.

#I don't have to follow anyone else's Rules—I'm in charge, and I make my own Rules.

"Well, you can't just go around telling other people what to do—"

#Yes, I can—other people are the ones who put me in charge.

"But I'm not 'other people'. I'm Asura, and only..." Her voice trailed off.

He leaned an elbow on the horn of the saddle, and stabbed an accusing finger at her.

#So only the Deva can tell the Asura what to do?

"I didn't say that!"

#So, I'm not Deva?

"No, I—"

#I forgot how high and mighty you think you are, compared to this Big Ol' Ugly Devil. You want me to bow at your feet? I already did. But even when I'm bowing at your feet, I'm still Deva. I outrank you.

"I didn't mean it that way—"

The Watcher unleashed his thoughts.

#Yes, you did, and I've got news for you, Princess: the Deva are the ones who put me in charge of YOU. Let me count the ways...

"Oh, you don't have to do that..."

He held up his gloved right fist, popping out a digit for each point.

#Let the record reflect:

ONE—The Deva made The System

TWO—The System appointed Warden Howell

THREE—Warden Howell deputized me as your Recovery Agent

FOUR—He put me under the Director's command

FIVE—The Director proclaimed me Deva under the System and Commander under the Lone Star.

All his fingers now extended, the Watcher held up his hand in an Oath, the sign of the Abhaya Mudra: compelled, Rose answered him, subconsciously raising her hands in Lotus Mudra. A flicker of aggravation at her own reflexive conditioning rippled across her face; the Watcher noted it. *I don't need AutoSpeex to tell me what you're thinking... you're thinking you shouldn't have to salute a Big Ol' Ugly Devil.*

He jerked an angry thumb at his Badge:

#Whether we're under the Eight-Pointed Star of The System, or the Five-Pointed Star of the Revolution, the result is the same; I'm in charge, I'm the Boss, I'm the Man—

Tossing Rose up into Oro's saddle, the Watcher retrieved a spoon from their interrupted breakfast setting:

#And I say you are going to eat this Amrita, or—

He looked for the jar where he left it on the log... *not there...* he looked under the log. *Nothing...*

You. He noticed the Chupacabra looked sheepish; walking over to the tree where Oskar was chained, he searched and found the jar in the fork of the tree next to the shame-faced beast, its empty glass spotlessly clean.

"Oh Oskar, you were hungry!" Rose said sympathetically, "It's a good thing I saved my Amrita for you."

The Watcher glared at the Afterling, then at Oskar, shaking the jar at the Chupacabra and scolding though the Text-2-Talk:

#WATCHER: NO, Oskar, BAD. Bad...

Oskar whined and groveled at the booming digital voice. Perturbed at the loss of their breakfast, and subsequent the delay of resolution in the Amrita Battle, the Watcher turned to Rose and held out the empty jar:

#You're not getting out of this, Rose—when we get settled in, I am going to make a new batch of this stuff, and you are going to eat Amrita if it harelips every mule in Texas.

Rose tilted her head, confused: "What does that even mean?"

A text box popped up in chat:

#EMMANUEL: o

The Watcher looked alarmed. Why is Emmanuel's Ring activating in chat?

Must be a glitch, or worse, a hack: he opened Emmanuel's directory to lock the security settings.

#EMMANUEL: oo owo,&°¤

"Oh, what... who is that?" Able to see the Xirxes chatroom directory through their linked devices, Rose swiped at her HeadsUp display. Suddenly intense, she turned to Oskar: "Oskar, is that you?"

Oskar whined.

#EMMANUEL: io&w,

Oskar? That's not possible. The Watcher snorted and continued to toggle settings—there was no beacon available so *it can't be a hack, it has to be a glitch...*

Rose patted Oskar: "Oh quick, if you really are Deva, read Oskar's mind!"

The Watcher unchained Oskar, who writhed and cowered; he patted Oskar to comfort him, then ascended into his saddle and linked again with Rose.

#I'll Deva his mind another time. We're leaving before someone sees the smoke from our bonfire and decides to investigate.

Rose grabbed ahold "But where will we go? Father said we were to all meet here in forty-eight hours."

#We will; but between now and then, we ride—we need to take shelter far from here, and we have a little investigation of our own to do. I have a hunch about the origin of those Serpents, and I intend to see if I'm right.

He opened Evangelo's uploaded map link and zoomed in on a green patch designated "FORBIDDEN ZONE—HAZMAT" on the map, a little more than a half-day's ride to their southeast.

#How are you at surveillance, Rose?

Intrigued, she replied: "Surveillance? You mean I get to watch someone else instead of them just watching me?"

The Watcher gave a quick nod of his head, then slapped the reins against Oro's neck; they were on the trail again.

———•—•—•———

From his perch up on the Ridge, Evangelo could see the lights of home. It had been a long trail, bypassing the usual stop at the Leyden Peanut Plantation with its grand balcony and familiar faces. He would have welcomed the chance to take another hot shower and stock up on salted peanuts, but it was simply too dangerous to stop.

The little Ranger breathed in the smell of hay and horses; the last of the sweetgum leaves were fluttering silver in the night wind. His mind wandered away to the first time he ever saw this place, how he chose everything, all for the love of Shaney... the cabins overlooking the arroyos thick with yaupon and pecan, the rock walkways, the comfortable bathrooms, the abundant water—it was all for her.

Behind him in the saddle, the Director tapped his shoulder. They had tied Dominic's horse, Charger, in a secluded, secure barn one mile to the southwest, and the Director had mounted William behind Evangelo. The Director motioned for the Ranger to stop and slid off the horse's crupper; he spoke low and quickly:

"We start our comms blackout now and continue until we are clear of the Checkpoint Black Beacon. Give me at least thirty minutes to get in place for entry. Flash your Ring's WeLites, facing north, when you leave your cabin and head towards Shaney: I'll make my way to Emmanuel's cabin at that time. Cough twice when you leave her cabin if the scene is secure; cough three times and I'll know to take cover." He pulled up his gray bandana to obscure his face. "We'll rendezvous at the southern crossroad; I will make a whippoorwill's call, and you answer back with a tap on a tree trunk. Take care." The Director vanished into the gloom.

The only thing that's missing is the secret hi-sign and handshake, the Ranger thought wryly. He turned to his task, and his heart sank with an iron certainty that life would never again be the same after tonight. *There will be no turning back...* Riding the out of the oak and pine woods, he headed for the high wooden gate of Checkpoint Black. William snorted in anticipation.

"Halt; who goes there?" A shadowy figure at the lanterned gate called into the darkness.

"Ranger Captain Evangelo, Tejas Co-op, " Evangelo replied.

"Advance to be recognized."

Evangelo stepped into the light; he removed his cowboy hat, allowing the flame from above to illuminate his high, fine-scaled cheek bones, plated prominent brow ridge, and chiseled jaw line.

The guard grunted the callsign: "Moon—"

Hungry, Evangelo called back, "Pie."

The guard peered at him from beneath a great sloppy-brimmed sombrero. "Hey, Captain, welcome home—all's well. Sergeant Federer was hoping you'd come! He's down at the stable. Sunshine is fixing to foal."

"Thank you, Corporal Louis; I'll head that way." He clicked softly and turned William down the path towards the barn. The warm glow of the lanterns made bright the path to the stables, and William's hooves clopped down the familiar ironstone path. Here he felt most at home, more alive than he had anywhere else on earth; the soft breaths of his horses greeted them, and William answered each in kind. The Ranger spoke in subdued greeting to them:

"Daddy's home."

Ambling up under the gazebo, he tied William, still tacked out, next to a water trough and a manger of hay. "I'll be back soon, Will—stay ready." Patting the big Bay, he made his way down the lighted path to the Great Barn. Once an open-air picnic pavilion of red stone, steel, and cedar, it was now a sheltered-in barn with fully accommodated stalls. Spacious and close to the pond to allow for easy watering, Evangelo was proud of his barn, and proud of his horses within.

Captain Evangelo's Horse Ranch was the pride of the Rangers and his very own Haven of Joy. The little Ranger had dreamed it from the first day he had tamed his first horse, Star—a snow-white yearling, destined to become the first of nearly one hundred horses he would break and breed over the course of four decades. The breeding program was slow going at first—the bio-agent disrupted equine breeding cycles, somewhat like it did human fertility—but after the first decade, the horses gradually started to become fertile once more. Then the work of the breeding program began in earnest.

Myriad beautiful colors and patterns bedecked Evangelo's warhorses. He bred them for intelligence, soundness, and size, but their own markings and tonalities he allowed to manifest as Nature willed it. He considered it an embodiment of the creativity of God, to see their uniqueness revealed upon the day of their birth:

dapples, appaloosas, palominos, paints, grullos, sorrels, creams, roans, grays, buckskins, blacks, duns—

No matter the coat, they were all beautiful in their own right, glorious and shining as the hand of God who made them. They tossed their satiny manes as Evangelo entered, a King among his adoring court of princesses and their progeny.

Down the center aisle, flanked left and right by his brooding mares, he made his way, reaching out to wordlessly touch each waiting nose as he walked by, until at last he came to a stall, where an anxious Hombre was playing midwife to a beautiful gold Buckskin Dun mare. Evangelo could hear the man muttering unawares as he approached, the mare lying on her side in the hay.

"There's a girl, you've got two hooves out—let's give a push and see a nose..." The muttering Hombre reached out to pat the flank as he made his way around the sweating horse; deep in labor, she whickered.

"Good evening, Sergeant Federer; how is my Sunshine?" Evangelo leaned over the stable gate. The other Hombre jumped—

"Cap! Ah, God—don't scare a man like that. What the actual hell, are you trying to give me a heart attack?"

"It's good to see you too, Andre... how is she doing?" The Captain entered the stall and reached over to stroked the mare's neck. She snorted, and pushed.

"She's doing better than I am right now, no thanks to you. It's almost ten o'clock at night—why are you dragging in so late? Where have you been? We've got a bunkhouse full of Rangers who are chomping at the bit for your sage advice on their horse problems, but they're stuck with me and Rigsby. What's the deal? You usually don't just disappear like that—"

"I had unexpected business." Evangelo stroked the horse's black mane and inspected her.

"Yeah, the Commander just said you were busy. We all know what 'busy' means; but it's just been a while since you've been busy like that."

Evangelo nodded. "Do you have it all under control?"

The Sergeant grimaced. "Yes, but that doesn't mean anyone likes it—and that includes horses."

Tasked with giving the Director time to set up before breaking into Chief Emmanuel's cabin, Evangelo contented himself with the solemn sanctity of the foaling barn. Minutes passed as the men commented on the nature of the mare, of the foal's cream-colored sire, and the probabilities of the foal's coat pattern and color.

Sunshine groaned and whickered, straining. At last, a push, and another, then a wriggling foal poured out of the dark-maned golden mare—*life*.

Evangelo felt a bubble of joy. "That's my girl, Sunshine! Oh, it's a little filly, a beauty—" still cowled in the whitish amniotic sac, they could see a tiny Dunalino foal, pale, white mane and tail—golden, perfect. The Lieutenant pierced the sack at the tip, and pulled out a soft little nose, wiping the fluid out of the foal's nostrils with a soft cloth.

The Lieutenant beamed, glad that all seemed well with mare and foal: "I'm glad you were here—Sunshine tolerates me, but she's your girl. She's not happy when you're away."

Evangelo rubbed the mare's ears, "I don't like it either, but there are some things that simply can't be helped, Andre. I've got to go check in with the Commander." He stroked Sunshine's velvety muzzle and she huffed, sniffing his hand before nosing her filly with interest. "That's my girl—

A vicious pang seized him, the realization that this might be the last time he would see his beloved mare. His hand lingered on her silky mane as he whispered to the Sergeant: "Take care of my baby for me."

Reluctant, the Ranger took his leave.

Carefully securing each gate behind him, he made his way across the wooden footbridge, stopping to gaze out across the arroyo briefly; the horse pasture, with its glistening pond and pavilions, had been his island of serenity for the past four decades; within its confines, he had shared the closest relationship to Shaney he would ever enjoy. As Horseman and Horsewoman, together they had created this little slice of Horse Heaven. Evangelo looked up at the moon with its white veil of wispy clouds, closing his eyes to remember always this moment. Crossing over the ravine, he moved up the trail past the bunkhouse to his own cabin.

His dusty boots had no sooner hit the steps of his screened in porch then he heard a grumbling voice call out:

"'Bout time you came back, Cap... where you been?" The voice floated up from a darkly rugged macho whittling in a rocking chair next to the wood stove. "People have been inquiring 'bout you."

Evangelo felt a warmth at the familiar greeting. "Hello, Quincy. I suppose those inquiring would be you..."

"Maybe. Me and some others. You might ought to tell a body when you decide to disappear." The Lieutenant kept whittling, trying to look unperturbed.

"It was unexpected. Is everything in order around here?" Evangelo looked around for any signs of disruption of his personal belongings.

Lieutenant Rigsby appeared irritated. "As much as usual. I'm having to fend off questions from certain people about where you've gone and what you're doing—can you at least give me a warning the next time you decide to leave without warning?"

"If I could, I would, Quincy. You know that."

"Fair enough. Have you heard from Chief Emmanuel? Shadow's up to get shoed—you know he's got tender feet." The Lieutenant said it with pointed interest.

"No, Chief hasn't messaged me in the last few days." Evangelo answered honestly, then walked over to his bunk, with its faded patchwork quilt and comfy pillow. *It would sure feel good to just lie down and go back to the way things were, before Afterlings and Revolution...* He thought about his future, sighed, and pulled out a worn leather knapsack from beneath his bed.

The fine string he had looped around the buckle was broken... *Someone searched my knapsack.* Wary, he turned to his other personal effects to inspect them.

A thick book in a cracked black leather binding lay upon the table next to Evangelo's bunk. Gilt letters, worn with age, testified to the nature of the Book, the ancient blue-ribbon bookmark frayed. The Captain's hand ran across it, and he opened it to the bookmark—the Gospel of John, Chapter One, Verse Five:

> *And the Light shineth in the Darkness, and the Darkness comprehended it not...*

Rigsby leaned forward and lowered his whittling to look up at his Captain. "It's not for me to say, Boss, but times have changed. I know you love being a Ranger—but that Book is holding you back from everything you could be in this Organization. You could've been Chief if it hadn't been for that Book. You should've been Chief..." The Macho jabbed his knife towards the Book, resentful. "Maybe it's finally time for you to choose—that old relic, or the Rangers?"

Evangelo closed the relic lovingly and slipped it in his knapsack. "Perhaps you are right. Thank you for the kind advice." He looked up at his bunkmate with sad eyes. "Quincy, if anything should ever happen to me," he spoke casually, "...you and Andre are to take care of the horses. My things, you can split them up between you."

The Macho looked up, "That dangerous, huh? Well, count me in, pardner—but you know that final decision on the horses and your stuff is up to her Majesty in yonder castle." He jerked his head towards Shaney's cabin. "And you need to know she's one of them that's been asking if you checked in."

Evangelo set his jaw. "I suppose I better check in, then."

He stepped out the cabin, and flicked on his WeLites once, discreetly, facing north...

Time to move, Dominic.

Through the darkness, the little Ranger could see a lantern sparkling through the twiggy brush. Familiar sorrow twisted his heart as he set his Ring to play Cindy Walker's ballad of love unloved, unending:

> *...You don't know me*

His foot fell along the well-travelled path towards the lantern, drawn like a moth to her flame. On the wind, he could hear a pert feminine voice talking to Storm out in the personal stable next to her cabin, and his heart became heavier with each step.

"You big baby, don't you make me smack you—Mamma's got a right to check your feet..." He heard her grunt and heard the horse snort. "There's nothing wrong with you. Stop complaining."

Evangelo walked around the side of her cabin, where he had built Storm's stable all those years ago; unable to bear being away from her beloved horse for one moment, Shaney had begged for a stable to be attached to her cabin so she could spend more time with the animal... and as usual, Evangelo made it happen. He looked over the stable door to see Shaney leaning against the Appaloosa's flank, fussing; undressed for bed, her curves strained against her beige, long-tailed t-shirt, her bare, sleek-scaled legs glittering in the lantern's glow. He cleared his throat and swallowed hard.

She gasped, drew her snub-nosed .38 and turned those blue eyes round towards him; his earth stood still, but not because of the gun. Had she fired, he probably would have never noticed until he bled to death... *Oh God, why did you make her eyes so big and blue?*

She lowered the gun in her hands. "Oh, it's you Raffi! I didn't expect you until tomorrow morning—" She smiled, and the whole world was suddenly beautiful to Evangelo; a warning inner thought tapped on his shoulder; *why did she expect me tomorrow morning?*

She laughed. "Why are you standing there all tongue tied—speak up and tell me what happened!" Shaney pushed back her white hat, revealing her perfect, fine features. Satiny scales followed the curves of her face, tracing the arc where her eyebrows once grew, as if she were covered in lacy copper tracery.

He gathered himself. "I'm sorry, C-Commander; I ran into some complications. But first, what's the problem with S-Storm?"

She seemed taken aback at his lack of kowtowing. "Oh, well, he's been favoring his left front foot. It's not laminitis, and I can't figure it out." She ran her fingers through the horse's streaked gray and white mane. "He's probably just spoiled, aren't you, you giant slacker..."

Slinging his knapsack off, Evangelo backed up and pulled up the horse's foot between his knees. He probed gently with the hard tips of his fingers, running them along the inside edge of the hoof, at the white line; then clamping the hoof between his knees, he opened his knapsack and pulled out a large set of tweezers and a sharp, hooked probe. Resettling himself, Evangelo dug into Storm's hoof with the probe. He pulled forth a hidden bit of wood, then dropped the probe and grabbed the sliver with the tweezers; a wicked, narrow mesquite thorn slid out of the tender tissue between the horny hoof wall and the thick padded sole of the horse's hoof. He held it up, then laid it in Shaney's hand.

"There you go—it was hidden, just a small thorn—but it would have become infected eventually. Small things can cause big problems." He patted Storm, then rinsed off his tools in Storm's water trough and put them back in his knapsack.

She smiled that brilliant smile, all her shining teeth showing. "Well, you are the man when it comes to horses. But I'm the 'man' when it comes to who's the boss around here. So, update the boss... where's the Afterling?"

Keeping his broad-brimmed hat pulled low and his face as expressionless as possible, he tried to keep himself unmoved by her physical proximity. "There's s-some small things wrong with this investigation, and they threaten to become big problems. I need some answers, Shaney."

She looked surprised at his insistence. "I'm Commander—I don't have to tell you anything. But what do you mean, wrong?"

"Tell m-me—who else is involved in this investigation, and who is your client?"

Her expression became guarded: "I don't know what you mean..."

Pulling a bundle from the pocket of his army jacket, Evangelo tossed it on a square work table. The bloody Reunion badge from one of Warden Howell's deputized, dead El Trafico thugs shone dimly in the lantern light. Evangelo pointed at it, accusatory: "This was found on scene..." Shaney picked up the badge to inspect it with a keen eye. Evangelo asked her: "Did Agent Azarian have a badge like this?"

Inquisitive, she picked it up, brushing a crumble of blood away from the battered tin star. "Agent Azarian is dead, then?" She turned the badge over to look at the identifying marks. "Where was it found?"

"On the body of a dead Deputy." Evangelo was careful to speak only the truth—Shaney was sure to be recording this conversation through her WeSpeex Ring's DocuMental program, and the TrueSpeex lie detection mode would be on. "An encounter of some kind took place south of the Reunion Camp. And as you can see, I do not have the Afterling. Too many cooks spoiled the stew." Evangelo spoke in a measured voice. "Director Santos said to tell you he sends his regards."

A cunning look flickered across Shaney's face, rapidly replaced by her usual imperial affability. "I really should check in on him." She demurred.

Evangelo hardened his heart against an onslaught. "You really should have told me you hired him to tail me. Why did you keep that information a secret from me?"

She pushed back. "I have a right to run an investigation any way I see fit."

His displeased expression didn't go unnoticed by Shaney. She suddenly became soft and hurt: "Raffi, what's gotten into you? You never act this way." Her hand rested lightly on his forearm, but it seemed to burn like fire through his gabardine jacket sleeve. "Why are you questioning me as if I were a criminal?"

His voice became rough. "I know there are others involved in this investigation, and I can't go any further in this briefing until you tell me who else you have brought in, and for what purpose your client wants the Afterling."

"That's nobody's business but my own, Captain." The blue eyes became cold, but she quickly thought twice about her anger. She smiled again. "What difference does it make? The Afterling gets turned in, and you get a reward—" she slid her warm hand down to his bare, cold fingers. "I need someone I can rely upon—"

Evangelo's heart flared up with a jealous heat. "I thought you were relying on Chief Emmanuel."

Undaunted, she ran her hand up under his sleeve to touch his scaly forearm. She gazed up under his hat, into his hazel eyes now streaked with green.

"I was, but he is proving—unreliable." She bit her lip, looking vulnerable and lost. "He's gone rogue. You are the only one that I can count on now." She took his hand and pressed it to her heart; his rough fingers felt cold in stark contrast to the warmth of her skin radiating through her t-shirt. Each pulse of her heart reverberated through his body, and Evangelo felt the walls start to spin...

"I need you to help me, Evangelo. I need the Afterling. Chief Emmanuel has taken the Afterling all for himself, but there are others who want her more, and I know they are willing to give the Rangers whatever we ask in exchange for the Afterling. But I can't go to the table with an offer unless I have her firmly in hand."

The overwhelming, musky-sweet scent of Shaney's skin was drowning Evangelo; "You didn't recover the Afterling." Eye to hypnotic eye, she moved in closer to him. "You failed."

He knew she was manipulating him, but it still didn't stop his ego from falling into a bottomless pit of despair. *I failed...*

Shaney's breath played against his cheek as she whispered. "So, Emmanuel got to the Afterling before you did, and you lost the trail. You are always second place to Emmanuel, no matter how hard you try." Her hand crawled up to his bicep and stroked it. "But I believe in you, Evangelo—I'll give you a second chance."

Her tender voice burned in his ears; *always second place to Emmanuel...*

"I need you to take out Emmanuel and bring me the Afterling. Then deals can be made, the highest bidder can win, and the Rangers can break out of this backwater to become more powerful than you ever dreamed. Just think of it, Evangelo—the ability to ride far beyond the confines of the camps, to have all the weapons, all the gear... to be the ultimate authority!" She was becoming aroused, her breathing erratic, her face flushed. "You could be King of it all, and all I need to make you King is for you to bring me that Afterling."

He could scarcely breathe. "You are the C-client! Y-you..."

Her tongue flicked out between her lips, and she reached out to put her hand on his chest—"Help me, Evangelo."

The universe rolled wild, and he struggled to stay in control. A thought pierced the fog and he spoke it. "I am s-sworn to d-defend the innocent and the d-defenseless..." he gasped. "I can't just use this innocent human b-being as a p-pawn."

Shaney put a hand to his cheek: "She's not a human—she's just an Afterling, Raffi. Look at me—I'm Human..."

Her eyes glowed, bluer than his sorrow, brighter than the stars that sparkled above them in the midnight Texas sky. Fighting for air, Evangelo softly pushed Shaney away from him, holding her at arms' length, both hands on Shaney's shoulders. A battle was raging inside him: *this is madness —why am I holding her back? She's finally turning to me, and I'm pushing her away?*

He stammered. "I c-can't—I can't d-do that. Even if she's less than human, she's more than a p-pawn..."

She was squirming beneath his hands, trying to reach him. "Tell me you'll bring the Afterling to me—just tell me. You don't have to do anything else..." Shaney moaned, unrequited. He felt her body pulling his, a gravitational sexuality that threatened to rend him asunder. "Bring me the Afterling, and I'll take care of the rest." She reached towards him again.

Evangelo thrust his arms out, pushing her back away from him, into the soft hay. He breathed a deep breath, clearing his head.

Shaney pleaded—"All you have to do is go get her from Emmanuel."

Evangelo made a calculated play: "How d-do you know this? W-Where is the Chief?"

Shaney's voice became smug, her smile flirtatious and coy; "I have my ways. Let's just say Emmanuel's somewhere in the area—I got a message from him last night, with only two communication nodes between us. He has the Afterling, and he's too drunk to fight."

"How am I supposed to f-find him?"

A sly look shone in her cerulean eyes. "You silly nilly—I'll do it like I did before—I'll message him, then hack his device with an embedded bit of code in an image. He'll open it, and BOOM, we'll have a location and then you just swoop in to save the day..."

She's hacking our devices—that has to be how she found out about the assassination, the Afterling, and Azarian in the first place... he made a mental note; *time to lock down all images in outside messages.*

Evangelo pushed into the next stage of his interview of Shaney. "You want me to hunt d-down an innocent being, just to use her as a bargaining chip for weapons from some two-bit LandLord?" He turned away from her. "It's against everything in the Ranger Code."

She sprang up from the hay behind him and clutched at his coat. "Damn it, Raffi, can't you just forget the Code for once? It's not just some two-bit LandLords who want the Afterling—it's the Masters of the Universe, and without that Afterling, their Universe will implode," Shaney wheedled. "You have no idea what is out there—you know nothing of the world outside our bounds. I can set you free, I can give it all to you—" Her hands slithered up his spine, and a shiver followed them.

He tried to ask with a disinterested air, but his voice cracked; "What do you m-mean?"

"There are secrets you've never known; I have knowledge, access, influence with powerful people you don't even know exist. It's all there, waiting for you, and more. But I know what you want more than all the secrets in the world: I know..." Her silky fingers touched the coarse, bronze scales on the back of his neck, then crept around to stroke his chest.

A lump in his throat rose, more than lust; it was the loneliness of decades, a hope of love, and here it was at last, in the touch of her hand. That hand crept over to his Badge, and ran a soft finger around the silver rim...

"Emmanuel is the only thing standing between us. He should never have been Chief. That title should have belonged to you," she breathed. Leaning against his back, Evangelo could feel her breasts pressed against him, warmth seeping through the leather and into his own body. "I should have belonged to you. I know that now."

Oh God... He felt his heart melt. It was everything he ever fantasied she would finally say—*except it was for all the wrong reasons.*

Shaney whispered over his shoulder and into his ear: "But you always have to play the Hero—so play the Hero. Emmanuel has the Afterling, and you know how rough he gets with little things... you need to save her from him, then we can decide who gets her next. Maybe I could even keep her as a pet, and you could protect us..." Her fingers toyed with his earlobe, and he shuddered with desire.

"Y-You want me to kill the Chief?" He asked, incredulous. "You aren't going to try to compromise somehow?"

She leaned her head against his back. "It's the only way. You know what must be done if you are going to take Emmanuel's place..."

She's dangling herself as bait. Nibble on the bait so she'll let out more line...

He turned to grasp her hands. "What about the D-Director—you hired him to follow me. W-What are you going to do about him? " He was fighting to keep his head clear.

"He's not going to be involved much longer." She squeezed Evangelo's hands eagerly: "Don't worry about Director Santos, you jealous man." She chuckled softly. "He'll get handled, soon... " Flustered, she realized she had said too much, and tied to reel the words back in; but Evangelo took her, hook, line, and sinker:

"Handled by who, Shaney? Who else is p-part of this operation? You told me I was the only one on this assignment. You told me all you had I was to bring a runaway creature back to a Client that would c-care for her —you didn't tell me she's an oppressed pawn in a global power struggle. You didn't t-tell me you wanted fellow lawmen dead." A cold indignation start to rise. "You l-lied to me about the assignment, you l-lied about the client—what else are you l-lying about?"

Stunned, she jerked her hands out of his grasp, blinking at him, uncomprehending. "How dare you! I'll bust you back down to Private—"

"Go ahead! Strip me of everything you ever gave to me—it's all a lie, like everything you told me—The System, the Co-Op, the Happening— it's all a l-lie! All of it—" He threw his hands up, animated with a righteous anger. "I helped start this organization to help bring L-Law and Order to Survivors left behind in a world of chaos and disorder. I d-didn't start the Rangers just so we could help some cabal of power-hungry overlords enslave the human race. But that's what we are; we are s-slavers, and this is slavery." His eyes suddenly turned silvery-gray. "And now you w-want me to go hunt down this defenseless Afterling and trade her for more power from this unseen group of would-be gods." He pointed to his Badge. "But that's not the W-Way of the Rangers—that's not the W-Way of the C-Code. Yet you ask me to forget the C-Code..."

In a fury of passion, he grasped his Captain's bars and wrenched them free from his jacket lapel. "Take back your damned bars! I no longer recognize you; you are no longer a Ranger. You have no Honor—you hold nothing holy... and I was too b-blind to see it! But I am no longer blind—" He slapped his silver bars down onto the small work table beside Shaney, and she flinched, blindsided. "I will NOT abandon all that I hold Holy for a promise of your unholy joy... I am a Ranger—" Evangelo thundered, and the stable shook:

"I am the Code!"

"So, you're saying you won't help me?" In the lantern's glow, he saw tears glittering in her eyes. "Long ago you said you loved me... are you saying you don't love me anymore?"

Christ, give me strength...

"Please—Rafael..." In her eyes he saw a desperate longing, a real hunger—but not for him. In her eyes, he could see the lust for power burning away all her goodness. Evangelo covered his face with his hands, his heart breaking—

Shaney leapt into his arms, her body invading his embrace like a conquering army.

"Say you love me!" her little snub nose brushing against his own blunt one, her slender arms snaking around his muscular frame, she pressed her mouth to his, and his lips found hers. He felt his eyes rolling back in his head; a heat rose inside him and threatened to burn down his very soul.

From far away, a voice cried out—an inner Guard from the Ramparts of his own Heart, calling out a forgotten line from the poet Lovelace. His lips lingered, and longed to stay; still touching, he breathed deeply, then whispered;

"Lillabeth, I..." He looked full into Shaney's eyes, resolute:

"I could not love thee, Dear, so much, Loved I not Honour more."

With a monstrous effort, Evangelo tore himself free from Shaney's arms and strode out into the chill night. His steps were propelled by an unseen Force, something beyond himself or he could not have borne it to walk away.

"Raffi?"

Behind him, he heard his Love of a lifetime calling: "Where are you going?"

Evangelo oriented himself towards Emmanuel's cabin and coughed loudly, twice. *Time to go, Dominic. Hurry, before I crumble into a heap of weakness.* He heard Shaney's voice crying through the darkness:

"You can't just walk away! What about the horses? What about us?"

He stopped, and turned to view her standing on the edge of the porch, the clouds casting a moon shadow across her face and into the dark arroyo separating them. Silent moments passed, then at last a desolate Evangelo answered out of the shadows. A lone beam cast down its light to illuminate him starkly against the pitch darkness of the arroyo:

"This is us."

He walked away.

A cold wind blew him down the path towards the pavilion where William was tied. Swiftly, he loosed his steed and mounted, then clicked his tongue and the horse loped down the path and out of the gate, past the guardsman, who opened the gate and asked, "When will you return, Captain?"

"When I return with Honor." The Ranger's eyes glinted as cold as steel, then he galloped away into the night.

———◆———

When the Director gave the signal, he heard the answering sound of a tap on the trunk of a tree. Just to make sure, he gave the whippoorwill's plaintive call again, and the tap once more sounded. The Director walked into a patch of moonlight, and Ranger and Horse stepped out of the shadows from the opposite side of the road.

Even in the pale light, Dominic could see the scars of battle etched into Evangelo's face. He swung up behind the Ranger in the saddle and tapped his shoulder to let him know he was fully on board. They rode silently, lest the wind carry their voices back to camp. Departing the trail, they headed back a roundabout way to the barn where Charger was secured; making their way southwest one mile, the Director dismounted as they approached a sturdy metal shack:

"How are you, compadre?" He looked up at the Ranger's emotionally battered visage.

"She offered me the world in exchange for my soul." Evangelo looked downcast. "It is as you said—they are corrupted to the core; even Shaney. She is the Client—she wishes me to abandon the Code, kill Chief Emmanuel, and seize the Afterling from him. All this for the purpose of trading the Afterling to the highest bidder in The System, in exchange for power."

A shadow hid his face, and the Director could not see with his eyes; but his mind could detect the anguish in the quiet man's heart.

"I tried to think of something bold to say that might change her mind, but all that came to mind was Lovelace's line from 'To Lucasta on Going to War'..."

Dominic grunted with approval. "It is the appropriate time for such a quote."

"You were the one who first taught it to me," Evangelo sighed. "And for the love of Honor, I have broken ranks with Shaney. I turned in my Captain's bars, and told her she was no longer a Ranger."

Dominic nodded wordlessly.

"This means those who used to be our allies are now our enemies. In trying to recruit me to kill Emmanuel, Shaney got sloppy and revealed she has sent others to 'handle' you, just like you were sent to 'handle' Azarian. She also told me she didn't expect me until tomorrow morning—meaning she must have received word we were at Purgatory this morning; she would have expected us to take the approved route and stay overnight at the Leyden Plantation."

The Director appeared pleased with their own travel arrangements. "I am sure a welcoming committee was waiting for us there; it was wise we chose a different route. I found excellent accommodations in Chief Emmanuel's cabin, so it all worked out." He smiled with a satisfied air. "Did she mention me otherwise?"

"Regarding you, without my prompting she said nothing; I believe that was because she still doesn't know if you talked to me about your role in this little drama yet."

Dominic waved a deferential hand. "Fair enough. She will talk about me when she realizes who broke into her cabin while you two were whispering sweet nothings in the night."

"Really?" Evangelo raised his brow, impressed.

"Absolutely." Dominic flicked his sleeve and a small box tumbled out of it. "It was... fruitful. We will discuss my findings later." He caressed the iridescent embossed metal box, then placed it in his pocket for safekeeping.

Evangelo thought back on the details of the interview. "I believe Shaney sent her so-called Rangers to your known haunts to try and take you unawares; when they saw me with you at Purgatory, they retreated so they wouldn't blow their cover. They have no Rings, so a radio dispatch would have been sent from a Purgatory comms outpost informing Shaney we were there, asking for further instructions."

"That would explain their unhappy demeanor—Shaney's thugs could not act on orders as long as you were there." The Director grunted.

"I imagine they will have their further instructions now." Pulling down his hat against the wind, the Ranger continued: "We will need to deal with them before they deal with us."

Dominic pulled open the door to the shack and brought out Charger, who was chomping at his bit, eager to leave the dark barn. Mounting his blue grullo, the Director rode alongside the Ranger to grasp his shoulder in friendship.

"You shall not ride alone, then. To Purgatory—there are foes to fight, and a Revolucion to plan."

His unbroken spirit rising in him, the Ranger set his face to the west, and proclaimed to the wind:

"Let's ride."

———————

II

The Watcher held up his hand and adjusted the Palm Cam on the Ring, trying to zoom in—*still fuzzy*. In the daytime, the zoom worked as well as old-fashioned binoculars, but without the annoying need to be adjusted for sight. But at night...

He groaned inwardly. The Nite-Eyes tech had always been touchy; fine when new, this Ring's infrared sensors had degraded from overexposure and use over the years, and were now next to useless. He scowled and turned back to Rose.

Unable to see the action in the deepening darkness, the Watcher kept his eyes on his surroundings and pondered the incredible helpfulness of the Afterling's full-spectrum detection capabilities. *It has to be a natural by-product of her genetic chimerism, possibly related to her jellyfish gene?* Even excluding infrared night-vision technology, she had certain capabilities that went far beyond what technology could produce. He wondered what he could have done with such an asset as a Private Investigator in LifeBefore.

He admired her assets.

Lying belly-down upon a limestone escarpment, she was busy being a spy, knit-clad legs splayed out behind with the toes of her pink boots dug into the dirt. With her chin in her hands, propped up on her elbows, she reveled in her newfound occupation as investigative assistant. Absorbed in her adventure, Rose had the gleeful air of a person who doesn't care if she is belly down on the cold ground.

You might want to not lay down in the grass here... he noted sourly that her leather apron was getting all dusty in the limestone caliche. Wisely, she had hung up her cloak, not wanting to sully it.

The Watcher chose this site for a surveillance post because of the thick overhead brush cover, clear view of the strip mines, and its marked Forbidden Zone to the south. A white, miles-wide gash in the limestone soil stretched far away and to the northeast; in it, a black river of exposed coal seams wound through artificial hills created in the wake of the old strip mines. These small, rounded ridges were a repentance, the reconstruction from the hand of humanity attempting to heal the earth. A whiff of acrid smoke hung in the air, the product of coal fires deep in the earth where unsuppressed fires had raged in the absence of the suppressive hand of firefighters. Now surrounded by little clumps of scraggly mesquite trees, the entire area had a gloomy look in the waning moonlight, a wispy pall of smoke hanging eternally over the man-made valley, cloaking it from ready view, even in the day.

Their surveillance target was a mile to their southeast, a minuscule island in a moderately large pond; it had been created when enormous earth-moving equipment had once dug trenches with massive buckets. Most of that equipment had long since been removed by enterprising Visionaries keen to profit from the closure of the mine, but some remnants still lingered, rusting precariously away on the edges of open pits. What had once been a bustling hub of wealth and energy for the people of the area had become a dismal reminder of lost prosperity and pollution of humans.

They had ridden all day to get here from the safe house, through dangerous territory; what had presented itself as an easy half-day's ride had become a torturous route studded with hazardous obstacles. The smoke from the smoldering coal seams helped shield them from view as they skirted dozens of miles of reclaimed strip mines. Primarily hogs had greeted them, and the SHIVA device—set low to the second notch with a wide aperture—turned away the slow-moving herds without requiring him to engage in a noisy shootout.

This was a welcome discovery—the energy weapon could prove useful in stealthily clearing paths ahead of parties moving through the wilderness. Still, he preferred the Mariner or Remington when it came to quick lethality. The SHIVA device was a weapon best suited for deterrence against large groups or lethal force in a confined space—the slow start-up was a challenge, and the accuracy was marginal.

Utilizing the SHIVA device for that purpose of deterrence, the

Watcher scanned the woods around them, seeking threats. Normally the Watcher would have taken position on the roof of the nearby abandoned garage where Oskar and the Horses were secured, but the prospect of aircraft equipped with Nite-Eyes capability left him cautious. With multiple buildings around them, and abundant trees, the Afterling and the Watcher would be harder to see even if the enemy used infrared detection. The Watcher kept himself and Rose close to the earth and behind trees, good to avoid detection, but this left them vulnerable to attack by nocturnal creatures. Still, it couldn't be helped; the infant Revolution needed this information about El Trafico and transport, and now was the time to get it.

A little judicious time invested in this job now would make way for a more intimate job later... another half-hour or so of surveillance would soon give way to the need for shelter from the night-time WildLands. Then would finally come his chance for a little romp with Rose.

He had already taken pains to set up his lair in the old utility building. Tying Shadow and Oro up in the enclosed garage, he had secured Oskar with his leash, a blanket and a bone scavenged from the Bar-Be-Que before leaving the smoldering remains of Mystery Outpost. With their own cozy bedroll tucked in the corner behind closed doors and the red-checked Comfy Pillow laid out, it wouldn't be too hard to get her to snuggle under the covers with him on that cold concrete floor...

Rose scooted forward to get a better view, scooted again, then began to hiss, abruptly sitting up and frantically dusting at her ankle—

"Ow—ow! They're biting me! Ow..."

Yanking her up off the ground by her grab strap, the Watcher jerked off her pink cowboy boot and flung it to the ground, followed by a slightly grubby ankle sock. Large black and red ants, stingers flailing, jabbed at her tender golden skin, leaving behind large red welts.

He judiciously stepped away from the disturbed fire ant nest where her boot toe had scooted.

Business-like, the Watcher pulled up her pants leg and vigorously rubbed Rose's bare calf, ankle and foot with his calloused hand, oblivious to the vengeful insects. Stripping his hand downwards, the ants were crushed and rolled away. He swore under his breath as one vicious fire ant managed to find the only nanometre of tender skin between his fingers and clamped down with its mandibles, plunging its wicked little stinger into his flesh.

He smashed it with satisfaction, then twirled the dangling Afterling from her grab strap while dusting off any remaining ants. Inspecting her ankle and foot, he noted the ugly bumps left behind.

Rose whined: "I hate fire ants."

#*I told you lying on the ground was a bad idea; maybe next time you'll listen.*

The Watcher retrieved her boot and sock, beating them against a tree trunk to knock off any lurking ants. Rose pulled the footwear back on her foot, then pulled them off again as she found more ants. This pattern was repeated twice more, until the last of the ants were removed.

She sighed and scratched. From somewhere in the distant past, the Watcher heard his Mother's voice float out of his own mouth:

#*Don't scratch, it will get infected.*

"Ugh—what next?" Agitated, she retrieved her deerskin cloak from the tree branch, and pulled it over her head.

#*Infrared capability no longer works well on your device—your magical eyes are still the best option. Tell me what you can see from this distance, and we will attempt to puzzle it out.*

Rose was amused. "My eyes aren't magic—they are just eyes. I can't believe you can't see like this."

#*Well, I can't believe you can't save yourself from fire ants, and yet, here we are... we each have our strengths. Now get busy.*

"My, you are fussy-wussy tonight. You should eat some food..."

#*All I have are these sweet potato slices. Vegetables are not food.*

Hulking in the darkness, he pouted, his crimson-scaled lips turned down in disapproval at the lack of meat.

"Well, when we get to a nice hidden place where we can build a fire, I will make a lovely sweet potato pudding with some sugar water..." She knelt gingerly in a new spot far from the ant bed, then peered into the darkness, back to her usual bubbly self: her bright eyes sparkled with intrigue as she looked though the brush atop the ridge. "There are so many hotspots just below the surface—you say it's coal?—burning, there must be dozens of them on fire. It's hard to distinguish... What exactly is it we are looking for out here?"

#*Any kind of confined movement; any light patterns.*

"So, you are expecting an aircraft here?" She rubbed her eyes. It was getting dark, but she was too entranced by the thought of spying on Deva to sleep yet. "Do you really think they will come?"

#I'm looking for aircraft or anything that would need to recharge or refuel—but there's no way to know if this is spot or not until one shows up. Evangelo believes these Forbidden Zones may be some kind of refueling stations. So, we'll watch—but surveillance is always a gamble. This is the closest Hazmat Area to Mystery Outpost, and it has been twenty-four hours since the aircraft's last contact with whoever sent them —if hostile forces are ever going to use this station, it will be tonight, under cover of darkness.

He knelt on one knee in the dirt beside her, one hand linking to hers and the other clutching his weapon; head still up, he was scanning their surroundings for threats. He explained more about surveillance to his new assistant:

#Investigators may watch for hours and never see anything while on surveillance, or it could be the big win, and we see everything we need to see. We were just close enough by, so this is logistically expedient—stake out this Forbidden Zone and see what shows up here. Evangelo said the secret Tesoro entrance you found is also marked as Hazmat by Ranger leadership, so let's find out what the Powers That Be forbid us to see.

"What exactly IS Hazmat?" Rose was curious.

#HAZMAT—an abbreviation for Hazardous Materials; toxic areas.

"Well, that certainly applies to this place." She waved the haze of sulfuric coal smoke that lingered over the area. "But I can't see it from here and neither can you, so let's get closer." Rose pointed down the slope to a clump of scrubby oaks some several hundred yards distant.

#No; I'm the investigator in this operation, and I say we base ourselves up on this ridge, far away from any activity. I don't want to tip off any hostiles that might be nearby.

"I think I see movement, but it's so faint..."

#What kind of movement?

"A big squiggly ball." She pondered—"like the one I saw in the Feathered Serpents' den at the safe house, but much larger..."

Bingo.

#I think this could be the source of your fabulous flying snakes. It's night, and it's cool, so they'll be denning—that's why they are in a den- ball now. Evangelo and Dominic mentioned that fantastic monsters are usually seen close to Forbidden Zones, Hazmat Areas, and in the BorderLands—

"Oh, that would make sense! Our Bestiary Book says that the most wonderful creatures are found where Angels fear to tread..."

#They are probably being used to guard this station and to frighten off or kill any locals who come too close to the island. A few must have escaped somehow, perhaps when a drought made the pond's water low. Fortunately for us, the pond is high now due to recent rains. Did your Asura's Bestiary say anything else about these snakes?

She closed her eyes and recited a snippet of poetry from memory.

"Feathered Serpents swoop and glide

their plumes all shimmery-shiney

if you see them, run away

or they will bite your hiney."

He looked at her, askance;

#That's it? That's the best they could come up with?

He had expected better poetry for this fearsome creature.

Rose looked hurt. "Well, it is a children's book..."

Rubbing his craggy jaw, the Watcher thought for a moment, then cranked out a brand-new verse.

#"Quetzalcoatl, come to life,

god of wind and wisdom;

Who brought you forth upon this earth

or framed your fearful length and girth?

Glittering, your sharp tail-knife

Plumed, a rainbow prism..."

Rose looked up from the dirt. "Oh—that is absolutely perfect! Did you rhyme it just now?"

#Yes—I created a sketch and a rhyme for every creature I encountered while I was in the service of Reunion Camp; but the notebook was left behind with my personal effects at the gate when I left.

"Well, we shall just have to make a new rhyme-bestiary, then!" she proclaimed, cheery.

We... it was the first time she had ever spoken the word in reference to just the two of them, alone. *We...* a couple. Blushing, he remembered the

Director's admonition—*Distraction hones Death*—and focused his attention on his surroundings. Still, Rose's admiration felt oddly delightful; the Watcher nodded, satisfied, and entered the rhyme into his We-Notes app. *Time to create a new book.*

As he wrote, the Watcher heard a distinctive sound—a small chirp in the night:

tsees... tsees...

A sparrow called to its flock mates, and they answered back. The trees were filled with their little chirps as they called to each other. He raised his hand to point towards the sound of the birds.

#Do you hear that bird call? It is the flight call of the Chipping Sparrow; they are a small, striped sparrow with a rusty cap, and during their great fall migration, they travel at night to avoid detection by predators. Using that one small chirp, they call to each other in the darkness, that they might find each other.

Rose listened, fascinated; as they called, she joined in, mimicking their call perfectly—a short, up-inflected chirp:

tsees... tsees...

"That would be ever so handy; I have been lost so many times." Cheerily struggling with an unspoken emotion, she said nothing more, but the Watcher could tell by energy flowing though her fingers, there was so much more she wished she could say. He pondered the lostness of Rose, and her long journey to find the Flower, now cut off from her flock.

#If you are lost, call to me, and I will find you.

She looked up at him, eyes shining. A great flurry of wings suddenly surrounded them as the flock of sparrows rose from their hiding place. An edge had disturbed the peace—out there...

#Stay still, and eyes up—I detect some kind of odd vibration. Tell me everything you see, and don't assume I can see what you see.

"See, you have magical powers, too! You seem to sense everything unseen, and you never need sleep." Rose observed. "Do all Devils have the same powers?"

#No. I'm an anomaly. I don't know why, I just am. I wasn't always this way, but I am now.

"Do all Survivors live as long as you?"

#If the WildLands or the Ooze doesn't kill them, then yes. Survivors age only very slowly, although they do occasionally get sick or have medical conditions, like diabetes and heart conditions...

"If I may ask, Deva?" Curious, she leaned in to study him. "Just how old are you?"

A flicker of reluctance crossed his face, as the gulf between their ages yawned wide between them.

#I was twenty-seven when the Happening occurred.

"But Father said you all haven't really aged since you all became Devils —sorry, I mean Survivors?"

#I've aged little in the fifty-four years since the Happening.

"But that would make you... um, fifty-four plus twenty-seven is... us, I'm sorry, I don't have a calculator—"

#Eighty-two upcoming this next birthday.

"Oh! I love Birthdays! When is your Birthday?"

#When it should be.

"Well, if what father said is true, you could potentially live for hundreds of years; if you stopped aging when you were twenty-seven, then that makes you only one year older than me!" She was puzzling a great mystery. "But I will die of old age before I am thirty-five. How old does that make me in Survivor years?"

He didn't want to think about it. It seemed inconceivable that this little clone woman could consider herself old.

#You are young. Don't worry about it.

"Oh no, I am very old. You just can't see it yet; Asura are just made that way. We don't show it until the last minute, then everything falls apart all at once! But age is already affecting me a little. My knees are giving me some trouble. " Sitting upright in the dirt, she straightened her leg, and they heard an audible pop. She thought on it for a minute. "I was created three years before the Great Cleansing, so that would make me..." She waved her hands to him, helpless to calculate without her WeSpeex Ring.

#When is YOUR Birthday?

"Oh, Asura don't have them. We have a hatch day, and mine was February 21 of Year 28 after the Great Cleansing. Hatch days are celebrated by all when they occur, but not after. A Hatch Day is not the same as a Birthday." Animated at the thought of all the boy babies born to the Asura of Tesoro, she bubbled at the Watcher: "Hatch days are very planned, with a special ceremony celebrated at that time. But a birthday is mysterious and wonderful, and is celebrated every year! No one knows when it shall happen—the Asura hope and pray, but a Birthday comes when it will, and then POP! Out comes a Baby Boy—"

The Watcher calculated in his head, no need for a calculator.

#Counting from the time of your creation, you are almost sixty years old. But you're actually only twenty-six. Being created doesn't count—you have to be actually born before it counts.

"But that's not true... I wasn't ever born; I was hatched from a Tesoro Cradle, and I'm still alive!" Crushed emotionally at his pronouncement, her face fell. "And that would mean that Angelina was never alive..."

Dammit. Caught in her personal dilemma, the Watcher flagellated himself mentally as tried to think of something to say that would extricate him from this ethical trap. Rose's eyes were glimmering in the deepening shadows gathering about her:

"I saw her alive... Angelina was alive, even if she was never born..." Her face was twisting in the gloom, trying to wrap her heart around what the Watcher had said. "I saw her—I felt her!"

A tremor ran up his spine as he remembered his own vision of the Child-turned-foetus, tiny mangled body quivering upon a metal table beneath a scalpel. He could hear that odd whimper leaking out of Rose as her heart unspooled in the darkness. Unwilling to go down this path at this inconvenient time, the Watcher decided the best play was to punt.

#Stop it. Stop it now. She's alive, you're alive, no matter which way you count it—

"Angelina was alive—" Rose's tender fingers curled between his gnarled ones, clinging to a reality only she could see. A cold ripple of despair pulsed through her hand and up his arm, seeking recognition; fearful of her emotion invading his heart, he grabbed her shoulder and shook her:

#STOP—that's an ORDER...

His callousness made plain, she stopped mid-sob, clapping her palm to her mouth to staunch the noise. Detecting a vibration, the Watcher placed his hand on a slender oak trunk and felt it through the branches; he waved away Rose's distress and pointed her towards a new interest.

#Now is not the time or place for this; we have an incoming aircraft. Find it.

Stung by his rebuke, she retreated from him, taking her despair with her. Trying to focus her on the incoming mystery craft, the Watcher shushed Rose's remaining sorrow with a raised finger, and pointed upwards. They stayed low, kneeling; Rose wiped her eyes, regained her composure, and hardened her heart against any sympathy from the Devil.

She swiveled to look all around, then subtly pointing her demi-gloved finger to their northeast, whispering: "Just above the tree line, moving southeast, fast—a faint glow." She tracked it with her hand, tracing an arc in the air: "It's headed to your target..."

Jackpot.

The Watcher felt the thrill of the hunt. Holding up his hand, he began to holo-graph the target area, hoping to zoom in later for analysis.

"Oh, now lights are blinking on the island, down between the trees—" Renewed by curiosity, Rose sniffled as she watched from beneath the barren oak branches. "I can just barely detect the reflection of the flash on the trees around them." The Watcher peered into the darkness, still seeing nothing.

#Those are probably infrared landing lights.

Back to business, a coolly intense Rose narrated: "The flying object is tightly circling over the island, but I'm too far away to see clearly. It appears bright, so it must be very hot internally... would that be the engine?"

#Hybrid engines—they must have switched to internal combustion for long distance flight.

"It's hovering now, directly over the clump of trees—is it landing? It's moving downward—I can make out an oval-shaped glow, but that's all."

#If it's just one glow, then it's probably a Boone & Hainey HeliScram Gazelle. Will seat two personnel, including the pilot, and has a small cargo bay. It's smaller and lighter than the aircraft we encountered last night and is used for reconnaissance.

She watched, fascinated. "I never thought I would actually see one of these—they never let the Asura talk about the flying machines, but we surmised they exist because some Clients accidentally mention it when they come in to visit."

Still concentrating on his immediate environs, he felt a brief flare of something akin to jealousy at Rose's mention of her Clients, but dismissed it as nonsense and kept working.

"The bigger light is lowering down to the island. I can't really make out anything else—the flashing lights have stopped..."

They waited for any sign of activity on the pond island. Wondering what the HeliScram's mission might be, the Watcher surmised it might have flown by the scene of the safe house to the northeast. The flames would still be visible, and the burning house would give off a visible and infrared glow. Any enemy scouting parties would be on the lookout for movement they could see from the air. He momentarily regretted his decision to burn the safe house, but he reminded himself it was full of giant flying snakes with stingers and therefore justified the risk.

Through the tips of his rough fingers, he could feel the faint thrumming of the HeliScram's whirling blades coursing up through the branches of the slender sapling. In all his years guarding the gate of Reunion Camp Prison, he had never experienced this vibration since the Happening—not until the battle with the HeliScram and their Asura Hunter Squad at WildLand Express' Mystery Outpost safe house. *The area between here and Reunion Camp has to be a no-fly zone...* the Watcher briefly considered scanning for beacons, but realized that his "ping" could be traced—he preferred to leave the heavy tech investigations to someone more experienced. They watched in silence.

After five minutes, Rose finally piped up:

"Deva, the lights are flashing again, and the large light is rising into the air." The Watcher knit his brows, puzzled—this was a fast turnaround.

Rose watched the target area as the glow ascended. The Watcher felt a nervous tension; the HeliScram was close enough for Rose to see its heat signature—was it close enough to to for a pilot to spot them with Nite-Eyes technology? It was a definite concern to the Watcher, but he noticed that Rose seemed to detect infrared signals at a further distance, at a lower resolution.

Watching the HeliScram, a wondering light filled Rose's eyes. "Oh, now that's interesting; some smaller things burst from the main glow and are flying up from the island now; several, very slow and low above the trees. They look like little faintly glowing balls of light..."

Long-dead dread floated to the surface of his consciousness.

"How amazing—the lights are rather pretty, bobbing along all together in harmony, almost like a dance!"

It can't be...

A cold terror settled into the pit of his stomach.

#*Quickly, back to the shed. No noise, no light, just hurry; we've got to get to the horses, and get out of here—*

"Why are we running? What are they?" She reflected his fear.

#*It's a swarm of drones—Aerial Lethal Global Orthogonic Searchers: automated killer drones that use a customizable artificial intelligence interface to create algorithmic searches for fugitives on the run.*

Rose shook her head. "I don't understand."
#ALGOS—Intelligent flying death-bots are hunting us.
The Watcher grabbed her and fled.

———◆———

Oro and his riders were moving stealthily eastward through the brush, leading a spooky Shadow as Oskar loped alongside.

Rose was struggling to keep her eyes open, watching for the ALGOS in the event that one would come near them. She had lost sight of them, meaning they too were probably out of range of the drones' infrared and voice detectors. She whispered over her shoulder to the Watcher:

"What will we do if we see a drone up close?"

#If you can see it before it sees us, point me at it and I'll blast it out of the sky; that's why we have to get some distance between us and the other ALGOS. This was a batch release from a central drop point—they will methodically search a grid of likely locations, slowly moving further and further apart, each in a circumscribed area. For now, the drones are still too close together—if we shoot one, the others will quickly respond to the last known location of the destroyed drone and kill us if we are spotted.

She was terrified yet strangely intrigued by the deadly drones. "But what's so dangerous about these robots?"

The Watcher was grim.

#They never sleep, never rest, and are equipped with thermal imagers. They possess voice detection capability, holocams, flame throwers, stun loads and heat-seeking mini-missiles. They are gyroscopic constructs, constantly scanning, they can pinpoint the location of unique identifiers such as your nano-transmitters. The ALGOS have medium-range infrared capability, which means if your infrared detection can 'see' them, they might 'see' you. However, you did see it and they didn't come right at us, so heat from the burning coal seams must be cluttering their detection field. All the more reason for us to put distance between us and them.

Rose frowned and looked miffed. "If you would be so polite as give me my gun, I could shoot one out of the sky, from a comfy distance…"

#Maybe—if you can see the drone before it 'sees' us, you might be able to shoot it down. However, if you destroy one of the ALGOS right

now, the team that released them will be notified. If the HeliScram is still in the area, we would have to fight that team as well as the other drones. Our best course of action is to escape to a place where the ALGOS won't expect us to hide, and allow the drones to get further apart from each other before we engage any of them.

"But how do you know where they expect us would we hide?"

The Watcher used the same trick he always used when investigating his subjects—think like them. *It's good to have personal experience with the subject of your investigation*—in this case, flying death-bots:

#I worked with ALGOS, before the Happening. The ALGOS programming team will have already programmed our respective profiles into the drone database, allowing the ALGOS to create a search algorithm that automatically hones in on the most likely spots an Afterling would hide or be hidden. You are very different looking than the local populace, and easily recognizable. The algorithm will assume you are xenophobic and afraid of anyone different than yourself, so it will be expecting you—if you are alone—to hide in buildings far away from the Damned, or in an abandoned house.

Oro descended hesitantly into a limestone ravine which descended eastward through dense Oak and Ash forest towards the lake. Shadow began to slide, first one hoof, then another, snorting; turning Oro, the Watcher gently pulled the reins back, then dismounted to take the reins of both horses and guide them by starlight into the dark ravine. Presently the bottom of the ravine revealed an open, dry creek bed, mostly clear of brush in the white limestone ravine. Better able to see dark obstacles against the light backdrop, the Watcher climbed back into his saddle and let Oro lead the way once again; the high, arching branches of oak, sycamore and ash intertwined overhead, creating a canopied corridor winding away from the mines and towards distant lights. The Watcher resumed his narrative:

#The ALGOS may also have connected my profile and Chief Emmanuel's as well. The ALGOS make a 'social connections map', analyzing the likely hiding patterns of associates, so they will be able to create a map of places they believe I or Chief Emmanuel might hide you if you are in our respective custodies. In my case, that would be out in the wilderness, isolated, away from searchers, where I could take advantage of you without danger to us.

He pondered: *Like a little safehouse in the woods, far from civilization...*

Rose appeared relieved, but she had a strange look on her face. "Oh, but they don't know you. You would never do anything like that..."

Surprised. he almost laughed, but kept it to himself. *So, you think I am that much of a white knight, do you?* Amused, the Watcher cleared his throat and patted her hand on the saddle horn as she rode in front of him:

#*You better sleep now—morning will come early, and I have to come up with a plan.*

Rose stretched. "Well, I too would like to make a plan. In order to safeguard you, I think I should plan to stay awake so I can watch for drones with you..."

He grunted amicably; *if you can stay awake.*

Yawning, Rose leaned back against him, warm beneath his encircling arm; the stars wheeled dimly above the ravine in the smoky night sky, and he made his plans...

What would hide them from the infrared and audio pattern-seeking ALGOs drones? He called up his AI assistant to take notes:

###ACTIVATING HELPER BOT###

#<3 SPEEXBOT: *Hello, I'm Talisa, your comfortingly calm SpeexBot Personna*

#WATCHER: Talisa, open Archive 13; compile notations and highlights from all previous classified data on Aerial Lethal Global Orthogonic Searchers.

#<3 TalisaBOT: *I'd love to, Saul <3*

Opening the file, he scanned highlights from his previously compiled notes. A quick overview suggested what he had already surmised: in order to hide from the drones, the Watcher would need to hide Rose where no one thought they would go. In this case, that would be closer to densely populated areas, where their heat signatures would be less unusual and their voices would be drowned out in cacophony of nearby humanity.

There was only one place nearby where this could be accomplished— he grimaced at the thought: they could hide out closer to Purgatory to confuse the ALGOS.

Still, Rose's voice was distinctive, and if the directive came from Jarrod, an exact match could be made to her voice. But if the drones were sent from James, the programmers might not have access to Rose's voice files... still, she would need to be carefully hidden and silenced for her own protection.

What about the ALGOS scanning of known frequencies? The drones were programmed to scan all available frequencies for any digital communications. The Watcher entered his known data: Level 3 was the official Tejas Co-op Network of nodes; Level 7 was the secret shared network of El Trafico's and Tesoro—and Level 10 Network was internal to Tesoro. Since there was a high-level agreement between the Tejas Co-op and the Commandant's Insider Empire, ALGOS drones would undoubtedly be scanning the Tejas and Tesoro Networks 3 and 10...

Could the Revolution scavenge communications nodes? The Tesoro WeSpeex Beacon that he had looted from the Asura Hunters was a one-in-a-million find; it had been reprogrammed, but working beacons were a precious resource and weren't readily available. He entered his next step of action:

#WATCHER: Talisa, open MapPix program, set to location, overlay recent image files 835.mpx, merge, reroute.

#<3 TalisaBOT: *That sounds like fun, Saul<3*

A detailed LifeBefore area map in unfurled in his HeadsUp display once again. Barns and houses glowed a soft green beside clear roads and well-marked settlements of rural Central Texas. Toggling on the WeSpeek MapPix program, the overlay the Director's hastily sketched map, completely with Tech DeadZones and current landmarks. The DeadZones intrigued him—entire sections of the map were marked as digital and tech Dead Zones, unavailable to technological or mechanical capability.

How were they being operated? It had to be remote, through a network of jammers, or maybe even a satellite... someone, somewhere knew how. He wondered if those someones would be among the Highest Ranking Survivors in the Tejas Co-op—Ultimates, Visionaries in the Consortium.

The MapPix pinwheel icon spun as it merged the two maps to create an updated map. The Watcher set the old map as a translucent layer in the background to allow him to explore old infrastructure if needed. Fifty years of abandonment led to an overgrowth of Mesquite and Red Cedar, destroying the roadbeds and obscuring houses and buildings. But the infrastructure was still there, and the old information was valuable. That information pointed himself and his dozing Afterling towards that den of iniquity the Damned called Purgatory.

What is the opposite of an abandoned hut in the woods?

That was the plan.

#EMMANUEL: *tinaf*
#EMMANUEL: *ofnW*
#EMMANUEL: *N bot wkna; o*
###ACTIVATING HELPER BOT###
#<3 SPEEXBOT: *Hello, I'm SQIRLBOT, your cheery chipper SpeexBot Personna* <3
   <3 SQIRLBOT: Oskar's *SpeexBot* <3
#EMMANUEL: *jka,χ'*
   <3 SQIRLBOT: *I don't recognize that command* <3
#EMMANUEL: *goiaatpχχχχ*
   <3 SQIRLBOT: *type—h for help menu* <3
#EMMANUEL: *dsioi idfakdsm,sdcpofdaee;kaetmadmkmagej'adfjef,MAEF '*
   <3 SQUIRLBOT: *Do you need help? Y/N* <3
#EMMANUEL: *giokvzkj; aago[ma'viiiiiiiiiiiiiiiiii*
   <3 SQIRLBOT: *Do you need help? Y/N <3*
#EMMANUEL: *Y bkjlaefw,n*
   <3 SQIRLBOT: *Running WeSpeex Assistive Suite v17.3; enabling predictive spelling; enabling gestures; enabling pictograph keyboard please hold...<3*
#EMMANUEL: ☺

Fog filled the ravine as morning sun filtered in dimly though the mirk. A shadowy canopy of dark branches wove their random basketweave pattern over the narrow limestone ravine, and the air smelled of river bottoms and oxbows. Ahead, an overhang in the dry limestone ravine provided a temporary shelter large enough to hide the horses from overhead threats, and would give them a place to rest while he plotted their next move.

Something crashed behind them; Oskar wheeled around and bounded off into the thick fog, the Watcher heard a shriek and a snarl, then the sound of wet fur and flesh being torn. He tried to see a target, but could not find one—

Dread filled him. What would he tell Rose? *That's just the way it is,* he would say. *Oskar had a good life*. But what if Oskar was killed by an ALGOS? He reined Oro into a rollback with Shadow in tow, turning them down the trail and pulling his shotgun to prepare for the worst.

Much to his surprise, Oskar was not dead.

The cub came trotting back down the trail dragging a long, limp hunk of bloody tan fur. The Watcher gave the hand signal, and Oskar loped towards him, whipping a shredded animal from side to side as if playing with a whip. The Watcher was impressed: it appeared a young cougar had given chase to the party, but Oskar made short work of the cat—the Chupacabra had broken the predator's neck.

Amazing, the Watcher thought, how powerful Oskar already was—he was still a baby, but after just one week he was probably ten pounds heavier and six inches longer, running alongside the horses rather than being carried by them. Plentiful protein and protection from the elements had allowed the Chupacabra cub a chance to invest all his calories into growing rather than trying to stay warm.

Observing the blood staining the beast's wickedly recurved claws, the Watcher was grateful Oskar had not savaged Rose when she shot the cub's mother—still a joey in the pouch, Oskar may have not yet recognized enemies... or maybe he just recognized a friend?

Checking once more to make sure Oskar's Text-2-Talk was toggled on in the encrypted Chat Room, he motioned for Oskar to sit, and the Chupacabra did so.

#WATCHER: Good Boy, Oskar! Give...

He gave the hand command, and the cub dropped the dead cougar. The Watcher shook Rose to wake her and dismounted, leaving the groggy Afterling swaying in Oro's saddle. The horses snorted and bobbed their heads, sniffing the ravaged cat. The Watcher picked it up and inspected it, then placed across Shadow's saddle.

Rose rubbed her eyes and gasped. "Oh—I'm sorry! I didn't mean to fall asleep... what happened and why is Oskar covered in blood?"

#He killed a cougar before it killed us, and I am going to give it to him as a meal later.

He messaged Oskar again through Text-2-Talk:

#WATCHER: Good Boy—Treat! Sit—

Oskar sat, eager for his reward. The Watcher pulled a piece of sweet potato out of his pocket and tossed it to the cub. A mouth lined with razor-sharp fangs opened wide as Oskar's tongue uncoiled to snatch the treat out of air.

#EMMANUEL: *goow@*

Bemused, the Watcher decided this was a great opportunity.

Well, obviously Oskar is randomly accessing Chief Emmanuel's VisualTrax technology. It would need to be toggled off later, but here was a chance to impress Rose with some subterfuge in the meantime... *This should be fast and easy.* Never one to let an opportunity go to waste, the Watcher got busy.

Taking the reins, he walked the horses back up the trail and tied them fast.

#*I would like to know more about the fight—I am going to read Oskar's thoughts.*

Suddenly awake, Rose swept back her tangled curls to blink at the Chupacabra. "Oh, yes, go Deva his mind now, please! I want to tell him something."

Disconnecting from Rose, the Watcher prepared to impersonate Oskar.

The Ring still had Chief Emmanuel's identifying information on it—this had served them well in spoofing the dead man's identity. Good thing the ring couldn't tell the difference between a dead man's hand and a Chupacabra's tail...

But that spoofed ID made interactions on the stolen ring confusing. The Watcher decided to remedy this situation.

First, let's give Chief Emmanuel's Ring a more Chupacabra-appropriate Chat Room nickname:

#OSKAR

Then, to ensure we pick up some kind of signal, we turn on AutoSpeex in Oskar's directory—

###AUTOSPEEX v.4.7###
###LOCAL SERVER ACTIVATED###
#EN-US#
#DIALECT - CTX#
#AUTO-TRANSCRIBE - Y#

WeSpeex Rings had been specifically designed to neuronically link up with speech centers of the human brain. Before The Happening, researchers had tried without success to use it to communicate with higher mammals, but the intricacies on interspecies communications always just beyond their understanding. A string of garbled nonsense was the only "language" researchers ever heard...

Just as well, the Watcher thought smugly. As long as Rose wasn't there to "see how the sausage was made," she could see Oskar's AutoSpeex transmit gobbledy-gook, then the Watcher could "translate" it for her. He nearly chortled to himself, but quickly stifled it. He pondered telling Rose that Oskar thought the Watcher was a good Deva. *This could be very helpful...*

He turned on his DocuMental program to record; perhaps some entertainment value might be worth the playback. Linking Rose's embedded software to the encrypted Xirxes WeSpeex ChatRoom so she could hear Oskar, the Watcher wondered what kind of information an Afterling would share with a Chupacabra.

Time to have a little fun and score a few easy Deva points.

#*Very well, Rose; you can tell Oskar what you wish, and as Deva, I'll interpret his thoughts for you. But do it quietly and hurry up—I need to interrogate him on his fight, and we are still on the run from the ALGOS drones.*

"Well, with killer robots chasing us, I must make my statement count, as I may never get another chance to speak to him this way again." Eyes alight with curiosity, Rose reached out to touch the little Chupacabra on his warty cheek, and the cub's eyes sparkled with joy, pink nose quivering...

A surge of warmth flowed out of Rose's fingertips, rippling up the Watcher's arm. It caught the Watcher unawares, and he felt the thrill of her touch, even though it was not meant for him. The Afterling murmured with an earnest sweetness into Oskar's round, hairless ear:

"I love you."

The Watcher felt it like a wallop in the gut, knocking the breath out of him. Three words, not spoken in his presence since childhood. A wild panic welled up in his heart, but he bridled it with irritability; the sight of her delicate hand caressing Oskar's grubby, goofy face kindled a sense of injustice. Rose cast love to all things, everywhere, as if it was available for free—pearls before Chupacabras. And yet...

This has nothing to do with me. An unfamiliar indignation simmered: *you offer love to the animal that ate your breakfast, but not to the animal that saved your life.*

Recognizing the ridiculousness of his recurrent romanticism, the Watcher immediately hurled it into the bonfire of reason. His Mentors chided from the lecture hall of memory:

"Sex. Sex is the word you're looking for, not love. Sociopaths don't feel love, but

they can see its value. Get it and use it, but always remember—what the Normz call 'love' is just another flawed chemical reaction for you."

Just a chemical reaction...

His own biochemical imbalances were a result of nature and nurture, the melding of DNA and childhood trauma. Fortunately, the Firm's careful cultivation of the Watcher as a gifted young Sociopath—or as the Firm like to call them, Socio-Automanauts—meant that the Watcher had been trained to recognize and utilize his own unique personality traits for the greater good of the Firm and everyone it served. The Watcher had been trained by the Firm's Mentors to turn to food, comfort or sex for dopamine and oxytocin stimulation, and he understood his own seeking behaviors.

I'm just looking for a natural high.

Having properly stoked his own cynicism, the Watcher deconstructed the Afterling's emotion. Superiority in his own self-awareness gave way to detached analysis: how might this knowledge help him gain what he was seeking from her? He opened Rose's profile in the Ring's HeadsUp display, and entered his observation:

#PROFILE NOTES: *after the loss of her unborn children, and rejection by her tribe, sociophilic Rose is depressed. Oxytocin is at a low, and she is seeking a flood of dopamine to comfort her aching heart. Oskar is a substitute. Oskar is obviously reacting to her in the natural way of a young animal to any mother creature who presents the right cues.*

As he closed his notes, the Watcher's eyes narrowed in thought. Here might be a pathway into her heart...

Oskar leaned his head against the Afterling's shoulder, burrowing into her arms with a sigh. Through his shared neural portal with Rose, the Watcher could feel another surge of mysterious warmth engulf Rose and Oskar. There beneath the twining branches of Elm and Ash, two unnatural creatures met in an innocent Eden, walled away from the Watcher, who observed from the parapet of his own emotional fortress. Obliviously relentless, Rose's love hammered away at the Watcher's stony heart, and he could feel every hammer blow:

Hada Pequeña—what fairy power is this?

The Watcher felt stupid at his visceral reaction to her gooey affection for Oskar. He tried to dismiss it, but—*the emotion is real to them*. A twinge of shame sprouted in his soul for having subverted such a pure connection between two living creatures. Nagged by unaccustomed guilt, he awaited a string of text-nonsense from the little beast; then the ruse could be ended...

Through the Watcher's Ring to Rose, the voice of Oskar's Text-2-Talk boomed out in the Ring's pre-set voice filter:

#OSKAR ASv4.7: *treat*

The Watcher stared at Oskar, flabbergasted.

"Oh, Oskar—you can talk!" Rose sputtered with joy. "I'll get a treat—oh Deva, this is a wonder!" She reached into her pocket and pulled out a peanut, and the cub flicked his curling tongue to take it from her fingers.

Amazed, the Watcher opened the Ring's message settings. Somehow, the AutoSpeex program was detecting human speech patterns in Oskar's brain, and the Text-2-Talk was voicing him through the Watcher's chosen filter: the boisterous voice of Jim Lowe's Iconic State Fair Cowboy, Big Tex.

#OSKAR ASv4.7: *treat treat*

She gave him another peanut—Oskar gurgled enthusiastically and waved a paw.

#OSKAR ASv4.7: *treat   treat treat   treat*

More peanuts tumbled out of Rose's pocket; Oskar rolled over and she patted his belly.

This is—unnatural. Apprehensive of talking Chupacabras, the Watcher decided enough was enough.

#There. I helped you hear Oskar's thoughts, I'm Deva. 'Nuff said. We're done.

"How marvellous! Oh Deva, this makes me so happy. We can talk now, any time!" Rose was ecstatic at the thought being able to communicate with other friendly genetic mutants. The Watcher put his finger to his lips, shushing her once more—he pointed to the sky.

"Oh, I'm sorry. I was just so excited; but that was simply amazing! Could you train me to hear thoughts too?"

#No. Deva only, sorry.

He disconnected from Rose, unwilling to share his own secrets. Rose went over to pat Shadow, who was now snorting with jealousy at all the attention paid this unwashed interloper. Chattering away, Oskar leapt around the Watcher.

#OSKAR ASv4.7: *treat treat treat*

#OSKAR ASv4.7: *treat*

Unnerved by this latest development, the Watcher scratched his chin as he surveyed the talking Chupacabra.

#WATCHER: Good boy, Oskar. Down.

#OSKAR ASv4.7: *treat*

Holding out his hand for the Chupacabra to sniff, the Watcher suddenly felt as if he needed to ask permission. This wasn't just some wild animal... Oskar was now a cognizant, sentient being. *Or maybe Oskar was always cognizant and sentient, and I just never realized it.* A queasy unease settled in to the Watcher's mind; Oskar was a chimera—just like Rose— and the Designer of both seemed to have no qualms about pushing the definitions of "Humanity" to its limits. *Does this uncanny beast have more than just a little of humanity in him?*

Oskar flopped out a long slobbery tongue and looped it around the Watcher's forearm, eyes shining.

#OSKAR ASv4.7: *treat*

He motioned for the cub to sit, and Oskar obliged. A slight twitch of a grin worked its way around the Watcher's scar as he rubbed Oskar's warty round ear. *Ah, Dopamine.* The pleasant sensation reminded him of his visits with Reunion Camp's old black Tomcat, Waylon; it was one of the only tolerable memories from his imprisonment at the Reunion Archway. He wondered if Waylon ever missed him...

more likely the old beggar misses my food. Stepping into a hog wallow, where the sight of a carnivorous mess might be obscured from the herbacious Afterling, the Watcher tossed the dead cougar to the cub—

#WATCHER: Good. Eat.

Chortling, the Chupacabra slithered his tail in the leaves, and proceeded to devour the carcass:

#OSKAR ASv4.7: *treat treat treat treat treat*

Turning back to Rose and the horses beneath the overhang, the Watcher readied himself for a cold breakfast and perhaps a chance to cool his heels before planning his next course of action. Had they not been absconding from death-bots, now would been a good time to enjoy Rose's promised morning sit-down together and let her listen to a little music— and let him Deva her mind as well. But the Watcher now had to spend this time listening to the WildLand and thinking of ways to stay alive.

Grumping to himself over opportunities lost, he decided he would be willing to forego the music and simply hold hands. The Watcher dusted off a fallen log and patted it, beckoning to Rose. *Come here—*

An urgent notification tone—much like an old-fashioned boxing-ring bell—jangled the Watcher's Ear. A red notification box popped up, blinking:

##WESPEEX BEACON ZERO - LOCATED##

He disconnected from the Xirxes Chatroom and enacted the lockdown security check before proceeding. Rose, still coddling Shadow, continued her spoiling of the petulant horse, oblivious to the Watcher's burst of activity; unwilling to connect with her in the event of a breech, he moved forward with the designated protocols as set forth by the Director before they parted. Having checked off all security measures, he scanned—no other beacons were detected, so they had to be within the 2.5-mile signal radius. He opened the message.

A long burst of static crackled out over the encrypted channel. It sounded for all the world like digital or radio signal interference; *Dominic's deception*, they had dubbed it. As the Director instructed, the Watcher played it back at one-tenth speed.

Three short bursts of static, followed by three long bursts, then three short bursts again. the Watcher scowled involuntarily.

dit-dit-dit

daw-daw-daw

dit-dit-dit

The Watcher was not proficient with Morse Code, but even he knew these dits and daws. *S. O. S.*—a distress signal.

The Watcher activated the third layer of encryption. An image of a gaily-feathered purple parrot popped up, dancing and chirpy little tune—a meme designed to bypass digital searchbots scanning for voice files. He slowed the holo-video to one-tenth speed, and watched frame by frame, then froze playback as a faint white-font text image flashed sequentially on the white tipped feathers of the parrot's wings. The font was a fancy cursive, hard to distinguish against curving tips of the feathers. The Watcher struggled to read it:

F-E-N-I-X

C-R-E-C-I-E-N-T-E

The Director's beacon was paging the Watcher—but the message was not from the Director... the parrot looped, and continued singing.

The Watcher took a deep breath.

Danger's calling.

With the ALGOS drones tracking behind them and WildLand Express agents waiting ahead of them, it was hard to find time for breakfast. Oskar had no such problem; having made a grisly feast of the cougar's carcass, the cub shuddered with delight and snuggled down next to Rose, who was sitting on a large rock under the limestone overhang. The Watcher wished Oskar would have caught a rabbit or a snake to share for breakfast—he himself had no love for the meat of most carnivores— but no such luck. Times like these, the Watcher most keenly missed Abuelita and her cooking, not simply because he was hungry, but because her meals were woven into the fabric of his life and now that pattern was gone. He sighed and pulled a pear out of his coat pocket.

"Is Father in trouble?" Rose's face was drawn with worry, a little crinkle appearing between her brows. "And what of Evangelo?"

The Watcher reached over to connect with her via the Ring between bites of pear:

#*Their status is unknown. We received a distress signal, and it's the parrot macro and the embedded "Fenix Creciente" sign, pre-set by the Director—that means someone is "parroting" instructions, so it's not the Director who sent it. They would only know the steps with specific instruction from the Director, so I've bounced the same holo-meme back, with an embedded callsign—We Will Be Free—and am waiting the return message.*

Glancing up, he saw her trying to hide her face—but not really. *You want me to know what you're feeling, but you are too proud to say it...* he pulled out another pear and handed it to Rose.

#*Oskar had his breakfast, and so should you. Don't worry—I'll take care of the problem, whatever that might be.*

Not looking up at the Watcher, she talked to the pear: "Oh, you don't have to do that, I can do it if I need to..."

This game again... pretend you don't need help when you're just too ashamed to ask for it. Without skipping a beat, the Watcher fired back.

#*You're right, I don't have to help you. Now, do you want help, or not? Because either you think you can handle it, and you don't need my help, or you need my help. What'll it be?*

Shocked, she backpedalled. "I didn't mean it that way."

#*Yes, you did. Your Church Fathers taught you to reject what you need. You are taught to refuse to see your own needs, your own limitations. You've been taught to do it yourself, even when you can't— and to turn back allies who would willingly help you. That's how they are keeping you enslaved, by teaching you to reject what you need. So I'm unteaching you; what do you need?*

Embarrassed at her own confusion, she balked: "I don't know, yet. I'm sorry. I just didn't want you to think I'm weak, or that I can't do it myself, or that I need you to rescue me."

#You're not weak. But you can't do it all, all by yourself; that's just reality. No one can. There is nothing weak about asking for help when you really do need to be rescued. If you ever figured that out, maybe you'd stop rejecting me every time you need me.

Ruffled at his bluntness, Rose bit the pear. "Well, what is good for the Goose is good for the Gander. So, if you ever need me, or need rescue, does this mean you'll tell me, too?"

She looked up at him, a subversive twinkle in her eye, clearly enjoying her turnabout. The Watcher almost snorted.

#When that happens, you'll be the first to know.

They both ate in subdued silence, wondering what had happened to their friends. Evangelo's moccasin boots weighed heavy upon the Watcher's feet; just like Abuelita's absent cooking upon his empty stomach, or Montel's badge upon his chest, it was a reminder of persons not present. He was tired of caring about dead people, and hoped this wasn't yet another prelude to sorrow. *If Dominic and Evangelo are both dead, then why even try?* If that was the case, he was taking Rose far away from this hellhole of a life to someplace—

The message notification bell jangled once again.

#A response just came in—stand by.

Downloading the message, he disconnected from the beacon and went through the layers of protocols until, at last, the singing parrot once more gave its dance.

"I want to see, please? I like mysteries!" Rose held out her hand, inquisitive.

Well sure, why not... the Watcher secured all data and hooked her up.

Just as the Director had previously instructed, he froze the frames every 123rd frame of the holo-vid, to reveal its embedded message. Every 123rd frame was a pastel picture of a stylized autumn tree, each seemingly the same, with a few leaves clinging to a branch over a grassy field littered with fallen leaves.

The Watcher scratched his head.

#*It has to be a code—*

Rose tugged on his hand—"It's a pun! The message is 'Leave', like leaves on a tree…"

Studying it with careful eyes, Rose suddenly gasped. "Each branch is the same, but look at the number of leaves on the ground—it changes every few frames."

The Watcher suddenly caught it: every tenth frame of the embedded image, a word appeared, or a different number of leaves on the ground. *Leaves, the word "decimal", and more leaves: then a blank, the word "negative" more leaves, the word "decimal" again…* puzzling at it, the Watcher turned it over in his mind:

Ah HA - there it is!

three leaves

one leaf

decimal

three leaves

eight leaves

four leaves

three leaves

BLANK

negative

nine leaves

six leaves

decimal

three leaves

…

He flung open the Map in their HeadsUp Display, and typed it in.

#*These are location coordinates.*

The Map spun and zoom in, down to the lake, down to a peninsula, down to a ravine in a dark, forested crevice of the world—just a half mile to the north of Purgatory, a little more than two miles from their current location.

It would still be outside the Purgatory Dead Zone, which encompassed the entire city. The Watcher would be able to communicate with anyone who had a functional Neural Port, even if they didn't have a working WeSpeex Ring; that was a welcome location feature, as not everyone could read handwritten notes.

The Watcher leaned back and closed his eyes. To take Rose so close to the City with its twelve hundred or so debauched Survivors—was it worth the risk? It was exactly where the ALGOs wouldn't be looking for either of them...

#There's only one way to find out what's happened to Dominic and Evangelo—are you ready for an adventure?

She jumped up from her seat: "Oh, that sounds lovely! I'm always ready for an adventure..." She patted Oskar awake. "Come on, Oskar, we have to 'leave'." She muffled a giggle: "I really do love puns."

The Watcher retrieved her moccasins from the gear bag.

#The first part of this adventure is to play a little dress up—

"Dress up, here? Now?" She looked up at him askance: "Okee dokee, Deva, I'll do my best... but I didn't expect you to enjoy roleplay and dress-up in the great outdoors. Plus, it's cold out here—"

Flustered, the Watcher turned red and shook his head.

"Oh! You mean not for fun?" Slightly disappointed, Rose flipped off her boots and replaced them with the fringed deer hide moccasins, pausing to admire her feet while the Watcher packed away her cherished boots. Fixing his mind on the road ahead, he pulled the deer-head hood of her furred cloak firmly in place, then swung into the saddle behind Rose to take the reins once more.

#Now hunker down and stay quiet beneath your furs. Where we're going, deer hides are always in fashion...

Agent Mansour lay low in the shadows, hiding his coppery leathered face beneath his camouflage boonie hat. Glittering ice-blue eyes peered out over a prodigious nose, giving the Survivor a hawk-like, predatory appearance. In the twiggy resplendence of the lakeside forest, fog crept between the massive elms, making them appear ghostlike in the early morning gloom; the diffuse sunlight filtering down between golden skeletons of elm leaves gave an otherworldly half-golden cast to landscape. His makeshift ghillie suit—cobbled from old lawn-chair webbing and earth-toned rags—was supplemented by fallen leaves and twigs from the forest floor, and his muscular, compact frame became one with the rocky limestone crag on which he perched.

He hoped Agent Azarian would show up and bring whatever sort of amazing prize he had with him. The Director had informed Sam about a "package" of such extraordinary importance to the Cause—and its heir, the newly-minted Revolution—that the Director had recruited this extraordinary new Special Agent for the sole purpose of protecting the package. Agent Mansour wondered what it might be; *advanced weaponry, perhaps, or an experimental technological device?* Whatever it was, Mansour hoped the Special Agent would hurry up. Even with the current crisis, it was time for morning workout, and then rounds...

Sam would be insisting on a fitness check, and she was a stickler for making sure her agents were up to any task, physical or mental. He took a bite of deer jerky, and contemplated Sam, AKA Agent Ellison, AKA She Who Must Be Obeyed.

Rank is an absolute bitch.

If he outranked Sam, he would have insisted they blow Purgatory and everyone in it to smithereens a long time ago. But no, Sam outranked him —and she wanted to go save the damn world.

To be fair, that was very admirable, but admiration wasn't the reason he kept hanging on; he hung on because there was absolutely no one in the world like Stormy Sam. That very first day he walked into Purgatory, on assignment from the WildLand Express, he saw her and thought he had won the Love Lottery. A statuesque goddess greeted him from the steps of the local whorehouse, clad in black leather pants and a studded biker vest. But even if he hadn't already been warned by the Director that Sam was embedded on assignment, Mansour would have sought out Sam. Sleekly lethal, hypnotically gorgeous, high-strung, hot-blooded, and demanding—Sam was just his style.

Clearly Sam appreciated his military bearing and his overall incredible good looks. A body builder and fitness buff, Agent Mansour was always appreciated by the few ladies still out there, and as Sam was ex-military herself, it seemed a natural fit. He expected to partake of her charms, perhaps share a laugh or two, then roll out with his next assignment.

He did not expect to be broken.

For the next three days, Mansour hung on for dear life as she put him through his paces, worked every angle he had, explored every nuance of his body and soul—and by the end of the run, Sam declared that he was fit for duty and she had chosen him for "Special Assignment." And here he still was, sixteen years later, doing her bidding...

Sam needed his muscle and his military skills to complete her entourage, and the Director found it a good use of Mansour's skills to place him under Sam's command. The assignments were intriguing, and sufficiently dangerous, but it was Sam who kept him coming back, year after year. It wasn't a bad life. But he wanted a life just with Sam, without the whole sordid cast of characters woven into the vivid tapestry of sin that made up Purgatory. Still, Sam had to go deeper down that world-saving rabbit hole... she wanted to fight for the Cause.

The Director had made a way for Sam to do it—but all Mansour wanted was for Sam to make him a priority. *Well, that did happen from time to time,* he remembered with an ardent sigh. Adjusting his seating, Agent Mansour toggled his ring on, scanning for signals. *No new messages.*

He heard a rustle and the sound of horses' hooves.

Into the ravine leading down to the water, an ominous, slightly hunched figure rode in on a pale horse. He was swathed in a black trench coat with a bundle of deer hides draped across the saddle in front of him, and a magnificent black pack horse ambled behind him in tow.... the horse looked familiar. *Chief Emmanuel's horse?* A horned, scarred red skull framed piercing eyes peering from beneath a black oilskin hat. Unflinching, the red man stared directly at Mansour...

Agent Mansour felt a wary appreciation at the rider's quick detection of him... *so this is the fabled Watcher of Reunion. You are one big, ugly... sucker.*

A leather-gauntleted hand was raised in salute, then tapped a badge pinned to the red man's coat's lapel; Agent Mansour nodded. A message hailed the Watcher on the encrypted channel, and an avatar of a half-nude, tanned bodybuilder in full pose popped up in the HeadsUp display:

#MANSOUR: Fenix Creciente

The red man hailed back and Mansour allowed the connection: an icon of a neatly-bearded man with straight shoulder-length hair and a lean, athletic build appeared—

#WATCHER: We Will Be Free

Mansour stepped out of the shadows. "I am Agent Lazarus Mansour, and you are Agent Saul Azarian—the Watcher of Reunion. Where is the Director's package?"

#WATCHER: What you see is what you get. Call me "Watcher," and tell me why you called me here.

"Follow me and we will discuss it in a place of greater safety. Do you have any uninvited guests accompanying you?"

#WATCHER: One might call him unexpected rather than uninvited. Do not draw your weapon—I am summoning an experimental animal the Director is training.

The Watcher raised his hand, then made the motion to come—and from a tree above the ravine, a ridiculously ugly creature appeared, then leapt down to the Watcher's feet—

"Mother of God!" Nervous, Agent Mansour toyed with his hatchet, but did not raise it. "How on earth did you end up with a chupacabra?"

The Watcher motioned, and the chupacabra cub sat beside the horses, his tail coiling and uncoiling behind him.

#WATCHER: It's a long story.

"Anything else I should know about?"

#WATCHER: ALGOS are searching for me, dropped back at the mine from a HeliScram last night. I have not yet been spotted.

Agent Mansour's eyes narrowed, and his hand drifted to the hefty tomahawk on his belt. "You are lying. No one has seen ALGOS drones since the Happening, much less any HeliScram."

#WATCHER: I would make you eat your words, but I would have said the same thing two weeks ago. No matter—you will apologize to me in full when you realize I am telling the truth. Director Santos himself will tell you when we meet with him. Where is he?

"Why should I trust you?"

#WATCHER: Because you have to—you need my help, or you wouldn't be here. Now, take me where we are going, or let me go my own way and you can deal with your problem on your own.

Mansour studied the Watcher. Already he didn't like him, and he had no reason to trust him. If it weren't for Sam, this man would already be dead. Still, the directive came not only from Sam, but from the Director—and that meant putting up with this arrogant son-of-a-bitch until such time as it was deemed expedient to axe him. He snarled. "Follow me. If you cross me, you die."

#WATCHER: Likewise.

Following Agent Mansour down the ravine, they turned north to make their way between thick, overgrown elm and willow trunks, through a cold marsh and towards what appeared to be a cleft in the rock face of a limestone escarpment just beyond the view of the lake. Here, they entered an alcove where green briar hung down in curtains, dotted with red heart-shaped leaves and small crimson berries. Mansour took his tomahawk and pulled a particularly heavy curtain of thorns back with the head of his hatchet; it revealed a heavy cedar door barring a narrow cave entrance. Carved into the rock by wind and water, made larger by human hands, the cave entrance was just large enough for the horses to pass through; Agent Mansour held up his WeSpeex Ring and adjusted the light to a bright setting, then knocked twice, followed by two more knocks. A voice wheezed:

"Agent Renfro. Salt."

"Agent Mansour, Pepper—"

The door swung open, and footsteps retreated back into the cavern. The Watcher patted the deer hide bundle and dismounted to lead the horses through the cleft and down a short, winding passageway into an airy cavern, dotted with vents to the surface; these allowed light to filter into the cave and illuminate a primitive but well-appointed stable. From behind a boulder, he heard a familiar snort, and his horses answered in reply.

Past the boulder was a carved stone chamber where William and Charger were tethered to a cedar post—and with them, a wiry old codger cuddling a double-barreled shotgun in his embrace. The ancient edges of his speckled, ivory scales curled up like feathers, giving the Survivor an avian visage.

Six stalls with water and feed were set aside for visiting Agents' horses, and a set of clean dog-pens lay open and ready for the hounds of the WildLand Express. One old bloodhound lay snoozing in the corner of one pen; she blinked, and her great droopy snout twitched along with her tail before uttering one solitary, soft "woof."

"Agent Saul Azarian, otherwise known as Watcher—this is Agent Leroy Renfro, otherwise known as Gunny." The old man spit from beneath a beat-up brown hat, and said nothing. The Watcher nodded and grunted. Mansour continued "He's not friendly, but he's good with horses, dogs, and weapons. Gunny, the Watcher cannot speak—he has a pet chupacabra and a bad attitude. I'm sure you two will get along great."

Renfro scowled. "Charmed." He held up his hand to reveal his own ring, then hailed the Watcher on the encrypted frequency. The Watcher linked in.

Mansour removed his ghillie suit and placed it in an old metal locker wedged into a niche chiseled in the wall. Beneath the suit, a simple t-shirt and old military-style cargo pants accented the massive biceps and well-balanced physique of a body-builder. Except for his heavy brow ridge and cracked, leathery skin, Mansour could have passed for a LifeBefore man.

He pulled out a dusty tan jacket and donned it. "The Director has informed us of your new System status as Privilege Level Four Personnel; but since you are new to Purgatory, let me brief you—Purgatory is a Privilege Level Two Facility, an intake and processing facility for unassigned, promoted, or newly discovered Survivors. Purgatory is supervised by five town Bosses, each one a Privilege Level Four Visionary; they supervise one thousand, two hundred and sixty-three Privilege Level Two skilled workers and craftsmen, who count themselves as citizens, twenty-seven private contractors and thirty-six public servants at Privilege Level Zero."

Mansour pulled the tail of his shirt loose to hide the tomahawk in his belt. "Purgatory Hostess Club—established over thirty years ago—operates within System guidelines, but it has been co-opted by Agent Sam Ellison and is now run as a deep cover for WildLand Express Covert Operations, under the direct supervision of Director Santos. In order for us to operate undetected by the System at Purgatory, Director Santos has approved undercover activities consistent with all System Hostess Clubs. No freebies, so don't ask. There are five women, each of them Agents or Specialists, and all are here of their own free will—four serve as Hostesses and Agent Ellison presents as their Madame, as cover for their covert activities on behalf of the Cause and the WildLand Express."

The Watcher shook his head, incredulous.

#WATCHER: That's all in the whole town? Five?

"Have you been living under a rock?" Mansour answered, surprised at the Watcher's reaction. "How long you been a prisoner at Reunion Camp?"

#WATCHER: Forty-three years.

"Well, that explains it—you've been living under a rock pretty much since the Happening. I guess you just got used to all the Chicas and Hembras that gathered inside the walls of Reunion Camp—but trust me, Buddy, it's not that way in the World Out There. Every Femme the Judge could gather up, she did, and brought them inside the walls and under your safe keeping. The highest concentration of women still living in the WildLands exists behind the fortified walls of Reunion Camp."

A flash of shock crossed the Watcher's face.

#WATCHER: I knew the virus was more deadly to women than to men, but I had no idea it was this bad.

"Well, you're in for a rude awakening; it's a feminine wasteland out here." Mansour waved a hand. "I'd say we've gotten used to it—but that's a lie. You can ask any man on this detail; it's a plum assignment just for the fact that we get to interact with the girls on a regular basis. That's why so many fight to get on with this unit. It's the only place to find feminine company outside of Judge Leona's 'Sugar Sanctuary'. She cornered the Market..." He gave a cool look to the Watcher. "If you're coming aboard expecting to find romance, you'd have been better off staying at Reunion."

The Watcher didn't seem to be concerned.

"Nine other associated WildLand Express Agents and Specialists are on permanent assignment here. You will be introduced to undercover personnel on a need-to-know basis. Our job here is to find and recruit willing Survivors to join the Cause, and set them free. Under cover of regulated activities, we help them escape the System and Purgatory. I use my skill as a construction worker to provide cover for my presence at Purgatory. I have a shack in LowTown and work with an ally, Boss Winston and his work crews. I am also Agent Ellison's second in command." Mansour removed his boonie hat and replaced it with a work-worn straw hat:

"The WildLand Express gains approved entry and exit from Purgatory once a month thanks to the orgy of gambling and fighting known as Purgatory's Market Mayhem Weekend; at that time, the Wagon Teams come rolling in from Plantations all over the Tejas Co-op. From as far north as the Granbury Gates to as far south as the Tomball Turnaround, from the western walls of the Brazos River Bear Camp to the far eastern reaches of the Trinity River Trapping Zone they come—all headed to trade goods and peddle flesh at the center of the Tejas Co-op universe, Purgatory."

Gunny nodded at the thought of the upcoming weekend. "It's grand to see the WildLand Express Wagon Teams rollin' in, loaded with produce from all over the Co-op—when it started fifteen years ago, there was hardly anything except sweet potatoes and peanuts. And now look at it— scavenged goods, fruit, and products of all kinds! Survivors have come a long way since those first days after the Happening—"

A pride edged into the old soldier's voice, "If it warn't for the buyin' and sellin' of people, the Tejas Co-op could be a great place."

Mansour nodded in acknowledgement of progress, then tossed his locker key to Gunny: "No firearms except on waiver, no ring comms, no unauthorized entrances or exits. The local citizens are largely ignorant of the world outside Purgatory, and the Bosses prefer to keep it that way. Only a few nosy busybodies keep track of life outside the walls, and even fewer care what happens there, as long as the Mood-Wagons keep bringing their pay."

As Mansour talked, Gunny scoffed at institutional intemperance.

"Upon entering Purgatory, remember—no System Awareness; all government is local, horses are only for Law Enforcement, and Rings don't exist. Purgatory is a Dead Zone, just like Reunion and other low-level facilities, so don't expect to use your tech, even if you do manage to smuggle it in..."

A questioning look crept over the Watcher's face. Mansour questioned him back: "You do know about the DeadZones, right?"

#WATCHER: The Director and Captain Evangelo mentioned the DeadZones, and they are included on my Map. I want to know why there are DeadZones.

"Good luck; if you figure it out, let me know." Mansour harrumphed. "Leave your ring, livestock and gear here with Gunny. Come with me, do not make any loud noises, and I will take you to meet Agent Ellison. Do you have any questions?"

Scowling, the Watcher motioned to Oskar, then the deer hide bundle, and grunted.

"No pets allowed inside the facility, and no gear unless it has been searched. No negotiations."

Crossing his arms, the Watcher sat down.

#WATCHER: Then bring your people to meet me down here— I will not leave my gear or animals in the care of unknown parties until I have a reason to trust you.

"That is not up to you—ask Agent Renfro; he is in charge of the stable, and he decides who is allowed to wait here." Waiting for Agent Azarian to make his request—the Watcher could only message one Ring at a time here, as the Chat System was not set up—Agent Mansour looked to Agent Renfro, expecting a rejection. But much to his surprise, the old man grinned in approval, his wrinkled, brown-speckled hide gleaming in the cave's dim light.

"I wouldn't do it neither." The old man spit again. "I wouldn't leave my Sassy with strangers." The bloodhound did not rise, but her tail twitched once more.

"Suit yourselves—I will have to request Agent Ellison personally, since Ring comms are forbidden inside the walls. If she chooses to not meet with you here, you will be asked to leave and not return."

The Watcher gave a curt nod and continued to stand by his steed.

Something's sketchy about that deer hide bundle—possibly contraband or the Director's mystery package hidden within it? Normally Mansour would initiate a search, but according to the Director's instructions the Watcher ranked Level Four in the System, and that meant *rank has its privileges...*

Agent Mansour couldn't help but notice the beauty of the horses, and wished that he too could have one—his previous assignment had been with a WildLand Express Scouting Unit and he missed riding. It was a privilege that only came with a badge. A suspicion arose in him. How was it this former prisoner rose through the ranks so quickly? Two weeks ago, the Watcher was considered Privilege Level Zero in The System—now he was a Level Four VIP, equivalent to a Boss.

It could only be explained if the Watcher was a high-ranking Visionary. Mansour eyed him suspiciously—*has Azarian been embedded as a System spy all along?* Sam would need to be advised—there were very few Level Four or higher personnel in the WildLands, and their exact number was hidden from lower-ranking personnel. The Director was one; the Watcher appeared to be another. still, if the Director trusted him...

Mansour secreted his ring in his coat pocket. "I'll return in one half hour. Gunny, shoot him if you want to."

"You've got it." the old geezer patted his shotgun.

Mansour ducked around a boulder, and pulled a string to draw back a bundle of reeds, revealing another heavy wooden door. He lightly tapped twice, waited a beat, then tapped again. A knock answered, then the door swung outward, and a lanky guard whispered, "Who goes there?"

"Agent Mansour, WildLand Express...Syrup."

"Agent Wilcox. Pancakes."

Stepping into the small, torch-lit guard chamber, Mansour drew the reed curtain back into place, and pulled the door shut behind him, barring it with a heavy oaken timber. "Let no one through either way until I return."

Grabbing a torch, he lit it, then strode down the manmade four-by-

eight-foot corridor, walls shored up by cedar timbers; their fresh
condition was testament to recent construction and constant maintenance.
The corridor descended into the darkness at a steep slope, carved
limestone steps leading down into a damp subterranean walkway below a
narrow inlet of the Lake. Moldy puddles made the footing treacherous,
and he made a mental note to order more gravel brought down to fill in
any slip hazards. The last thing their "guests" needed was an injury while
fleeing for their lives...

After five hundred feet or so, the steps ascended once again and
leveled off; the passage was well-maintained, but dark. Armed only with
torchlight, Agent Mansour seemed to know intimately every step of the
long limestone corridor.

How many times had he led guests to freedom in the middle of the
night through this tunnel? How many times had he helped others flee
down the limestone steps towards their own liberty, only to have himself
return to this glorified prison?

Too many times—all for the love of a woman who wanted to save the world.

Next to a slender chain loop dangling through a hole in the ceiling,
white shoe-polish letters proclaiming "SHHHH" were painted along the
wall, reminding guests to keep silence. Mansour reached up and gently
pulled the loop of chain to change the small garden flag from blue to red
—the sign to the hostesses in the cabin that a guest was taking shelter in
the tunnels. Coming to the end of the corridor, he entered a guard
chamber much like the last, with a short tank of a macho sitting on a
stool. The stout Survivor looked as if he could punch a hole in the stone
wall, provided there was a meal waiting on the other side.

Agent Mansour whispered to the guard:

"How's the morning shift?"

"Fair to middlin'—who goes there, Agent?"

Mansour sighed. "Agent Mansour. Eggs."

"Agent Mancini—Bacon."

He worked his way through the next door, towards a ladder climbing
some twelve feet up the far limestone wall of a circular chamber. "See you
in a minute, Joey. Don't get comfortable." He set the torch into an iron
sconce, then pulled on a braided cotton cord; twice, a pause, then twice
again. A small chime sounded each time he pulled the cord.

A soft voice answered; "Who goes there?"

"The best thing that ever happened to you, Coffee."

"Agent Ellison—Cream," From the floor of a dank basement store-room, Sam opened the hatch, her dark eyes shining. She peered down into the hole: "Where is Agent Azarian and the Director's package?"

"He refused to leave his horses and gear. He's is waiting at the stable with Gunny, asking for you to come to him. Azarian's not exactly System compliant, even though he's Privilege Level Four. He acts like he runs everything. Sam, this guy makes no sense—how did he rise through the ranks that quickly? He can't talk, he's the ugliest man alive, and he was a prisoner till just a few days ago... is it possible he's a System spy?" Mansour backed down the ladder.

Sam straightened herself, her slender fingers adjusting the backs of her tiny hoop earrings. "Lazarus, I told you—Dominic himself recruited this guy. I trust Dominic, or I wouldn't be doing this job; still, I'll take your concerns under advisement. I wouldn't be much of a commanding officer if I didn't listen to my second in command..." She swung her long legs down into the hole, then pulled an empty crate back over the hatch, closed it and slid down the rails. "Let's find out what it is he's hiding, then we can determine whether or not he makes it inside the walls."

Back past Fat Joey and down the hole, all the way to the other side of the inlet, Sam blew through the secret passage until she came to a nervous Agent Wilcox, who forgot to call the sign and was promptly lambasted in hushed tones. Finally making it through the last doorway, Mansour and his Commanding Officer came into the stable, where a dour Agent Renfro and a reticent Agent Azarian stood next to the horses. The Watcher had not moved from his station next to the deerskin bundle; *sketchy indeed*, Mansour noted.

Sam drew herself up to her full height and made herself known.

"Agent Sam Ellison, WildLand Express, Covert Ops, Purgatory Unit —thank you for answering the distress ca—what the *hell* is that thing?"

Agent Renfro was patting a beaming, affable Oskar. The small Chupacabra coughed up a ball of soggy cougar fur.

"That a good boy, that's what it is. Don't fuss and he won't bite." The old man offered a piece of jerky to the cub, and Oskar nibbled it down. "I always wanted me a pet chupacabra. I'll set him up in one of the WildLand Express' dog pens; they're good n' sturdy." Hassling, the little chupacabra uncoiled a gooey tongue towards Sam's perfectly manicured hands.

"As you will, Gunny—just keep that thing away from me," she hissed.

The Watcher tipped his hat and pointed to his ring. She nodded and opened the encrypted channel for messaging; the avatar of a dark-skinned, dark-eyed woman in a blazer presented herself from a Visionary conference long past, her short, silver-streaked afro a crown for a woman who considered herself queen.

The Watcher made his introduction.

#WATCHER: Special Agent Saul Azarian, Ranger Command, WildLand Express Detachment. Call me Watcher.

He thumped his badge—then flipped the leather badge cover down to reveal the Rising Phoenix with its Five-Pointed Star.

"Fenix Creciente," Sam whispered.

#WATCHER: We Will Be Free.

"Do you have the Director's package?"

#WATCHER: Yes. I will reveal it to you when I am ready. Now, why are we here?

"The Director and Captain Evangelo were ambushed this morning, less than three hours ago—one of our own girls was taken hostage without our knowledge during a client call, and she was used as bait to lure the Director and Evangelo into a trap. My Recon Specialist, Kendra Qin, witnessed the entire thing." Agent Ellison's expression was grave.

"The Director and the Captain tethered their horses in this location and checked in at four-thirty a.m. with Agent Renfro; as is standard protocol for all personnel under cover, they made their way on foot to the main gate so as not to attract suspicion. As a Privilege Level Two Facility, no horses or higher-level privileges are allowed inside the gate, except on Market Mayhem Weekend, so they checked all tech and gear in here—but as badged personnel, the Director and the Captain have weapons waivers so they were allowed to keep firearms with them."

Fear mitigated by anger, Sam recalled the events of that morning: "Kendra said she saw runners from the gate before the Director and the Captain entered. Rangers posted outside the gate probably saw their approach to Purgatory and sent advanced word to co-conspirators inside the walls. Around five a.m., just as the Director and the Captain entered the gates, Jip McMasters came around the corner of Boss Zhu's house—he had Destiny hollering for help in one hand, and he had a knife in the other hand. He conveniently ducked into Boss Chartreaux's house, and the Director and the Captain pursued Jip into the cabin."

"Our recon specialist tried to get in closer, but the cabin was locked from the inside and the blinds were drawn—it sounded like a scuffle was underway, then shots were fired. Two minutes later, at least twenty men came streaming out of the cabin carrying the Director and the Captain, bloody and unconscious; they were whisked down the street to the Jail. Several injured men were taken to a medic station, and four bodies were brought out of Boss Chartreaux's house as well—they look like the Rangers who have been hanging out here since last week. The dead men are laid by the gate awaiting burial outside the walls—they were shot at close range."

The Watcher nodded grimly. *Dominic and Evangelo would not go down without a fight.*

"Shortly afterwards, a message was found in the yard behind Boss Chartreaux's house, Kendra picked it up—Destiny probably dropped it out of his second story window." Sam held up a scrap of paper with a note written in a loose scrawl, and she read it aloud.

~~~~~

get this to sam
directer and captin in truble
boss shartro has them
jip cot me at boss zus house they hurt him and i cride for
help
but it was a trap the director and captain was jumpt
i herd boss shartro say she was comin to git them
i dont no who she is but she gets hear for market mayhem
weekind
Forgiv me

-D

~~~~~

#WATCHER: 'D' is Destiny, then? Does she have any skills in evasion or escape?

"Destiny is excellent at escape, but she is no fighter." Sam appeared perturbed, passing the note to the Watcher. "She one of my best girls for personal intel, but she's lost her nerve lately. She's not paying attention to her surroundings, and this is what it cost us. All she's supposed to do is go to the clients, find out who has private contractors, and set us up to make contact." The Agent pursed her lips. "She's been helping us find willing recruits for the Cause, but she's been at it so long, I think it affected her judgement. Besides, she has no stomach for the kill. If I can recover her, I'm going to release her from duty...but that may be a moot point."

The Watcher looked at the note, his eyes guarded.

#WATCHER: She was recruiting for the Cause?

"Dominic said you were in—you should know what I mean."

#WATCHER: I do—I'm just surprised you've been recruiting this long.

Sam looked at the Watcher, with fire in her eyes. "We've been fighting for the Cause—Freedom—for the last two decades, risking our lives to free imprisoned survivors. While you were strung out at the gates of Reunion, keeping people enslaved to The System, we were breaking people out to serve the Cause..."

His eyes turned cold.

#WATCHER: You never tried to set me free.

Sam answered heatedly. "You wouldn't let us. We couldn't get anywhere near you or the Camp—the one time we almost breached the gate, you killed two of my men. You were your own best Slave Master." She pointed to the Watcher. "You were at that gate for forty-three years, thwarting us at every turn; and yet, here you are, now—with a Ring, on horseback, with full rank and privileges. Tell us how you managed to ascend to Privilege Level Four in these last two weeks, Agent Azarian."

The Watcher leaned back, and spoke through steepled fingers:

#WATCHER: The Warden had a problem, and I offered my services in exchange for my freedom.

"So we heard. Judge Leona was assassinated under mysterious circumstances. Some outlandish rumors have been floated—but we do know that you personally shot three sentinels that day. That is admirable and leads me to believe you might be an ally to the Cause. It still doesn't explain how you merited a Ring, a horse, and the Director's favor."

He looked circumspect.

#WATCHER: I acted on behalf of innocent bystanders—and I was rewarded through a series of fortunate events. Now I need to use that rank and privilege to act on behalf of the Dominic, Evangelo, and your specialist, or the Cause will lose valuable manpower. But we are also under orders to carry out the Director's

plan for his fledgling Revolution. Set up the meetings and arrange for the unit leaders to gather their recruits over the next twelve hours. The LoneStar Revolution will rise on schedule—

He studied the note in his hand.

#WATCHER:—and the investigation and rescue operation must get underway within the hour. Set up an interview with Specialist Qin in fifteen minutes. But first, I need to secure the Director's Package.

"Hold on—I am the one who calls the action here." Sam rankled. "You can't just walk in here and assume command. Until the Director is freed, I'm the one who decides what we do next—and I'm the one who determines how you 'secure the package.'"

#WATCHER: I'm not assuming your command—I am assuming my own command. Did the Director get an opportunity to brief you on the package he entrusted to my safekeeping?

Sam frowned. "The Director was supposed to debrief us all when he returned from his mission with the Captain, but that may never happen now..."

The Watcher gave a sly sideways grin, and softly smacked the deer hide bundle lying motionless across Oro's saddle.

#WATCHER: I proudly present to you the Director's Package —the Heart of the Revolution.

Two small golden hands slowly stretched out as the hides began to ascend from the saddle; a pair of floppy doe-ears flicked atop a fur hood, then rose from the pile of furs. Ellison swore in disbelief as Mansour and Renfro tried not to gape in sheer amazement. Face still obscured, the deer hide bundle rubbed her eyes:

"I'm awake! I'm awake—I'm just stiff, that's all..."

The Watcher pulled the doe's ears back and a cascade of frizzy hair pouffed out from under the deerskin hood, revealing a smooth, sleepy golden face with big dark eyes. The skin was soft and unprotected, the body small and round, no bigger than a child.

In shock, Sam reached for Lazarus' hand just as they both heard a thud hit the dirt—Renfro had fainted.

Rose blinked at them in surprise, then whispered into the Watcher's rough red ear. "They act as if they had never seen a human before..."

The Watcher just grunted, and reached down to make sure Renfro was still alive.

———◆———

While Renfro was recovering from his shock, chaos broke out at the New Reality.

Sam glared at the Watcher. "You can't keep her here. She'll get lost, killed, or stolen. Take her back to wherever you found her."

Rose piped up: "I can hear you all, you know..."

Ignoring the Afterling, Sam continued to rail at the Watcher: "Look, this isn't supposed to be 'Rebellion of the Baby People.' We aren't here to free them—" Sam jabbed a finger at the Afterling, "we are here to free US!"

An indignant Afterling bristled: "We are not 'Baby People', thank you very much. We are full grown people, and we don't need your help anyway..."

Specialist Renfro was leaning against Agent Mansour; every so often he would cough, then look at the Afterling and get queasy. "She looks like my Lulu when she was little."

"Oh, did you have children?" Rose's eyes glimmered in the soft cave light; the old Survivor's hands shook. "Tell me a wonderful story about them..."

"You—shut up. You're triggering me." Pointing at Rose, Sam looked like she was about to blow a gusset. "I don't need your yapping right now."

"Well, that isn't very polite." Rose started to tune up. "I didn't ask to be here in the first place."

The Watcher put a hand to his temple. This was not exactly the response he had envisioned. He closed his eyes to recalibrate his mind.

#WATCHER: When we rescue Director Santos and Captain Evangelo, they will explain everything in greater detail. Until then, we need to stick to the plan the Director worked out with you originally and get them back in the game.

"And what are we supposed to do with her until then?" Sam hissed. "Just look at her! She's going to die—the WildLand is no place for this creature." Turning her back to Rose, she continued to wave an indignant hand: "I already have one weak excuse for a woman I have to save, and I don't need another to take on. I am not responsible for what happens to this... this Afterling."

"It's Asura, not Afterling." Rose snapped. "Why do you all insist on calling me that?"

Agent Mansour took a closer look at the Afterling. "What does she do?"

#WATCHER: The same thing women always did—but she can still reproduce, and she has a natural infrared detection capability.

Agent Ellison was coldly assessing all assets. "I already have almost passable infrared capability with my Ring, so that makes the Afterling's skills redundant. And as for 'reproduction': Survivors don't need it. Survivors live extraordinary, long lives—we don't need to 'reproduce' anymore." She glared at Rose—"We have gotten past the point of needing to reproduce. I had children, and now I don't have children—and yet, I live. Reproduction is no longer a necessary function for females."

Rose visibly flinched. Sam continued:

"Survivors have a need, now—to live as we are now, to deal with this world now. It is a ridiculous waste of our time and resources to bring in a new set of needs for a completely irrelevant group of weak people; if this Afterling has a place to live in safety, where she can be born, replicate, and die, then she should go there."

#WATCHER: That is no longer a viable option for her.

"Then the Afterling is useless baggage, to be relegated to the role of non-combatant: she will be kept in the safe room until the Director is rescued and can tell us his plans for her."

Rose was unhappy. "We are not useless—we do many things! And we are part of this world. That is the reality, and you can't just dismiss us because you don't like us."

"It's not that I don't like you; I just don't think you belong here."

Agent Renfro looked hopeful. "She can stay down here with the Chupacabra and me—she shouldn't be in harm's way." Reaching into his pocket, the scaly sesqui-centenarian pulled out a piece of sugar cane, holding it out with a trembling hand. "I always carried candy for my Granddaughter, but I ain't got no candy now... all I got is this. Here ya go, ya lil' booger."

Rose looked confused, but took the sugar cane. "Oh, thank you—I'm old, but I do like sweets."

#WATCHER: She has to stay with me. She is my assignment, given to me personally by the Director.

Rose pled her case. "Please, I'll do whatever you ask... just let me help somehow." She turned to Sam: "Please—I have to help them. They're our Friends—and the Director's my Father..."

Sam passed her hand over her eyes, then pointed at Rose. "What do you mean, he's your Father?"

"He's just that; the Director is my Father." Rose tried to figure out how to say it where it all made sense. "I'm a genetic experiment gone awry from LifeBefore, and now I'm here to avenge him." She smiled brightly. "Oh, and I'll save Evangelo and your Specialist, too. Give me a gun and I'll make it happen."

#WATCHER: No—no guns.

Sam waved a hand: "You aren't allowed to have a gun, and yet you call yourself a part of this Revolution?"

"Yes! I helped start the Revolution." Rose looked pleased. "I'm a fugitive from the System because of it."

Pointing to the Watcher, Sam barked: "Explain."

#WATCHER: Rose is the Fugitive that Warden Howell of Reunion hired me to hunt. But I decided to keep her for myself instead of remanding her to the Warden, and I tricked him into signing a deal with the Devil, so to speak. After that, the Captain, the Afterling and the Director convinced me to fight for the Cause, under the new standard of the Revolution. Rose and I keep our roles as Fugitive and Bounty Hunter to provide cover for working within the System. And if she's a Fugitive, she can't have a gun.

Sam huffed. "Well, she can't fight for the Revolution if she has to ask permission to use a gun."

"She's right, you know..." Rose muttered. The Watcher shot back a sharp look.

#WATCHER: You are the Heart of this Revolution; your job is to inspire, not fight. Fighting is MY job. I'm your Weapon and Defender—and I'm going to do my job.

Rose pouted in return. "I have proven myself to the Director—it was he who chose me to help organize and lead this Revolution. And look at my actions; surely they count for something!" Rose appeared genuinely wounded.

"Look at you," Sam snorted. "You're hardly big enough to hold a gun, much less fire one. I'll bet you get knocked on your ass every time you fire off a round."

"That is not true!" A shocked Rose yelped. "That only happens when I shoot a shotgun!"

Turning her back on Rose to address the group, Sam's smooth, steel-blue scales flushed dark with anger. "I don't know the Director's reason for choosing someone so ill-suited for this mission. But I do know what it means to be a woman and a warrior; I have suffered in this world, and I have risen above it. I have done so by being a warrior—and she is no warrior."

A sharp gasp of indignation escaped from Rose lips. "I am too a warrior—" she ran up to Sam, eyes lit up like firecrackers. "I am the deadly Fugitive that killed Judge Leona!" The Afterling shook her delicate fist at the Hembra. "I am the one who did what you could not do: I assassinated the Judge, and freed all the Survivors of Reunion Camp—but only the Watcher dared to follow me and walk away from his prison..."

Sam stared at the Afterling, incredulous.

"I am the one who led the Watcher of Reunion to Freedom!" Rose was now crackling with energy, hair standing on end, deer hide cloak flung behind her, her dusty leather armor now exposed. "And I could lead others, too..."

The Hembra towered over the Afterling, her face an unreadable storm of emotion. Agent Mansour braced himself to intervene against an onslaught; the Watcher stood ready—

Sam snarled. "Do you really think this man followed you because you are a leader? You're delusional. He didn't follow your 'leadership' because he was inspired—he chased your tail because he was horny!"

Agent Mansour looked to the Watcher, who coughed into his gloved fist and said nothing.

"You are wrong!" Rose was incensed.

One hand raised, Sam gave a murderous look to Rose. "You dare backsass me in my own house?"

Mere inches of physical space separated the two women, but the gulf of their differences made them miles apart: one an imperial, dark Boudecia, towering and tactical—the other a rebellious, bright Joan of Arc, ad-hoc and irrepressible...

Suddenly realizing she herself was not a giant, Rose blanched, but kept her chin up. "I killed the Judge and set the Watcher free! What do you say to that?"

Looking up into Sam's eyes, Rose become keenly aware of her true state—a very small Afterling staring down a very large and angry Devil Woman. Sensing Rose's vulnerability, Sam brought her intimidating presence to full bear; a look so merciless, so brutal, that few could hold up beneath her withering gaze. Head thrown back, the Hembra sneered, her full, flushed lips curled back in a ferocious snarl, revealing perfect white teeth with small, sharp canines. Staring up at the fierce Devil Woman, Rose felt a familiar weakness start to wash over her—*oh God, not here, not now*—her hands started to tremble, and her knees became wobbly.

Sam noted the Rose's obvious distress and flashed a snarl of triumph at the hapless Afterling: "I say you are puny and fearful," Sam declared harshly. "I could crush you right now."

Wilting, Rose glanced back over her shoulder at the Watcher standing behind her.

He nodded to Rose, and she remembered his declaration: *I am your Weapon and Defender.* Suddenly all was made clear... the Afterling felt her fear drain away and her confidence return. Emboldened, Rose looked to Sam:

"You may be right; you could do all that, if I didn't have help. Alone, I may have a few disadvantages. But I am no longer alone—" The Afterling swept her hand towards her Champion with a flourish: "God is on my side, and He has sent me the Watcher!"

A thrill seeped into the Watcher's heart, and he gave a nod, vindicated.

"With him, I can do all things, and I will fulfill my mission. But even if all abandon me, and all hope is gone, I will still fight on—"

In the gloom of the stable, the Light came rippling from out of her now, a force field of Living Energy. She somehow appeared larger, stronger, fiercer than before, and once again raised her fist, defiant: "I will fight to my dying breath—and if not in this life, then in the next, We Will Be Free!"

A shockwave of Will burst forth from the Afterling; stunned by the Afterling's metaphysical transformation, Sam involuntarily stepped back. Fascinated, the Watcher tore his eyes away from Rose to glance around the room—the effect was extraordinary, universal; even Renfro and Mansour seemed to respond with a certain instinctive awe at whatever power this might be within the Afterling.

Had Rose been physically impressive like Sam, or frightening like the Watcher, she could have commanded armies based on that moment alone. But the reality of life intruded, and the glow incrementally faded, leaving behind only a slightly chubby Afterling with a grandiose attitude in its stead. But her image was burned into the Watcher's mind, and he reveled in the afterglow:

#WATCHER: I rest my case.

Agent Mansour cleared his throat: "Permission to speak freely, Agent Ellison." Brusque, Sam nodded, and Mansour continued. "Whatever the reason, Dominic has chosen her for leadership. Her leadership will declare itself in its own way, when the moment is right—and it will be your leadership which defines that moment."

Sam turned away from the group, hands clasped behind her back. Silent seconds passed, before she finally spoke. Turning once again to the group, Sam looked down fiercely upon Rose, then looked at the Watcher;

"Do not challenge me again." She then addressed the larger group:

"The Afterling's words are eloquent, but my assessment of her limitations as a warrior still stands. She is small and weak. I have grave concerns in allowing anyone on my team other than myself or my own chosen associates, and I have even greater concerns that innocent non-combatants may be involved in missions that may bring them or others to harm. A crisis is underway, and members of my team are in grave danger; we must rescue them, and that will require additional skilled, experienced personnel with nerves of steel. It is my assessment that Agent Azarian meets this standard, but the Afterling does not. He will be incorporated into the rescue team, and until we hear from the Director, the Afterling will remain restricted as a non-combatant."

Rose's face fell.

"Nonetheless, you are right, Agent Mansour." Sam inspected Rose with a calculating eye:

"Agent Azarian, keep your Afterling under control... she may yet serve the Cause in her own way." Sam's beautiful face became cunning. "Turn over your Ring to Gunny, grab your gear and come with me. We have friends to rescue—but when the time is right, we will loose the Afterling upon the World."

⊷———◆———➤

Gray light seeped in between his eyelids—just a little a first, so small an amount that Dominic could not tell if his eyes were opened or closed. In due course, he finally determined that he could not completely open his eyes, as they were swollen and crusted with blood. He tried to move his hands to wipe his eyes, but could only wiggle his fingers stiffly in the air, unable to bring his hands towards his face. At last, he discerned his position—*upright*—and his circumstance—*dangling from iron shackles on a concrete wall.* He attempted to straighten his posture, and was punished by a searing pain which notified him of at least two broken ribs. He couldn't adjust his stance—*shackles and chains at ankles.* An ache in his skull near the right parietal lobe let him deduce that someone had hit him in the back of the head...

That would explain why he couldn't quite tell which way was up. Disoriented, Dominic let the room spin until finally it stopped. While waiting, he worked his way back through his memory.

The last thing he remembered was the horses, and nodding goodbye to Renfro in the pre-dawn darkness: *Charger needs his left front shoe checked.*

But what happened next? *A pebble's stuck in my boot—hold on;* he dumped it out.

The gates opened—he noticed one of the guards was casually waving a blue bandana.

What is that noise? Shrieking, then running towards the shriek—he felt a sort of *pop* as everything snapped back into memory: Evangelo was running towards a squealing Specialist Rogers, her white lace dress torn and her red crocheted cap slipping down across her eyes as some big thug of a macho dragged her into a building. Dominic could feel the warning bells go off in his head, but Evangelo was already entering the luxury cabin. Confident of his ability to fight, and pumped full of adrenaline, Dominic jumped in behind the Ranger...

And that is where you made your mistake, Amigo—you didn't pay attention to the warning bells.

He listened, and could hear heavy breaths next to him, drippy snorts, the kind that come from a swollen nose.

Evangelo.

Dominic assessed the situation.

You always were a white knight, and that's how they trapped you.

Discreetly scanning his surroundings, He saw they were in a long, shallow cell; narrow windows blocked by rebar lattice pierced the outside wall, and flanked either side of a single door opening into hallway in a crude cinder-block building.

Second story, Purgatory Jail.

Well, at least Evangelo's alive—for now. Dominic took a deep breath and held it, clearing his head, and let it slowly out, feeling each rib in his chest move. He could hear other breaths nearby—the sound men make when they are waiting for someone to wake up.

Time to gather info. He continued to let his head roll forward, loose— breathing shallow and slow. *Let them think you are still passed out.*

It paid off.

"God almighty, did your goons have to nearly kill him? Her Majesty will not be happy if the bastard dies."

A thick New Orleans basso oozed out of a refined mouth, a deep mint julep of a voice in a whiskey world. "I really don't care what your Head Bitch thinks—these maniacs killed four of your men, and badly wounded six of my own. I am going to lose two fine, strapping hunks because of this little enterprise, and that pains me greatly. What you do with your men is no concern of mine, but I have an empire to build, and my subjects are valuable; I don't usually allow my investments to get killed, as the 'Powers That Be' aren't making replacement people anymore. People only get killed when I want them to get killed."

Boss Chartreaux, Dominic thought with a wince—he would know that voice anywhere; *he's in with Shaney now?*

The cell door opened, and Dominic could feel fetid breath from a large man slide against his cheek; a thick finger prodded his ribs. With extraordinary discipline, he fought off a yelp, playing possum as the man continued to poke his broken ribs to try and awaken him. The sweaty hands groped his pockets, then felt around his fingers to where his ring usually rested—but like Evangelo's Ring, it had been left back in the secret stable with Renfro and the horses, in deference to Purgatory tech restrictions.

"Keep me informed—as soon as he comes around, I need to interrogate him about some activity I've noticed around Purgatory. There's word he has influence here, and as we all know, no one is allowed to have influence at Purgatory but me..."

He gave the Director's face a slap. No response.

"Shaney's going to pay extra for this little favor—I have a new position I want her to assume, and it will require her to be acrobatic." The Boss growled and slapped the Director again. "Set up our delicate guest in the next room over. I want these gentlemen to hear her when she cries. Perhaps that will help them talk." Boots stomped away, and Dominic heard a heavy door slam behind the massive macho.

Faintly from the hall, Dominic heard the sound of nylon fabric being dragged across damp concrete and another heavy door creaking open. A flurry of footsteps followed the dragging sound and shuffled in the hall—men were jockeying for position, excitedly murmuring—then catcalls as a heavy zipper unzipped. A restrained jeer from someone in the hall echoed into the Director's cell:

"I betcha don't think you're so high and mighty now, do you, Destiny?"

"Shut up, you undisciplined imbeciles..." Dominic heard Boss Chartreaux's deep croak. "Not everybody in town is on board with this hostile takeover—but that will change soon. The other so-called Bosses of this fine city will capitulate once the rest of their whorehouse is taken hostage, and with the drug and liquor trade locked down, all fealty will be soon sworn to us."

Murmurs greeted this statement.

"I have made the necessary arrangements to keep the Jailers quiet, but we still have much work to do over the next twenty-four hours. For now, keep your mouths shut, your eyes open, and allow no unauthorized personnel on this floor." Now the scuffle of small bare feet could be discerned, and muffled shrieks as shackles closed—then door squeaked shut.

"Gentlemen, you may look all you want, but do not touch the merchandise, yet. You will get top pick once the takeover is complete. Landon, Germaine—you control this cell. Do not disappoint me—and you know I am so easily disappointed."

Plodding steps echoed down the steps, and out another door.

Dominic could feel chill air blowing in from an open window somewhere—the wet slap of a cold autumn storm. He continued to listen and was assaulted with more nasty chatter from multiple unknown parties:

"Lookie here boys, we got us a show."

"Hey—hey, Pinkie..." Smooching noises filled the hall, then ugly laughter.

"She's alright, but not my style. Sam's pretty hot. The others? Meh..."

"Anybody compared to Queen Shaney looks like a toad. But trust me, these girls look good if you get lonely enough."

"The twins are mine."

"They ain't twins you dipwad, they just dress that way. One's black-eyed, the other's green-eyed, and you can only pick one for your round."

"That sassy tomboy is on my list, and I plan on taking her down a notch..."

"Somebody better tell Shaney to offer a little more incentive to us working stiffs or we may abandon her for a shot at the girls here."

He counted—*five distinct voices. All Rangers?* The tone changed from jeering to anticipatory—longing and resentment mixed together in a cocktail of yearning.

"When'll she arrive? I gotta get myself cleaned up—I ain't a filthy pig like the rest of you."

"Queen Shaney's not going to get out until the storms stop; you know she won't ride her spoiled pony anywhere if she thinks the weather is less than perfect for his delicate constitution."

"His delicate constitution is no match for my need for a shot of Shaney. I wish she'd ride me into town."

"Yeah, well, I wish she gave half as much of a damn about us as she does about her stupid horse. Four Rangers are dead because she wanted the Director and the Captain in chains. There better be some good explanation as to why she thinks we are all expendable—"

Suddenly the tone of the conversation turned painful.

"I'm still tore up from wrestling with Director Santos. That son-of-a-bitch was an absolute animal; he shivved three of Chartreaux's thugs in the throat, busted out the kneecaps of two others with some sort of karate kicks, and gouged out an eye of another goon—all in thirty seconds. They're all in Chartreaux's infirmary, and last report says two of them are cut up so bad they'll be dead by noon."

"Well hell, it's not like Captain Evangelo was easy pickin's. I don't know how he got off the shots in the first place—there was two of us on either side of him, and he still drew faster than we could grab him. He was shooting with both hands, and he took four Rangers down before we could pin him. Cap was still fighting when he hit the floor with all of us on top of him—and I had to kick him in the head three times before he stopped moving"

"If Chartreaux's goons hadn't knocked the Director in the noggin with a baseball bat, I'm pretty sure we'd all be dead by now. It took twenty-five men to take out these two hombres; I think the Commander will have something to say about that."

"Damn. Four dead, two dying and another four wounded..."

"Maybe we need to spend more time on training?"

"Shut up, Danforth."

"I bet the Chief won't be happy."

"The Chief doesn't care about us any more than the Commander does—since he started running with his Courier group, AKA extortion racket, he doesn't have time for the rank and file anymore. At least Shaney offers us the time of day, and an occasional glimpse of paradise."

"Yeah, Jessup got more than a glimpse the other night. But it's been so long for me, I'm starting to think these Purgatory Hostesses look good..."

"Someone tell the Commander to hurry up. I need some inspiration to stay on her team."

"You can tell her yourself Saturday morning; she'll be arriving with her own personal security detail sometime Friday night, according to her last radio message, but I imagine she will stop in at Chartreaux's to pay the piper first."

Groans of disgust erupted from the five men.

"God, what a horrible thought."

"So, night after next? Why is she waiting so long?"

"No, tomorrow night. She'll be here tomorrow, Friday."

"Dammit, I forgot—I thought today was Wednesday. I just got back from assignment at Reunion last week, and I forgot to reset. Geez... a Reunion Wednesday is now a WildLand Thursday. Why the hell did Judge Leona make such a stupid move as to change their calendar?"

"I have no idea—it's got everyone screwed up. The Judge demanded the calendar change, and someone told me that the Chief's Courier Group synced with the Reunion calendar, too—something about a correction to line up with an 'official' calendar."

"Well Judge Leona just implemented it two weeks ago, and now the Judge is dead. All that rigamarole for nothing..."

"Yeah. What a waste of a great body."

"Is there any other news on that?"

"Reunion's in an uproar, six personnel are dead, and the Warden is tightlipped. When I saw Chief Emmanuel last Friday, he said he was personally handling the investigation, then he put the kibosh on all discussion and dismissed me. But the big news is, the Watcher is missing..."

A shocked moment of silence, followed by urgent questions and pointed commentary.

"Missing? Like, gone?"

"Well, that explains the carnage."

"What the actual hell—if that savage is loose, I'm not going anywhere near Reunion."

"I heard he got deputized, by the Warden no less—even after he killed the sentinels."

"That's gotta be a lie. If that's true, Reunion's turned into crazy town."

"Well, I got a sneaking suspicion that the Captain here has some insight on the deal at Reunion—and Shaney's gonna make him sing on it."

Now feet approached the cell nearest Evangelo. The men became contemplative.

"Why the Captain, though? He's always been good to us..."

"No matter... she sent word: we each get paid personally by the Queen herself, plus a secret bonus for bringing in the Director."

"Yeah, sorry Cap. I gotta get some action."

"For what she's offering, I'd sell my own mother—it's nothing personal."

"I don't think Cap ever got paid personally by Shaney, though... he's that crazy in love. He could have charged her a monthly fee for the horses at least."

"Well, there's a lot fewer of us to pay for this job, now. Who's left— just us five? That'll make it easier on her."

"At least she's not having to pay that unwashed mob out there. Boss Chartreaux's plying them with drugs, liquor, and the promise of a turn at that pink whore when the takeover is complete."

"Chartreaux needs to supervise, or that pack of jackals will ruin her. That would be a shame."

"Well, she's in safekeeping for now—but that won't last long once we get these guys in the ground. His boys will demand payment, and that pink girl is the full check."

Dominic heard someone come closer in, breathing through the window.

"But what about Director Santos? Won't the WildLand Express go to war over this?"

"Not if we get our own guy in as the next Director. Besides we have an official line. Just remember what we practiced—the Director and Captain started this fight, not the other way around. If Santos' boys complain, it'll go back to the System, and the WildLand Express can deal with The System instead."

"So, the story is that Cap went crazy over the pink whore? That doesn't make sense... everyone knows he loves Shaney. We should say the Director went nuts, and Cap backed him up..."

"Naw, it's already been decided. Don't confuse people."

"But won't someone from Purgatory say something?"

"Nobody witnessed it but Boss Chartreaux's thugs, the gate guards, and this pink-skinned chippy from the Hostess club; but Boss Chartreaux's got them all covered."

"Well then, it's decided—Santos and Evangelo shot up Purgatory, and they have to pay for the crime. Better luck next time, guys. Oh, I'm sorry, there's no next time..."

A smattering of laughter erupted, the kind of that let Dominic know that there would be no mercy given. The chatter continued on, then he heard Evangelo stir next to him—a groan escaped the younger man's lips, and the chatter fell silent. Footsteps approached the cell...

Eyes swollen shut like slits, the Director glanced furtively at Evangelo. He was upright, wrists shackled to the wall; he had a red lump just above his eyebrow and a bloody gash slitting the side of his brassy-scaled jaw where it appeared he had been kicked by a steel-toed boot. His russet flannel shirt was ripped open from the brawl inside the cabin, and his beautiful double-huckleberry gun rig had been confiscated.

"Hey Cap, how you feeling?" A voice called through the rebar window.

"Where am I?" Evangelo's groggy voice cracked.

"Sorry, I gotta keep that info from you, just like you're keeping something from Shaney. You ought to give her whatever it is she wants, Cap..."

Another groan from Evangelo. "Gupta? I trained you. We rode together. Why?"

"Shaney made me an offer I can't refuse, and she sweetened the deal with material bonuses."

Looking up from beneath his battered brow, the last true Ranger gazed at the men that he once considered his brothers. Evangelo voice broke open like a wound. "The Code..."

"The Code is just words, Cap." Gupta's voice was tremulous, as if his mind was teetering on the edge of regret. "You would have done the same thing if she had offered you what she offered us..."

Evangelo spit, and a bloody tooth ricocheted off the wall and rolled, roots up on the floor. Gupta retreated.

Dominic could no longer hang idly by and let Evangelo suffer alone. Raising his head, the Director smiled and his lip split, trickling fresh blood. "The Code is more than just words, Hijo." Stiff, Evangelo turned his head to look at Dominic through his own crimson veil. The little

Ranger nodded, then sucked in a sharp breath through clenched teeth, leaning his head against the wall.

A whimper was heard from the cell next door, and the sound of rattling chains. One of Shaney's Rangers laughed in the hall.

"Destiny Rogers—The Hembra with the red cap," Dominic jerked his head towards the other cell; "she was brought in just a few minutes ago." Evangelo eyes grew cold and gray, then tried his own shackles. They were steadfast.

Now footsteps were coming down the hall outside the cell, heavy and slow. The door opened, and a mountain of muscle and fat squeezed through the doorframe; moist ivory warts and perpetually watering eyes gave the big macho an appearance of a bullfrog in a stained white cotton shirt. Clad in worn khakis, folded blue handkerchief in his pocket, a fine panama hat and earth-toned silk scarf around his neck, the man was trailed by two slender hombres, each dressed in ancient black spandex running suits, blue bandanas tied about their necks, carrying small duffle bags. He snapped his heavy fingers, and the slender men scrambled in front of him, lizard-like, bags at the ready.

Outside the cell, Shaney's five accomplices gathered, staring through the rebar lattice with a mix of horror and glee.

The bullfrog macho doffed his hat, then stroked a burly hand across Evangelo cheek. "I've been admiring you, boy. You could make a lovely compliment to my entourage, along with Sugar and Spice here. I'd name you 'Spankie.' I bet you'd like that, wouldn't you, Captain?" The voice was deep, smooth.

The little Ranger snarled up at the big man through his bloody teeth and said nothing.

"Alas, the incomparable Shaney has not yet agreed to turn you over to me—but if you are lucky, I may be able to negotiate a bargain in exchange for your crimes. You shot four Rangers, all in a jealous rage over that little pink strumpet. For shame, Captain—who would have ever thought you could do such a thing?" He patted Evangelo's cheek, then pulled out a blue bandana from a deep cargo pocket and shoved it in the Ranger's mouth. "I am sure arrangements can be made—but Shaney wants you untouched, and she wants you first." He tied the bandana, and his sweaty paw lingered on the back of the Ranger's neck, before creeping down the front of his open shirt. "Pity." The massive macho turned to Dominic. "You, on the other hand..."

Dominic smiled affably as he could though bruised lips. "Reginald Chartreaux... I didn't expect to see you up so early. How's the rape and murder business treating you?"

A massive fist jabbed Dominic in his broken ribs, and the Director coughed up red sputum. Still grinding his knuckles into Dominic's ribs, Boss Chartreaux leaned down to breath directly into Dominic's face; his immense, tumorous jaw and jutting mouth drooled just inches from the ebony, swept-back scales that adorned Dominic's upper lip.

"Come now, Dominic. You and I have known each other how long now? Forty years? What's a little blood between old enemies?"

He pressed his enormous body against the Director's lithe, muscular torso, and the smaller hombre gasped in pain; then Chartreaux brushed his wet, thick lips against Dominic's lacerated forehead—a kiss of death. Pulling out another blue bandana, he gagged the Director; Chartreaux spoke menacingly as he tied it in place between Dominic's teeth:

"I am going to relish this encounter, Dominic. Were I able to take you out of this intrusively public jail cell, I would relish it more; but for now, we have an audience, and that means I will have to keep this less—intimate. But trust me, you will still consider it to be personal... Sugar, the bag, please."

Sugar's sleek, tan lizard-skin was coated in sweat as he opened his duffle-bag to pulled out a long, bright orange rod. The exposed metal tip glinted in the faint morning light, and two lead wires dangled from the other end.

One of the men in the hallway giggled.

"Spice, the other bag please. Hop, hop—" Chartreaux clapped his hands. "The Seven O'clock electronics window is open, but not for long, so I intend to make every minute count."

Mahogany scales glistening in the jail's dim light, Spice set down his bag upon a side table nearby and produced a small, hand-cranked generator. The slender men moved as a unit, expertly hooking up the cattle prod's lead wires to the generator. Spice turned the handle quickly A spark crackled from the tip as Sugar squeezed the trigger, and he nodded to Boss Chartreaux.

"My business with you is unrelated to Shaney's request, but I believe now is an excellent time to review WildLand Express operations in my city, Director. You have been a thorn in my side for decades, always questioning my associates and thwarting my attempts at increasing my collection of sweet Survivor flesh."

Chartreaux ripped open the Director's blue plaid shirt, then casually glanced at the faintly glittering silver strands on his left pectoral, the barely visible ghost of the Visionary tattoo on Dominic's chest. Without the right frequency of light, it could not be readily detected; but for one who knew of it, it could be discerned.

Chartreaux placed a meaty palm over Dominic's tattoo, and stroked it briefly. "Ah, old alliances. I will go easy on you, my brother—if you tell me what I need to hear." Chartreaux pulled the collar of Dominic's shirt up to obscure the tattoo. "You and I are not so different—we both like to work on the margins of polite society. You should have taken my offer to help me find suitable subjects for Purgatory's many enterprises. But you always had to go your own way..."

Boss Chartreaux leaned in close to whisper huskily in Dominic's ear. "I have some questions I'd like to ask you about the disappearance of several valuable Hostesses and Private Contractors over the years in my district. It's as if they had help escaping, but we all know the System doesn't allow that. Let me help you remember anything you might be willing to share—or maybe your little friend Evangelo would care to speak out on your behalf about his knowledge of any illicit escape operations at Purgatory."

Dominic steeled his resolve. He glanced to Evangelo, who had a look of barely concealed terror upon his face—

Boss Chartreaux's bullfrog face split into a slimy smile as he picked up the crackling cattle prod:

"Let's take it from the top, Gentlemen."

———◆———

Rose was waiting in the safe room at Purgatory Hostess Club. Hood pulled back up to hide her hair and face, she sat quietly while the Watcher secured the room. Thus attired, he had carried her through the tunnels, obscured from all the guards, visible only as a small person bundled under a deerskin cloak. Putting their personal gear bags beside the bed, the Watcher awaited the next set of instructions from Agent Ellison.

Unhappy with the loss of his Ring to Purgatory tech restrictions—which had been left behind with Oskar and the Horses, in the care of the Stable-Master, Gunny—he pulled out his notepad-pencil set and prepped them for use. He had already destroyed all his previous sensitive notes before he left Mystery Outpost, and he looked around the room, making plans on how to destroy any new ones he might write.

The safe room was cozy, long and narrow to hide its space profile—

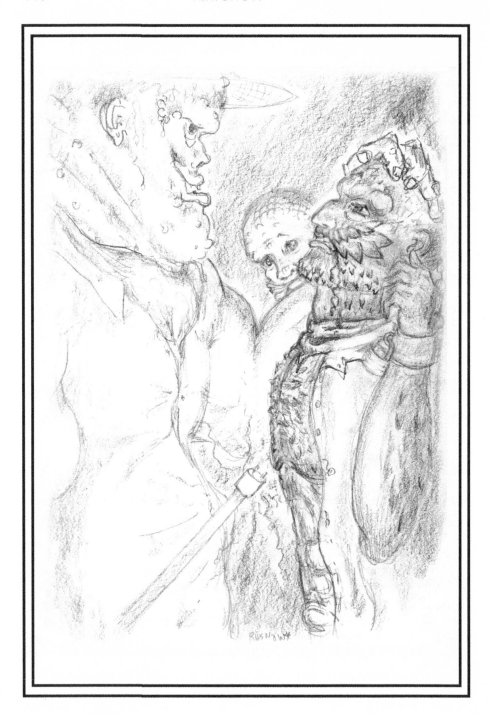

some eight feet wide and sixteen feet long, it ran along one end of the basement of the large, two-story cabin. Made to look like a hidden "client" room, its presence could be explained away upon potential discovery as a place for unauthorized meetings between the girls and paramours. A queen-sized bed with a worn red velveteen coverlet was tucked into one end of the dark, wood-paneled room. At the foot of the bed sat a bench with an inset, lidded chamber pot, the receptacle discreetly hidden from view by a striped, cotton-ticking bench pad. Next to this was a mirrored wooden washstand with an old-fashioned, floral-painted ceramic dry sink and matching pitcher filled with water; a glass cup and a bowl of dried sweet raisins completed the comfy corner.

A small metal wood stove was situated at the other end of the room, the stovepipe running up through the basement ceiling and presumably connecting with a larger, main floor stovepipe to hide its smoke. *Toss sensitive communications in there,* the Watcher grunted.

Between the two narrow ends of the room, a red lantern with a candle hung above an overstuffed loveseat and faded, floral-print rug. Beneath that rug, a hatch was located, and that hatch led to a small storage room filled with casks of Reunion's Finest Brew and boxes of Johnson Plantation Premium BudWeed. *That should sufficiently distract anyone looking for hidden treasures*—but should prying, sober eyes look further, under a crate filled with dirty laundry, searchers would find another hatch that led to a narrow circular chamber, with a ladder descending to a limestone corridor...

The Watcher checked the door—it was heavy and wooden, with a narrow, vented transom above the door which could be cracked open to allow fresh air to enter. The door was barred from his side; a string to raise the heavy oak bar was only accessible when run through a hole in the door, and he had pulled the string through the hole to their side, rendering the door inoperable from the other room. Likewise, the hatch below was barred from their own side, making the room fairly secure. Before leaving them alone in the safe room, Sam had informed them that a guard, Agent Sampson, would be stationed on the other side of the door, disguised as a drunken lout sleeping it off on cot situated in front of a false wooden rollaway wall.

The guard, like everyone else under Sam's command, had been informed there would be a guest tonight. However, they had not been informed of the nature of their guest. Now the Watcher pondered what to do with her...

It seemed the height of cruelty. Here he was, finally alone with Rose in a comfy, secure love nest—and there was not a moment to spend celebrating that fact. Instead, he was desperately trying to come up with a plan for saving the Director, Evangelo, and some unknown female—and that left no time for love nests.

He scowled.

The Afterling looked up in alarm. "Is there something wrong?"

He shook his head, grumbling to himself—*No, just trying to save the world again, as usual.*

He unpacked her books and put them down beside her on the couch; then pulled out a rag, a clean t-shirt, and an overshirt for himself. He wrote on the notepad:

> *—I need to patch myself up and get ready. You should do likewise; even though you are a non-combatant, you should ready yourself now, and tend that cut on your shoulder.*

She read the note and nodded. "Okee Dokee... you go first. I will clean up next." Slipping her deerskin moccasins off, she tucked her bare feet up under her legs, between the warm cushions of the loveseat.

A slow blush crept up his cheeks; he hoped she wouldn't notice.

She noticed. "Oh, don't worry—I won't look!" She responded cheerily, then grabbed her book and sat on the loveseat, turning her back to him.

Pulling off his coat, vest and shirt, he stripped from the waist up, then poured water from the pitcher into the ceramic sink. The scars from his battle with the chupacabra by the Water Treatment Plant were almost completely healed now, except for one deep gash across his back. He looked in the mirror—

Not half bad looking.

He flexed his biceps and pectorals, admiring himself and his magnificent, scarred muscles. *Amazing*—his slouch had started to disappear, replaced with proper posture; being freed from his chains for the past two weeks had allowed him full range of body motion, and he was already looking straighter, taller. Soaking an available rag in water, he rubbed it with soap, then scrubbed at the wound... in the mirror, he could see Rose.

She wasn't looking.

He felt slightly disappointed, and unzipped his dungarees to finish cleaning himself up, irritable and ignored. Rounding out his grooming with a quick rub-down of DubbDee-40, the Watcher donned his clean clothes and replaced his red bandana. Glancing once more in the mirror, he again felt civilized and clean—a welcome development that would only be made better if he could find some real breakfast.

He pulled the plug on the ceramic bowl, and it drained into a plastic bin underneath; pouring a little clean water into it, he grunted to the Afterling.

Rose looked up. "Yes?"

He scribbled out:

> *—Get dressed and ready. We have a busy day ahead, and you may not get this chance again for a while.*

"Aren't you going to leave, or go out of the room for a moment?"

> *—Not here—until I know who's keeping watch, I won't leave.*

She sighed. "But this is not a show?"

> *—No. I won't look, now get busy.*

She removed the deer hide cloak; he parked himself by the wall and stared at Rose's book, but was interrupted by the sound of her fussing. "Oh! You'll have to help me take off my armor—I can't reach the buckles. Are you sure you didn't design it that way on purpose?"

He grunted—he hadn't really thought about the logistic of buckles. *Ah, well, too bad for you. This should be pleasant duty.*

She swept the cascade of dark hair up into her hands and held it, exposing the smooth citron nape of her neck. Unexpectedly, the scent of her hair and skin wafted over him, back to normal now, warm and sweet without the bloody undertone... the Watcher felt faint. Unbuckling the neck of the gorget, then the chest—his thick fingers suddenly turned clumsy, and he fumbled with the buckles as he swore under his breath. Finally freeing the waist of her duty pinafore, her leather armor fell to the ground.

She stepped out of the pile of dusty gear; befuddled, he knelt down and picked them up—*these need a wipe down with a damp cloth and some good ol' DubbDee-40.* Rose tapped a small unshod foot next to his hand; neat, translucent nails topped round little toes. One touched his clawed red thumb...

He froze, unable to think about anything else.

To his surprise, Rose donned the deer hide cloak once more. "This is actually quite handy..." Buttoning the toggles, she pulled her arms up under the cloak and began to wriggle. A few seconds passed, then to his chagrin and amazement, all her clothes fell to the floor around her ankles beneath the cloak. "See? It's like my own personal tent!"

Barefoot and barelegged beneath her fur cloak, she stepped out of the pile of knits and over to the washstand to grab the rag and soap. Pulling her arms under the cloak, she began to wriggle again, mere feet away.

He was still kneeling on the floor, leathers in his hands, unable to think or move.

She batted her eyes at him. "If you don't want to watch, then you should look away now..." She turned towards the washstand, and once more piling her hair atop her head, she washed the back of her neck with the soapy rag.

Standing there swathed only in the deer hide furs, Rose was completely covered—but the Watcher couldn't help but think of the clean and warm barefoot Afterling up under the furs, dressed in only what Nature gave her. The Watcher blushed a deeper shade of crimson as the room began to spin... he grabbed his head in his hands, struggling with himself.

Why not? Why not now?

Overwhelmed, the Watcher clutched a deer-tail tassel at the hem of her cloak. Back to him, Rose was busy with the soap—

A soft tap-tap rapped at the door, then a pause and another tap-tap.

Interrupted, a flustered Watcher froze again. The knock repeated, then repeated again. Rose looked up, unsure, and at last he grunted and pointed at Rose.

"Oh! Fenix Creciente..." She whispered.

Sam answered, "We Will Be Free—let me in."

"Okee Dokee—hang on." She reached over to lift the bar.

Stopping her, the Watcher scowled and pointed at her clothes on the floor. He shook his head.

"Oh, don't be a fuddy-duddy, I'm completely covered."

Reluctantly, the Watcher raised the bar to let Sam in—she poked her head in the door:

"I have another one of our personnel with me—Specialist Kendra

Qin. She will be the Afterling's designated handler while she is secured in the safe room. Permission to enter?"

"Permission granted!" the Afterling replied cheerily, pulling up her hood. The Watcher growled, frustrated with this unwelcome intruder.

Sam came in, followed by a lanky, boyish figure clad in a rhinestone-studded blue ball cap, blue jeans, and a dingy white t-shirt beneath a denim vest. Her beaded ivory snake-skin accented black eyes rimmed with a smudgy black eyeliner, and a pert nose; a jaded expression completed her ensemble.

"Well, I thought you were lying to me, but I guess I was wrong, Sam. Look at this." Specialist Qin poked at the furs. "Are you for real? Show yourself. I want to see you."

"Oh, I'm not dressed under here." Rose chirped.

Specialist Qin glanced over at the Watcher. "What—couldn't you wait? Disgusting."

Shaking his head, he grunted, irritated.

"Fine. Lie to yourself." Specialist Qin turned to Rose. "Listen, I'm Kendra. I'll be your handler. These people have to work on stuff. Don't give me trouble, and I won't give you trouble, okay?"

Rose appeared somewhat saddened. "Hello, Kendra! I'm Rose, and I want to work on stuff, too. But if I can't, well, I don't need a handler—I will be fine by myself."

"That's not what Sam says." Kendra pointed at Sam, then bent down to look the Afterling in the eyes—she spoke very slowly and clearly:

"This is Sam. Sam says no. You stay here with me."

Sam nodded her head smugly. "Listen to your handler."

"May I at least get dressed before I have this conversation?"

"Sure—do you want us to step out?" Kendra asked almost politely.

"Yes, that would be lovely to have some privacy."

"Well, what about Big Boy over here—" Kendra pointed to the Watcher—"do you want him to leave?"

"Certainly! I'd love to have a moment to myself." Rose nodded enthusiastically.

"Okay, you heard the Midget—everybody out." Kendra pointed to the door. "You have two minutes. Hurry up." Kendra and Sam stepped outside the door.

The Watcher shook his head again.

"Step out." Sam spoke to the Watcher with firmness. "Within these walls, our girls get to say yes or no." She motioned, and a towering, ham-fisted macho stepped up behind her. "This is Agent Herman Sampson, and he handles men who can't take 'no' for an answer."

The Watcher pulled out his notepad and scribbled quickly:

> *—This is my assignment, and these are my rules—I don't*
> *leave her side.*

He walked up to Sam to give her the notepad—

The door closed firmly behind him, and the bar slammed down in place. *You little...* the Watcher turned on his heel, then rapped on the door.

"Whoa there, Hoss—" Sampson spoke in a deep, calming voice, hand on the Watcher's shoulder. "You can give her a moment. What's a couple of minutes?"

The Watcher whirled to glare up at Sampson. *I'll introduce you to my fist, Hoss, if you don't back up.* He snarled.

"Settle down, Agent Azarian, or you will be asked to leave. You can handle two minutes, and if you can't, you need to reconsider whether you are actually fighting for the Cause of Freedom or not." Sam was deadly serious. "She's safe, and you can trust us. Dominic trusted us."

I don't trust anyone, he thought—*not even Dominic.*

Rose was humming in the safe room. He breathed in a deep breath; yes, he could take them all out, even while unarmed; but what would be gained? Just a pile of dead bodies, and an unhappy Afterling. He breathed back out, slowly, then wrote another note.

> *—You are absolutely right; I can probably handle two*
> *minutes without her. But what about you? If she says no to*
> *you, will you also leave her alone?*

Sam looked fierce. "No, it's my house, my rules. She doesn't stay here without a handler. It's too dangerous, and she doesn't know anything about this place—everyone who comes here has a handler, and we ourselves do not go out without a buddy. It's standard protocol."

> *—Good, now we're getting somewhere. Who's my handler?*

"It was supposed to be the Director himself—but now it will be Agent Mansour."

> *—So, you are splitting us up, for safety, but also to make us*
> *easier to manage.*

"No, I didn't mean it that way—"
The Watcher furiously scribbled:

> *—I am the Afterling's handler. So, you are just choosing your own handler over Dominic's handler, your own system over the other System. If you are going to force a handler on both of us, then stop playing this divide-and-conquer game. Stop pretending you are giving her freedom from an oppressor when you are just trading one oppressor—me— for another oppressor—you.*

The entire group looked tragic. One moment they had been so sure in their virtue, and now they were all confused.

Sam glared at the Watcher. "You are dangerous as hell."
The Watcher smirked.

> *—You're right.*

Sam gave him a cold look: "I don't know what your angle is, or why the Director chose you, but I'm only going to say this once. Purgatory is my Command, and I'm in charge of this unit."
The Watcher nodded and pointed at the safe room door.

> *—And she is my Command, and I'm in charge of her.*

The door creaked back open, and Rose came out. Her face was bright and clean, but her hair was a wild mess, frizzed out and completely unmanageable, hanging down to her hips in a tangled cloud. "Does anyone have a comb?"

Silent stares greeted her. She looked less like a child now, minus the deer hide cloak, plus fresh leggings and a sleek flowered tunic; with her choli top, her outfit accented her exaggerated curves, and gave testament to her status as an adult. Only the child-sized pink boots hearkened back to her child-sized stature.

Sam was aghast. "You're full grown?"

"Well of course I am. Why wouldn't I be?" Rose seemed surprised. "Nobody nice would let a child run loose in the WildLands."

"I just, I..." Sam regained her bearing. "You look like a little girl under that cloak and armor. But you're not..."

"Oh no, I'm very old. Now, what's next?"

Kendra poked a languid finger at Rose's hair. "This is real. It's real hair..."

Sampson, dazed by the Afterling, backed out of the room to duck around the corner.

Sam spoke: "We need Agent Azarian's help, and that means he needs to come with us. We can't leave you here alone, but you are too different-looking to go out there. Specialist Qin will stay with you." Sam demurred. "If you are comfortable with that."

"Oh." Rose thought for a moment. "If it helps rescue my Father, Evangelo, and your friend, then yes, let us do whatever it takes—I shan't complain."

"Shan't?" Sam asked. "That's... different." She turned to the Watcher; "Come with me—I can't expose her to the whole organization yet; her existence will be on a need-to-know basis, and we need to go upstairs to debrief."

The Watcher looked to Kendra, small but still a head taller than the Afterling. Kendra stared back at him, deadpan. *Is this Hembra a threat?* Time for an assessment.

—I request an interview with Specialist Qin now.

"Very well. She doesn't read script well, so I'll read to her. Specialist Qin, Agent Azarian needs a short interview with you before we go upstairs."

Kendra reclined against the door, thumbs hooked into her bejeweled jeans pockets. She gave him an apathetic shrug. "Go ahead and take a swing at it—but I already gave a statement to Agent Ellison. What do you want to know?"

The Watcher passed Sam the notepad to read aloud to her Agent:

—What did you leave out of your report?

"What? Nothing—"

—Think again.

Kendra protested to Sam: "He can't just come in here and accuse me of not giving a good report!" Sam glowered at the Watcher, who calmly wrote:

—It's not an accusation, it's a statement of fact. You left something out; why?

The slender Hembra kept her face deadpan, but her eyes belied her calm. Meeting her gaze, the Watcher subtly flicked his eyes towards Agent

Sampson, who turned white. Sam made note, but said nothing, watching intensely.

>*—Perhaps you'd like to rethink what it was you left out.*
>*Are you usually on duty outside the Hostess Cabin by*
>*yourself at 4:30 a.m.?*

"I can answer that, and the answer is no." Sam leaned forward. "This is a valid question—I was in such a hurry to find out what happened to Destiny, I missed this detail. Good catch, Azarian..." She turned her keen eyes to her Specialist. "Care to explain, Kendra?"

Agent Sampson started to sweat.

Kendra's eye twitched imperceptibly. "Oh, yes. I thought I heard a dog barking outside my window. I love dogs, and sure enough there was a really big dog outside my window... " Kendra kept her face straight. "He looked lonesome, so I snuck out the window to pet him."

"That is completely against protocol!" Sam was clearly displeased. "You know you're not allowed outside by yourself—and dogs are banned inside the city limits anyway. You're going to attract the wrong kind of attention."

"Oh, but I understand; I love dogs, too!" Rose sympathized cheerily.

The Watcher smirked ever so slightly, and continued:

>*—So, while you were busy petting this 'big friendly dog'—*
>*when did you notice the action taking place at the gate?*

"The dog had just run off and—and I was trying to get all the... drool off my jeans. " Kendra's eyes met the Watcher's gaze, still calm, but her fingers began to tap her jeans pocket nervously "He was a really droolly dog."

Agent Sampson swallowed nervously.

"I was sneaking back into my window, and that's when I saw runners coming up to the gate."

>*—I need to know if there was a signal of any kind.*
>*Between the gate and action on the ground, something*
>*happened. Close your eyes and see it.*

"Huh..." She knit her brows. "I saw a guard waving a blue bandana. I guess I forgot that detail."

>*—That's what I needed. The blue bandana is a signal or an*

identifier—we need to look for them around town and see
if they are connected. Anything else?

Eyes still closed, Kendra recalled: "The sound of the back door closing to Boss Zhu's place, and feet running away—but that was at the same time Jip was coming around the corner..."

—Thank you. Someone else was leaving the house. If you
recall anything else, write it down. Enjoy your dog.

The Watcher gave a nod to Sampson, who tried not to notice. He passed a note to Rose.

—I'm just upstairs, and I won't leave you behind. You are
first priority, and I won't abandon this mission just to save
someone else—even when that person is the one who
entrusted me with you. I am your Champion, and you alone
will be the one to tell me what to do.

He did not wait for a reply, but simply walked away with Sam and her entourage. They disappeared through a door at the far side of the other room, leaving a bewildered Sampson guarding the door. He gawked at the Afterling.

⋆———◆———⋆

"You go take a nap or something, Herman." Kendra said bluntly, closing the door to the safe room. Suddenly the world seemed not so safe to Rose. It felt like Tesoro all over again—handlers everywhere.

"Gah. they're finally gone." Kendra secured the door "So, what's the deal with you two? Is he your LandLord or something?"

"LandLord?"

"You know, your owner, your Boss, The Man. Whatever. What is he?"

"Who, Agent Azarian? Oh, no." Rose said simply. "He's my Champion. I chose him. He's supposed to protect me when I need it, set my people free, and do my bidding."

"Hmm" Kendra paused. "So, there's no ringy-dingy-ding going on with you two?"

"I'm not sure I understand..."

"You know—the horizontal boop. Plowing your muffins. Buttering your bean field?"

Rose looked sad. "We have no butter."

Kendra groaned. "No, you dimbulb, I mean you know..." She sighed—she had been trying to avoid the emotional fallout from the word. "Sex."

"Oh oh OH, well why didn't you say that? Sadly, no, it is not that way for us."

Kendra seemed surprised in a very laid-back fashion. "Really?"

"Well, one time, but I seduced him first, then hit him in the head so I could escape, and that spoiled the whole thing."

"I can imagine." The Specialist replied helpfully.

Downcast, Rose continued: "I've been trying to make up for it ever since the Church Fathers declared the Watcher a Deva—"

"Church Fathers? Deva? Are they like some kind of Bosses?" Kendra maintained an air of indifference, but her curiosity bubbled out at the idea of this unseen world.

"I suppose one could say that—" Rose had never thought of a world where they didn't have Church Fathers or Deva. "Anyhow, since they declared him one of whatever-he-is, I've offered myself to him over and over again to try and make amends, but so far I've been an abysmal failure. He's constantly irritated at me, and he won't play games or wrestle. He occasionally flirts with me and makes me feel all ridiculous inside, then... he backs away." Rose pouted.

"Then why is Agent Azarian with you?"

"It's his job. He was deputized to hunt me down after I killed someone..." she thought about it, "twice."

"So, you killed someone... Nice. Did they deserve it?"

"I like to think so. Each time I did do so as humanely as possible, but I still feel terrible about the whole thing." She folded her hands, silently asking forgiveness of the dead.

"If that's the way it is, then Sam is right—you're no warrior. You sound like Destiny; she can't stand killing anyone, even if they deserve it." Kendra said it quietly. "That's probably how she got in trouble this morning in the first place."

"Well, I did it, and I still got in trouble for it. They sent the Watcher after me as a Bounty Hunter." Shaking her head, Rose tried to make sense of it all. She whispered confidentially to Kendra. "It's all so confusing. I think he is only with me now because of power, and because he feels beholden to me, since he gave me a Project..." Remembering her lost conception with the Watcher, she became despondent.

Unaware of what a project was for an Afterling, Kendra asked, "What kind of project? You mean a mission?"

"I suppose you could say that. But I failed to complete our Project." Rose was on the verge of tears.

"Well, if he trusted you to complete a project and you failed, maybe he's just disappointed with you." Kendra shrugged. "That's understandable."

Rose put on her brave face. "But even so, I hoped the Watcher would allow me to make up for my losses with offerings of personal pleasure. Although I'm hopeless with projects, I usually do pretty well with pleasure." Baffled at his behavior, Rose wondered: "Perhaps he just likes the company of men better? That's the way it was with Jarrod, my Group Leader." Rose paused, then rephrased it. "My ex-Group leader."

Kendra was blunt. "Well maybe the Watcher likes guys, but it also could be that maybe he just doesn't like the way you look. You don't look like any Survivor I know."

Rose bit her lip to stop it from trembling. *That is not comforting—but the truth hurts sometimes.* Rose remembered how Evangelo described his Devil-Love, Shaney, as being so beautiful. From the look on the Watcher's face when they saw her holo-video, Rose knew the Watcher thought so, too. *And why not?* These Devil Women were all so sleek and diverse, with myriad skin colors and beautiful eyes of all different hues...

Rose felt a twinge of jealousy at the exotically attractive Survivor Women.

"I suppose you're right. I probably look very ugly to him... I'm just not his type." Rose winced. "I should just accept him for who he is, and give him his space. I should respect his preferences, and I shouldn't try to seduce him anymore." Mortified by her own attraction to the Watcher, she wondered why it should bother her so much that a Devil rejected her.

"Well, it could be a power trip, but I could've sworn something was up with you two when I walked in earlier..." Kendra was still not convinced. "I think he might have some feelings for you—maybe we just need to work on your looks."

"I've done the best I can, considering the circumstances!" Wounded at the critique, Rose murmured, "It's hard to find time to attend to one's looks, when one is fleeing for one's life." She sat on the couch and picked up Wister's book, running her hands over it. *What would The Virginian do if Miss Molly didn't have time to attend to her looks? Well, that romantic Cowboy certainly wouldn't ignore Miss Molly if she was only dressed in furs...*

"It's all to no avail, anyway. The Watcher doesn't want me. He only wants what I represent—power and an opportunity to kill things." Throwing her hands up over her eyes, Rose breathed out slowly to center herself. She thought of the beautiful red and yellow book, and chastised herself for ever reading Western Romances. *That book should be banned, it's a corrupting influence...*

She stifled a sob: "I'm a job."

"Well, I'd feel sorry for you, but that happens to me all the time." Kendra seemed unmoved. "You'll just have to get over it. Men are power-hungry animals, but so are women, so I guess we deserve each other." Staring at the Afterling, Kendra's eyes took on an intense gleam: "Stop whining, and do something about it. You have more important things to worry about."

"Oh, you are right. I have to save the Director and Evangelo somehow." Rose hid her face in her hands.

"No, you moron." Kendra Qin grabbed a curl hanging down in front of the Afterling's dejected face, and her eyes lit up with interest. "Your hair..." She twisted a lock. "Curl Pattern Type Three 'A' to Three 'B', medium texture, thick, black, medium porosity, green undersheen, with a tendency to frizz. Needs an oil-based moisturizer, plus folate, cobalamin and pantothenic acid."

"What?" Rose looked concerned. "Is it a health condition?"

"No," Kendra said flatly "it's more serious. You're not taking care of your hair properly. It's dry and lifeless, and you need to seriously moisturize." Kendra pulled on a lock and watched to see if it sprung back; it just flopped, and a strand of hair broke off. "When's the last time you oiled your hair?"

Remembering the weekly hair sessions with her sisters, Rose became nostalgic for scented oils and loving hands braiding, oiling, and coiling hair: "We used bear grease scented with wax myrtle - but that was three months ago, before I was banished from home."

"Well it's no wonder your hair is fried; that's too long to go without oiling for your hair type. If I was smart, I'd tell you to shave it all off - that would make you appear more like a normal Survivor - but before I was an Recon Specialist with the Cause, I was a Beautician in LifeBefore. I haven't seen a full head of hair in fifty years..." Kendra took Rose's hair by handfuls, and the hair crackled. "Beauty is my art, and hair and skin is my medium. It would be like denying Picasso the last painter's palette and brush in the world. Since you are the only one in the WildLand currently with hair, this is a crisis. Do what I say, and we can save your hair."

"They tried to warn me, but I wouldn't listen." Rose whined. "It's all my fault - I stopped eating Vitamin B foods, and now I will be bald and dead!"

"No, we can save you. Your hair will be natural, curly-coily and gorgeous... just help me out this one time, and I will help you."

Rose looked up from between her fingers. "What do I have to do?"

"A dangerous mission." Cunning, Kendra twirled a lock of Rose's hair around her finger. "I need a partner in crime to help me save my friend, Destiny. You are going to help me, and in exchange for your help, I will save your hair... but we have to disguise you first. You are useless like this —but with my expertise, even with all this hair I can pass you off as human."

"But I already am human..."

"No, I mean a real human—one of us. Look, I'm the main recon specialist, and as a Beautician, one of my jobs here is to disguise people when they are escaping into the WildLand. I change their looks, and they flee to their new life. If I can change their looks, I can change yours too— and in return, you can help me save Destiny."

"But how will we get this past the others? You see how the Watcher and Agent Ellison are acting—they are refusing to let me even leave this safe room."

"Leave that to me. I'll not only get them to allow you a disguise, I'll get them to ask for it." Kendra gave a confident nod. "You help me save Destiny, and I will help you save your hair. Perhaps we can make you more attractive and normal-looking to the Watcher. You'll be happy, he'll be happy, we'll all be happy."

Hopeful, Rose nodded. Kendra peeked out the door. "Herman... psssssst, Herman, go get my kit."

Sampson's expressive brown eyes peered around the door jamb, his giant frame hunkered down in a too-small chair. "But what about the sign and call sign?" he whispered.

"Listen, you big Palooka, I don't need a call sign—now get me my kit, and tell Araceli and Lourdes to send a jar of bear grease and to give you that long black stocking cap they crocheted—the one with the pompom on the end."

Slamming the door, Kendra took a deep breath, grabbed a fork, and turned back to the Afterling.

"I don't have a comb. I haven't needed one since the Happening, so we'll just use this salad fork. Just relax, and this won't hurt a bit..." She ran the tines of the fork through Rose's tangled mess, and the Afterling yelped.

Kendra smirked:

"Naw, I'm lying. This'll hurt."

———————

A half-hour had passed, and Sam, Mansour, and the Watcher were closer to a plan than when they had started—but not there yet.

Sitting in great room, they perched among the yellowed remains of what used to be white wicker furniture. The entire cabin had been decorated by someone who felt too hot in the Texas summer, and the color scheme reflected that longing for coolness. Tattered ivory lace curtains—once white—hung over large, mostly-intact windows, and blue-ticking cushions adorned the white wicker couches and chairs. In an effort to make the room more cozy in the winter, Sam's specialists had taken up crochet; myriad doilies, lap robes, rag rugs and runners draped every possible surface. Multicolored afghans crocheted from scraps made the airy room warmer, and a fire roared in the wood stove. Next to the fire, the heavy Machos sat carefully on the wicker couch to avoid undue stress on the delicate furnishings.

Over eggs and fried potatoes, they had agreed on goals, and the Watcher scribed it out in between bites of incredibly delicious scrambled eggs—a treat he had not enjoyed since last summer, when eggs were plentiful at Reunion. He made a fast check to ensure the food contained no Reunion Masa, then shoveled it down, disheartened by the knowledge that his friends were in dire straits. He forced himself to eat it, remembering the words of the Director—*eat to fuel a Revolution.*

He didn't have to force too hard... he fueled up, scribbling notes between mouthfuls of eggs and gulps of hot chicoffee:

> *—Rescue Director Santos and Captain Evangelo from Purgatory Jail*
>
> *—Rescue Specialist Rogers from Boss Chartreaux's Thugs*

—Maintain cover for Agents at Purgatory

They had new intel:

Boss Chartreaux was seen walking to Purgatory Jail around six a.m. with his favorite attaches, Sugar and Spice. The two of them carried a large duffel bag in addition to personal bags; even as they left Chartreaux's cabin, it sounded like a party was underway, with occasional loud bickering and raucous banter breaking out. Specialist Destiny Rogers could still be upstairs—or she might have been moved to another location, to be saved as a final payment for services rendered. They had to locate Specialist Rogers. The Watcher added to his notes:

—surveil at Boss Chartreaux's Cabin

Specialist Rogers could be possibly be rescued without bloodshed, provided Sam used her cover as a Madame to demand her return from Boss Chartreaux. But once that option was exercised, it could possibly blow the cover on their intel gathering operation. Her last known official location was supposed to be Boss Zhu's house. Agent Mercedes went out under the pretense of escorting Destiny back home after Boss Zhu's scheduled monthly appointment. No one came to the door, and a cursory search of the grounds revealed nothing—perhaps Zhu was strung out? Or something worse?

—surveil Boss Zhu's Cabin

The Rescue Team all agreed a Jail Break was in order, but it would require additional reconnaissance to determine how many personnel were needed and how many enemy agents were in play. The idea of an open assault against the Jail was debated, as Purgatory security would be called in via the alarm bells. But some sort of reconnaissance was needed there.

—surveil the Jail

Purgatory Security Forces numbered approximately one hundred— five groups of twenty selected Survivors, each assigned to a particular boss at Purgatory: Boss Winston, Boss Zhu, Boss Chartreaux, Boss Balogun, and Boss Waitie. Purgatory Security Forces acted as combination fire brigades, reserve deputies, and work crews for Purgatory, and were rewarded by the bosses in liquor, drugs, or goods. In this case, Boss Chartreaux's Security Detail was accounted for—six thugs in the infirmary, with the fourteen remaining—all at Chartreaux's house, getting plastered as part of their pay.

Agent Mansour suggested an immediate outreach to Boss Winston be made, as he was an ally in the Cause and might withhold his security forces or interfere if they were called out for mutual aid by Boss Chartreaux. Boss Winston had been working with Agent Mansour for a number of years now, and had provided cover for escaping Survivors through his work crew.

—contact Boss Winston

This was agreed upon, but a cover would have to be given for the sudden lack of aid to the town. Perhaps mass sickness, or some other kind of activity?

—plan diversion for Security forces

During this period, the Jail would be most vulnerable.

—free the Director and Evangelo from the Jail

The details of this plan were yet to be worked out—but they needed to be worked out soon because Specialist Rogers' note indicated Shaney would be coming Friday night. From the Commons, the gate was in clear view; agents would need to be designated to watch the gate for Commander Shaney's entrance with her personal security detail, number unknown.

—watch for the arrival of Shaney

Shaney was coming, and so was the chaos and madness of the event known as Market Mayhem Weekend. Mansour looked as if he had a headache, and Sam looked harried. *In addition to everything else, here comes Market Mayhem Weekend...*

This coming Friday morning marked the beginning of Purgatory's monthly Market Mayhem Weekend. Under the protection of the WildLand Express, plantations and camps would send designated Buyers with wagonloads of goods and foodstuffs on the dangerous journey to Purgatory, with most arriving Thursday night. The third weekend of every month, Purgatory's population of twelve hundred would swell by an additional five hundred people as wagon teams of WildLand Express Agents, as Sellers, Buyers, and entourages rode in to set up designated booths inside the Commons. Purgatory craftsmen and merchants would have items to barter in return—leather gear, knives, scavenged items, furnishings, crafts, or hunting and fishing supplies. Here too, masons, blacksmiths, gunsmiths, construction workers, bricklayers, and other skilled laborers offered their services in exchange for goods or tokens. Only weapons sales were restricted, although everyone knew that—for the right price—certain people would peddle firepower.

But it was after Purgatory Market closed at Four O' Clock Friday that the Commons came to life—and then the Mayhem part of Market Mayhem Weekend would get underway. Sawdust laid and tables set up, an orgy of gambling and fighting engulfed Purgatory. Then liquor flowed, with drugs injected and smoke inhaled, and the first sample free. Tournaments of every conceivable sport would spontaneously spring up all over town— Horseshoes, Arm-wrestling, Checkers, Dominos—to be played for liquor, drugs, or goods. But down at the Commons, on the main drag, the "Big Three" games were for high-rollers only: Craps, Poker, and Blackjack. The pavilions would be filled with high-ranking visitors, who would gamble for mountains of goods at the tables—and the big winners would score an immediate appointment with one of Sam's beauties.

As always, gambling and drinking was highly encouraged over the weekend, and the bosses' constables were at the ready to put any ruffians in Purgatory Jail. A fine would pay off any laws that were broken, but if there was not enough to pay the fine, then the offender would be sent to the auction block. If the offense was grave enough, a malcontent could even be sold to one of the Co-op Prison Camps.

It was this debt mill that produced the star product of Purgatory— Survivor flesh. Friday's unlucky gamblers, dead-beat debtors, and petty criminals would hit the block, to be sold for the highest bidder on Saturday Morning. Camp Leaders and LandLords would bid for the labor or sexual partners they wanted, and leave that afternoon with their prizes. The coming weekend's crop of unfortunates would be held on the lower level of Purgatory Jail...

And Director and Evangelo would probably be held somewhere in that facility with them.

Of late, the winners at the Big Three were almost always WildLand Express agents. Card sharks and gamblers extraordinaire, they were fast at the tables and loose with their bets—and under orders from Dominic to never press for their winnings from the ladies. Most considered it a rescue operation; some considered it a chance at romance—but all WildLand Express agents considered their time at the tables a covert operation to provide cover for Agent Ellison and keep her specialists safe from unwanted sexual encounters with strangers.

Then at eight, the tables would close, Sam's girls would strut out on the arms of the night's big winners, and the main event would begin—Friday Night Fights. The sign at the Commons said it all:

> *8 FITERS, 2 POOLS of 4, NO CLASSES, OPEN*
> *SINEUP, FIRST COM FIRST SURV—NO*
> *HOLDS BARD. WINNRS ADVANS, LUSERS*
> *SOLD*

Criminals would be loosed from the Jail if they chose to opt for the Fights. The only way to avoid the auction block was to fight. Fights usually ended with one party in jail and the other party dancing with a hostess. But for freedom-minded diehards, the "Death Match" was available, only at the top-level Championship Fight when all other options had been exhausted. This option allowed the fighter to gamble for their lives. The Winner of a Purgatory Death Match would win the prize, plus a date with one of Sam's girls—and the loser would lose their lives.

The group of rescuers decided that Market Mayhem Weekend and Friday Night Fights would provide the Watcher with adequate reason to be there, and that he should disguise himself and head to the front gate with all the other WildLand Express Agents, who would arrive starting tonight.

Under this guise, WildLand Express Unit Leaders for the Revolution would arrive in town and recruit. If the Director was unavailable, the Watcher, through Agent Mansour, would be the one to relay instructions.

> *—have Agent Mansour and Agent Azarian meet and*
> *instruct Unit Leaders tonight*

But what of the Afterling? The Watcher needed to confer with her before he made a final choice as to his role on the Rescue Team, as his current assignment as Rose's bodyguard superseded all other roles.

> *—talk to Rose*

He showed his notes to Sam, then put down his pencil and rubbed his eyes. How to resolve this conflict—to protect the Afterling, help rescue their leaders, and start the Revolution all at once?

Sam nodded to Mansour: "Escort Agent Azarian downstairs while I get the girls ready to do a little surveillance of Boss Chartreaux and Boss Zhu's cabins. I have Specialist Diaz scheduled for Boss Waitie tonight, and he may yield some valuable information. But before then, I will have her and Specialist LaFleur sashay through town with Agent Mercedes to see if they can pick up any additional information from Shaney's Rangers. Perhaps the promise of a few freebies will help loosen their tongues." She stood up and walked to a door to the other side of the great room. "Araceli—Lourdes! Let's dress for success—Destiny isn't going to save herself." Sam paused, then remembered: "There's a chill today, so make sure to lay out your socks; you'll need to warm your feet when you get back."

Two svelte hembras, one smaller, dark-eyed, and sultry, the other taller, green eyed, and lithe, flitted down from the loft and into the great room, cool and confident. Dressed in faded knit tunics and leggings, their flat scales complimented their large eyes and fine features. Soft crocheted berets made them look almost LifeBefore level fashionable—except for those bare feet. Purgatory's barefoot ruling on Hostesses was enacted several years ago to stop them from escaping into the thorny, fire ant-infested Texas WildLands; Sam made them comply to maintain cover while in Public.

Glancing down, the Watcher flushed red and tried to not openly admire their sleek figures and delicate little toes. Sam whispered instructions to them, and the girls nodded in tandem before linking arms and walking down out the door, an alert Agent Mercedes following behind them.

"Now you two; take some breakfast to Kendra and Rose, and get this done quick. We need a decision in the next fifteen minutes." Sam shoved a tray in the Watcher's hands, stacked with two breakfast plates and cups of hot chicoffee.

Mansour and the Watcher made their way to the basement stairs, balancing the tray carefully as they descended into a dark, crowded cellar. Here were piles of goods laid back by the girls, wealth accumulated through judicious saving: fabrics, yarns, leathers, barrels of salt, and other assorted luxury goods. They knocked on the door at the far end of the room—*tap-tap, tap-tap*—

"Who goes there?"

"Agent Mansour—Peach."

"Agent Sampson—Cobbler..." the door creaked open, and Sampson stooped to look through it. "Any luck with the plans?"

"Almost done. Are the ladies available? We need to talk." Mansour ducked into the small storage room, then rolled the wood-paneled false wall to the side. He knocked the secret knock.

"Who goes there?'

"Fenix Creciente." Mansour whispered.

"We Will Be Free." The door opened just a crack, and Kendra stood in the breach. "You'll have to wait; she's busy. What do you need?"

Holding the breakfast tray, the Watcher tried to peer around the lanky little Hembra, but she blocked his view.

Mansour spoke on his behalf: "Watcher needs to inform the Afterling about his plans—we've only got fifteen minutes before we have to leave."

"Okay, well, she's right in the middle of something—I'm disguising her, just like Sam requested."

Mansour looked puzzled. "Disguised? I don't recall Sam asking for that."

"It's wonderful! She oiled my hair, and now it's much better." Rose sounded chipper.

"We always disguise our guests; you know that, Lazarus. I just did what Sam always requests. The Midget should be able to pass for human once the process is done—you can thank me later."

The Watcher appeared dubious of the claim. He tried to peek around the Specialist once more...

Without warning, Specialist Qin snatched the breakfast tray from the Watcher's hands and slammed the door in their faces. A narrow, long window opened above the door.

"You can't come in—she will need six hours to set. Talk to her through the transom."

An exasperated grunt burst forth from the Watcher. Agitated, he thumped on the door. But Specialist Qin was not to be intimidated. "Beat on the door all you want, you big ape—you're not getting in."

"Kendra, we've got no time for this." Mansour was trying to be patient, but all the planning was wearing thin, and talk needed to be replaced with action—soon. "Herman, ask Sam to come on down... Kendra needs her attitude adjusted."

Sampson scrambled upstairs, then returned, Sam following close behind. "Kendra, what's the problem?"

"There is no problem—Agent Azarian wants to come barging in, but we are oiling the Afterling's hair; let him ask through the transom."

Sam remembered a time when she had hair, and the delightful

necessity of oiling it. "I really don't see what the problem is, Gentlemen. Her hair is a mess." The tall Hembra thought about it: "Kendra, tell the Afterling she needs to spend time on the rest of her, too—her skin is getting ashy."

"We're gonna need a bigger jar of grease."

The Watcher's ears blushed red.

"Make do with what you have—dump a tiny dab of vanilla in there to make it smell nice." Sam headed back upstairs to prep for their mission. "Agent Azarian, ask through the transom."

Intrigued, the Watcher colored a deeper shade of crimson. *They're oiling her hair... and whatever else needs moisturizing.* Suddenly distracted again by the thought of a vanilla-scented Afterling, he tried to refocus; he was having to make important decisions about whether or not he should leave her behind to free the leaders of this Revolution, and *she's oiling her hair?*

This next hour of reconnaissance, and her response to his absence, would determine whether or not he could leave her side; he trusted no one to be with her, and yet—here she was, locked in a cozy safe room with a guard and a personal handler, doing her hair. The Watcher looked at the door and pondered the Afterling behind it. *Dominic's personally chosen guards in a secret fortress... and Rose safe inside it, playing dress up with a friend.*

It sounded boring, compared to doing reconnaissance. Suddenly, it didn't seem that hard a choice to make. *Babysit the Afterling, or start the Revolution?*

"You should really be nicer to Kendra," proffered Sampson.

Mansour grumbled. "Kendra has you hoodwinked." Then he turned to the Watcher: "What do you wish to ask her?" Aggravated, the big brawler scrawled out, then handed a note to Mansour.

> *—I'm leaving with Agents Mansour and Ellison to do surveillance at the Jail—I'll be away for an hour. I don't want to leave you but there is no choice if we are to rescue the Dominic and Evangelo. Do you want me to stay or to go?*

Reading the note aloud, through the transom Mansour wondered just how difficult it must be to have any kind of relationship when one party can't talk without permission or help from the other...

"Oh yes, please go! Save them, please—I promise I'll be fine here without you."

Fine here. without. me. Hot injustice stabbed his soul at her dismissal of him. *Fine.* He had hoped she would at least act somewhat clingy at his departure. He scratched out his next missive for Agent Mansour to read.

—Very well. Don't leave this facility. That is an order.

"Oh, absolutely! Be careful, everyone!" Rose bubbled.

Everyone. The Watcher grunted, unhappy.

"Watch Kendra, Herman... she's up to no good." Agent Mansour gave a private nod to the sentry, then turned to leave.

The Watcher stopped him—

—If you do not trust Kendra then why should I?

Mansour spoke plainly. "I'd trust Kendra with my life. She is a fantastic friend, and she would never allow the Afterling to come to harm. But she likes to buck the system. That's why she's still just a Specialist and not an Agent. She's independent, outspoken, and likely to do things on impulse—it's part of what makes her a great field operative. Sam found her alone in the Great Suburban Badlands south of the TroPlex, living on cockroaches and cigarettes—Sam rescued her, and Kendra became a daughter to her, like all her girls. If I had to choose anyone to act independently on a mission, it would be Kendra; she works well alone, is resourceful and is capable of taking care of herself and others." Mansour clapped Sampson on the shoulder: "But just in case Kendra needs a reason to follow orders more closely, we've got Agent Sampson here to guard this door."

Sampson looked up: "Kendra is a good person. She just has a bad attitude."

Mansour opened a locker in the storage room. "I just know Kendra's got a mind of her own. If that's a problem for you, Watcher, then don't go."

Grunting acknowledgment, the Watcher nodded.

Mansour continued: "We'll only be gone for an hour. You can see how The Afterling does with our team and make your decision when you come back."

Do the Afterling's hair, or save the Revolution? Rose's breezy disregard of the Watcher chafed him no end; injured, he nodded to Mansour.

—Let's roll.

Grabbing work clothes from a stash in the basement, Mansour gave them to the Watcher: "Put these on; with a balaclava and work gloves, I can pass you off in Boss Winston's work crew. We'll meet with him afterwards."

A reluctant Watcher headed up the stairs, followed by the stalwart Mansour.

Minutes passed, and the Recon Team assembled with Sam, Mansour, and the Watcher to head out into a cold rain. Specialist Qin, hearing the door slam upstairs, poked her head out from the room. "Is the coast clear?

Sampson leaned back against the wall: "Yes, it's just us for now. Can I get something for you?"

"We'll get it ourselves—we're going upstairs to get the Afterling some more bear grease. It may be a while, so don't worry."

"The Afterling isn't allowed upstairs, Kendra—orders are for her to stay in the safe room." Sampson spoke softly but firmly.

Specialist Qin came out, followed by a friendly Afterling, her hair obscured under a long black stocking cap. "Herman, everyone's gone, and there's no reason for her to stay hidden. It will only be a few minutes..."

Sampson looked determined. He rose up from his seat. "No, Kendra. Not this time..."

Kendra leapt up and grabbed Sampson by both ears and pulled him down to eye level. "Keep it quiet, you big Palooka, and we can argue about it later." The slender Hembra pulled his enormous face down to hers and gave him a sudden, passionate kiss on the lips.

Overwhelmed, Agent Sampson struggled briefly, then gave up completely, whereupon Kendra released his ears and patted his chest to whisper: "Don't forget who gave you a treat when you came howling at my window, Big Dog..." He stood there, dumbfounded as he always did when she acknowledged his existence.

Freed, Kendra and the Afterling scurried up the basement stairs and darted up a loft ladder to the empty barracks room where all Sam's girls slept, locking the bedroom door behind them. Grabbing a hooded gray jacket from a dresser drawer, Kendra scanned her surroundings, then opened a cracked second-story window on the back side of the cabin. Chilly, damp air washed in, bring a fine misting rain with it. "All clear?"

Rose looked out the window. "All clear."

Kendra hiked one leg out the window, then held her hand out to the Afterling. "We're headed to the Roof. No one likes to look up on rainy days..."

Rose pulled up the hood of her black sweater. "Where shall we go?"

Kendra pointed to a cabin two doors down.

"Time to raid Boss Zhu's house."

———◆———

III

From the window to the tree, from the tree to the roof, then from roof to roof. *This isn't so bad*, Rose thought. *It's just that whole broad daylight problem, but...* that could be handled.

Kendra was remarkably adept at climbing; she seemed to have a natural sense for what foot to put where. They were atop the ridge of one of the many two-story cabins that had originally graced Purgatory when it was a gated, mid-level luxury community; the cookie-cutter log-cabins were upscale but still had a rustic quality made even more rustic by age and neglect. The coated metal roofs had survived tough Texas weather, but panels showed signs they had been pierced by hail or bent by wind. Rose and Kendra crept along the battered ridges of the rooflines, slow and low with their bodies flat against the corrugated metal.

Raising a hand subtly before her, Kendra waved, and the curtain of rain briefly parted, revealing the woebegone metropolis before her:

"Welcome to Purgatory—a Hell of a Town!"

In some ways, Purgatory was pretty for a run-down hovel. Some of the cabins were well tended, with small gardens or lawn furnishings; the Hostess Club even had a little bird feeder and a small flower garden with wind chimes, complete with a decorative flag made of bright blue crocheted yarn. Other cabins had similar treasures, but for the most part, yard decor consisted of weedy, overgrown lawns and broken-down picnic tables.

Motioning to the cabin beneath their feet, Rose whispered in Kendra's ear—"Tread softly. Someone is motionless in the room directly below us."

Kendra cocked her head to look at Rose: "Really? You can see that? Sam said you had mysterious powers but I thought she was just high or something." Kendra crept softly. "It's probably Hizzoner Norris, sleeping off another bender. He's supposed to run this town, but that's hard to do when he's sloshed all the time—that's why the Bosses are the ones really running everything."

A few small groups of Survivors were out in the morning rain, mostly work crews. Nine bells had just sounded, and the townsmen were still sleeping off their sins. Kendra looked up, then pointed down the street and whispered: "There's our Recon Team—keep watch. That slender hombre is actually Sam; underneath that long tan coat, with shoulder pads and a scarf pulled up to hide her jaw, she's tall enough to pass for an Hombre. Sam will look for anything out of the ordinary, but she can't really see that far—just lay low on the rooftops and keep out of her view. The shorter, buff macho beside her is Mansour: Don't ever stand up if you know he's within line of sight, because he'll see you right away; his eyesight is incredible."

A brisk wind blew from behind Rose's back, and a spattering of rain fell across the roof. Below them in the Recon party, a broad-backed Macho with a battered felt hat turned his dark eyes to look back their way. The rest of his face was obscured by a tan balaclava, but he had a familiar red bandana tied at his throat. His eyes scanned the street—

The Watcher. He seemed to be sniffing the air...

Rose flattened herself, and pointed in his direction. Kendra nodded, and they both slid below the ridge line to hide their silhouettes. In the fogging mist their outlines would be harder to see, but noise would carry further in the moist atmosphere, so they maintained silence. They lay motionless as the Watcher continued to search his surroundings. He even glanced at Hizzoner's roof before Sam touched his arm and pointed down the street towards the Jail. Reluctantly, he moved on and turned the corner beyond their sight.

"Well, that was exciting. Is Watcher always this observant?" Kendra whispered.

Rose nodded. "Yes, he always seems to be able to track me somehow —it's rather terrifying." Rose thought for a moment, "Speaking of terrifying; you may wish to know that I have an annoying tendency to go limp when I am terrified."

"Well, it can't be that bad, or I doubt you could have survived this long. Just don't get terrified... think happy thoughts." Kendra instructed. "Now, let's vamoose. We need to get to that next house over there—through that ash tree, the oak next to it, and then onto the roof, then into that window on the top floor. That's Boss Zhu's house, and he never uses that upstairs room. I've been there plenty of times, he just keeps to himself down in the bottom bedroom where he can shoot up the Stuff."

"With chemicals? Oh, that is so sad." Rose pitied Boss Zhu. "Is there no one to help him?"

Kendra scowled. "Destiny has tried to talk to him, but he just keeps hitting the Stuff. I guess he wants drugs more than he wants her. She's his favorite girl—but not favorite enough for him to quit using drugs and buy her out."

"Oh—would she really go with him? Even though she's fighting for freedom?" Rose was curious.

Kendra pulled no punches: "We all have our price."

They crept further down the roofline to a branch from a spreading white ash overhanging the roof of Hizzoner Norris' house. "From this tree we can reach the Oak nearest Boss Zhu's house and duck into the loft. Before we go in, use your secret powers to see if you can spot him. If the coast is clear, we'll check it out and find some clues."

"Okee Dokee, but be aware that I can't see through water or thick walls. These logs may be too dense."

"Shhh, it'll be okay. Let's go."

Grabbing a sturdy branch, they scampered through the treetops, limb to limb; the small yellow leaves on the limber twigs of the ash bridged to the leathery brown leaves on the sturdy, unbending wood of the white oak, providing ample cover for the climbers; two more weeks, and the trees would be bare in the late Texas autumn.

They stepped lightly onto the roof of Boss Zhu's house, keeping their profiles low. Rose closed her eyes to blot out distractions and searched the room below, trying to detect any heat or movement.

"I can't discern anything on the upper level—and just a faint glow downstairs. It doesn't seem to be hot enough to be alive."

Kendra's brows knit together as she puzzled. "He was supposed to be with Destiny until eight this morning—I don't get it. He has to be passed out downstairs. Can you pry down there?"

"I can detect something not moving in that bottom corner—but it might just be a cold wood stove, not hot enough to be on fire. Maybe it's just a cold person? Give me a minute to see if it will move..."

Waiting a few moments, Rose watched for any movement. "Nothing."

"Let's move—I'll get the window open." Clinging to the narrow edge of the roof, Kendra swung her legs down to the wall. Low branches from the oak helped block the view but did not provide access to the loft. Improvising, Kendra lowered herself down to a decorative external cross-beam that delineated the first story from the second half-story; setting her foot on the ledge, she gripped the logs with her slim fingers and inched her way to the loft window. Peering in, she saw nothing and slowly pushed up on the glass, careful to not cut her hands on the fractured panes. Sliding her body into the loft, she motioned to the Afterling to follow her.

Mimicking Kendra's movements, Rose scooted across the shaded exterior wall of the cabin then eased into the opened window. Kendra crouched in the darkened loft, cautiously hunching down between piles of old furnishings and discarded papers. Half a century of dust covered the wooden floor of the loft, and evidence of rats was everywhere.

Rose wrinkled her nose at the smell. "Are you sure this is the right place?"

"Yes," Kendra whispered. "Boss Zhu treats this like an attic. The downstairs parlor is nice, but the rest of the house looks like an abandoned homeless shelter. Destiny cleaned it up for him once or twice, but he could never keep it decent."

They crept through the dark, cold loft towards the stairs. Upon reaching the loft door, Rose closed her eyes again: "The glow is still in the same place, and growing fainter—it must be dying embers in a fireplace." She opened the door—

Pale light leaked in from around drawn blinds, revealing a house that once had been loved. The kitchen was filled with dirty dishes and empty cups; a small, round table with one chair was centered alone in the middle of a bare floor. Kendra and Rose made their way down the decrepit stairs softly, slowly.

The portion of the house directly in front of the door was cleared and cleaned, with a small couch made cozy; a gray fleece blanket and mismatched lace pillows lay rumpled on the stained tweed cushions. Remains of a carrot cake and a chili dinner for two were on a coffee table, the bowls still partly filled. It was a glimpse of a life where hope and beauty still existed. A scribbled note on a ragged piece of paper appeared to have a letter written upon it, held down by a burnt-out candle.

But a partially opened door revealed a bedroom beyond, where an unmade bed and piles of dirty clothes lay untouched; beyond that, shadows framed a backlit silhouette of a faded hyacinth in jar.

"The faint glow—over there:"

In the darkness of the lonely bedroom, a man lay on the floor.

"It's Boss Zhu..." Kendra whispered. His upturned face, almost beautiful in the half-light, was pale, the scales turning livid blue around their smooth copper edges.

"Oh! He's getting cold." Rose reached over to touch his hand and found it stiff. She withdrew her hand from his, and they saw the blood on her fingertips...

"Holy crap, he's dead." Kendra hissed. "We gotta go."

"That's odd..." Rose opined. "There's blood on the floor but I don't see a wound."

"Well, Zhu didn't stab himself in the back—he got dead some other way." Kendra was backing up slowly, looking all around. "Let's get the hell out of here." Kendra grabbed Rose's hand.

"Oh, we cannot leave him like this—it's not right. A ceremony is in order." Rose took the faded hyacinth and laid it upon Boss Zhu's chest. Putting out her hands, she began to wordlessly pray, just as she had over her brother and Chief Emmanuel. Kendra, however, was not in a prayerful mood.

"He died, AMEN. C'mon..."

"Wait—look, a pokey thing." Rose pointed at an object beneath his back.

"That's an ice pick, it's a murder, let's GO."

Backtracking out of the room, they made their way past the scene of Boss Zhu's date with Destiny; Rose picked up the note and tucked it into her shirt, between her breasts. "This may be a clue."

"Screw clues. " Kendra started hauling Rose bodily back through the abandoned furnishings and up the stairs.

Halfway up the stairs, Rose froze:

"By the back door—in the kitchen—there's a glow, two big people are outside the door."

A knife was scraping against the doorjamb; someone was attempting to force the door open.

"Come on we have to get out of here NOW—" closer to the loft than the front door, Kendra dragged Rose up the stairs behind her, dodging boxes and piles of books. They raced to the loft, pulling the door shut just as they heard a boot kick down the back door down in the kitchen. A man's gruff voice growled low:

"Take lookout, and keep an eye on that open window upstairs. I gotta finish this up—if someone asks, tell them you're here to do maintenance, then tell them to scram."

A deep voice answered from outside: "I told you we should have done clean-up on scene, Dornak... Are you sure that window wasn't open before?"

"I'm sure, and no, I couldn't do clean-up with Destiny screaming in my ear. If you hadn't gagged her, I would have knocked her out... too bad Jip didn't."

"Zhu's drunk neighbors wouldn't have ever woke up at that hour. I would have done more than just gagged that little ho', but Chartreaux was wanting to stage her right away."

"Well, pocket the ice pick, and get the kerosene rags laid down—we have to get this done pronto. This was not well thought out."

"Gimme a break, will ya? We never expected Zhu to fight back. He's usually so hopped up, he wouldn't even flinch. I figured we could take her without a struggle, but this stupid junkie had to go act the Hero with Jip —and now he's dead."

"Just hurry up already, people are starting to wake up around here."

Kendra pulled Rose down behind a large stack of empty "Reunion's Best" crates piled precariously against the wall, next to a mountain of drained bottles of varying shapes and sizes. Hearts hammering, they listened as heavy boots made their way slowly around the room downstairs, kicking boxes, pushing furniture aside.

The steps stopped near the front door, and a voice called out in hushed tones:

"We got someone snooping about over here... Boss Zhu's had company since we left. Someone left a flower on his chest—that wasn't there when we offed him."

"Are you sure? Destiny's chained up at the jail, so we know it wasn't her. But who else would do such a thing for this loser?"

"A girl. This was a girl thing... one of 'em must've come looking for Destiny." The voice turned venomous and moved towards them, footsteps lumbering from the bottom of the stairs. "Get ready to torch this place."

Kendra and Rose held their breath as the footsteps stopped.

The gruff voice wondered aloud: "What the hell?" a sniffing noise. "Hey, Harper—"

"What?"

"Our little intruder is so scared she just peed herself on the stairs. It's still warm—she's hiding in the loft. Watch that window."

A stifled guffaw wafted up from Harper outside the door, as Kendra shot a horrified look at the petrified Rose leaning against her arm. The gruff voice hissed from down the stairs:

"Hey lil' pissant, I got news for you. You ain't seen scared yet—just wait 'til I get ahold of you."

A hollow, muffled smash echoed through the empty house, the sound of boxes being crushed by a heavy, blunt object. "Which one of you nosy bitches is poking around here?"

With each heavy step, another swing, another crushing blow, another threat:

"D'ya know what I do to meddlin' little girls?"

smash

"I'm gonna make you cry"

smash

"I'm gonna make you beg"

smash

"But no one will hear you"

smash

"With your mouth crammed full of my—"

SMASH

The big boot kicked open the door at the top of the loft; it slammed into the pile of boxes hiding Kendra and Rose, toppling the pile down on top of them, and covering them completely. They huddled, motionless.

Kendra could see him now through a gap in the boxes, a heavyset, scarred Macho in a gimme cap and a dirty t-shirt, his back turned to them. Yellowed cloth, soaked with sweat, clung to the heaving muscles of his back, and Kendra could smell his rank odor from across the room. His voice had that depraved malevolence that oozes from those who relish the fear of the small. Working his way around the other side of the spacious loft, Dornak methodically knocked down piles of junk with an old aluminum baseball bat; his eyes were on a storage closet tucked beneath the angled roof of the loft. Breathing heavily in anticipation, he rapped on the hatch, his bloated, red face dripping with excitement:

"Daddy's got a present for ya..."

Dornak kicked in the door of the closet, and stuck his head into it, holding the bat high. "Surprise, you littl—"

A bottle sailed through the air and connected with the back of the Macho's head with a solid *thwack*. He groaned, and put his hand to his head—blood dripped from a cut. "What the f..."

Another crack echoed through the loft as Kendra delivered a solid overhand fastball of a bottle to his temple. Staggering, Dornak fell to his knees and toppled into a jumble of empty cans and glass bottles.

Kendra jumped out from behind the boxes, dragging a floppy Rose, running for her life. They heard a bellow behind them as they flew down the stairs.

"Harper! Harper, dammit..."

The back door flew open, and a lean, hungry-looking Hombre glanced in front of him just in time to see Boss Zhu's front door swinging in the breeze and the bare heels of Kendra's flying feet as she fled—

The Hombre came thundering behind them as Kendra hauled the Afterling through the neighbor's yard. They were just two doors down—

Just two bases to round.

Kendra rounded the corner just as she used to round the bases in softball, carrying a rag-doll Rose in her arms. One door down—

One base to round.

Flying into Hizzoner's yard, past a pile of ancestral lawn tools left out to decay in front, Kendra threw her feet forward and slid under the Abelia bushes in front of Hizzoner's porch—

And Kendra Qin slides into Home base!

A sharp *thwack* was heard from under the bushes.

Seconds passed, and a huffing Harper came around the corner of Hizzoner's front porch, barreling towards the bushes. Grabbing a rake from Hizzoner's ancient tool pile, Harper began to poke around for any signs of the intruders, sputtering to the abelias:

"Come out, you little bitches! I know you're in there—"

A smell of smoke tinged the air.

Now neighbors poked their heads out their windows, clamoring about the ungodly hour of this disturbance. A steady, cold rain was falling, and they stayed on their porches and out of the chill.

The squat rotundity of Hizzoner came staggering out onto the porch, cuddled in a well-loved terrycloth robe. "Why the hell are you yelling in my yard at an ungodly Ten a.m.?"

Harper jumped into the bushes in front of Hizzoner's cabin, poking with a rake. He got down on his hands and knees—

"She was here! I saw her—she was here—I swear it... Kendra and a small golden girl disappeared into your bushes..."

"You're drunk and high, Harper. Go hallucinate somewhere else." Hizzoner was not amused. A stronger smell of smoke now wafted over to them, the smell of burning kerosene. In the rain, the smoke was being damped down—

Harper was beating the bushes with the rake. "Where are you, you little—"

Hizzoner sniffed the air, then looked over, and saw smoke drifting up from Boss Zhu's loft window. Still addled by sleep, it took a moment to register—

"Fire—FIRE!" Hizzoner yelled of his front porch. "Fire—sound the alarm!" He waddled to a small, fabricated bell next to his door and began to beat it with a piece of rebar hanging from a cord. He did this for a good minute, then a house up the street sounded the alarm, and then another, the alarm spreading all over town.

A neighbor ran up the street to the next bell man: "Fire—Boss Zhu's house!"

The makeshift bells' brazen alarm drilled a hole in the drunken repose of Purgatory. Grumbling Survivors stumbled into the street, clutching their heads, bleary and rancorous; this changed to consternation as they realized their aging wooden cabins were tinderboxes, and all Purgatory was in danger.

Survivors shook off their malaise and tried to open the front door, but it was barred. One stocky Hombre, clad in a heavy tan coat with a peeling yellow letters 'VFD', took an axe and broke a window on the front porch; flames shot out, and the porch roof began to burn. Other Survivors ran to the back door, but it too was locked and barred.

Dornak appeared from across the street, walking calmly, looking unruffled. He glared and whispered low. "Come on, Harper. We'll deal with them later."

"But they're here! I saw Kendra and that little golden Chica hiding in these bushes..."

"Rein it in—we'll ask the Madame herself..."

Down the street they could see her, coat tails flying, striding like she gave not a single damn:

Sam.

Araceli and Lourdes came running behind her, crocheted scarves flapping fashionably behind them, with an intense Jorge gathering the tension in their wake. They made their way through the chaos just as the first of the fire brigades arrived on foot, buckets in hand. Passed hand to hand, Survivors clad in decrepit fire uniforms threw buckets of water into the broken-out window. Another group of survivors grabbed hoes and rakes from Hizzoner's tool pile, clearing a firebreak around Boss Zhu's house to contain the spread.

Firebrands floated high in the air, then fell helplessly to the saturated ground around the burning cabin; they landed upon the metal roofs and sizzled to death in the misting rain. Not to be defeated, one fell against a sheltered wooden board on Hizzoner's porch, and began to smolder. Hizzoner screeched, and stomped on it with his slippered foot, then a fireman beat it out with a homemade flapper engineered from a crumbling rubber doormat screwed to a broom handle.

What was once a yard now became a sea of mud, as each clomping boot sank up to the ankles. It was a slippery mess made worse by floating ash and rising desperation as the firemen tried again to make entry from the back side of the cabin, but could not break down the back door—it seemed to be barred from the other side. Smoke was now pouring from under the metal ridge line of Boss Zhu's aging cabin; a sick dread ran through Sam. She stopped to confer with Hizzoner, who huffed, anxious and allergic to smoke: "Boss Zhu's house is burning and nobody can find him—wasn't Destiny in there with him this morning?"

Sam nodded curtly.

Abrupt, Hizzoner demanded: "Well, go find her and ask her what she knows about this..."

Turning away, Sam pondered her choices. This looked like arson, and it would be pinned on Destiny if she couldn't be found. If Sam told Hizzoner that Destiny was missing, he would have her declared a runaway and would search the Hostess Club for clues. That could possibly expose their own covert operations...

Looking up, she saw two unwelcome figures lurking in the Hostess Club yard; leaving Hizzoner's anxious earshot, she approached the thugs.

"Dornak, Harper—I told you to stay away from the Hostess Club."

Dornak sneered. "Well, if it isn't the Head Ho."

Sam eyed him coldly.

"We go where we want." Harper spit at Sam's feet. "We have business with your slut Kendra and some sort of little bitty golden chica. They broke into a private property."

"Whose property did they break into?"

"I don't wanna say. You need to deal with her, or we will." Harper's eyes darted to the crowd gathering around the burning building.

"Maybe a deal can be made. Where is Destiny?" Sam asked flatly.

"I don't know nothing about no missing whores." Dornak retorted. "But everybody knows she was scheduled for Boss Zhu last night. Maybe your little pink playtoy set a fire to cover her little pink tracks while she was trying to escape. Go find her yourself, before the Bosses do."

"Maybe I will. Send word to Boss Chartreaux that we are looking for her."

Dornak bristled. "Good luck finding her, bitch. See ya soon." He grabbed a gasping Harper by the scruff of the neck and clomped off down the street. The neighbors gawked at the fire, more of them shaking off their stupor to help with the bucket brigade.

Sam stood immovable in the street, impervious to stares and threats.

Jorge backed Araceli and Lourdes into the front door, taking care to check for any unnoticed entries. Jorge whispered: "Senora—there are muddy footprints, leading from the loft to the basement stairs."

Without turning her head from the retreating Dornak and Harper, Sam whispered back: "Agent Mercedes, get Sampson to bring Kendra and the guest to the great room, then go help with the fire brigade."

Sam watched until Chartreaux's thugs disappeared around the street corner, then casually walked over to the Abelia bushes in front of Hizzoner's house. All attention was on the inferno, the fire brigades now watching helplessly as the roof began to buckle.

Sam peeked into Hizzoner's bushes. *Nothing there...* she pulled the branches back, and noticed a scrape in the wet soil where water had washed away the soil under the porch skirt. *Hmmm... a split in the thin skirting, right above the scraped soil.* Ambling to the back of Hizzoner's house, where the ash tree grew next to the wrap-around porch, she saw a similar-sized depression where water ran under the back porch—and more scraped soil. Looking up, she traced muddy splotches up the trunk to where the tree's branches intertwined with a cedar elm growing behind her own open loft window...

A muddy hand print sullied the log window frame.

Very clever.

She took another look around, then turned sharply on her heel and strode into the Hostess cabin.

Sam locked the door behind herself, then simply stood, silent, not acknowledging the anxious crowd gathered behind her. They held their collective breath, waiting for the tempest to hit... hands clasped behind her back, Sam stared out the window at the raging fire, and it reflected her own burning anger. The heat built in her, and her minions steeled themselves.

A sudden burst of words shot forth from her lips as she whirled to meet them, finger jabbing, spitting verbal bullets from an angry gun:

"I am short-staffed, and I don't have time for all y'all's bullshit. Specialist Rogers is missing, and her last official location is on fire!" Tears were glittering in her eyes, rage just barely contained. "Agent Sampson, you had one job: you were in charge. You are busted to Specialist. Enjoy your new rank."

Sampson stood stoic.

She swung around to take down Kendra, who was unrecognizable under a layer of cold, gray mud. "I know it was you—I don't even have to ask. What the hell is your problem? What were you playing at, and where is our Guest?"

"I'm over here—" A voice answered, hesitant, from behind Jorge. He stepped aside to reveal the Afterling, also coated head to toe in mud. Wet and trembling, Rose still had an affable innocence in her manner, which infuriated Sam.

Araceli and Lourdes both murmured, repelled and fascinated at the general appearance of the Afterling, and aghast at the condition of their beautiful crocheted hat. Sam, however, was beyond aghast—she was furious. "Specialist Qin, you are busted in rank to Probationary, and you are no longer on the recon team. Tell me what happened here."

The gray mudwoman spoke. "Blame me—It's not Herman's fault. I wanted to find Destiny and see the Midget use her mystery powers, so I arranged for both. We climbed up the trees and went rooftop to rooftop to gain access to Boss Zhu's house. Rose can see through walls; she has great recon skills but turns to jello as soon as she gets scared. Also, she peed on me... it was still worth it."

Sam expression was grave, "Afterling, is this true—you disobeyed orders, then collapsed under pressure?"

"I was trying to help find Destiny," Rose felt shame, "but I'm genetically predispositioned to become limp when I'm frightened or angry. It's called cataplexy, but I am learning how to control it by learning to control my fear—"

"I don't have time for you to learn. Rose, you are a danger to yourself and others in any high-stress situation. Agent Azarian's concerns about you are vindicated."

Rose lowered her eyes, frustrated with her own limitations. "I'm not afraid if I have a gun." Rose noted, hopeful.

"You are not fit for combat." Sam was adamant. "Perhaps you would like to speak on Kendra's behalf before I banish her to kitchen duty."

"Please don't punish anyone else—it's my fault entirely. I wanted to help and asked Kendra to help me find a way to do so. She offered me a chance to do some reconnaissance, and I jumped at the opportunity." Rose didn't flinch. "I understand this has caused problems, and I'm so sorry." She shook her head, and a plop of mud fell from her hat onto the floor.

"Screw your being 'sorry.' How did you both get away from Chartreaux's thugs?"

"Oh, Kendra slid under the bushes in the most amazing way—"

"Softball practice came in handy." Kendra grinned through her mud mask. "Hizzoner's porch is my designated home base—I use that maneuver at least once a week, but this is the first time I've ever had to 'slide into home' in broad daylight—and carrying this much dead weight." She glared at Rose. "You're heavier than you look."

Araceli and Lourdes gasped at this affront, but Rose appeared oblivious to it.

Rose effused: "Kendra was fantastic—we slid right between the panels and under the porch so I had a moment to regain my composure. Everyone was looking to that awful man while he was carrying on, so we utilized that distraction to find our way out. We burrowed up under the porch's crawlspace and made our way to the other side, where that tree is growing—then climbed the tree while everyone was gawking at Harper. We snuck back downstairs, but Sampson caught us while he was watching the fire from the door."

"Creative, but muddy." Sam said, irritated, "And utterly foolhardy for you to go out in the broad daylight, no matter the reason. It was also against orders, and Rose will not be allowed on any of my teams as a combatant, period."

Sam turned to Kendra. "Give your full report now, Kendra, without any wry commentary."

"Boss Zhu is dead, and Destiny is in Jail. Boss Chartreaux's goons murdered Zhu and are holding Destiny hostage. Dornak and Harper broke into the house while we were there, and we heard them say they were going to burn the cabin to hide the evidence. We found a meal, interrupted, and Boss Zhu lying dead on the floor. What we found on Zhu's body confirms their words—he was stabbed in the back with an ice pick when he fought them."

Sam's jaw clenched, chewing her own emotions and swallowing them whole. "Boss Zhu? Murdered? And Destiny is being held in the jail?" She breathed out. "But thank God—she was not still in the house. I was afraid they might take her back there."

A muddy Rose chirped: "Oh! I recovered some evidence from the scene. I'd imagine it's a clue..."

Sam held out her hand to Rose. "Give me your evidence, Afterling."

Reaching into her soggy shirt, Rose pulled forth a penciled note, wet and muddy around the edges but still relatively intact. She handed it to Sam, who read it in silence; looking up at last, with tears in her eyes, she passed the note to Sampson. "Read it to the group, Specialist Sampson."

Sampson cleared his throat to begin reading in a halting voice:

~~~~~

My Destiny

I've been clean for three days now. This is the longest I've gone without the Stuff in 32 yrs and its all thanks to you. You make me want to live again and I can see the lite at the end of my tunnel. You are the reason I am finally free of the Stuff and I want to return the favor—I will buy you out and help the cause of freedom.

I love you Destiny Rogers

always

Jack Zhu

~~~~~

Voice cracking, it was clear Sampson was miserable, brown eyes welling with emotion. Araceli and Lourdes burst into tears simultaneously, and tough old Jorge turned his face to the wall. Rose, stunned, stared at the letter in Sampson's trembling hands:

A man loved a woman—just like the Virginian loved Miss Molly in the wonderful Cowboy Book...

Only Kendra seemed to be unaffected. Nonchalant, she shrugged her slender shoulders: "Who'd a thunk it... the bastard finally got clean."

Turning her back to the group, Sam struggled to regain her bearing— but her tears flowed freely, and she hated every single one of them. *Weak. They make me look weak.* She pinched the bridge of her nose, hiding her face until the tears stopped. Her team wisely pretended to not notice.

"I had a nasty encounter with Chartreaux's goons, Harper and Dornak —they accused Destiny of setting the fire to cover an escape attempt. They are going to frame Destiny." Sam blew her nose into a worn bandana, dabbing at her eyes. "This letter proves Destiny didn't set the fire. She has no motive to try and escape Boss Zhu, or harm him—and besides, I know her—she's too meek to kill anyone," Sam waved at Sampson: "Secure the evidence in my desk; I'll send it with Mansour to brief Boss Winston of the discovery of Boss Zhu with an anonymous report from an undercover agent, so no one will be the wiser. Boss Winston will need it to determine how to proceed with the System regarding Boss Chartreaux. Boss Winston has been concerned that corruption has become rampant in Purgatory municipal workings."

Covertly wiping her eyes again with the bandana, Sam assumed her bearing once more. "Araceli, your appointment tonight is cancelled—it's too dangerous with the current state of unrest. I'll send word to Boss Waitie that you are sick."

Araceli looked tragic. "What do I have?"

"Diverticulitis." Sam thought. "I don't know exactly what it is, but it sounds bad."

Sam motioned to Kendra and the Afterling. "Both of you need to clean up yourselves and this muddy mess. I hate mud." She looked out the window again. "Kendra—you're on probation, and you will prove whether or not you can be trusted as the Afterling's handler with this next assignment. You still have to cook lunch and dinner, so plan accordingly."

Kendra muttered to herself, sullen, "Get back in the kitchen, Kendra..."

"And YOU—" Sam pointed a finger at Rose: "Kendra is going to disguise you as a regular human. I have a special assignment for you both." Plotting, the Agent was crafting a battle plan. "I need every trained Agent I have for the fight ahead—but I need one basically useless person to do nothing but turn some heads from a safe distance. The most useless person I have right now is Rose."

Visibly upset, Rose squawked: "I helped! You can't say that's useless."

"You helped cause a problem—Boss Chartreaux's goons know there's another girl at the club, and they will tell him. But you also found what I needed to prove Destiny's innocence, so it's a net balance of zero. What gives you a plus is your ability to think on your feet and work with Kendra to cause a diversion—and that's exactly what I'm going to recruit you to do."

Kendra demurred. "You're the boss, lady. But what about Agent Azarian? Won't he nix the whole idea, especially after he hears how the Afterling disobeyed his orders?"

Sam frowned—"What he doesn't know won't hurt us, and I think y'all need a reminder as to who is in charge of this operation in this territory. I am the Commander here, and I will make the decisions on how to run ops and utilize personnel. First order of business: everyone in this room is now sworn to secrecy. Understood?" Reluctantly, they nodded. "Jorge and Sampson, you are released to help with the fire brigade and to monitor whoever comes around to pry. Let me know when you see Mansour and Azarian."

They exited out the door.

Sam stepped over to the sodden Afterling, and bent down to speak to her confidentially. "Rose, I appreciate that you are a good scout. But you can't be used in a combat situation; we don't need you folding in the middle of a fight, still there are other ways I can utilize your skills. Do what I say, and I won't tell Agent Azarian about your blatant disregard for his orders. Cross me, and I'll have you both ejected from Purgatory for *your* insubordination."

Rose gaped, fishlike, then shut her mouth.

A flurry of activity commenced to clean up the mud, which smeared all over the wooden boards. Still, raggedy mops and threadbare towels made short work of the muddy mess on the floor. The muddy women, however, were quite a different problem altogether.

Kendra looked the Afterling up and down: "Well, you look a little more normal now—but we may never get it all out of your hair..."

The knock resounded softly—*tap-tap, tap-tap.* Jorge ran in from outside and whispered in Sam's ear.

Straightening herself, Sam snapped her fingers in the air. "Get moving, ladies—Kendra, head down to the basement with the Afterling—Boss Winston, Mansour, and Azarian are headed this way. I will stall them outside—you have five minutes to clean this up, get down to the basement and look innocent."

"Araceli, Lourdes; prepare to outfit the Afterling by this evening." Sam pursed her lips. "We're going to need a major distraction—and Rose is that distraction."

———◆———

Chaos ensued—the Chief Had Arrived On Scene.

Mansour and the Watcher ran behind Boss Winston, who was striding ahead them in mismatched turnout gear and bunker boots. A scuffed white helmet of unknown vintage was perched atop a tall, trim Hombre, Nomex hood pulled down so he could bark orders to the rest of his brigade. Torn bunker coveralls, their red suspenders stretched and frayed, overlaid a soot-stained shirt, and he hefted a battered halligan in his hand —as Boss, Winston was Fire Chief, Police Chief, Crew Chief, and Security Chief for his brigade, all rolled into one.

Billowing black smoke attempted to rise but was weighed down by the heavy mist and spattered rain; it filled the main street and hung in the air. Winston shouted—

"Mansour—scene size-up—give me a report."

Mansour ran ahead, shouting for command on scene. A voice on the far side of the smoke column shouted back, a barrel-chested Macho with a black helmet on his head and a shovel in his hand.

"Walters, IC—Boss Zhu's house is fully engulfed. Location unknown —attempted entry, exits locked, fire out of control early."

The chaos of the situation was palpable—*chaos*. The Watcher broke out in a cold sweat. Even here, chaos came with the Afterling, a pet familiar, always near when she was present. *She is chaos, personified. But where is she?*

The smell of smoke was overwhelming—but even now, the Watcher could catch the faintest whiff of her in the air—eau de Afterling. Surely he couldn't detect her scent through the walls? But he had smelled her on the wind earlier, through the rain—so faint even he wondered if he was hallucinating...

Or she disobeyed orders and left the safe room.

The Watcher leapt through the crowd, his bulky, over-muscled legs catapulting him forward through the haze, running towards the Hostess Club. Vaulting up the steps, he wrenched the door handle and found it locked—he prepared to kick it down.

Sampson came running up behind and tapped the Watcher's shoulder —"Whoa there Hoss—let me get you in." Gently blocking the Watcher, Sampson spoke calmly, tapping the code. "She's safe, she's safe—just hang on; Kendra is with her now." The Giant smiled broadly, standing between the Watcher and the cabin door.

A sense of unease filled the Watcher—his internal lie detector was going off—too many back teeth showing. *Eyes don't match the smile, and the situation doesn't lend itself to smiles—*

Sam opened the door just a crack. The Watcher growled and pointed at the door.

"Hey, hey it's all good." Sam cajoled. "The girls were having a hair party downstairs, and the fire broke out down the street. The Afterling is perfectly safe." She smiled broadly.

There's that smile again.

He whipped out his notepad—

—then let me in

"No need to panic, Agent Azarian—" Sam was still placid, overly calm. "Araceli and Lourdes are indecent—they were chilly, their clothes were damp from the rain, and they're getting undressed by the fire. Surely you wouldn't want to walk in on them?" Sam asked pointedly. "Or would you?" She closed the door again and locked it quickly.

Irritation rising, the Watcher wrote to Sampson:

—let me in—I have to determine the Afterling is safe.
Something is wrong, and I can tell—you are lying.

Sampson balked. "That's not true. We wouldn't—" the Watcher snarled, showing his sharp canines, ivory teeth glinting back to the molars —

—Sleeping Dogs shouldn't lie. If you want to keep on
meeting Kendra in the moonlight you better talk NOW

Thinking fast—for Sampson—he came up with a new story. "Okay Hoss, you caught me; I might as well come clean."

The Watcher could feel his hot anxiety balling up into a fist.

"We didn't want to tell you, because it seems like so minor an infraction, but... Kendra went to the ladies room, and I stood guard; but when I ran upstairs to look at the fire, the Afterling snuck out of the safe room. She got into my stash of homemade sassafras candies." He hung his head. "It's all my fault—I've been busted in rank, and the Afterling is safe—she's just full of my candies."

—I'd like to see these candies

"Oh, I still have a few left!" Sampson grinned. "But I don't see how— they are delicious."

The Watcher's eyes narrowed... pushing past Sampson once again, he rapped the code on the door. Just as he raised his fist to hammer on it again, to his surprise, the door swung open.

Two barefoot hembras in bath towels answered the door. Lourdes scowled at him, pale green eyes flashing—"C'est rude!"

Araceli squealed, her sienna-scaled shoulders gleaming in the flamelight: "You do not have an appointment—get out!"

The door slammed, and he could feel his cheeks burning. He turned to Sampson, and pointed to the door, grunting.

"Give them a few moments, and they will vacate the room with their gear. Then you can stomp around all you want."

A roar rang out behind them, the shout of men and the trample of feet; they turned to see the roof of Boss Zhu's house fall in with a crash then a horrible scream of metal and cracking timbers. Mansour was pushing the crowd back, while Boss Winston shouted orders for the firemen to fall back. Hizzoner stood on his porch, stomping out firebrands as fast as they could fall.

On the wind, the Watcher thought he heard the scream of a man, faint and far away. A cold feeling flooded his soul—*the little Ranger? The Director? Too many people to care about—too many choices.* He made his choice and knocked on the cabin door again.

A window opened above Sampson, and Lourdes called out from the loft—"You may come in now, but no free peeks."

The Watcher tried the handle and found it unlocked. Bounding through the door, he rounded the banister to the basement entrance— nearly slipping on the fresh-mopped floor—and made his way down, three steps at a time. He slowed down to inspect the scene. An almost-full bowl of orange-yellow sweets was out on a shelf nearby—Sampson's candies, untouched? *So, the candy is a lie, a diversion from the truth...* and the basement floor was also newly mopped. He muttered to himself. Why would they mop the basement floor if Araceli and Lourdes took off their wet clothes upstairs?

He grabbed a couple of candies, pushed aside the false wall, and rapped on the door.

He scribbled a note.

—Fenix Creciente

Tossing the note through the still-opened transom above the door, he heard Kendra's voice: "We will be free."

Then Rose—"We're coming, we're coming!" A shuffle of feet approached the wall, and the door barely cracked open.

"Are you sure you want to come in? There are beauty treatments in progress, and you don't look like a man that appreciates beauty treatments."

He growled, and Kendra swung the door open wide. Standing side by side, small and smaller, he saw two barely recognizable forms covered from head to toe in mud, wrapped in dilapidated print terrycloth bathrobes. Rose waved, and crumbles of mud drizzled from her hands to the toes of his moccasin boots... *matching the mud already on the treads...*

Two big eyes blinked up at him from the smaller mud figure. "I'm going to be beautiful, just wait and see," Rose warbled. "Kendra is giving me a special, super-secret beauty mud treatment." A braid, entirely coated in sticky, gray ooze, flopped out from under a towel. Kendra grinned, and a chunk of mud fell off her face.

Well, this seems unduly... innocent. He eyed them suspiciously. *No questions from a curious Rose about the fire next door—that's because she already knows.* Flipping his notebook open, he wrote—

—I would like a word with you alone

From under her layer of mud, Rose murmured, " Oh yes, you certainly may. Kendra, may I have a moment alone with him please?"

Kendra muttered indignantly. "By all means, you big lug. Just barge in and demand time." She wrapped her robe tightly around herself. "I can't leave, I'm covered in beauty mud."

—park yourself over by the stove then

"Whatever. This is my safe room and my assignment, though, so don't forget it." She balanced herself in the small armless rocking chair near the wood stove and turned her face towards the fire. "Let me know when you two are done."

Turning to Rose, the Watcher could see an unease in her. Dressed in his work crew disguise, with a torn gabardine shirt and jeans, he looked more like the Watcher of Reunion than Special Agent Azarian. He pulled down his Nomex balaclava to let Rose see his face beneath the battered felt hat.

Seeing his familiar scars and scales, she perked up. "It really is you under there!" She laughed, and he felt a twinge of remorse at his suspicion; she seemed to be genuine, her smile matching her eyes... almost glad to see him?

Someone's lying—time to find out who. But first, a cover and a chance to get some business done—he went to his gear bag and pulled out one of the Supra-Warmeez UltraFoil Emergency Blankets. Handing it to her, he wrote a note.

> *—I need you to line your cape, hood, and moccasins with this foil—shiny side facing your skin. If you can scrounge up a pair of mittens, do the same with them. Do it, and it will hide you from the drones' infrared detection when we go back out into the WildLands. Tell the others you are lining them for warmth.*

She seemed disappointed. *Expecting something else?*

Sampson peeked in from around the corner "Sorry, Agent Azarian, but Agent Mansour is calling from upstairs—he says you've got five minutes, then you have to leave if you're going to finish this job."

What to say? So much going on—

Turning back to Rose, the Watcher hastily scribbled out a message:

> *—Thanks to our intel, we have confirmed your Father and Evangelo are at the jail. I am leaving to stake out the location and gather intel, perhaps pass a message.*

"You found them? Oh, Deva! Are they well? Did you see them?"

> *—Answer my questions, and I will tell you what you want to know.*

"Please tell me!" She cajoled, but he hardened his heart against her.

Taking a long look at Rose, he studied her face as well as he could beneath her layer of goo. He scrawled:

–Did you enjoy breakfast?

"Absolutely, it was wonderful to taste eggs again—and potatoes too. I'm just too nervous to eat much—what of Evangelo and Father? Are they okay? Are they scared?"

–I'll take care of them. Are you still hungry?

"Oh no, I couldn't eat another bite. But I'm not really hungry knowing they are in danger." She clutched at her stomach, and under all the mud the Watcher could not tell if she was being overly dramatic or was truly anxious. "Almost everybody I love is in danger. My Father, my sister Amelia, and poor Evangelo, too..." She looked up into his eyes: "But at least Oskar is safe for now."

Rose's face nearly crumpled, and that genuine angst almost tugged at his heartstrings—but it fell just short of a full pull, since the Watcher was irritated that he was left off her list yet again.

Fine.

Back to lies and truths—*time to test the tale.* Reaching into his pocket of his work-crew coat, the Watcher pulled out one of Sampson's lumpy orangey candies, holding it delicately between two thick, gloved fingers.

–I'm sorry, I brought you a homemade Sassafras Candy
from Sampson, the guard. It will help your stomach.

"Ooh how pretty! But my hands are all muddy—will you?" she opened her mouth, eager.

His chest was starting to feel tight again; distracted, he popped the sweet in her mouth and she tumbled it around with her tongue, "I like it! It's different..."

–so you never had one of these before?

"No—I would remember these. They are delightful!"

–that answers my question. What are you hiding?

A look of panic crept across Rose's face. "I'm not hiding anything—just mud under my robe." Her voice rose in pitch and caught the notice of Kendra. "There's nothing else under here..."

Kendra jumped up. "Time's up—she's got to wash it off right away, or her hair will be mud stained forever..."

Blocking the door, the Watcher wrote, then tossed his note to Kendra:

*—I get my question answered first. Someone is lying. What
are you two hiding from me?*

Hands on her hips, Kendra flew at him. "Gah! You're dense as a
brick!" Pointing a mud-crusted finger in his face, she railed. "Isn't it
obvious? We're hiding how she's been crying over you—but you don't
even care, you big blowhard..."

His jaw dropped.

"But you're oblivious! She ran after you squalling when you left, but I
tackled her in the mud and brought her back in. And you didn't even turn
around..."

"That's not what happened!"

Kendra waved a dismissive hand into Rose's face. "No wonder she's
always trying to get your attention—you didn't even look back!"

Rose's eyes flew open in shock. "Kendra how could you? I mean, no
—" flustered, she sputtered just like the fire—"that's not true at all and I
shan't stand for this foolery. I am not at all crying over this—" She
pointed at him, stomping her foot—"this Devil!"

Mouth a-gape, the Watcher stood flabbergasted, his train of thought
completely derailed.

Kendra swung for the bleachers. "Yes, you did. You cried and mooned
over him, saying he didn't want you—"

"But—but—"

"There you go—confession time." Kendra pointed at Rose, looking
properly disdainful. Rose bit her lip, sure that the truth was worse than the
lie itself.

Lifting the notepad, the Watcher tried but could not think; pencil to
pad, he could only tap the paper and stare blankly at Rose.

From behind the befuddled Watcher's back, Kendra and mouthed the
word to Rose: *NOW*...

A look of sudden understanding crossed a flustered Rose's face, and
she tugged on the sleeve of his bedraggled work coat. "Please, come
down here—I need to tell you something privately."

The Watcher bent down and without warning, Rose jumped up to hug
his neck. She whispered in his ear, wrapping her arms tight around him:
"Thank you, thank you for finding them! Oh, tell Father." She thought for

a moment. "Tell Father I love him. I always wanted to say that to Baba."

Love him? You just met him...

"You are absolutely wonderful—" pulling aside the edge of his knit hood, Rose planted an ardent, muddy kiss on his rough cheek.

Even through the mud, tendrils of warmth uncoiled from her soft lips and radiated down his neural pathways, rippling through him, blinding him with a brilliant flash of white Light, burning away all coherence...

He forgot everything he ever thought, all at once.

Then as quickly as she kissed him, Rose let go, and he found himself being pushed out the door by Kendra. "Goodbye and good luck—out you go."

The door slammed behind him, and Sampson stood by, looking on in pure sympathy. Still befuddled, the Watcher trudged up the stairs, not sure of what just happened.

At the top of the stairs, Mansour was waiting. He eyed the Watcher dubiously: "What got ahold of you?"

From the loft above, he heard Lourdes giggle, the Watcher looked down—little muddy handprints were smudged all over his broad chest. Cheeks coloring deeply, he was getting the oddest sensation creeping up through his entire being...

Sampson gave a knowing nod. "Well Hoss, it looks like you got what you came to get."

Mansour seemed all too familiar with the situation. "Brush yourself off, Watcher—we've got to get down to the Jail. We have new information and a new assignment—if you are finished checking up on the Afterling, we need to prep to leave after our stakeout. I'll brief you en route." He reached over and helpfully pulled the Watcher's balaclava back up and placed the hat back on his head, dusting the mud from his shoulders. The Watcher just stood there, blinking like an owl.

"Be careful," Sam whispered to Mansour as they passed by her post at the door—grasping his shoulder, she squeezed it. "Please." She struggled, wanting to say something intimate, but could not bring herself to say it not here.

Mansour nodded wordlessly and patted her hand, then strode out of the cabin with a blindsided Watcher in tow.

They made their way past the flaming wreckage of Boss Zhu's cabin. Mansour stopped to pick up a rake and hand it to the Watcher as a prop. "Did you find out if your Afterling left the safe room?"

The Watcher shook his head slightly, still dazed.

Mansour looked at him with a pitying resignation. "You didn't even get to ask the question, did you?"

Once again, the Watcher shook his head, as the light of reality peeked through to his befogged brain.

"They're covering for someone. Sam briefed me on new intel; according to a reliable anonymous report, Boss Zhu is dead, and Destiny is in Jail; two of Chartreaux's thugs, Harper and Dornak, interrupted Destiny's date with Zhu, kidnapped her, and murdered him. Our witnesses heard the thugs discussing the murder, the arson, and how to frame Destiny so they can hold her. Our witnesses also recovered this—"

Surreptitiously, Mansour handed Boss Zhu's mud-stained note to the Watcher, who read it quickly. "This is Destiny's alibi—written in Boss Zhu's own hand. Whoever snatched this note risked their lives to get it."

The Watcher stopped dead in the middle of the street, a slow burn starting to rise in him. The edges of the paper were stained, crusted... *Muddy—just like the Afterling.* He lifted it to his nose and closed his eyes—

The scent of her body infused the paper, the warm, fermented aroma of Rose on the run, top notes of joy mingling with base notes of fear...

He handed the note back to Mansour. Curling and uncurling his hands, cracking his knuckles and staring into the distance, questions were popping into his head. Without warning, the Watcher turned on his heel and stomped down the street towards the Hostess Club, rake still in hand. Mansour grabbed his shoulder and whispered low and quick:

"Hold up, Watcher. We already know it couldn't be them, you saw them in the basement, and you know they are safe." Mansour pulled the fuming Watcher to a stop. "There's no way those girls had enough time— we were only gone a little more than a half hour. Besides, Sam told me as much already—she wasn't forthcoming, but I used my manly wiles to get what I needed to know from her." Mansour gave a smug grin. "She all but said it was Herman; he's got a bad case of Kendra, and Destiny is Kendra's best friend. Herman would do anything to impress Kendra, and I think the girls are covering for him being gone."

The Watcher gave a skeptical look.

Red Flag Warning—each story was different.

Candies, crying Afterlings, and love-struck intel agents—was one, all, or none true?

The crying, muddy Afterling story made the most sense. It was certainly the most flattering. To think of Rose running behind him, calling for him was very appealing; it was also very dangerous for her to be out in public. But why the disparity in stories?

—Why is the note muddy, and why does it smell like Rose?

"Oh, Sam said they all passed the note around, cooing over it and being tragic. Araceli and Lourdes especially love that kind of stuff, all that tragi-romantic garbage makes them giddy."

Staring down the street at the Hostess Club's peeling green door, the Watcher wondered; *is that all she's hiding?*

"Look, you can deal with the Afterling later—she's in the safest place in Purgatory. We have friends and a Revolution to save. I've got to brief Winston about Chartreaux's treachery—the Director usually handles Winston, but we have no choice. I'll walk you up to the Jail to assign you some busy work on the grounds, and leave you to handle surveillance while I meet with Winston. But whether we complete our rescue operation or not—tonight, without fail, the Revolution starts."

Mouth set in a grim line, the Watcher reached into his shirt pocket and withdrew a green-gold folded washcloth. He carefully wiped Rose's still-damp muddy kiss from his cheek, then glanced down at the smear on the cloth—

All's fair in love and war—

then carefully tucked his prize away once more.

———•———

Closing the door behind Mansour and the Watcher, Sam dashed down the stairs; "Herman, what happened with Agent Azarian?"

"I don't know—he went in mad and came out stupefied." Sampson replied. "It seems to be catching around here."

He ate a candy, and offered one to Sam, and she willingly accepted. "You have a gift, Herman. You should make these more often."

Sampson gave a self-accepting nod of approval. "Good candy tastes like love."

Through the door, they could hear Rose whining: "But why did you tell him I was upset? That was supposed to be private."

Kendra answered: "Yeah, well, he was hot on the trail of figuring something out—I don't know how, but he's pretty good. He had to be stopped by any means necessary, and you were the means necessary."

"But you fed his already-overgrown ego with that preposterous story. Running after him crying? That's just humiliating. I'm a grown woman— why must you all infantilize me so?" Rose's high-pitched Central Texas twang was indignant.

"Because it's easy. You're little, you have a tendency to squeak, and you have big eyes. Plus, let's not forget who peed on the stairs."

"Those are genetic traits, not a character flaws—so please stop. And as for the whole tantrum in the street fabrication, that's not even believable."

"He totally believed it. Your reaction to the truth sealed the deal— you're scared he'll find out the truth."

"Well, that other part was a lie; I wouldn't ever do such a thing."

"Well, Azarian doesn't know that—and he bought the story hook, line, and sinker." Kendra mused. "But I figure this settles the question if he likes you or not."

"Oh, fiddle faddle, he doesn't like me. He didn't kiss me—I kissed him. And he said he wanted to talk to me alone, but he didn't even say wonderful things—he was just barking orders and trying to catch me in a lie," Rose tried to say it in a matter-of-fact voice, but she just came across as petty.

Kendra was not to be dissuaded. "One little peck on the cheek made him lose his mind. I count that as a win."

Having heard enough, Sam knocked on the door, and was answered in kind—she entered. "Did Agent Azarian find out anything?"

Kendra gave a satisfied smirk. "Nope; he started to nose around, but the Midget gave him a smooch on his scarred mug and he forgot which way was up. Nice going, Afterling..." Kendra gave a muddy thumbs up.

Looking the Afterling over, Sam offered, "You might make a decent intel officer—if you looked human and if you could just stop falling out each time something scares you. At least I know you're not afraid to lie."

"But I didn't lie—I just didn't answer the question." Rose seemed confused. "And I just gave him one little kiss on the cheek—I really didn't expect him to have that reaction. I mean, it seems odd that a kiss would make a man lose his entire thought process.... that never happened back home. Men don't usually want kisses, not on the cheek at least; kisses on the cheek are for babies and friends, not for acts of pleasure."

Kendra laughed. "That's because you're thinking like a Ho'. Come on, you mean to tell us that you've never been kissed by someone that desperately wanted just a kiss?"

"Well, no, I mean, none of my clients ever wanted just a kiss—they can have a whole menu of scintillating acts they can demand, so long as they are not taboo. Why would they want just a kiss?" Perplexed, Rose thought on her entire existence with men. "They want other things."

Kendra nodded to Sam. "Yup—she's one of us."

Sam grasped the teachable moment. "Afterling, wherever you're from, it's different out here. The few Survivors who love each other want and give kisses. That's still the currency for bonding—you give one, you get one. A kiss is still a sign of love." A bemused Sam instructed. "Agent Azarian became addled because he thought it meant you love him. You know—love. Right?"

"No, I guess I don't know love." Rose's eyes were averted, trying to hide her inner turmoil. "But I wasn't trying to mislead him—I really was glad when he told me they had found my Father, and it made me happy enough to kiss him."

"Don't let her fool you, Boss." Kendra drawled. "She wants it."

"Well, maybe I do, but that doesn't mean love for anybody. Besides, Kendra kissed Herman and it worked the same way. And she doesn't love him, does she?"

Kendra gasped, shocked at her sudden outing by the guileless Rose. "You little rat!"

"But I thought Sam knew you were kissing Herman!" Rose blanched.

"So I kissed the big Palooka—what of it? It don't mean anything to anyone but him."

"So that's what's been going on! No wonder you sneak past Sampson so easily—he lets you." Sam glanced at Kendra, clearly displeased. "I'll be changing your outside guard, then—you know you aren't supposed to fraternize."

Sam stuck her head into the basement and barked: "Specialist Sampson, get your gear and prepare to switch with Agent Walters to the Outside team. You are busted to Probationary for fraternizing with Kendra." Stony silence greeted her from around the corner. "I'd bust her again, but there is no lower rank." Without waiting for an answer, Sam slammed the door.

"We're a team—" Sam scolded. "You're playing with fire when you mess with your teammates' heads or hearts."

"Yeah, how's that working out for you and Mansour?" Kendra asked, flippant.

"That's none of your damn business." Sam hissed. "What I do off the books is not fraternization, it's sanctioned by the Director himself, and we have an Arrangement."

Kendra fumed.

"What's an Arrangement?" Rose asked, curious. Sam was genuinely surprised at her question.

"Say... where are you from, that they don't have Arrangements?" Sam pondered the Afterling—she had so many questions but had no Director to answer them—yet. *All the more reason to rescue him, pronto.* "They used to call it 'Marriage' in LifeBefore... two people would agree to be just with each other, because of love. Sometimes it would last their whole lives." Sam mulled it over. "Mansour and I agreed to an Arrangement, and the Director blessed it. We even had a little ceremony..." Sam's eyes became soft for a moment.

"Oh! You mean the Patriarchy?" Rose was mesmerized.

"No, it's not—" Sam spat at the idea.

"Yeah, it is, because Mansour wouldn't stay if she didn't have an Arrangement with just him. The jealous bastard couldn't take it—so Sam changed everything just so she could keep him on. Now, everybody but her has to pitch in, and Sam's the only one that doesn't have to meet with clients." Kendra confronted Sam.

"If you've got a problem with the way this organization is run, get out." Sam snapped. "I'll personally escort you to the exit if you don't shape up."

"Fine. FINE." Kendra rubbed her head and turned toward the wall. "Look, Sam... I can't help it—I just want something different. I want to quit the whole client merry-go-round. I'm just tired of it all, like Destiny. It's getting old." Kendra seemed suddenly deflated. "We're getting old."

Sam listened.

"The Cause was fun today—the intrigue, the adventure. But the grind of this whole racket—giving away sex just to buy someone else's freedom —I'm not sure I can take much more." Her shoulders sagged. "I know this ain't no LifeBefore fantasy world—the Happening ruined everything, including stupid crap like romance and happiness. All we've got left is us grinding away at each other's groins in exchange for a secure society. I understand it's that way all over the world now, except for the lucky few like you. But I need a break from reality..."

No one spoke while Kendra wrestled with stupid crap.

Finally, an elegant hand came to rest upon Kendra's shoulder. "Kendra, I've known you for fifty-one years. I don't blame you, but I promise you, tonight it will all change." Sam's face was alight. "The Revolution starts this evening, and I don't know what happens next, but our world won't ever be the same again. Just stick with me, and I guarantee you tomorrow will be a brand new day." She patted Kendra's back, a comforting, gentle tap. "And I need both you and Rose to make this happen—so stop screwing up."

Kendra rubbed her face and turned away from the wall. "Well, I guess we better get ready." She looked over at Rose and sighed. "You're gonna be a lot of work."

"Kendra, get this straightened up and gather your tools. You can clean yourself up after the Afterling is done." Sam held the door open—"Let's get you upstairs, Rose. Araceli and Lourdes are working on a disguise, and Kendra can make anyone look like they belong here. They're old hands at this." Still coated in drying mud, Rose followed Sam, the long tail of her bathrobe trailing behind her.

"Will it hurt?"

Sam smiled. "Maybe a little."

They headed around the corner, leaving Kendra grumbling in the safe room. She grabbed the broom, and swept up the clods of mud that festooned the floor. Sweeping it all completely out into the basement, she closed up the safe room behind her.

Sampson was stretched out on his cot by the door, hands linked behind his head, his too-long legs hanging off the end. Hat pulled down over his eyes, he appeared to be asleep. Now was her chance, before he got transferred out...

She crept over to the shelf where he kept his candy bowl. *Gone?* She approached the cot and picked up his hat, revealing a sullen frown.

"What do you want?" He was cold, distant.

"I want some of your candy."

"Well, maybe I don't want to give you any. It don't mean anything to you anyway." He grabbed his hat back and rolled over to face the wall. "Go eat someone else's candy."

"So, you eavesdrop on all my conversations?" Kendra asked. Sampson remained silent. "I didn't mean it, you big Palooka." Kendra poked him.

"Quit being a baby."

Sitting up abruptly, his feet hit the floor with a thud as he swung them out of bed.

The cot groaned as he perched on the edge, looking almost eye to eye with Kendra. Lantern-jawed beneath a rough, crinkled tan, his usually placid face was agitated. "You just gotta poke the bear, don't you, Kendra? You think I'm some kind of fool? You just got me busted in rank and transferred, and you don't give a damn..." Sampson stood up, his head nearly brushing the basement ceiling. "But I give a damn."

"C'mon, it was just talk." Kendra looked at him, face deadpan under her slimy gray mask. "I'm not going argue with you."

"You don't have to argue with me—if it means nothing to you, that's your right. But I don't have to give you my candy, neither." He gathered his gear, deliberate and steady. "I'm taking it with me while I go bust rocks with Mansour."

Kendra retorted: "What the hell has gotten into you, Herman? I'm a whore—that's it, that's all. None of it means anything." For a moment, the facade cracked and a tremor came into her voice.

Sampson slapped his bag down on his cot. "I don't let anybody talk that way about you—not even you. You take it back." He poked a sandpapery finger in her face. "You're not just a whore—you're living in this world here and now with all the rest of us, and you can't judge yourself based on what the world was back there and then. We're all forced into this, and we can't help what we've become—but what we give each other means something. What Destiny gave Zhu meant something, what you give me means something—" he was struggling contain himself: "I'm scrambling for the crumbs you throw me like you're some kind of goddess throwing away manna from Heaven... "

Normally so calm, so gentle, Sampson was now defiant, on fire: "You might be no goddess, but you're no whore, neither." He grabbed her mud-crusted shoulders— "It means something—it means something!"

His eyes were searching, searching for some sign of meaning in her; but Kendra was crushing her emotion down into the bottomless pit of her own bitterness.

Exasperated, he flung his hands off her shoulders and turned back to his gear. "Fine, it 'don't mean anything' to you. It can 'don't mean anything' while I go fight for the Revolution. Maybe it'll mean something to you then." Slinging his duffle bag across his broad back, he walked away, leaving a muddy Kendra bewildered in the basement, alone.

———•———

Down at the jail, a lonely figure was raking the grounds, searching for clues. Felt hat pulled low over a balaclava and a red bandana, he hummed tunelessly, raking piles of leaves and moving them into the muddy street to fill up the puddles near the walking path to the front door. Every so often, he bent down to pick up an item and placed it in a belt pouch...

Once, he leaned on his rake and stared back towards the Hostess Club, and the hazy column of smoke that hung over that end of the street. His face bore an expression of simultaneous wonder and skepticism, before being replaced by a look of pure determination.

Tell Father I love him...

Rose had finally given a quest to her Champion—and he was going to deliver.

Mansour had given him a briefing on the way to the Jail, under his breath, without stopping; get in, get the intel, make contact if possible, then get out to bring the info to the rest of the team at the Commons tonight, followed by a meeting with Unit Leaders for the recruitment. This would be a team effort, a major planning project, and if all went well, the Fenix would rise.

The Watcher surveilled his objective.

The new Jail was the pride of Purgatory; the construction of this spartan cinderblock edifice by Survivor work crews was lauded akin to the erection of the pyramids of Giza. This year was a turning point in LifeAfter history—no longer just living in cast-off houses of the Unhallowed Dead, Survivors had toiled together to construct something new, at great peril to themselves. Standing atop makeshift scaffolding, men labored day after day, lifting, pouring, hammering, chiseling—concrete was born of ash, sand, and quick lime; brick was salvaged from crumbling homes south of Purgatory. Rebar was scavenged and brought to the site from afar, and simple pulleys, forms, and cranes were constructed from timbers, blocks, and chain. Two men died when their scaffold collapsed; another lost his leg when his saw slipped—but the building still rose. Construction workers were hailed as Warriors of a new age, celebrated alongside Farmers and Tradesmen as proof of that civilization had survived along with the Survivors.

Of course, the cost in blood meant the Jail needed to be put to good use. Downstairs, blocky rooms housed a few meager municipal offices; most official business was still done at the Bosses' cabins. The rest of the downstairs were devoted to barren cells, each with a rebar window and a bucket for necessary business. Upstairs, holding cells for violent criminals were available, with shackles and chains for the most dangerous. These were considered to be overnight facilities, so accommodations were sparse, intended for short-term only.

For the most part, the cells were empty except for the weekends. But not today...

Channels cut into the small form-poured slabs allowed for overflow waste and blood to be rinsed out at the end of use, weeping down the sides through seep holes drilled through the wall at floor level. But a sour smell was already wafting out the windows—prisoners were in there, and no sanitation work had been done since last night. Sanitation was a major issue, handled by a few Public Servants or work crew personnel, and usually done as a punishment. *Nobody likes to haul waste,* the Watcher noted with distaste. He continued to rake and waited for a breakthrough.

He had found nothing of note so far—heard nothing except for the occasional burst of laughter from depraved men. It was calm for the moment. But according to the earlier report, it had been anything but calm during the two hours Boss Chartreaux had been here.

In the early-morning mist, Agent Goins heard muffled groans and soft sobs. A small, wiry Hombre who had been an oilfield driller in LifeBefore, Agent Goins had been left in place by Mansour, under cover of a work order to fix a clogged french drain beneath the Jail. Still on duty across the street, Goins told the Watcher that while he was on stakeout, he noted frequent laughter, a jeering catcall, and murmurs of shocked disgust from observers. Attempting to gain entry via subterfuge, he was turned away at the door. Goins also observed the Jailers at gunpoint being forced to accommodate the Rangers and deduced that Boss Chartreaux was now in charge of the Jail. It appeared the Jailers did not care for it at all.

Goins reported to Mansour: just after the fire started, Boss Chartreaux and four of his minions were seen leaving the premises with a large bag of equipment. When Winston, Mansour, and the Watcher responded to the fire, Goins observed Chartreaux's subsequent departure and quick closure of the top floor to even authorized personnel. This closure was unusual; Mansour determined to bring in an inside man.

From out of the corner of his eye, the Watcher saw a stranger approach the Jail: a heavy-set Macho with wide, blocky scales and keen, dark eyes approached the red metal door of the jail. A well-worn pair of discolored khaki dress pants was topped by a carefully preserved tweed sports jacket, still bearing its dignity even while worn with a stained t-shirt and ragged sneakers.

Without looking up, the Macho tapped the left brim of his gray fedora twice as he passed the Watcher. *The inside man.* The Watcher responded by giving two short scrapes of the rake in the leaves at his feet. The man approached the door, then gave three knocks, followed by a kick to the bottom of the door.

"Who goes there?"

"The way you get paid. Let me in, or the Bosses will hear about it."

The door opened. "We ain't receiving visitors today. Come back tomorrow."

From the back, a voice sounded the alarm—"Let him in—Habib works for all the Bosses, so let him in or face the consequences."

Another voice called through the door. "What's your business?"

"Purgatory bidness. Who is this?"

"Speak to Chartreaux."

"I will—and I'm gonna ask for your asses on a platter."

A flurry of voices in the back—

"Come on, man; what's your problem? We work for him, let him in..."

"No, I got orders. No one without Ranger pre-approval."

"Screw your orders—we live here. You can leave, we can't. Let him in..."

A squabble broke out, then at last a skinny hombre was shoved out the door—a public servant, his necklace chain tucked under his coat. Habib nodded to him. "Sanders? Go get word to Boss Chartreaux that if he wants the Jail to hold the merchandise this weekend, he has to let me in to get it ready."

Habib leaned in slightly and whispered into the man's ear, dropping something on the ground: the runner nodded and coughed, bending forward to pick up a scrap of paper. He then raced down the street towards Chartreaux's cabin. Habib paced back and forth, impatiently, glaring occasionally at the door. He came near the Watcher, and whispered:

"When he comes—" Habib turned and paced towards the door, away from the Watcher. Repeating his actions, he turned and made his way back.

"He will fall and fake injury—" pivoting on his heel once more, Habib paced back up the path, then towards the Watcher again:

"you'll take his place—" the scene repeated itself.

"Play dumb."

Habib kept pacing and the Watcher kept raking.

He made his way around the grounds, looking up at the second story—there were no ladder or gutters, as would normally be found on other multi-story buildings—in a world where death was a way of life, no one was worried about fire escapes. It appeared all windows on the top floor were covered from inside, perhaps by heavy blankets. Through the rebar windows on the north side, he could smell that sour smell, the stench of fear and sweat.

Torture. He grimaced inwardly, and kept raking.

The Watcher mapped it mentally—a central hall would likely be upstairs, and this smell was strongest on the back side of the Jail. The windows were too small to be accessed by any Survivor, and the rebar was impossible to cut without a grinder. Another method would have to be used if a jailbreak were to be attempted.

The Watcher heard the sound of running feet approaching. It was Sanders, returning with word from Boss Chartreaux. Habib raised his hat; the public servant suddenly slipped in the mud and fell to the ground.

"My leg! Ah! Ow!" Sanders groaned, clutching his knee. "It's twisted..."

Habib hammered on the door. "Come out—Chartreaux says to let me in. Ask my slacking lackey here... Get up man, you aren't hurt."

"No, Mr. Habib, I'm hurt! I think it's sprained." Sanders gritted his teeth and howled.

Now a Ranger peeked out the door at the commotion: the Watcher stood to the side, awaiting his cue.

Habib looked up: "What did Chartreaux say? Speak up, man—"

"He says let you in—ow!—here's the note." He held out a scrawled note, written in script, then went back to coddling his knee.

"It's from Chartreaux; now let me in." Habib flashed it at Shaney's Ranger.

"Lemme see that—the Hombre looked at the paper, and puzzled at the writing. "I can't read this—this hen scratch is terrible."

Habib spat. "Perhaps you'd like to tell Boss Chartreaux that—now let me the hell in this building, I've got work to do. But I need a laborer, and this old coot is obviously injured." He tapped the left brim of his hat again.

Goins scrambled up from his work crew to help Sanders, and the Watcher ran to help. He stumbled a bit, and grunted, dropping his rake.

"You," Habib called to the masked Watcher; "you big oaf—come with me; I've gotta fun job for you."

The Watcher scratched his head and stared blankly at the MoneyMan.

"Yes, you, simpleton. You'll be my assistant today. I'd bet you'd like that—now make it snappy."

Nodding, the Watcher dropped Sanders with a thud—who appropriately yowled—and lumbered forward towards Habib and the door. The Ranger at the door balked. "Hey, we said no unauthorized personnel. That includes the big dummy."

Habib crossed his arms—"Which one of you is going to take his place and dump out the latrines? Because if he doesn't do it, you will..."

Another cacophony of protesting voices filled the halls. One called from the offices: "Stop this crap, Carmine—I don't wanna do that job; let Habib's dummy do it."

Looking suspiciously at the Nomex-hooded Watcher, the Ranger at the door begrudgingly acquiesced. Patting him down around his waist, back, and chest, the Watcher received a cursory weapons inspection. "Fine —only him allowed upstairs, not you. Just don't let him talk to anybody. "

Habib laughed cruelly. "Look at him—I don't think that will be a problem...".

On cue, the Watcher grunted, then belched.

"Whatever. Keep your idiot in line."

Squeezing through the red door behind Habib, the Watcher found himself in a narrow hall with small rooms on either side. *Eight feet wide*—wide enough for a man with a guard on either side. The rooms were also eight feet, sectioned off into sixteen-foot sections. Rooms to the north side had narrow tables for official business, and the one nearest the door was filled with five Rangers drinking chicoffee. They glared as the hooded Watcher stumbled by. "What you lookin' at, you dope?" they jeered as he ambled past.

Bile rose in the Watcher's throat; he tamped down his rage and moved on.

The next room to the north contained three sullen Survivors with badges, obviously unhappy with the interference from Ranger outsiders. Atop a plastic bin in the corner, Dominic's blue-gray hat, his poncho, and gun lay in a pile with Evangelo's russet hat, army jacket, and gear. The Jailers seemed closed mouthed around the Rangers; they glanced up, nodded at Habib, then went back to their nervousness.

Noting the acknowledgments between the Jailers and Habib, the Ranger who the others called Danforth came out to monitor the situation from a chair at the end of the hallway.

Three mirrored rooms to the south were set up as cells with bench seats, buckets, and shackles, complete with square barred windows to each side of each door for jailers to view prisoners. All the downstairs cells were empty.

Habib motioned to the door at the end of the hallway: "That's the stairwell, Big Dummy. Next to it's my office; come in, and I'll tell you what to do next." He pulled a key from his pocket and unlocked the room, peering around a corner to make sure the coast was clear.

He locked the door behind them and pulled a thick curtain shut on the window. The room was more luxuriously appointed than the Watcher had expected—an antique writing desk was graced by a massive, slightly tilting Eames chair; a shabby brown and gold area rug made the whole set look almost rich. Lighting a kerosene lamp on the heavy oak desk, the MoneyMan nodded: "Proceed."

The Watcher stuck out his notepad, and scribbled:

—Azarian. Call me Watcher. Assignment?

The MoneyMan whispered "I'm Habib; I'm the Accountant for Purgatory, and a Bidnessman." He said the word the old Texas way, back when anybody doing Business in Texas needed to know how to do Bidness as well.

"I work for all five Bosses. I'm on board for the Cause, and I help hide outflow of goods and people. Boss Winston and Mansour advised me of your speech impediment and your credentials. Here's your equipment." Habib handed the Watcher two five-gallon buckets with their decrepit cleaning tools, a balding string mop, straw broom, and a rag. "Just keep up the simpleton act and head upstairs. I'll harangue the Rangers while they let you in and out, and I'll make sure to ask questions and cause trouble. My Jailers are unhappy—I can tell. They work with me on a regular basis.

I'll get them on our side."

Habib turned to the door and barked. "No no no—that's a mop, not a broom!" He paused then whispered to the Watcher again: "Get in there, clean up any messes just for show, and assess the prisoners. Then flash a note telling them we are aware and moving to break them out tomorrow night when we storm the jail with additional men. I will call you to my office one more time to noisily chew you out before we depart."

The Watcher nodded, then burned his last messages in the lamp's flame. Grabbing the rag bucket of full soapy water, an empty bucket, and a mop, he opened the door.

Habib snorted and shouted: "Quit lollygagging and dump those latrines. I don't have time to babysit you."

The Watcher grunted as he shambled to the stairwell door, fumbled with the round knob, dropped the bucket once, then bent down slowly to pick it up. He heard one of the Rangers snort derisively behind him.

The Watcher's eyes narrowed. How many times had he heard that mockery from citizens and prisoners alike at the Archway of Reunion Camp? How many times had his mutism triggered hate, humiliation, and abuse from someone just beyond the reach of his chain? At least he had strength, size, and wits. What kind of hell must it be to have neither strength, size, nor wits to defend oneself?

He felt a thrill of contempt for his tormentors. *Soon enough you'll know, jackasses—paybacks are hell.* He opened the door and clomped up the stairs, making the tight turn to a landing, then another turn before entering the landing at the top of the stairwell. Above him, he saw a padlocked rooftop hatch, but no ladder. Screw holes in the wall below the hatch indicated someone had removed a ladder recently. *A smart security move...*

Down in the hall below, the Watcher could hear Habib complaining loudly about the mess in the hallway.

As soon as he opened the stairwell door, the Watcher felt sick. He had a horror of torture, made more intense by his own experience as a prisoner. To see the chains, and to be so close to the cells made him feel physically ill. He damped down his nausea and moved through it. The cell nearest the door was empty, but he could hear the breaths of prisoners in the south center cell. Dreading what he might see, he bit his emotional bullet—

The door at the top of the stairwell slammed open behind him. "Get moving, crapsack. I don't like this job as much as you do." It was the stout Ranger, Carmine—the voice was impatient and overbearing. *How did these people ever become Rangers?* Evangelo had been so careful when letting the Watcher join in—going so far as to make him swear the Oath before he would even work with the Watcher. *Where did it all go so wrong?*

Lurching to the end of the hallway, the Watcher scanned the rest of the cells on the upper floor; except for the center cell to his north, all cell doors were open, so it was easy to check which rooms were occupied. Damp streaks marked the floor where someone had been dragged through vomit or urine and out of the now-empty cell closest to him. *Destiny?* He turned slowly towards the Ranger behind him, a stocky Hombre with shifty eyes and a careless attitude.

The Watcher looked in viewing window of the only occupied cell; there he saw a pair of stormy hazel-gray eyes glittering against the grim darkness of the cell—

Evangelo.

The little Captain, gagged, was dangling from shackles on the wall, his hands dark and swollen where the shackles had been clamped too tightly. His chiseled features were distorted by swellings and lacerations, but carried the light of a man lifted in angry prayer; evil had confronted Evangelo, and left him unbowed. He did not seem to recognize the Watcher beneath the mask...

Shackled next to him was the Director, head rolled forward as he drooled through a bandana onto a pile of blood and vomit at his feet. His swollen eyes indicated trauma at the hands of his enemies, and his clothes were ripped open.

A coldness overwhelmed the Watcher's soul—not a broad explosive heat, as his usual rage, but a pointed hatred as sharp and precise as the steel blade in his boot.

"Don't stand there and gawk; get out of the way, moron." Carmine shoved him aside, and pulled a tarnished key out of his badge pocket.

Behind the Ranger, the Watcher bent down as if picking up a bucket. The stout Hombre fitted the key into the padlock upon the door, but he could not finish the turn of the key—

An iron hand gripped Carmine's face from behind; hot breath prickled the back of his neck, then cold steel slit his throat... the Hombre tried to grab at the Watcher's hand, but the strength flowed from him; he tried to scream but only air bubbled through blood. Scrabbling weakly against the door, crimson rivers flowed down to the Hombre's hands, leaving great bloody streaks when he finally slid down to the floor.

Behind him, the Watcher loomed, almost clean except for the bloody Bowie knife and the hand that held it. He wiped his blade on the dead Ranger's pant leg, then pushed it back down into the sheath hidden in his boot.

With little effort the Watcher picked up the man and dragged him into the far cell, away from the staircase where it could be easily seen. Throwing Carmine onto the cell mattress to absorb the tell-tale blood, the Watcher searched pockets, but found no additional keys—*someone must have a set for the shackles. The Jailers...*

He took the holstered Colt 1911 from the Ranger and stuck it in his waistband at the small of his back, then retrieved the key from the lock.

He could see Evangelo trying to catch a glimpse of the action outside his cell, but the small rebar windows made it hard for the prisoner to catch any view. Putting his face to the window, the Watcher pulled down his mask, and put his finger to his lips. Evangelo eyes opened wide.

A dutiful employee, the Watcher then performed his sanitation duties, quickly swabbing down the blood from the door and hallway, rinsing it to run down the grooves cut channeling it into the weep holes. Within a minute, all trace of struggle was gone. He scribed a note and waited for Habib.

"Ya dumb brute—hurry it up!" It was Habib, checking in... the Watcher crept to the door, and cracked it open to pass the note.

> *—tell a Ranger I'm accidentally hung up in a shackle and must be freed. Tell him his friend asked for him to bring the shackle key.*

"What?' Habib hissed, "Where's the other Ranger?"

> *—change of plans.*

Habib blanched just a little under his bronzy scales and ducked back into the stairwell. Striding down the hallway, he stood near the Jailer's room, and barked to Shaney's Rangers—

"Hey! Danforth—your buddy says my idiot got hung up in a shackle —if you don't want me up there, go take him the key."

Grumbling, the Ranger in the chair called into lounge—"Leroy! Handle it."

A scrappy Hombre approached the head Jailer, who had a suspicious attitude and a trucker hat. "Gimme the damn keys—are all you Purgatory

Men this stupid?"

The Jailer held up the jingling ring, and Shaney's Ranger, a skinny pale hombre, yanked the keyring out of his hand. "There's gonna be some changes around here..." He stormed down the hallway and into the stairwell.

Coming out of the stairwell, he heard a confused grunt from the end of the mopped hall, from the room where the pink girl had been held. "Carmine, are you saying this stupid goof couldn't clean the room without getting trapped?..." Fumbling with the ring, he picked through keys as he walked towards the room, searching for the shackle key. As he rounded the doorway, he looked up—

In the dark cell, he saw Carmine lying on a bloody mattress. From behind, Leroy felt a hand upon his shoulder, and the dim awareness of something very wrong as a curtain of warm, sticky blood covered his chest. The hand propelled Leroy down upon the mattress, muffling his last scuffling movements, soaking up his life.

Once more, the Watcher wiped his hands and blade clean, this time using the soapy water left in the bucket. Tucking Leroy's snub-nosed .38 into his back pocket, the Watcher stripped off his own dripping work jacket so he would leave no bloody trail. He then retrieved the key ring with its selected key from Leroy's dying grip. Rounding the corner, the Watcher strode silently to the prisoner's cell door, fitting the door key into the door lock—it opened.

Evangelo's eyes lit up as the Watcher closed the gap. The selected key opened the rusty padlock on the wall, and the shackle swung free. First one hand, then the other; the swollen fingers, almost purple, were numb from lack of circulation. He tried to pull down his gag, but could not. The Watcher moved to free Evangelo's legs from their chains, then yanked the bloody bandana out of the Ranger's mouth.

"You're here!" He gasped under his breath, harried—"I prayed for help, and here you are..." The little Ranger was trembling with emotion. "The girl, Destiny... is she here?"

The Watcher shook his head.

Legs stiff, Evangelo ran to the Director, patting his face. The crusted eyes opened.

The Watcher tried the padlock on Dominic's shackles. Each padlock had the same key, made possible by innumerable raids on the various hardware stores over the last half-century; he was glad for lazy Jailers.

Dominic slumped against Evangelo. "Dios Mio—" he groaned.

Evangelo propped up the Director as the Watcher freed him from his shackles—"Keep silence. We're getting out of here, and we're going to save that girl."

The Watcher handed them each a gun.

Dominic stretched, then groaned softly. "Three Rangers left? And Boss Chartreaux's friends are on standby down the lane..." Dominic rubbed his head; his voice sounded shaky, breathless. "Gunfire will alert the entire Purgatory that a jailbreak is in progress, so a silent option is still the best option; we must get clear of here without them any the wiser if we are to escape and still meet with the Unit Leaders tonight." With a cleaning rag, Dominic wiped the dried blood from his eyes, and hugged his ribs again.

The Watcher put his finger to his lips again; downstairs, they could hear the sound of chairs scooting on concrete tiles, and voices rumbling:

"This is taking too damn long—come on, Perry, we're fixin' to put Habib's idiot out of his misery."

Habib grumbled—"You can't just go around killing my workers."

"We can do whatever we want."

An argument broke out between Rangers—

"Guys, wait—I didn't sign on to kill innocents. This is starting to feel bad…"

"Shut your yap, Gupta—we got orders from Shaney."

"I know, but... I thought we were just bringing Cap in for Commander Shaney. I thought we were just going to rough him up a little bit; but this whole thing... it's—"

"If you don't like it you can turn in your bars, just like Cap and the Director—and you can get the same treatment. Nobody walks away from the Rangers. What'll it be?"

A pause, then the sound of a chair scooting out again.

"Yeah, I thought so."

Evangelo grabbed the broom, gripping it as tightly as he could with his swollen hands. They could hear boots scuffling down the halls, making their way towards the stairwell. The Watcher motioned towards the empty cell near the door.

Dominic whispered: "You take that position, Compadre—let them see us here." He pulled the bandana back into his mouth.

Gritting his teeth against the pain of his broken ribs, Dominic grabbed the mop and twisted off the head, transforming it into a bo staff. Secreting it behind his back, he coolly propped himself back against his cell wall, arms up as if still in chains. He wiped his eyes on his sleeve to clear them, then let his head droop forward.

Evangelo followed suit, taking his place back in his original position with the broomstick behind his back; the Watcher took his position in the first empty cell, crouched behind the wall and below the viewing window.

Protesting, Habib grew louder. "This is Purgatory jail—not Boss Chartreaux's palace or Ranger Headquarters. All the bosses run this joint, not just him."

The Jailers' voices joined in, sullen, angry—the Watcher heard the sound of a pistol clearing leather, and a hammer cocking.

"We run this Jail now, and if you don't like it, die."

The stairwell door screeched, and footsteps echoed. The second-story door swung open; a loaded gun peeked through, followed by an arm; creaking open wider, one of Shaney's Rangers entered: "Leroy? Carmine?"

Two Rangers now came into view in the upstairs hall; they glanced at the rooms, then headed towards the prisoner's viewing windows. "Both of these traitors are still in the cell—"

The Rangers' heads slammed together as a massive fist grasped each man's collar from behind. The Watcher smashed them into the wall next, then fell on top of them, pinning their bodies beneath his own.

As the Watcher grappled with Danforth and Perry, Evangelo came flying through the cell door, his broomstick smashing down on Danforth's head, then kicked the gun away from Danforth's jerking fingers.

For a man with broken ribs, Dominic moved with surprising alacrity. Wielding the mop handle like golf club, he gave a savage swing to Perry's temple, rendering that man dead. But the scuffle did not go unnoticed downstairs...

Footsteps were bounding up the stairwell. The Watcher leapt into the cell nearest the door. Dominic followed—

Gupta shoved the door open to see a bruised and beaten Evangelo standing only steps away, bodies surrounding him, gun in his useless fingers.

"Cap... how the hell—"

The gun in Gupta's hands trembled. Leaping up from behind the cell window, Dominic's hands whipped out, reaching through the bars to wrench the weapon free from the Hombre's grip.

Silver metal flashed behind Gupta, one, twice, three times with lightning speed; a dagger pierced the Hombre's kidneys, lungs, and heart, and Gupta crumpled to the floor. Red-handed, a calm Habib stood in the stairwell behind him—and behind him, the three Jailers gaped, agog at the sight of their cantankerous MoneyMan turned stone-cold killer.

Habib turned to the slack-jawed Jailers behind him. "Do any of you got a problem with this?"

They all shook their heads.

"I thought not." Straightening his jacket, Habib flicked a chunk of flesh from this lapel.

Evangelo knelt next to the Ranger he once counted as a brother. "Cap... I—" Gupta gurgled. "Cap—" He grasped Evangelo's hand with slippery fingers.

"Gup, where did they take the girl? Tell me, and die with Honor..."

Gupta tried to talk; he desperately wanted to—but now, in the hour of his death, the words that could have redeemed him could no longer be spoken. Only bloody froth came out, until at last it trickled to a stop. Evangelo bowed his head.

Wiping the blood from his hands, Habib nodded to the Watcher. "Big Brute, you don't follow orders too well—but you are a straight-up gangster. I'm glad you are on our side."

The Watcher nodded back, stripping the Ranger's bodies of all guns and ammo. *Time to score some weaponry...* From the Rangers who died of blunt force trauma, he took their unstained clothing and gear; he took gun belts, holsters, and badges from all.

Habib glanced at the bloody mess in the hall. "Guys, get these bodies out of here. Put 'em in that back cell; tonight, they're going to take a little trip down to the alligators..."

The Jailers dragged the bodies to the end of the hallway, then scurried back, still dazed from the killings. Habib wiped a splatter of blood from his face, "Now scram downstairs and secure this building. Let no one in."

Eager feet trampled down the stairs again.

Still leaning against the wall, assembling himself, Dominic pointed to Habib: "Captain Evangelo, this is Agent Habib of the WildLand Express, Covert Operations Field Unit. Agent Azarian, you've already met."

Evangelo extended a swollen, purple paw; Habib grasped it gingerly and grunted, "Likewise, I'm sure."

Dominic called to the Watcher: "Agent Azarian—I'm most impressed by your performance here and am sure a fascinating story accompanies your sudden appearance. Write out your briefing, and while you are doing that, Agent Habib will apprise us of the details of the events at the Jail."

Speaking quietly, Habib washed his hands in the soapy water of the mop bucket. "It appears Boss Chartreaux is attempting a coup. Our Jailers on duty say they have been putting up with his goons and the Rangers since midnight. I received word of an 'incident' around five this morning from Agent Mansour and have been working with Boss Winston to notify the other Bosses. So far, the general consensus has been to see how this all plays out—Winston is on our side, no one can find Boss Zhu, his house has been burned, and now Bosses Waitie and Balogun don't want to rock the boat."

The Watcher handed the Director a terse note:

—Boss Zhu is dead. Murdered by Chartreaux's goons.

Dominic read the note as an epitaph.

"Damn." Habib's expression was regretful. "So, this is confirmed?"

—Intel agents overheard his thugs Harper and Dornak discussing the murder and arson.

The Director scrubbed the blood from his wounds, then grabbed one of the dead Ranger's clean, salvaged shirts; switching out, he took his own torn rags and began to wrap his broken ribs. Blisters marred the ebony scales where the cattle prod had lingered too long upon his chest and lower abdomen. The Visionary tattoo on Dominic's chest was barely visible—as he touched it in silent salute, Habib touched his left pectoral in acknowledgment, and continued to speak.

"There's some crazy stuff going on in The System—Chartreaux's reaching outside Purgatory, and there's rumors everywhere, things we haven't heard in years. I won't mention them here, but if the rumors are true..." Habib looked away.

"It will be clearer after tonight. Hold the fort here—send for your most trusted staffers, and tell them to bring extra supplies." Dominic motioned to the Watcher—"The Jail is now the Armory. It is time for us to prepare to outfit an Army. Arm yourselves and secure any additional guns and munitions brought to you—they will all be disbursed by tomorrow evening." Emptying the buckets, the Watcher filled them with salvaged gear.

Evangelo wrapped Dominic's bandages around his ribs and over his shoulder, then pinned it with one of the Scavenged Ranger badges, above his heart. "It seems fitting—the last time the Rangers were really the Rangers was when you were there." The little Ranger's eyes were alive with some undisclosed emotion. "I would wish you had never left us, but then, I would not be here now."

Odd, the Watcher noted. *Lose your girl, lose your way of life, and get tortured, all on the same day—and be glad of where you are?* Evangelo had Hope in his heart again... the Watcher determined to find out why.

Grunting with effort, Dominic tucked in his shirt and patted the younger man's shoulder. "Ay, Hijo. We are here now, all in God's good time, and for His purpose."

Anxious, Evangelo cleared his throat. "With all due respect, Director, God himself demands I act in His time. I must—" His eyes grew strange with wonder. "She saved me."

"So she did, Captain. Assemble a rescue team and lead it. Gather your intel from the Jailers in the next two minutes, and we will do as God bids."

The Watcher looked at the Director with surprise. He had never expected to hear a high-ranking Visionary talk that way; it was everything Visionaries had sought to destroy. But just like the virus that transmutated Survivors, some sort of spiritually infectious agent had mutated Dominic's Visionary ideological purity over the decades and it was now affecting the Director's behavior.

Observing the Director's obvious admiration for Evangelo, the Watcher had a hunch what that infectious agent might be.

The Goodness in Evangelo is spreading—and Dominic caught it. The Watcher made note for future reference. *This could be helpful.*

Habib led Evangelo downstairs, where the Jailers were already securing windows with storm windows made from previously fitted sheets of salvaged plywood. The Watcher heard Evangelo speaking in urgent, hushed tones to Habib, and wondered about the Ranger and this unknown woman. As they descended the stairs, the Watcher asked the Director:

—How did Specialist Rogers save Evangelo?

"She offered herself in his place for torture. When Chartreaux openly threatened to abuse Evangelo if we did not give up our secrets, Destiny took the bait—she unwisely, boldly offered herself and her own information, in Evangelo's stead. She could not bear to see him subjected to the depravities she herself has suffered from men."

The Watcher felt an unspeakable joy in knowing he killed Shaney's Rangers, and an unbearable sorrow that he had not yet killed Chartreaux.

Dominic pressed on. "Now Chartreaux knows what Destiny is willing to protect—innocence—the vile beast will use it to break her. Specialist Rogers is well meaning, and she may believe she can withstand his brutality; but she not psychologically prepared for Chartreaux's interrogation techniques." His eye twitched: "Chartreaux is a monster."

—Does she know Boss Zhu is dead?

"That is unclear." He stood, guarding his ribs. "We must make haste; it is time to rescue Destiny and put the next phase of our plan into effect. Come with me down to Habib's office."

The Director eased down the stairs. "Habib, Evangelo—meet us in the Office in five minutes. Bring all our gear from the Jailer's storage."

Alone, the Director entered, closed the door, and held out his hand to receive the Watcher's report:

> *—The Safe house was filled with Feathered Serpents; they are not a drunken myth as many have speculated. I destroyed them all and burned the safe house to the ground.*

> *—Seeking the source of the Feathered Serpents, we made our way to the nearest forbidden zone site, and located an air station seventeen miles to the east of this location, inside the Burning Mine boundaries. Feathered Serpents may be used as a lethal deterrent in the landing zone to discourage exploration; they escaped and have infested the countryside. Other secret sites may be found if Feathered Serpents are located nearby.*

> *—A Boone & Hainey HeliScram Gazelle landed and released a swarm package of ALGOS drones at that location at approximately 18:14 hours.*

> *—We retreated to a remote location closer to Purgatory's physical, electrical, and infrared interference to confuse the ALGOS, and came within range to receive an encrypted distress call on the secured server at approximately 5:30*

hours.

—The Chupacabra has learned to use available technology to communicate.

—The Package is secured in the predetermined location.

—You and Evangelo have been rescued, as per the Package's request.

—Specialist Rogers' rescue now in progress.

—The Package sends the message: "Tell Father I love him. I always wanted to say that to Baba."

The Director read quickly, his eyes lingering on the last line of the message. "For the sake of Rose's message, I wish I could save this, but..." he folded the note, then held it over the flame of the Kerosene lamp, allowing it to burn to ash. He leaned back and chuckled quietly. "Feathered Serpents and talking Chupacabras, eh? And they are but a few of her creations. Ay yi yi..." he shook his head.

"Saisha, Saisha, my little plum, what extraordinary terrors you have released upon the WildLands! And I'm not even including your most terrifying, adorable Creation..." he clicked his tongue. "But this news of the ALGOS—this is very dangerous. I don't know which Generales has sent them—James, or Jarrod. We must avoid them at all costs."

—I am addressing those concerns. I believe they are using infrared. A full-body ultrafoil cloak liner is in the works.

"Excellent forethought. You're remarkably well-educated about ALGOS, Azarian—especially considering you never made Visionary Rank. Soon, we must discuss your past and how you came to know so much about these classified drones." Dominic searched the Watcher's eyes. "We must discuss that, among other things. Something is changing inside you."

Giving a curt nod, the Watcher pondered his completed quest, and his thoughts turned to how he would claim his prize. Dominic opened the office door and motioned to his cohorts down the hall.

"Destiny—her name is Destiny—" Evangelo swept through the door with Habib, eager to start a rescue mission. "Destiny was removed from the Jail to an undisclosed location less than an hour ago, encased in a large duffle bag. Boss Chartreaux himself has taken her, and that means his movements should lead us to her."

"Agents are already tailing him," Habib noted, locking the door behind him. "Agent Goins sent for Agent Walters from Boss Winston's work crew, asking him to tail Chartreaux, and once we have that information, we should be able to strike quickly."

"Excellent work, Agent Habib." Dominic smiled with genuine approval. The stout Habib bobbed his head in gratitude for the acknowledgment.

Dominic and Evangelo gathered their gear and reassembled themselves; they took the Ranger's hats, and Evangelo took a new shirt as well. The Watcher held up a blue bandana:

> *—I believe this is their method for identifying their group. Specialist Qin said a blue bandana was waved to signal your ambush from the gate, and all the rangers here have been spotted with these blue bandanas. Take one to hide your faces.*

Due to Purgatory's strict gun control measures, only their side arms had been allowed with them on "badge waiver," but their pistols were as dear and welcome as any bazooka or flamethrower could have ever been.

"With God as my witness, Director, I swear will never rush into a situation again without my gun drawn," the little Captain said earnestly.

The entire group grunted in approval, and the Watcher pointed to the holstered Colt 1911. Agent—now Quartermaster—Habib nodded, and the Watcher threaded the gun onto his belt, concealing it beneath his loose shirttail.

Dominic mulled over their options. "While in public, we will escort Agent Azarian as if returning him to the Public Servant bunkhouse."

He turned to Habib, who was sorting through the gear with a knowledgeable hand: "Agent Habib, your orders: you will stay here to prepare the Armory and keep Boss Chartreaux at bay. Please have a jailer quietly ask Agent Goins to dispatch a runner for Mansour and Boss Winston, and tell them to rendezvous down by the docks discreetly— meet us in ten minutes, and bring fishing gear as cover."

Planning ahead, Evangelo asked, "The Jailers say one of Chartreaux's agents is outside, in view of our door. Are we fighting our way out or disguising ourselves?"

"Neither." The Director gave a serene smile and pushed the antique desk to the side. It rolled smoothly away from the corner rug on its well-oiled brass casters, and Habib flipped the rug back from the four-foot by four-foot concrete floor slabs. Pushing his boot heel down on the lower left corner of the slab centered beneath the rug, the Director popped up the upper right corner, revealing a hollowed out, lightweight cover. Habib hooked his fingers under it to slid the slab aside and reveal a three-foot by three-foot passage into darkness. With a flourish, Habib tipped his fedora and offered the lantern from the desk.

Pleased, The Director took the kerosene lantern and lowered himself into the secret corridor.

"I prefer a more stealthy option."

* * *

"Agent Walters, could you please get Sam for us?" Araceli cajoled their new door guard from around the corner, batting her eyes.

"Keep your wiles to yourself, Woman, I refuse to be affected by you." Agent Walters said bluntly, "I should be working the fire or investigating Destiny's disappearance but instead—thanks to Herman getting hornswoggled—I'm running this daycare while other men do real jobs." The stout Macho turned his back to the door, disgruntled.

"Ah, Araceli, see? We are not all fools." Jorge mused in the corner while sharpening his knife. He pointed to Walters. "Cheer up, Vato. You get to take a vacation, and Herman gets to see the sights. He's been stationed down in this basement too long anyways. It was time for him to take a rotation, and you were next on the list for a break." Dragging the blade across the back of his arm to test it, the fine edge of Jorge's blade shaved back a curl of keratinous mahogany scale. Jorge nodded in approval. "Go up and take Sam's duty at the front door, and I will take your place down here temporarily while you monitor the situation outside."

"Mucho Obligado, Mercedes." Walters grabbed his shotgun and headed towards the stairs. "I owe you."

Peering through the door, Araceli tried her hand again: "Jorge, please —may I check upstairs to see if we have new word on Destiny?"

Agent Mercedes turned away from Araceli's dark, pleading eyes. "No, little Bruja., Herman has been sent to join Agent Goins in the search, and they should have a lead soon. I will tell you as soon as they return." He turned gruff again. "Now go, and do not ask me again, for I can't bear the way you look at me when I tell you no."

Shutting the door to the safe room, Araceli pouted. "You have ruined it for us all, Kendra—how are we to roam freely without Herman to be your fool?"

Kendra bit her lip and said nothing, but kept spraying her subject with insta-tan through scraps of lace netting.

"Besides, Agent—Specialist, er, Sampson is going to be out there looking for Destiny, since he switched posts with Walters. Aren't you even a little bit scared for him, or at least sorry you got him in trouble, Kendra?" Araceli demanded some sort of emotive repentance.

Kendra refused to repent. "No. If he brings Destiny back, I'll personally apologize to him. Several times."

"You should at least feel guilty. We have no candy now." Araceli's eyes filled with tears.

The secret knock confirmed their visitor, and Sam opened the door. "How is our Guest's disguise coming?"

Lourdes swept a flourishing hand towards the love seat. "Come in. Try not to stare."

The Afterling was perched on a sofa cushion, surrounded by bits and bobs of Kendra' scavenged beauty products. A ridiculously long, pointed stocking cap—crocheted from a nubby boucle yarn of black, gold and brown—completely covered her hair and hung down to the small of her back. The floppy pointed crown terminated in a big black pouf of fluffy curls where the ringleted ends of her braid was pulled through to secure it, imitating a faux fur pom-pom. Dramatic, dark eyebrows and the remains of her forehead's scar were hidden beneath the fluffy black edging. Ear flaps allowed the hat to be tied under the chin in a bow, with pom-poms dangling from yarn braids.

"Her hair is her biggest giveaway, so we hid it under this specially crocheted tube cap—it can't come off accidentally, because I slicked back her hair into a long pony-braid and pulled the end of the braid through a hole at the bottom of the tube." Kendra tugged on the big pom-pom at the tip of conical hat, and the Afterling yelped.

"Ow! Hey—"

A fine tracery of orangey-brown lines covered her face, a temporary tattoo. Swirling patterns of varying thicknesses spread delicately down her straight, soft nose and fanned out around her wide-set, tilted eyes and across her forehead, and her smooth, soft lips tinted the same dark pumpkin color. Random overlaid patterns traced along her rounded, bare arms, across her décolleté, and down to the tips of her vermilion-stained fingers. The patterns trailing across her legs resembled burnt-sienna lace stockings, covering even the soft soles of her feet and the tips of her small rounded toes.

"Due to the fact that the Midget was covered in peach fuzz, her skin was harder to modify—" Kendra pointed to a pile of scavenged disposable razors next to the Afterling. "But thanks to Lourdes' obsession with shaving the pills off her old sweaters, we had the necessary tools."

Rose was indignant. "I have been fighting my way through the WildLands, and I haven't had time to defuzz my legs." She looked slightly uncomfortable. "Or anything else." She picked up several of the razors and tucked them into the gear bag at her feet.

"Well, the peach fuzz is gone now, and you no longer look disgusting." Kendra remarked. Araceli and Lourdes made approving hums.

"It wasn't disgusting, it was just... fuzz." Rose demurred. "It proves girls are all grown up, so I don't see how it can be such a bad thing. But for the record, we are forced to defuzz at Tesoro, too. Most clients demand it—it still gets tiresome."

"Well, tiresome or not, your fuzz interfered with your skin mods, so it had to go. Fortunately for you, my stash of Soo-Doe premium spray-on tans and canned tattoos has survived for over fifty years, and now is the perfect time to use them. This will last for around three weeks, as long as you don't use any petroleum products on your skin, so make it last. No DubbDee-40."

"Why on earth would I put that on my skin?" Rose was appalled.

"Silly Afterling, DubbDee-40 is good for skin. Destiny has to use a lot of it—her fuzzy pink skin is so very susceptible to dryness." Araceli's eyes welled up again. "I still have Destiny's can... I borrowed it from her accidentally last week while she was not looking, and now I am so very sorry." A single, perfect tear rolled down her soft cheek.

Frustrated, Kendra put down her tools. "Sam, let us look for Destiny. I'm begging you—I can't stand it anymore."

"Be patient... " Confidential, Sam whispered: "I'm waiting for one last word of her location. If I think there's a chance you girls can spring her out, I'll come up with a plan, and we'll all get her. Just give Agents Sampson and Goins a chance to see if they can pin down the last details, and I'll make it happen. We'll roll it covert, under cover of darkness tonight." Sam's eyes grew hard. "Nobody messes with my girls."

Kendra jumped up and hugged Sam.

"That's what I wanna hear!" Kendra seemed to have new life in her actions—"You heard the Boss Lady—let's get this done. We have a rescue to plan!"

The room became visibly cheerier. Lourdes clapped her slender hands: "Stand, Afterling."

Rose stood and dutifully twirled—she was used to costumers and stage managers. Pale green eyes glimmering, Lourdes addressed her captive audience. "As you all know, each of our Ladies has their own unique stage persona, thanks to the House of Lourdes Couture." Here, she pointed to each with dramatic effect:

"Sam—the Hot Huntress. Kendra—the Boyish Boheme. Araceli—the Delicate Diva. Destiny—the Girlish Gamine. And I, of course, am Lourdes—the Sultry Siren." She was entranced with her own creativity. "Now I have taken inspiration from the Afterling's rustic deerskin cloak to transform the Afterling into the latest creation from the House of Lour —" Lourdes picked it up, and it crinkled. "Is this a foil lining?" Shocked, she blurted, "Why?"

"Agent Azarian made me line it with a Supra-Warmeez UltraFoil Emergency Blanket for warmth. But it won't spoil the look if it remains hidden..."

"No, it is hideous. It ruins the look." Disgusted, she held it away. "Just knowing that ugly lining is there makes me nauseous." She flipped the cloak over; "I will tack one of my old cotton sheets to the inside and cut it to fit—that will hide the foil, and still allow you to have it lined if the Agent insists. But that seems so odd... even in the hood?" Lourdes scowled. "Araceli, go get that old sheet from the storage closet next to the door guard's cot."

Araceli scurried out, eager to respond to the Afterling's fashion disaster. After a few moments, she returned bearing the sheet in question —a light brown leaf print—and tossed it down next to the cloak.

"Now, if we have no more disastrous surprises..." Lourdes clapped her hands again. "I present to you the Afterling's persona—Deer Girl!"

Araceli clapped enthusiastically. Sam thought about it, and Kendra was busy.

"Deer Girl?" Rose was disappointed. "That seems rather un-sensual.

Why would anyone want to be with a woman who looks like a deer?"

Lourdes was hurt. "But you are the Spirit of the Wild! The Prize of the Hunter, the Song of the Moon..." Genuinely indignant, Lourdes continued, "Some people consider Her to be very powerful. Besides, beggars can't be choosers. I'm working with what I've got here."

"I'm so sorry, Lourdes, I truly am—I didn't mean to appear ungrateful; I'm sure it will be absolutely stunning," Rose apologized. "It's just that I was expecting an alliterative name. Everybody else has one."

Lourdes waved her hand dismissively. "You are a temporary Guest. All amazing alliterative names are saved for full-time Hostesses."

Rose moped.

Lourdes turned her critical eye to the Afterling's apparel. Rose's voluptuous figure demanded a soft, draping fabric, and her small stature required something short. Once again, cast off men's wear was enlisted, and a sleeveless men's t-shirt was up-cycled. Doe-skin leather thongs tied up the shoulders, lending some detail and structure, but without a defined waist Rose looked more like a potato than a deer.

All business, Lourdes studied the Afterling. "What is this?" She fingered the choker tied around the Afterling's neck—a pale yellow ribbon threaded through a silver chain and tied in a bow around her slender neck. "This doesn't go with your outfit. Get rid of it." She started to untie it—

"No! Don't—" Rose clutched the choker's bow. "The Watcher made it for me—it's my Brother's broken chain."

"You have a brother?" Sam was curious.

Downcast, Rose brushed it with her fingers. "Yes, a beautiful, wonderful boy named Joseph. He was enslaved with this chain, and the Watcher broke it away as a memento for me after Joseph was killed."

Araceli's lip trembled; Lourdes put a hand to her heart. "I'm so, so sorry! I had no idea—"

Kendra eyed the ribbon choker: "So the Watcher made you jewelry? Why do you keep telling me he doesn't want you?"

"Oh, there was nothing romantic about it at all. The Watcher said he made it to represent a contract between us. I'm supposed to always wear it to remember our agreement to follow him, trust him, and tell him; it commemorates our shared fight for Freedom."

"Well, I think that's romantic." Interest piqued, Sam interjected: "That sure sounds like you've got some kind of Arrangement between the two of you... did he give you a Ring? Or a kiss? Or a ceremony?"

"Oh no, just a handshake and a promise to follow the rules." Slightly alarmed at the thought of being roped into a Devil Arrangement, Rose paled. "That's all..."

Sam seemed disappointed.

"So be it: it is a sacred piece of jewelry. Still, we will cover it with a wide beaded collar instead to make it look less out of place..." Lourdes motioned to Araceli: "Find suitable brooches; gather the shirt to accent her tiny waist, and drape it toga-style to make a short shift. Then pull down the neckline of her shirt and gather it with a smaller brooch between her breasts to highlight her cleavage."

Dumping out her cigar box, Araceli beamed as a trove of glittering jewelry cascaded from it: gemstones and glass, precious metals, and dross, the desired objects of centuries made beautiful by the tarnish from their owners' touches. "I found these, alone and unloved. Now they are mine," she cooed and plucked out an amethyst brooch with a loving hand. "But this is my favorite of all—it was given to me by my lover, my dashing Cal—"

"Oh, for the love of—" exasperated, Lourdes frowned at her partner. "Stop it, Araceli. You found that at the dump. Winston never gave you that, he never gave you anything but heartache."

"That's not true—Cal gave me my freedom." Hurt, Araceli caressed the amethyst brooch. "But if he had ever given me anything else, he would have given me this wondrous treasure." She sighed and placed it back in the box, safe among her baubles.

Sympathetic, the Afterling remembered a similar heartache of her own, but she said nothing.

The little dark-eyed Hembra shook off her melancholy and rifled through her plundered goodies, then cooed. "This is exactly what Rose's dress wants!" Gathering the waist to the side with a silver crescent moon, Araceli created magic, and Rose morphed from dumpy to desirable.

Araceli hummed again, and chose a bewitching silver Celtic love-knot with a polished bead of hazel wood set at its center. Pinning it to the Afterling's shift, Araceli created the perfect plunging neckline, and the alchemy of accessorization was instantaneous—Rose's figure was transfigured.

"Enchanting!" Pleased with the Afterling's transformation, Lourdes smiled. "Those should certainly attract some attention."

"Are these rare?" Rose looked down at her fully rounded breasts, perplexed. "Every one of my sisters back home has ones like these—we feed babies with them."

"Babies? You mean, like real babies?" Lourdes asked, shocked. The entire room fell silent.

She hadn't considered what these Devil women would think of babies.

"Well, yes, I mean, that's how I got these... I was... I was..." Rose couldn't get past her training. *It's forbidden, forbidden to call it what it is*; she took a deep breath. "They come with the Project."

"Wait—" Kendra put two and two together. "Project—you mean... pregnant?"

Flustered, Rose put her hands up:"Shhhh! No, don't say it—we don't call it that! It's forbidden!"

"Holy crap, are you saying the Watcher made you pregnant?" Kendra grabbed hold of Sam's hand—"She told me earlier; I just didn't know what she meant!"

"Don't—don't say it..." terrified of the meaning of the word, the Afterling begged, distressed. "We aren't allowed to say it!"

Sam took Rose's hand.

"There's nothing wrong with calling it what it is." She looked at this small person before her, so afraid to acknowledge Life. "There's no shame in it. Call it what it is... with Child."

"The Church Fathers won't let us say it." Rose shook her head, almost in tears. "They don't want us to think of it as a baby. No one is supposed to know there's a child in there. But we all know... we know." She threw her hands up over her eyes. "The Watcher made one with me, but I lost it before it could implant."

"My God," Sam blinked; "the Watcher actually conceived a human being..."

Head down, Rose wondered: *my Devil-Baby was a human being?* She had imagined it with a tiny scaly face, red like its father; but to think of it as human made her feel guilty for doubting its humanity.

Leaning forward, Sam whispered to Rose; "Does the Watcher know?"

Still hiding her face, Rose nodded.

Stunned, the small group of women sat quietly for a while, until at last Sam gave her orders. "We won't talk of it anymore if it bothers you. But never be ashamed. It was a miracle—"

Spontaneously, Rose hugged Sam, and held on until at last Sam peeled her off. "But we still have to find a way to disguise you. Your breasts are rare out here in the WildLands."

Shaking off her shock, Lourdes got back to work; "Yes, very rare—

although a few breasts that big still exist in the WildLands, they are plastic. From a distance, though, it's hard to tell the difference, so you can explain them away. Your derriere, however…" Looking the Afterling up and down, Lourdes sighed. "Many clients will highly approve; but it is a dead giveaway that you are not from LifeAfter. You will just have to be a plump little autumn doe, and not a graceful spring gazelle."

"Yeah, she's got a booty." Kendra quipped. "And thighs."

Roused from her sorrow by body critiques, Rose protested. "May I at least wear my leggings? I will freeze out there."

"You are supposed to be a distraction—so show your legs." Sam was firm. "In order to do this job, we'll all be suiting up for tomorrow evening. You'll get more attention this way, and that will pull a crowd's eyes away from our field operatives. We just have to make sure your escape route is clear… once all the recruits have been armed, distractions will no longer be needed."

"But what about one of you? If I'm so odd looking, perhaps someone else might be better at distracting…"

"Trust us, we'll be distracting. And deadly…" Sam smiled to herself. "But you will be distracting, too. Listen, I know it's a challenge; you have a lot of shortcomings, it's true…"

Rose was amused at the pun.

"But you have some great assets, and they overcome any challenges. You are definitely a throwback, a real Chica—we haven't had one of those around here in years, and that will get some fast attention. When you walk out, all eyes will be on you."

Once more, Sam admonished the group: "Don't let anyone know what we're up to… Agent Mansour is diverting Agent Azarian to locate the Director and the Captain, and he will be rolled immediately to the Commons to recruit for the Revolution tonight. Afterling—if Agent Azarian shows up, just keep the lights off, pretend to be asleep, and we'll hurry him out. I'm pretty sure Agent Azarian will not approve this mission for you, Rose, and he is right—no combat missions, so you must stay here tonight."

Rose was downcast.

"But I think Agent Azarian will enjoy the show tomorrow night—enough he might forgive you if you let him." Sam looked into the Afterling's eyes. "Can you handle the pressure of being in front of a large crowd??"

"Oh, absolutely! The stage is not scary at all." Rose effused. "It is one of my great loves."

"Well, this might be a boisterous crowd. Kendra will be your handler tomorrow night, and she'll pull you if it gets rough." Sam snapped her fingers. "Araceli, Lourdes—finish up. We have to get upstairs to plan for Destiny's rescue tonight and get our gear together for tomorrow night— Kendra, you too."

"Just a few more minutes please: the color of the shirt, it is not the best." Lourdes studied it: "The dark brown compliments her dark golden skin base tone—but she needs contrast—" She pointed to Kendra. "The Afterling's lashes are showing, but we can disguise them at a distance..."

Lourdes called for the sacred relic. "Bring out the Black Charpeez Marker, and give her the eyes of a Deer."

A plastic shoebox was brought forth, and a white pen with a black lid was extracted from its reliquary. Excited to be using the ever-lasting Charpeez, Kendra flipped off the plastic lid of the pen, and a powerful odor of marker ink filled the room.

Rose's eyes watered. "Are you sure this is safe?"

"Beauty hurts, so suck it up, Buttercup." Kendra offered.

"Well, keep that garbage away from me." Sam scoffed. "But I will take one of your lip balms, if you don't mind—and this chunky necklace from Araceli's treasure chest." Her long, dusky fingers caressed a heavy silver chain then plucked a plastic tube from the pile of Kendra's goodies.

"Take it." Kendra waved, dismissive: she was busy creating a masterpiece. "Don't bother the Artist at work..." Rose sighed and tried not to let her lashes flicker as Kendra applied the Charpeez to her eyelids.

Beauty hurts.

———◆———

Waves lapped at the shore of the mid-day docks at the lake; the five-hundred-foot wide, circular cove had a narrow inlet barricaded by one hundred feet of decaying boardwalk-turned-wall, which extended to border the entire peninsula and its town, shutting out the rest of the alligator-infested lake. This rickety ruin still lived, thanks to penta and creosote coated timbers.

Cans and bottles bobbed lazily in the rippling waves, and some lily pads graced the cove, adding a peaceful serenity to the littered shoreline. Beneath the rustling cottonwood trees, a brown pelican preened upon a broken-down post at the end of the dock; it cocked its head, then flew off into the sky as two men approached from separate sides of the cove.

Mansour looked around, carrying his fishing gear; Usually, this time of day would see all manner of men crowding the docks, fishing for a bite of lunch, but all available men were at working the fire. Approaching the dock from the left, he nodded across the dock to a now-helmetless Boss Winston, who had draped himself in a shapeless coat and slouch hat to hide his identity from a distance. Sitting down on his helmet next to the shore, Winston took out a short coil of string and a hook from his pocket, then threaded a piece of jerky onto the line. He lowered it down into a crawdad chimney by his feet. Casually picking up an old can, Winston tossed it at a rusting hulk of a rowboat that was wedged up underneath a dry patch under the dock. Mansour likewise picked up a pebble, and chucked it at the rowboat. The sound of the two thrown objects made a rapid 'tap-tap' sound against the rusted metal.

The rowboat shifted slowly, and was pushed to the side by unseen hands. Two men dressed in Rangers' white shirts and hats emerged from beneath it—a lean, graceful Hombre and an athletic smaller one, with blue bandanas obscuring their haggard faces—followed by a broad-shouldered, hulking Macho decked out in a face hood and work gear. The men quickly dusted off and crouched down in the sand under the dock.

Hidden from prying eyes beneath the dock, the Director was visible to Mansour and Winston; he nodded to them, and whispered. "Welcome, Gentlemen."

Mansour sucked in a breath: "How the hell did you escape? You looked like you have tomatoes for eyes, Dominic. Not trying to be rude, but this was not the plan—still, I'm game. Are there twenty men after you this time?"

"Thank you for your concern. Agent Azarian became excited, and now all of the Rangers are dead." Dominic grimaced in pain as he crouched. "Of course, the Captain and I helped dispatch three of the five, but Azarian got the bloodbath kicked off to a rollicking start. All silently, with no gunfire. Agent Habib and his Jailers are now in control of the Jail, and the Jail is now a temporary Armory for the Revolucion. We have not yet been discovered, but that may change presently, so I should hurry with this briefing, gentlemen. Mansour, do you have a report?"

"Just... damn, Watcher. " Mansour marveled and pointed to Winston: "Boss Winston has been informed of Boss Zhu's death, and we are waiting for word from Agent Walters regarding Boss Chartreaux's whereabouts. Walters has been recalled to Sam for administrative duty, and a replacement is supposed to check in with Agent Goins for duty to locate Specialist Rogers."

The Director offered his gathered intelligence:

"With the death of Judge Leona two weeks ago, Boss Chartreaux sensed a power vacuum in the System, and he intends to take over Purgatory and become a leader of the Survivor factions in the Tejas Co-op. He is forging a New Leadership Alliance with Commander Shaney's Rangers, in exchange for personnel and firepower. To seal the deal, Shaney seeks a high-value Package that Evangelo and I secured for the Cause, and Chartreaux agreed to help her recover us and that Package."

The Director grasped his ribs, grunted, then continued: "Chartreaux also wants to end the WildLand Express' influence at Purgatory. Shaney and Chartreaux both want information from Evangelo and me, and they used Destiny to lure us into a trap. With the WildLand Express out of their way, they plan to force key Purgatory Denizens and Bosses into a hostile takeover, by holding preferred System rewards hostage. This includes liquor, drugs, gambling, food, and Hostesses."

"I figured Chartreaux was up to no good." Mansour spat and threaded a ball of stale bread onto a hook.

Dominic grunted. "Chartreaux plans to take the Hostesses hostage, then he can force Purgatory to capitulate to his New Alliance."

"Let the bastard try." Mansour plunked his hook into the water.

"Word and trusted reinforcements must be sent to Agent Ellison at once for her to harden security." Boss Winston chimed in. He had a strangely compelling civilian command presence, a blunt charisma that was both populist and elitist, a privileged man of the people who practiced power with a benevolent hand. "Murder, corruption and intrigue —just another day at Purgatory." Boss Winston muttered through gritted teeth, white beneath his soot-stained, armored carapace. "But it's time to clean house."

Winston tugged on his pocket line, and something tugged back. "Waitie is holding back—he's the true neutral in this drama. Balogun is tightly aligned with Higher Powers we won't name here, and he is hell-bent on Purgatory remaining loyal. He won't make any deals that cut us out of the System." He reeled the line in; "But Sam and her team are in enormous danger if Chartreaux is moving to take them under his control. Like most of Leadership, he doesn't know Sam's status as Fallen, and he definitely doesn't count her as his equal. To him, Sam is just an uppity Hostess, and he will treat her as such."

Giving an evil look, Mansour stood to go, suddenly anxious. He packed his fishing gear and prepared to head back to the Hostess Club. "Let him say that to my face—I'll chop him up and use him for bait."

Winston gave Mansour a sympathetic glance. "Nobody knows you're with her, Lazarus—as far as Purgatory's concerned, you're just another one of the Damned, living from day to day, hungry for your piece of the pie." A crawdad dangled from the piece of jerky at the end of Winston's line, and he flicked it off. "I'm gonna head back that way to investigate the remains of Boss Zhu's cabin, and set—" He stopped, held up his hand and listened. It sounded so faint at first, far away in the clearing rain...

Bells?

The alarm bells were ringing. Rippling towards them, first one, then the next as the alarm spread from station to station, a voice calling with each bell:

"Fire! Fire at Hizzoner's House! Fire at the Hostess Club!"

"No. NO—" Horror fell upon Boss Winston: "The fire was under control! Captain Swain was just relieved, and I left Captain Corey in place as Incident Commander..." The tall Hombre threw down his coat and grabbed his helmet, running up the hill to HighTown.

It hit Mansour out of the blue: "Oh God—Corey works for Boss Chartreaux's brigade."

All of them running now, they could see it as they topped the ridge above the docks—a billowing column of black smoke rising into the overcast sky, looming above luxury cabins of HighTown. Sprinting between the ramshackle shacks of LowTown, they made their way through the streets, past the Porta-Johnnies—LowTown was abandoned, with everyone running towards the fire, except for two men running towards the docks.

They saw a giant of a man bounding towards them, bellowing: "Mansour! The Girls—" Sampson caught his breath as they approached. "Sam sent me away to report to Goins, and we heard you were out this way..."

Agent Goins ran up behind and grabbed him by the arm, running fast: "I heard it from witnesses: Boss Chartreaux's Brigade has them— Sam, Araceli and Lourdes were seen being forcibly evacuated from the cabin. His thugs committed arson to make a kidnapping look like a rescue

—but now it's lit up Hizzoner Norris' house and he's still inside..."

"But the witness saw Kendra, too?" Sampson blinked. "Right?"

Mansour put his hand over his eyes: "Jorge? And Bob?"

Goins continued. "Agents Mercedes and Walters are not accounted for—and no one has seen Kendra or the Package."

Winston ran on, headed through the Commons.

Dominic pulled his bandana away from his face to take a breath: "Agents Goins, Sampson—head to the scene with Mansour and Azarian. Look for the Sign."

Breathless, Sampson nodded.

Dominic continued: "Evangelo and I will tail Boss Winston to the Commons—a crowd should already be there. Rendezvous at the Jailhouse afterwards." He pulled his bandana back up across his face, disguised once again.

"Let's go—" Mansour turned to grab the Watcher, but he was already running like the wind, heading for the Hostess Club.

———◆———

IV

Through the acrid black haze, the Watcher ran back up the street, then cut through an open yard, taking cover in the overgrown hedges. He ducked through a back alley and into the lane running behind the cabins, Mansour hot on his tail. Boss Zhu's house had completely collapsed, embers glowing, with clusters of fire here and there. Next to it was Hizzoner's house, fully engulfed, with a few of Boss Chartreaux's brigade standing, watching it burn—

Beside it blazed an inferno that was once the Hostess Club. The Watcher was thundering towards the conflagration as Chartreaux's brigade ran to intercept him. A fireman called out: "Hey buddy you're not supposed to be here—this is our scene. You've got no business here!"

Scanning the yard, Mansour saw it first. He grabbed the scrappy little driller beside him: "Goins—it's up! The Sign... let's get these thugs busy; Azarian and Sampson will go in and assess."

Goins and Mansour ran up into the yard, noisy and rough. Mansour shouted at Chartreaux's fire crew to draw their attention: "Where are they, you bastards—where are the Girls?"

With a bound, he jumped Captain Corey; Chartreaux's brigade jumped to tackle Mansour. Goins leapt into the middle of the brawl, yelling obscenities, and the rest of the Chartreaux's crew on scene ran to join the fray.

With Mansour and Goins on the ground, fighting, the coast was clear.

Everything became strangely sharp, each little detail etched in three-dimensional clarity upon the Watcher's mind. He was moving in slow-motion towards the fire with his heart in his throat. Flames were shooting up through the roof, roaring out the windows, burning through the walls —but there was no sign of anyone, anywhere. He tore a path around to the back of the cabin, but it seemed to him as if he was bound by invisible chains, slow and weak; he couldn't move fast enough.

The cedar elm next to the back loft window was one giant candle, lit from the ground up. No one could have possibly escaped the house that way. The loft window was open, a tongue of fire streaming from it, licking skyward.

Make entry—how to get in? Is she hiding? Is she waiting for rescue? He couldn't smell her—but he did smell another, more terrifying odor: the unmistakable stench of human flesh, burning. The outside world shrunk to a pinpoint dot in his mind, and he sorted his way through the information. *Someone is dead inside this burning house.*

Someone is dead. The Watcher's mind shut down.

Unimpeded by the brawling fire crew, Sampson was close behind. He circled, out of sight of the fire crew, searching for any signs of information, but neither man could get close to the cabin—the flames were too intense.

"Kendra knows the drill..." Sampson whispered with a desperate hopefulness. "She knows the procedure. If she wasn't with Sam and the others, then she has to be with the Package in the tunnel. We've practiced this drill a thousand times, she knows..." His eyes were searching the side yard of the Hostess club, where a small flower garden lay in shambles, trampled by fire crews; above it, a small red crocheted flag hung limply dangling from a small flagpole. Sampson saw it, and a grin of pure joy burst forth: "The Sign!" He looked beside him for the Watcher, to show him—

The Watcher was not there; he was moving toward the brawling mass of arms and legs on the ground next to Hizzoner's house. Crouching low, he sprung to the outside of the pile, and yanked a flailing Hombre out. With a deadly grip, the Watcher whipped the unfortunate Hombre around as a pit bull would whip a rat, gripping the Brigades-Man by his trachea and choking off all air. Dragging him towards the burning tree, the Watcher held the Hombre out at arm's length, towards the flames:

He pulled down his hood, exposing a face from hell—a slashed skull covered in sharp red-gold slabs of skin. Canines flashing, eyes blazing, the Watcher barked as the stub of his tongue strained to make words:

Tell me where she is—

A guttural snarl burst forth from his scarred crimson jaws. Frustrated, the Watcher snapped his teeth within inches of the Hombre's face.

Tell me where she IS—only a mangled howl wrestled its way out.

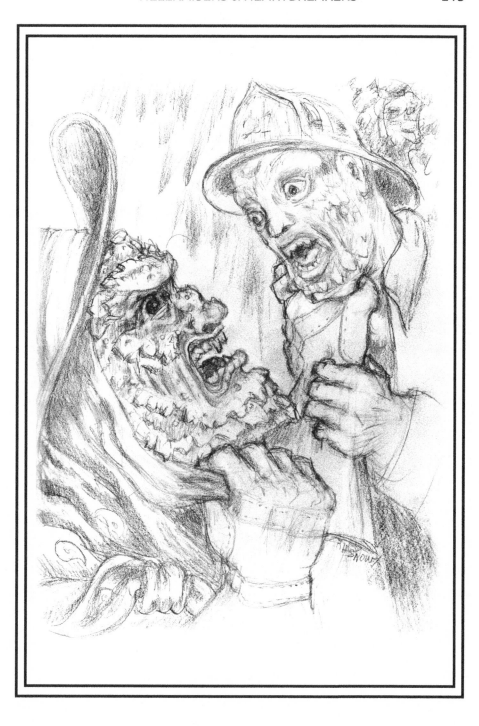

Saul tried to speak, but the Watcher could not. The Hombre's clothing started to smoke; he was trying to scream, but nothing came out—neither man could make the words they needed to speak. In a rage, The Watcher smashed the Hombre's face with his fist, flinging the now-senseless body to the ground. He turned towards the fire...

"Whoa Hoss, wait—" Sampson grabbed the Watcher's shoulder and whispered. "The Sign, I saw the Sign—they're in the tunnel! We gotta go —we gotta get to them."

The Watcher turned in a flash, gripping Sampson's wrist; his eyes only showed brutality.

Sampson recoiled. "The flag—it's red! It's a Sign from down below... it means a Guest is in the tunnel." Sampson struggled to reach the Watcher through his bloodlust. "The Package..." Seeing a flicker of recognition, Sampson tried again. "Your Girl."

My Girl...

My Girl?

Somewhere in Saul Azarian's distant past, The Person Who Had Just Completed Sensitivity Training knew that one should not refer to someone as "Girl" unless one was certain that the person in question wished to be called Girl, and one certainly didn't refer to said Girl as "My Girl" because one certainly shouldn't be a possessive, toxic Patriarchist. However, that past no longer existed, and all the people who insisted Saul Azarian take Sensitivity Training were now dead. In the end, all the Watcher could remember was some sweet song from far away, about Sunshine and a Cloudy Day...

My Girl.

For a moment, the Watcher's bloodlust dipped just a hair, and his expression went from rage to just almost rage. Sampson jumped at chance to stop him.

"Your Girl's in the tunnel." Sampson blew out a hard breath, relieved; he felt a bitter pang and wanted to call Kendra his Girl, too... but he didn't. It didn't mean anything to anyone but him. The Watcher was trying to focus; his hands began to shake, so slightly Sampson almost did not notice.

My Girl...

"Mansour and Goins are keeping the goons busy—we have to get down below. Stay low and follow me."

———◆———

Dominic, Evangelo, and Winston were running towards the huge crowd gathered in the Commons. Five blocks down from the scene of the fire, a group of men in fire gear stood in the street, blocking their path. A deep, bass voice bellowed orders:

"... and stay away from this dangerous scene."

From afar, they could hear Boss Chartreaux at the Commons Pavilion, holding an antique cheerleading megaphone in one hand and a rifle in the other. He was flanked by two Hombres, one short, heavily muscled, and serious, and the other a slender, tall man of elegant features. Key Brigade members were surrounding them as Chartreaux spoke to the amassed, grumbling crowd:

"This is an affront to Purgatory—Winston has failed in his duties, and he is no longer trustworthy as a Boss. Boss Waitie—" he pointed to the shorter Hombre, "and Boss Balogun," he pointed to the taller one—"both reluctantly agree an investigation should be launched into Winston's failure to act."

Attempting to barrel through the line, Winston was pushed back by a line of Boss Waitie's and Boss Balogun's men.

Winston exploded: "Don't tell me I can't enter my own scene! I have jurisdiction—where are the Girls, you son-of-a-bitch?"

A murmur washed over the crowd.

"Like all of Purgatory Public Works, they are no longer under your jurisdiction." Chartreaux's smooth patois floated above his audience, raining contempt. "This is my scene, and your Girls are my Girls now, Winston. It's true that you were in command of both elements, but you have been relieved of your duties."

The audience grumbled. "When your Captain released Incident Command to mine, Corey dismissed all other brigades from the scene. It is being secured as the scene of a crime, so you're not in command anymore."

Chartreaux gave a disdainful look. "The other Bosses are with me, Winston—this scene is now an arson investigation, and under the command of my brigade."

"Bullshit!" Winston bellowed to the crowd. "This fire was in mop-up stage when I left it to your Captain, and now you say it has jumped to two neighboring houses?"

Chartreaux sneered. "The fire must not have been under control then, Winston. Where were you? Out busy with other business perhaps? You were... negligent."

"You're a liar. This is arson, and your goons are at fault!"

"You are wrong. Men of Purgatory," Chartreaux's basso voice intoned through the megaphone; "A terrible tragedy has struck our home, and what started as a single structure fire has engulfed three cabins due to the malfeasance of Boss Winston. Our hearts are grieved over the loss of two of our own, Hizzoner the Mayor Bradley Norris, and Boss Jack Zhu, both killed in this senseless arson. Worse, more bodies may be in the burning ruins. The fire was started by a heartless runaway—Hostess Destiny Rogers—and the lack of a Hostess Oversight Board is clearly to blame."

The audience grumbled at this news. Runaways were highly despised, as it was unseemly for Public Servants to not acknowledge their duty to share their bodily goods with society.

"These are lies!" Pushing through the crowd, Winston yelled: "You are the arsonist—not Destiny; this will not stand!"

Chartreaux ignored him. "Nonetheless, we can all be grateful that the men of my Fire Brigade are now in command and were there to save some of our other beloved Hostesses; they are currently resting in a safe location, away from the stress of this terrible scene."

Winston gritted his teeth and gripped his halligan tighter.

"Now Purgatory must build a new Hostess Club, one with more controls to avoid such unpleasantness as runaway arsonists. We must choose leaders who will keep Purgatory and our Hostesses safe from such happenings ever again. In order to ensure that directive, I will keep the Hostesses under my watchful care at Pair'O'Dice Pier. And of course, my personal pick, the exquisite Araceli is among them." Chartreaux smirked. "But I'm certain that she means nothing to you—Cal."

"Like Hell!" Livid, Winston roared as he plowed through the line, waving his arm above his head—"Winston Brigade, follow me!"

Headed for the stage, Winston leapt into the thick of the line, and Captain Swain surged behind him. Fists flew, knocking Winston's white helmet to the ground. In a rage, Boss Winston wheeled a haymaker into the crowd, and the scene disintegrated into utter mayhem. Balogun's and Waitie's Brigades-Men joined the fracas, eager to defend the honor of their beloved Brigades. Men grappled, shouts rose, and all the firefighters jumped in—

A shot was fired into the air, then they heard the sound of a rifle bolt racking again. Boss Balogun stood with a rifle in hand, his features distorted with disgust. "Order will be restored, or death will be dealt." The crowd became silent.

One of Boss Winston's Brigades-Men retrieved his white helmet, and plunked it firmly upon the Boss' head.

"Men of Purgatory" Boss Chartreaux intoned: "We are free." The mob became silent as Chartreaux invoked the rallying cry of Purgatory Men: "Free to DRINK—" The mob listened. "Free to TOKE—" some of the mob began to chant with him now. "Free to gamble, RICH or BROKE—"

"Free to BANG and free to STROKE! Nothing stops Purgatory Folk!"

The mob shouted it, and the streets reverberated with the sound of their cry.

"But we are not free to live outside the rules of Society. We have a System, and all must submit to it. Clearly, there are those who do not appreciate our way of life here, and they only wish to destroy our access to our cherished freedoms. Drink, Toke, Rich or Broke, Bang, and Stroke —we are the Men of Purgatory, and we will not be denied!"

Cheers erupted, and hats waved in the crowd.

"These incorrigibles must be re-integrated into society. At this terrible time in Purgatory history, with the death of Boss Zhu and Hizzoner, we need to embrace strong Leadership on behalf of Purgatory Values—and Bosses Waitie and Balogun stand ready to support my Leadership. Here is a token of our esteem, and incentive for those already submitting to the System of Fairness..."

Boss Chartreaux motioned to his men, and from a nearby hand-cart, wooden crates were unloaded. The crowd murmured with approval at the sight of a highly respected name: Johnson Plantation Premium BudWeed.

"We now fairly redistribute these precious resources to you."

Chartreaux cracked open a crate, and pulled forth an enormous paper cigarette. Lighting it, he puffed then blew it out, holding it in the air to let the fragrance drift out across the crowd. The crowd cheered. "Boss Waitie, Boss Balogun and I offer incentives for you to return to your peaceful lives, and let us deal with the issues of Boss Winston and the Hostesses." Chartreaux waved the BudWeed in the air, then handed it to his Lieutenant, who clenched it between his teeth to take a long drag on the cigarette. Holding it in, an expression of pure indulgence washed over his face before letting the smoke curl out from between his lips, scrollwork litanies of artificial happiness.

The Lieutenant coughed and leaned over. "That's some good BudWeed!"

The men whooped.

"Thanks to an informant, we found these crates of contraband in a secret room beneath the basement of the Hostess Club, along with other items. These wayward Girls were illegally stockpiling BudWeed and Liquor, hoarding treasures of the Co-op to themselves, rather than allowing your Bosses to redistribute it fairly among the deserving Denizens of Purgatory."

"Wait—how could you find the contraband and take it out of the Hostess Club if the Cabin was already on fire?" Winston demanded.

"Pitiful." Shaking his head in disapproval, Chartreaux rebuked Winston to the crowd: "Denizens of Purgatory—don't let Winston's conspiracy theories rob you of your rightful access to this illicit contraband. He only wants it for himself." The men booed Winston.

Chartreaux's sorrowing voice spread across the gathered audience like a cloud of poisonous gas:

"But that is not all these Hostesses were hiding... The Hostesses were also hiding a new girl from you." A gasp, and a thrill rippled through the mob. The Director and Evangelo glanced at each other, guarded. "Not content to merely deny her own services to the Men of Purgatory, Madame Sam also denied another girl to you—a Chica, small and golden."

A voice shouted from the back: "Harper saw her! He said so this morning—he saw her with Kendra, hiding at Hizzoner's house!"

A shout went up from a brigade man: "Unfair! Unfair!" It caught, jumping from man to man, lighting them with anger:

"Unfair!"

A clearly saddened Chartreaux mourned to Purgatory: "The denial of services by Madame Sam to the Denizens of Purgatory are clearly in violation of our System of equal access for all. Boss Winston may have turned a blind eye to such corruption, but under my leadership, this blatant resource inequity will no longer be tolerated. Madame Sam's mismanagement of public trust may be repaid by her community service. Under the New Leadership Alliance, I will ensure access to the services of not just one, but two additional Hostesses for Purgatory—the incomparable Sam, and this new Chica."

Other voices rose in a wave of surprise and hope—new Hostesses meant new relationships, and less of a wait between appointments. Boss Chartreaux held up a cautioning hand:

"Alas, this Chica is missing, along with another Hostess, the misguided and naughty Kendra. In response, a reward is being offered for the safe return of Kendra and the Golden Chica—one months' ration of BudWeed and Liquor, plus a stack of tokens for tomorrow night's Big Three Gaming Tables. But that is not all—"

He held up a small repurposed prescription bottle, the old label peeled away and replaced with a duct tape label. "The Stuff—one month's ration, with a set of re-treaded syringes and washed needles."

Yelps of desire rumbled up from the crowd. Boss Chartreaux held up the megaphone again.

"But for all those who do not recover our mischievous Kendra and her little Companion, we still offer free incentives for your peaceful compliance. Their things are now our things... that is only fair." He smiled benevolently, white smoke wreathing his head in a hazy halo of promised bliss. "These are the New Leadership Alliances' gifts to you, if you wish to receive them: BudWeed, Liquor, and Hostesses—all you have to do is help us seize Winston."

Purgatory inhaled its collective breath.

Incredulous, Winston looked at the crowd: men who had fought alongside him just moments before were now moving towards him with a hunger in their eyes. Holding his hands out, he reasoned with the mob: "Guys, come on—I'm the one who distributed an entire crate of Reunion's Best at our last brigade meeting..."

Captain Swain advanced: "Yeah Boss—but what have you done for us lately?"

"That was just last week!" Winston said, backing away.

"Well, that's too long..." Captain Swain waved his hand: "Get 'im, boys!"

Mass hysteria descended as every man piled atop the Hombre formerly known as Boss Winston. A raging sea of concupiscence and gluttony washed over Winston, and he sank under it; his white helmet was seen briefly above fists before disappearing beneath a wave of inflamed Survivors.

Dominic whispered to Evangelo: "Grab him now, before they tear him apart!"

A sharp crack was heard as a swinging two-by-four hit Winston's head, and the white helmet flew through the air to land next to the stage. Boss Chartreaux inspected it, then solemnly placed it on his own head.

Then two shots, and the sea spontaneously parted.

Boss Chartreaux saw two masked Rangers, easily identifiable in their stained white hats, shirts, and blue bandanas. They were laying hands on Winston, shouting and brandishing weapons to hold off the crowd.

"Get back, he's ours!" Jumping the bloody Winston, one Ranger tied his hands with another blue bandana, while the other Ranger held off the howling mob. "It's off to the Jail you go, Winston!" the smaller one said, with a rather dramatic effect. "BudWeed for all!"

They hauled Winston off the ground, and walked him through the hooting crowd towards the Jail. Empty bottles and old batteries were thrown as clapping followed his departure.

From his power position beneath the pavilion at the Commons, Boss Chartreaux's eyes narrowed. Something seemed amiss; the Rangers had not been called in, and they should be at the Jail, watching the prisoners. He clenched his teeth and took his Lieutenant by the collar:

"Go follow the Rangers, and report back to me. I want assurances."

Watching the panoply unfold, Boss Balogun became nervous. He leaned into Boss Waitie and whispered: "Are we sure this Alliance is what we want? Chartreaux is already power-mad. This change may draw unwanted attention from unwanted eyes..."

"Look at these animals." Boss Waitie gave a subtle nod. "Chartreaux is nowhere near as dangerous as these ferals. Keep them quiet, or we lose everything—that's the deal."

"Welcome to the New Alliance, Men of Purgatory—" Waving the white Blunt of Peace, Boss Chartreaux held up the BudWeed cigarette for all to see, and he smiled:

"The line forms on the right."

•———◆———•

"Hey! Take it easy—" Winston snapped to the two Rangers hauling him not-so-gently down to the jail.

"Apologies, Amigo," Dominic said under his breath "We are being followed, and a show of force is in order." Evangelo glanced back over his shoulder:

"The Brigades-Man is still tailing us. Struggle some, Winston..."

Obliging, Winston tried to wrest free, and Evangelo knocked him in the head, perhaps a little too hard.

"Ow—watch it!"

They turned between the shacks of LowTown, taking a right at the Porta-Johnnies and down the narrow, twisting paths. Overhead, the rain was clearing, and stiff winds were starting to blow the smoke clear from the streets; the norther was coming through, and temperatures were dropping.

Angry, Winston shivered and muttered to his escorts: "Humidity is tanking—you can feel the air being sucked dry, and now the winds will rise. These idiots better watch that scene, or it'll catch more than those cabins alight. Boss Chartreaux's damn lucky everything is damp from this morning, or he wouldn't have a town left to tyrannize."

They turned a tight corner and came into the open, grassy area surrounding the Jail.

"Did you know this used to be a dump?" Winston grumbled. "I was the one that proposed this project in the first place. I was the one who led the combined Brigades to clean up that festering hellhole, and now look at it—it's a monument to Survivor ingenuity and determination. And what did they do?" Incensed, Winston flung his head back to rail at the Brigades-Man behind them, almost wrenching free. "You betrayed me, you ingrates—" His brassy scales flushed pink along their edges, lending his honest, blunt face a choleric cast.

Evangelo pulled his hat low. "Move along!" It was a very convincing show; they dragged him up to the jail, and gave the knock—three raps and a kick.

Dour, the head Jailer peered out the sliding hatch on the wood door and spied Boss Winston with the Ranger imposters. Dominic pulled down his bandana and whispered, "Tell Habib we have a guest."

The hatch slapped shut, then Habib showed up. Dominic whispered the passphrase: "Fenix Creciente"...

Habib muttered "We Will Be Free," and opened wide the door. They hurried in, leaving their observer behind. "Howdy, Boss. I see you're not happy."

"That's because I'm not Boss anymore." The imposters let go his arms, and Winston twisted his hands free of their half-hearted restraints. "The bastards abandoned me for Boss Chartreaux, all for the promise of BudWeed and Bitches."

"Fortune is a fickle mistress." Habib said flatly, looking out the back window of his office to watch their observer heading back to the Commons with a report for Boss Chartreaux. "It appears you have an admirer."

"Yes, I hope we provided convincing entertainment." Wincing, Dominic reached under his shirt to adjust his rib wrap. He sat down, temporarily winded. "I know I was convinced."

"Not as convinced as me. Who is this kid who keeps smacking me around?" Winston rubbed the back of his head. He missed his helmet.

"My regrets, good sir, I am Captain Evangelo, of..." he paused. He was a Ranger, but they were no longer him. He did not know who he was anymore.

Winston shook his hand. "I'm Boss... I mean..." He stopped, not sure of who he was, either. "I'm Winston."

Habib was impatient. "If we are done with all the finery here, may I ask what's going on?"

"Boss Chartreaux has made his move, and I'm out." Winston frowned. "My own men sold me down the river for the promise of free toke and some tail."

"My own men did the same." Evangelo was staring at the hat in his hand, unsure about anything anymore. "The Apple of my Eye offered them a bite, and my own Brothers cast me out of Eden." He put his hat back on. "And now they are dead."

Both men reflected on their lot; one brooding and silent, the other fuming and muttering.

"Loyalty don't come cheap," Habib said with nod, then leaned in confidentially to Winston. "But you can bet 'the Family back home' ain't gonna be happy."

The tall Hombre gritted his teeth; "They'll be hearing from me."

The Jailers stood to the side, watching the drama unfold, shaking their heads at the state of unrest. Habib called them over.

"Howard—whattaya got for me?"

The Head Jailer, Howard, stepped up: "We got inquiries. People asking things. We shut them down and told them to mind their own beeswax."

Habib snorted. "Yeah, you keep doing that. Keep them dangling outside, and refer all questions to me. If someone offers you something, let me know. I'll beat the offer."

"You're a straight up guy." Howard tipped his trucker hat.

"Time is running out." Winston pushed into their discussion. "Hizzoner Norris is dead, probably by the hand of an assassin, just like Boss Zhu; they thought Kendra and a mysterious golden Chica were hiding at his house. Now Norris' cabin and the Hostess Club is on fire, and they blame my negligence. Araceli and Lourdes have been kidnapped, and Boss Chartreaux's men have taken them to an unknown location."

"Sam..." A shadow crossed Habib's face. "The mobs were howling earlier. Packs of wolves, headed to LowTown..." he thought for a moment. "I might have a lead for you."

The three Jailers showed up in the office doorway, rapping upon the frame: "We've got company outside: Boss Chartreaux's Brigades-Men are here to make a deposit."

Habib muttered to his Jailers: "Let in prisoners only. Howard—get to the front door and hold them; DeRita, Fine—stand guard, and take the prisoners. Director, Captain, you may wish to ensconce yourselves in an appropriate location as a stand-in for Shaney's missing Rangers."

"I believe hiding in plain site will be the best option." Dominic said calmly: "Winston, you may wish to close yourself in a cell." The Director beckoned Evangelo, and they moved to the lounge, sitting with their backs to the door.

The sliding peep-hole on the door opened, revealing the glowering face of the one of Boss Chartreaux's men. He was with several other Brigades-Men, dragging two cuffed and beaten Survivors—Mansour and Goins:

Mansour yelled: "What have you done with Sam and the girls, you piece of ..."

"You're getting a fist upside the head if'n you don't shut up." The Brigades-Men looked a little worse for wear—it appeared Goins and Mansour had been trouble all along the way for Chartreaux's thugs.

Goins shouted, "You'll get a pipe-wrench up yours—"

Irritated, the Head Jailer pointed to the offenders. "DeRita, Fines—bring 'em in."

"Certainly!" Gleeful, Howard's assistants scrambled out. "Come in... I said come in!" The Jailers grabbed Mansour and Goins, dragging them inside. Eager to help deliver their own brand of justice to the captives, Chartreaux's thugs rushed the jailhouse door, almost trampling the Head Jailer.

Howard blocked them. "Just for that, you don't get to go in there."

The Head Jailer shut the door, but left the small sliding hatch open as he leapt in behind his assistants. Emphatic pummeling and gratuitous violence filled the hallway and echoed through the jail, titillating sounds of havoc streaming through the open hatch.

The Brigades-Men looked surprised at the level of outright brutality of the Jailers. They jostled to get a better look, but could only hear the fracas from their post at the door. They could see the two seemingly oblivious Rangers with their backs to the door, drinking chicoffee...

The Head Jailer reappeared at the door, glared at his assembled crowd, and shook his head disapprovingly. "This is getting on my nerves," Howard scowled. "Get outta here!" He slammed the peephole shut, and the Brigades-Men tromped away, dejected that they could not watch the show.

From the window, Habib monitored their departure.

"That's the ticket—Chartreaux's goons appear to be convinced we have their prisoners under our thumb—they're headed back without so much as a look." Habib peered from beneath the curtain as Chartreaux's men trailed back towards the commons, then complimented his Jailers. "You should start your own stage show—you put on quite an act."

The Jailers released Mansour and Goins; Habib nodded to Goins, then flipped off Mansour as he turned away, walking away at a quick pace.

Mansour snarled and said nothing.

Ignoring Mansour's and Habib's drama, Dominic called them all into Habib's office, where the three Jailers brought chicoffee, cornbread, and a curious attitude. "Gentlemen, you are genuine treasures," Dominic praised as the chicoffee was poured. "Habib for now, have your Jailers monitor the area and inform us of any unusual activity."

Flattered, the Jailers returned to their posts, scanning the streets and whittling.

Everyone but Habib and the Jailers had taken a beating. Mansour was rubbing a bruised jaw, Goins had a broken nose and a strained shoulder, Winston received a knot on the back of his head, Evangelo had a bruised forehead and a molar missing. But Dominic was the most visibly injured of the group, with swollen eyes plus broken ribs. All in all, they were a battered lot—but for each strike they had been given, they had given twice as much in return.

"Any of you beauty queens got an update?" Habib prodded as the group nursed their wounds; his head turned to the wall, gaze averted from Mansour.

"The Girls are gone, and bodies are burning. But the red flag was seen, and a Guest entered the tunnel." Trying to remain calm, Mansour focused on what probably happened, and not what might have happened. Sam was too valuable to be killed, *but it might happen...* "Azarian and Sampson were sent to the tunnel to hunt down Kendra and the Guest."

Winston grimaced. "She must be a helluva valuable Guest to cause this much mayhem."

Dominic smiled beatifically. "You have no idea yet—but you will." He hugged his ribs, and coughed. "Agent Ellison and her team have sacrificed much; we must recover them, and rendezvous in the tunnels by sundown this evening. Agent Habib, you were preparing to show us a possible lead for the location of Ellison's team?"

Habib grunted and reached into the desk drawer to draw out a mysterious cardboard tube. Flipping a metal cap off the end, Habib pulled forth a scroll of paper and unscrolled it—

A hand-drawn map was revealed, lovingly detailed with known features such as bushes and trees, houses, shacks, roads. The divisions between HighTown and LowTown, the new Municipal District, the sight of the old dump, and Pair'O'Dice—it was a masterwork of the draftsman's art, complete with flourishes and titled in elegant handwriting: *Purgatory.*

"As you know, gents, Purgatory is a Level Two Facility. No System awareness is allowed; even for those of us with Rings, Outlaws are forbidden to create full maps of the Tejas Co-op. You should appreciate that our Draftsmen have taken a bold, dangerous step in drawing this map, and I trust you will keep this private."

Dominic admired the beautiful map; "We shall talk afterwards. I believe you have a package for me." Habib grunted, and turned his full attention to the artwork before him.

Careful so as not to touch the blue ink itself, Habib took a dried-up pen and used the capped tip as a pointer. He tapped the cap to the southwest side of town where a twisting path delineated the backside borderland between the Industrial District and LowTown. There, a large blue-ink rectangle labeled "Barracks" huddled against the high palisade wall of Purgatory, out of sight from the main road.

"Boss Chartreaux's men requisitioned and received a metal vault door from our scavenging crews eight months ago; they also requested a portion of rebar and cinderblock from our acquisition teams but were denied their request based on availability. Wouldn't ya know, those materials plus concrete and mortar came up missing from the Jail construction site... being a dedicated accountant, I pride myself on knowing where my goods go, and I tracked the location of the missing material to HERE...". He tapped the inked rectangle. "It's the barracks for Boss Chartreaux's men, an old metal tractor barn its own little nook; you wouldn't go there unless you wanted to go there. There's a brand spankin' new cellar that's been added to the existing structure. I talked to Boss Chartreaux about it, and he assured me it was a storm shelter for his men. He's thoughtful that way." Habib said dryly.

"In exchange for my silence I asked for the specs and the ability to have his crews add one to my house at a later date. I appreciate smarts, and he appreciates flattery, so he gave me the details:

—Fourteen feet by twenty-six feet by eight feet, built directly under the barracks;

—the floor above it was removed and a concrete slab was poured over a wooden form, lined with cinderblocks;

—metal door with metal frame opens inward, flood proof;

—locks from the inside, but could be barred from outside if needed.

—No windows.

—No way out."

Habib leaned back and crossed his arms. "The only place besides the jail strong enough to hold Sam and her Girls is that cellar. I think you will find her there—and if she's there, Destiny will be there, too."

"Then we must be there also." Evangelo offered with grim determination. "Our Ranger charade has worked well, and I would think it will work in this case, too—who's with me to rescue them?"

"Sam?" Habib snorted. "Chartreaux's men are more likely to need rescue from Sam than vice versa. The others, though..."

Mansour glanced at Habib with a thinly-veiled jealousy. "Sam still needs the help. She's not invincible... Evangelo, you know I'm in."

Goins nodded; Winston waved a hand. "Put me on the list."

The Director rallied his men. "So be it. Get any Ranger gear that is useable, and be ready to roll out in ten minutes. Habib, send for one of our runners to bring a handcart and a blanket to the Docks, and we will take the tunnel to load up there. We have a special delivery for Chartreaux's men."

As the others walked away to grab their gear, Dominic closed the office door and turned to Habib: "It has been a long time, Amigo, but perhaps you would consider how we will need your expertise for the

Cause. We leave tomorrow night following the weapons disbursement. Things could become very dangerous around here..."

Habib took off his hat, rubbing the back of his thick, armored neck. "If Mansour is coming, I don't want to be there... Sorry."

Sympathetic, Dominic clasped an ebony hand to Habib's shoulder. "You are the consummate Businessman—no one can run numbers and logistics like you. I understand your feelings; but this is the big one, Frank. And it's been sixteen years..."

"Sixteen years don't seem so long." Habib walked out the door.

━━━━◆━━━━

Bustling through the halls, men were strapping on weapons, putting on gear, carefully constructing a ruse. There were five men to pretend to be five Rangers, and there were five hats, five badges, and two shirts; the shirts could be faked under coats. Dominic and Evangelo were educating the participants on Ranger passcodes and lore, so they would not be easily detected, and Dominic was planning the approach and attack. But what of the hostages? Evangelo set about to find out more about the people they would rescue.

Sidling up to Habib in the hallway, Evangelo asked quietly: "Do you have any intel or insights to share on our Hostages, Agent Habib?"

"Sure. I guess you can say I'm acquainted with them all, having partaken of their charms on a regular basis." Habib said it without boasting; that was just the way of society in the WildLands. He sat down and pulled a bottle of Reunion's Finest Brew from the top drawer of his desk. "Care for a drink?"

Taking a seat in a battered side-chair, Evangelo shook his head. "No thank you—I'm a Man of the Cloth."

"Ah, a Shepherd. Your call—" Habib poured himself two fingers of the amber liquor and leaned back in his chair. "Let's see... how to describe Sam's Girls? Araceli is a dramatic little Hembra, sure to make noise and cause trouble; she's not much of a fighter, but she's a thief par excellence, and an expert prevaricator. Watch for her to cause a diversion if you need it, but be aware—Araceli has a tendency to be clumsy."

"Lourdes is independent, elegant, and completely deadly, a cold-blooded killer—a real class act. Get a weapon in her hands early, and she will take care of any problems. She does not take instruction well. She's also a world-class sniper." A glint of awe shone in Habib's eyes.

"Kendra has a 'devil-may-care but I don't' attitude, rebellious, athletic and sneaky. She can climb anything, hide in anything. Recon is her game, and so is softball. Give her a bat and let her go."

"And Sam?"

"Sam is Queen." Habib's eyes were flooded with an unspoken memory. "She's without peer; whether she's a street fighter or a lover, Sam has no equal. No matter where she goes, Sam's gonna be the Leader. The only man she'll really work for is Dom; the rest are expected to bow down before her majesty—and they do, because she deserves it. She doesn't always say what she needs or what she knows; she keeps a lot to herself, and she expects a lot from her people—but she won't tell you. Just communicate clearly, and stay out of her way." Habib drained his shot glass. "She also used to be my Girl. Back before... things." He poured himself another drink.

Unsure of what to say, Evangelo simply nodded his head. "I'm sorry."

"I've gotten over it." Habib slammed the next shot down.

Leaning forward, Evangelo took off his hat and looked at it. "What about Destiny?"

"Destiny's excellent at human intel; she can find a man's weakness and get him to talk about it—or about anything, really. She's also the biggest creampuff to ever walk the WildLands." Habib said, concerned. "Even Araceli is tougher than Destiny. That's why it's such a disaster that she was taken by Chartreaux; she's a monumental pushover... whether it's a sad face or a strong hand, Destiny can't say no to anybody."

Surprised, Evangelo blurted: "She seems tough to me... she saved me from Boss Chartreaux."

Shaking his head, Habib looked out the window again. "That's Destiny. She tries to save everybody else."

"But that's what Heroes do... they try to save everybody," Evangelo murmured. He thought of how he had tried to save Shaney, and a bittersweet tang touched his soul.

"Not everybody... everybody else." Habib muttered, and put away his shot glass. "Destiny tries to save everybody but herself."

Somehow that didn't so odd to Evangelo. *Physician, heal thyself—Hero, save thyself... it's all the same.* Strapping on his guns, he set his hat, then set his mind to save everybody.

———————◆———————

Sam leaned against the wall and took a deep breath—it had been a fast trip down a bumpy road.

How did we get here?

A knock on the door led to an evacuation demand. That demand led to gunfire, and gunfire led to a raid carried out by a mob tasked to take out as many Hostesses as they could find—

but they did not find them all.

Sighing, Sam asked herself: *Where were the other brigades when the raid went down? Normally this could have never happened—someone would have noticed something out of place. Boss Zhu's men had been outside along with all the other brigades, fighting the fire all morning. Perhaps they were dismissed?* As far as noise, gunfire had been heard throughout the morning as ammo stored in Boss Zhu's house cooked off, so Sam had little hope the sound of gunfire would alert other bosses' brigades. It could be dismissed by onlookers as just one more sound at the scene of disaster.

Agent Walters lay in the doorway, cut down where he made his stand. Shots and shouts rang out from the basement as Agent Mercedes attempted to slow down the invasion and buy the Girls in the safe room time; then whoops and hollers were heard as Chartreaux's thugs discovered the cache of Liquor and Budweed in the secret stash below the safe room.

Chartreaux's men knew exactly where the stash was...

Sam grimaced: It could only mean one thing—Chartreaux broke Destiny.

But his goons did not find the Hostess Club's greatest hidden treasure. *Destiny must not have told the savages everything.* Chartreaux's men returned triumphant up the stairs bearing only the boxes of BudWeed and Liquor; lanterns in hand, they hastily stuffed and lit kerosene-soaked rags as they left...

Neither Kendra nor the Afterling was seen.

Savage faces and cruel eyes—these were not rescuers. She knocked out an Hombre with a wicked backfist to the nose, but ten men took his place...

Araceli was doing her job to cause a scene. Hysterical, wailing for Jorge, it lasted only as long as it took to slap her mouth with duct tape.

Conversely, Lourdes was not hysterical—she was ice cold, even in the midst of groping hands and rough treatment. She would be working on a plan.

The Hostesses stumbled through the smoke and chaos to a rickety handcart; Sam tried to drag her feet, leaving marks in the soil, but those were obliterated by the callous boots trampling behind her. She tried to leave a trail, casting down the silver necklace, but the foreman coming behind her knew the drill and picked up the tale-tale item as fast as she could throw it...

Bound and laid in the cart with a blanket to hide them, they were whisked away to an unknown location.

Sam reflected on her operatives and how they had fallen back on their extensive training. The duct tape gag was defeatable by puffing out one's cheeks and slobbering profusely, so the girls knew what to do—but the ropes would take longer. Still, they had all trained, they all knew the procedures.

Look helpless. Act boldly. Take surprise.

How many times had they trained for this very scenario? How many times had they playfully tied each other up and timed their escapes?

Not enough—they still got overwhelmed. She had worked hard to be realistic with her Girls: *Men are bigger, stronger, faster; you only get one chance to take them down, and in a group, they are almost unstoppable unless you've got a big enough gun.*

But Purgatory didn't allow guns except on waiver—and the Bosses wouldn't allow the Hostesses to carry. Sam's .9mm was still hidden by the fireplace where she could not reach it in time.

So much for equality.

And what of Kendra? Kendra, alerted by the door guard's alarm, should have fallen back on her training and evacuated to the tunnel with the Afterling. At least, that's what Sam hoped...

When in doubt, always fall back on training.

Wiping her eyes, Sam pondered the day so far, and all the chaos that had come with it. Best laid plans had gone awry, entire worlds had come undone, and to top it off, she had started crying in the middle of the ride.

Going to hell in that handcart, she knew things were forever changed. Jorge and Bob were dead. Tears started to threaten again, and with them, that old familiar humiliation; the more one fights tears, the worse they become. An audible sob racked her body, and she heard a man laugh; they laughed more when they removed the blanket covering the girls and saw the tracks of her tears.

Sam blew her nose on the bandana. She hated crying... *it makes me look weak*. But in the end, that was exactly what was needed—her perceived weakness made the Brigades-Men careless. She laid the bandana over the glassy eyes of the pale, scar-faced thug lying beside her; he was still warm, but cooling fast. His fresh blood was already puddling in dark, coagulated pools around the upper half of his mutilated body—and she just didn't like looking at dead bodies.

They underestimated us.

"How's our girl?" Sam whispered to Lourdes, who was tending to the waif lying motionless on the floor before them. Lourdes spit. "Chartreaux and his vile beasts have vandalized her. They should be castrated, all of them." Araceli held up Destiny's head, and made her take a sip of water.

Sam stared at the ceiling while the door behind her rattled. "Is there much blood?"

"No." Lourdes seethed. "Just the usual blood from the usual places. She will heal in a couple of weeks, but she can't serve until then."

"None of us are ever serving here again—this mission is now officially terminated." Resentful, Sam closed her eyes and thought back on the sequence of events:

Destiny was lying on a bare, soiled mattress in the corner of the room when Sam and the girls were pushed into their prison. Seeing her there, dress torn, clothes bloody and caked from the filth of abuse, Sam felt her eyes burn with tears again—and the man who brought them in made the mistake of laughing at Sam one last time.

Having loosened her ropes in transit, Sam made an assessment. The thug unlocking the door was a pale-skinned scar-faced man equal in height to Sam, but slightly heavier. They were being herded into a windowless cellar at the bottom of a narrow stairwell. The cinderblock-lined room had one metal door in a metal frame—a heavy, vault-style stainless steel slab which opened inward, now partway ajar to allow quick closing of the door in case one of the girls tried to run. Inside, a heavy ladder-backed chair sat beside the door, placed by the guard to the knob side so he could open it without having to get up each time. Araceli and Lourdes were ahead of her, and the rest of the men were a few steps behind her.

Just one chance...

Entering the door, Sam whirled, blowing the sodden duct tape gag from her lips as she hurled her muscular frame against the door, slamming it shut.

"Now!"

Araceli, still bound, fell against the guard, and he turned to shove her away; Lourdes—freed of her ropes by her own deft hands—grabbed the shotgun slung behind him and fell on top of him, grappling, wrapping her long legs around his hips. His brawny fist grabbed Lourdes' fragile wrist, twisting it, and she yelped.

One of the thugs in the stairwell outside hit the door, knocking it open a hair—but Sam rammed the door again. It shut, and she flipped the deadbolt, then jammed the chair back under the door knob, wedging it shut.

Araceli was drumming her bare heels against the man's head as he yelled for backup, but so far, the door was holding. Landing atop the man and Lourdes, Sam wrapped her hands around the thug's waist—his attention was on his gun, and she deftly reached under him to pull out his knife; Sam stabbed him in the shoulder, and leapt back. Gravely wounded, the Hombre roared and turned his attention to Sam. Lourdes freed his shotgun from its sling and fired, point-blank.

Blowing him in ragged halves, the bloody shrapnel of flesh and bone ruined Lourdes' ensemble entirely.

Enraged thugs were now kicking the door from the other side, but they could not get good momentum in the narrow stairway. Still, the chair by itself would not hold the door long. Sam slid down, her back against the door, then jammed the escort's combat knife into the half-inch gap between the concrete floor and door, below the knob. Scrambling around the room, she looked for anything else that could be used to wedge the door shut—

Yanking run-down cowboy boots from the guard's feet, Sam shoved both curled toes under the door to each side of the knife. Their thin rubber soles created an ideal, textured wedge to prevent the door from opening. But even if she had the only key, it wouldn't be enough to hold them for long. She lodged the chair tightly against the door and prayed for deliverance.

She counted the rounds in the shotgun. *Seven in the chamber and eight in the sleeve.*

Looking around the room, Sam looked for any additional resources—there was one canteen of water, currently in Lourdes' hands. Assorted litter was found around the room, as well as the heavy mattress.

Keeping her back to the door to hold it against the invading horde,

Sam beckoned to Araceli.

"Go around the room and find me every loose item. Bottles, cans, nails, anything you can find. Don't pass over anything, and flip the mattress; we'll use that to help block the door."

Araceli mutely nodded, then stood. Blood spattered her shift; Araceli attempted to sweep it off, but it kept smearing on her hands. "Oh! Get it off..." A sticky substance was wedged between her delicate fingers, and she flicked her hand to fling it away, then gasped as a chunk of the Brigades-Man's flesh dripped from her fingers to the floor.

Sam stood stiffly, then leaned against the door once more. Feeling the men raging through the door behind her, Sam determined to rally her troops.

"Well, it may not have gone according to plan," Sam noted with a wry voice, "but Strike Team Destiny has secured our objective." *Now would be a great time for someone with more firepower to finish this job... where are you, Lazarus?*

Groaning, Destiny opened her eyes. "Lourdes, I dreamed you were here." She was delirious—had she been drugged? Her head was rolling, her soft gray eyes wild. Thick yellow vomit stained the mattress next Destiny, bits of her carrot cake mixed with the effluvia of man-unkind's sin.

"Get it off." Hands shaking, Araceli was pulling Destiny off the mattress, trying to drag her away from the filth touching her. "Get it off... " She grabbed a stained red rag lying on the corner of the mattress and wiped the vomit away from Destiny's mouth.

Lourdes pulled the rag from Araceli's hands, and wetted it with water from the canteen. "Settle down. I'll take care of it." Lourdes wiped gently, but Destiny's lips still bled. Unwrapping the scarf still clinging to her neck, Araceli draped it around Destiny, attempting to cover her nakedness. The fringe of the crocheted scarf fell into the puddle of filth.

"Get it off." Araceli whispered, tugging it away.

Destiny's voice was flat, dead. "Sam, forgive me—I didn't mean to tell. I accidentally told them. The stash... the words just came out." Destiny held out her fragile hand, and the shreds of her white lace dress fell open to reveal red welts marring the pink, fuzzy plaques of her torso. "Please."

"You are not to blame." Still holding the door shut, Sam viciously kicked the dead man away from her, more tears rolling down her smooth-scaled blue cheeks. His leg detached from his torso, a tendon dangling between hip and socket. Blood spattered.

Araceli watched, shellshocked and silent, while Lourdes tenderly cradled Destiny in her arms.

Sam was snarling:

Nobody messes with my girls.

She kicked the dead man again.

Nobody.

———◆———

They were moving through the underbrush, Sampson in the lead with the Watcher right behind. Through the open yards of the lesser cabins of HighTown, off the main drag, they stealthed their way out to the Wall; there between the grown-up hedges they crouched, running north until they came to a broken-off trunk of a hollow Ash tree rising next the stockade wall. Behind it, a small section of the wall was cut and hinged near the bottom to allow unauthorized access to the WildLand; the Agents ducked in discreetly and started moving through the brush of the lakeshore.

All along the way, Sampson was looking behind to see if anyone had seen them or if anyone was following. But the Watcher was only looking forward—his job was to keep his eyes on any threats that might lie ahead and to neutralize them without undue commotion. Conscientious and careful, Sampson was sneaking through green briar and willow thickets—a narrow, winding path had been cut for ease and was well hidden in the almost impenetrable willow-wood. In the summer, this would be a haven for alligator and snake, but in the chilly midday, neither creature was to be seen. They were running the creek bottoms, skirting the shoreline of an inlet that separated Purgatory from the secret entrance to the tunnel. Tracks of deer and coyote filled the muddy bottoms where the creeks trickled into the lake, and great blue herons were wading in seasonal pools, looking for fish.

Past these, Sampson stealthily crept, alerting nothing to their presence; he seemed entirely at home in these backwaters, rifle slung across his back, machete in hand. Creeping past an abandoned den, he motioned for silence and moved along quickly—big as a bear and fearless as a boar, Sampson was a true man of the woods. Had Sampson been any larger, the Watcher would have taken him for the legendary Bigfoot, minus the hair; his massive growth resulted in an oversized, underslung jaw, and his bark-like sepia skin lent Sampson the appearance of an animated oak.

The Giant cleared his throat and straightened the straps on his mechanic's overalls.

"I've got a confession to make, Watcher, and you can fight me for doin' you dirty later. Just let me get us to the stables first... but you need to know, I lied to you."

Oh really? I would have never guessed, you Rube. The Watcher thought to himself with an exasperated growl.

"I lied about your Girl sneaking out and eating the candies. She did sneak out, but she didn't eat any candies... I fell prey to Kendra's seductress ways, and they absconded behind my back." Sampson was silent for a moment. "I guess I'm just stupid. I know Kendra thinks I'm stupid." The bitterness in his voice was thick.

You aren't the only fool around here. The Watcher commiserated. Was that kiss just another game for Rose?

"They snuck out the top story window and climbed rooftop to rooftop to Boss Zhu's house—in broad daylight, no less. By God, that's daring, come to think of it..." Temporarily blinded by admiration, Sampson kept sneaking down the trail.

The Watcher was not blinded. So, there was no piteous Afterling crying in the mud, calling for him—just a Minx laughing at his gullibility. *How stupid does she think I am?* Anxiety and anger were waging a war within him, but right now anxiety was winning, hands down.

Sampson slashed through a grapevine hanging across their path, then the Watcher tapped him on his shoulder and pointed: hogs were on an upwind slope some hundred and fifty yards away, rooting beneath a grove of young pecan trees. Their satisfied grunts and growls lent a peaceful air to the scene, which would have been more peaceful if the lead Boar had not weighed upwards of a thousand pounds. But the wind was strong, gusting the Survivors' scent away from the hogs' incredibly sensitive snouts, and the rustling branches helped to hide the sound of the men's movements. Sampson stopped talking, and they moved in silence through the willow-wood surrounding the lake. Several minutes passed as they travelled, slipping through the woods, away from the hog herd. Sampson continued:

"Anyhow, Kendra and your Girl discovered Zhu was murdered; they grabbed the note just as Zhu's murderers came back to burn the house. They were almost caught: your Girl is a powerful Sneak, but she ain't much in a straight-up fight. Did you know, if she gets scared, she falls completely apart?" He pondered. "You might wanna avoid carpets if you ever build a house."

Get to the point.

Unaware of the Watcher's irritation at his constant patter, Sampson chattered on: "We all got busted in rank; but I got busted twice—once because the insubordination went down on my watch, and twice for fraternization. The situation was left in my control, but I let it get out of control. So I was reassigned."

The Watcher could hear regret creeping up into Sampson's throat: "I should've been there, Watcher, but I got stupid. But I got even stupider, because I lied to you to protect Kendra, and she doesn't even care."

Woulda, shoulda, coulda...

For the Watcher, Sampson's ruminations mirrored his own...*I should've been there, too, but a little tart kissed me and sent me on a quest. I should've known it was all a ruse...*

As if "woulda shoulda coulda" were not enough, the Watcher could not stop "what if" from creeping into his mind; *what if only one person—or the wrong person—entered the tunnel?* Unable to speak to Sampson and not wanting to take the time to write, the Watcher could only follow along. He was consumed with a desperate need to see Rose now, to know that she was not cruelly left behind, or trapped somewhere... *and if she was left behind? What would happen then?*

There wouldn't be enough blood in the WildLands to sate that rage. Burning down Purgatory would not be enough to make the pain go away. Nothing might ever be enough again—and the thought terrified him. The Watcher briefly wondered—*how bad would it be this time? How bad compared to any other woman?*

It had been not quite bad with Kaitlyn; *more like uncomfortable...* that was the last real relationship he had, fifty-two years ago. Losing her hair, some teeth missing, and in transition to a strong Hembra—Kaitlyn had been desirable in some odd, indefinable way. Three weeks of sex and desperation, followed by a brief, brutal tooth infection and painful death —that was the be-all of their whole time together. She was an angry woman, but back then everyone was angry. Still, Kaitlyn had been company... he almost missed her when she was gone. Mostly, he just missed holding her, and that faded after a few days. As usual, he had taken precautions to not get too close.

Ever since his Mother's death, he had always been careful to never get too close to anyone. He understood the psychological implications, and he didn't care—his emotional aloofness had served him well in LifeAfter. Abuelita was an exception, because one cannot be fed and clothed by a person for over four decades and not become close to them. Montel was another break of the rules; a person who extends kindness when none is expected and none can be returned is a friend. Abuelita had nurtured him, and Montel had befriended him—of all the countless deaths, these two alone he had mourned.

Until now.

Suddenly the world was filled with potential for immeasurable heartache. The sight of Evangelo and Dominic enshackled had engendered a cold rage in him, but it was nothing compared to the unhinged heat the inferno at the Hostess Club had sparked.

Why the hell now? What's so different about the Afterling? It wasn't just that she was female. There were other females on the planet, just not very many and not as... female. Abnormally short, unbelievably brave, unbearably contrary to him, and infuriatingly conciliatory to others, he wondered if she was deliberately trying to make him insane. She was forcing him to choose between her freedom and her fragility, over and over again...

The dichotomy between Rose's willingly self-determinant self and her unwittingly self-destructive self was creating a state of perpetual war within the Watcher—his promise to set her free to be herself was grappling with his need to protect her from herself. The Watcher was constantly torn between the desire to take her in his arms, or take her over his knee:

You want your Freedom? I'll give you Freedom... You need the Patriarchy? I'll show you the damn Patriarchy...

Either way, the unending battle to defend Rose from the world and from herself had left the Watcher unable to emotionally defend himself. Deciding to "not get too close" was not working too well anymore. The only alternative to not getting too close was to take charge of the process and make it happen the way he wanted.

"I should've been there." Still turning over the whole fiasco in his mind, Sampson lead them into a clearing where the willow-wood was broken down all around them, and a trampling of dirt and stone had occurred. *Stampede?* They came upon a dappled horse lying sprawled in the path, still fresh from the morning. Sampson took a stick and whacked it just to be sure it was dead, then stepped around it. "I was left in control. I lost control."

I lost control. Smelling the singed leather of his gloves, scorched when he held that goon's feet to the fire, the Watcher realized he had been completely out of control, unable to stop the emotional crash. He had to regain control... An emotional nihilism seized him. What would it mean to purposely get close? What would it mean if he were the one to engineer this train wreck? *It would a be a hell of a ride, and a fiery crash*—but at least it would be his own hand on the throttle.

He would be in control again.

They rounded a bend in the willow-wood and came into the opening where the Watcher first met Mansour. Unable to bear the slow pace any longer, the Watcher bounded ahead of Sampson, recognizing the way.

Just a trace—

"Whoa, whoa, whoa, Hoss—slow down or you'll get shot by the Sentry." Sampson held out a hand.

A whiff on the wind—

"Stay behind me, Watcher: I'm more trigger-happy than you are. You're not the only one hunting someone."

Rose. Her scent was waving a banner to him, cheering him on to the finish line; stronger now, the Watcher was wrapped in the aroma of harried Afterling.

Entering the limestone canyon, the curtains of greenbriar mixed between stands of yaupon, they heard the chatter of plump red cardinals fill the air and the sound of sparrows in the nearby ash grove. Amidst the little birds, the Child looked up from the shadows beneath the trees...

The Watcher leapt into the narrow arroyo, pulling aside the greenbriar and knocking:

A voice whispered: "Salt." It was Agent Renfro—

"Pepper," whispered Sampson. The Door swung open, and both men jumped through, jamming their broad shoulders against the walls, jostling and shoving.

Renfro hissed, "Slow down or I'll shoot you myself." He glared menacingly at the two Machos: "Kendra and the little one, they're both in there—and they're out for blood."

Sampson mumbled, staring ahead into the darkness. "Outta the way, Gunny—"

Renfro racked the slide on this shotgun. "That's Agent Renfro to you, Sampson. This is my territory. You follow me, or you'll both get put in the ground."

Sampson blinked, and the Watcher simmered, but they both fell behind the old Hombre as he held his position: "You stay quiet and don't get stupid—they're already acting wild enough as it is, swearing death to Purgatory—and I don't need you setting them off. They came running down the tunnel pell-mell, saying the door guards were dead and men were storming the cabin. Agent Mancini is holding the fort at the far end of the tunnel; he heard heavy boots directly above the hatch, and loud voices. But now it's just silence, and the metal hatch is red-hot, like it's on fire. The concrete will hold, as long as no one sprays water on it while it's hot." Renfro tossed a request back to Sampson—"Update me."

Sampson's update was terse. "Boss Chartreaux's mounted a Coup in Purgatory with permission from Bosses Balogun and Waitie, and they deposed Winston. His men torched the Hostess Cabin, along with Boss Zhu's and Hizzoner's cabin, killing both of 'em, plus Jorge and Bob. Then his thugs stole the Girls, and probably put them wherever they took Destiny. The Director and the Captain are rescued, and they will rendezvous with us later." He set his jaw. "We're here to secure Kendra and the Guest."

"So, society's falling apart, eh? 'Bout time. I'll tell Agent Wilcox to get ready for trouble from either end of the tunnel." Renfro snarled, and a cold light was in his eyes. "It's time to kill the sumbitches."

They entered the stable; Oro whickered and tossed his head, stamping at the sight of the Watcher. William, Charger, and Shadow, agitated, danced at the end of their tethers. Ahead, they could hear soft voices in the living quarters of the tunnel:

"Warpaint—check. Weapons—check. Ammo—check." Kendra was counting off equipment; at the sound of her voice, Sampson hid his face in his hands and let out a pent-up sigh of relief.

Now a dreadful caterwauling sound filled the tunnel: it was the sound of Oskar, having caught the scent of the Watcher. Howling, the little beast whined and raced around his pen. Sassy raised her head and let out a soft woof, then laid down once more, wagging her tail.

"Don't forget my Chupacabra. He is a fearsome creature, aren't you, Oskar?" Mournful, Rose tried to comfort the young chupacabra from the other room.

"Chupacabra—check."

"Can we wait no longer? Maybe they are trying to find us." Rose did not seem to quite believe that everyone was dead.

"Nope, they're dead, and we're gonna avenge them all. We're the only ones left."

"Kendra, are you certain?"

"Everyone's dead. Jorge's dead, and you know that means Walters is dead. I don't know about Sam and the Girls, but it's just us that's free now, and Chartreaux must pay in blood." Kendra sounded dead serious. "All the rest must have been killed."

"Everyone? Even the Watcher?" Rose's sounded incredulous.

"Especially him. You know if he were alive, he would already be here. Watcher's probably dead outside the cabin lying on top of a mountain of bodies with a giant machete sticking through him, and the whole heap on fire." Kendra seemed to enjoy that vision. "You've gotta be brave."

"Saul always did so love killing things..." Voice tremulous at the thought of a heroic Watcher lying deceased atop a flaming pile of bodies, Rose was near tears.

Saul. At the mention of his own name from her lips, the Watcher blinked. *She called me Saul...* Taken aback at how close Kendra's vision came to being a reality, the Watcher was suddenly thankful for the patient Sampson as his guide.

Renfro held his hand up to halt them; they peered around the narrow opening to the living quarters to see a ferocious Kendra, bedazzled baseball cap slapped on backwards, black charcoal streaked beneath her eyes like warpaint. Beside her, a small hooded figure knelt in the hay with her back to the stable's tunnel; the toes of her bare feet peeked out from beneath her furs...

Rose.

He saw her, and his heart stopped. There was the Afterling, safe and sound, looking as if she had merely run down a tunnel and not like she had nearly died twice. Seeing her alive, a weakness washed over the Watcher, a feeling so intense it left him slightly queasy. The fragility of her life hit him squarely in the solar plexus; in her escapades, Rose was always openly taunting Death, daring it to come find her. *The little trickster deceived me with a kiss, then flirted with Death behind my back...* the weakness passed and was rapidly replaced by a growing feeling of anger to burn away the weakness. That irritation purged all sentimentality from him, a welcome development.

Musashi said to control anger—use it, not lose it. Time to use it. He had let her control his mind with her moon magic once again; now, the Watcher needed to bring everything back under his control. He felt for his notepad and pencil—they were still in his pocket. He mentally riffled through his analysis of Rose's psychological profile. *An update to our agreement is in order.*

On their way out of the burning cabin, the Girls had managed to grab two of the Watcher's gear bags from the safe room, and they were now divvying up the goods. Rose's small hand pulled his 12-gauge Remington from the bag, racked it open, and pushed it to the side with his vest, badge and hat. Her hand lingered on the vest, as if she were remembering. "So, you really think Saul is dead?"

"Yup."

"What about Herman? Did he die too?" Rose asked, trying to remain stoic.

"Yup." Kendra hesitated. Her eyes become bright, but she clamped her sassy mouth into a stiff upper lip. "I think he was eating candies and got taken unawares. It was a peaceful death. Herman probably didn't even notice I'm gone..."

"That's a damn lie, and you take it back!" Felt hat brushing the ceiling, Sampson burst into the living quarters, bellowing.

"Herman!" Kendra gasped, and for just a moment her mask slipped, all pretense of world-weariness gone.

"Ain't nobody eating my candies but you—" putting a humongous fist in his pocket, Sampson pulled out a little brown bag and threw it at her. "I hunted you down and you're gonna take 'em."

Kendra caught the bag, and also caught herself; she pulled her jaded facade back into place just in time. "These are mine now. But you're too late; we are off to avenge our fallen."

"Like Hell—after that stunt you and that Afterling pulled at Boss Zhu's you're going nowhere!"

"Good luck stopping us..." She did not get to say anymore, as Sampson leapt over the Afterling's head and hauled the protesting Kendra bodily around the corner of an empty stall.

"Hey! Stupid kids..." watching from the tunnel, Renfro spat and whispered to the Watcher. "Watcher, you're on your own—make it count. But don't you hurt that lil' booger, or you'll answer to Gunny." Deep in thought, the Watcher nodded. "C'mere, Sassy..." She wagged, slowly sat up, then ambled to Renfro's side. He headed back to patrol the outer door and stables, bloodhound in tow.

The Watcher's eyes narrowed, *That stunt at Boss Zhu's...* he walked over to Oro and stroked his mane, then reached into his equipment bag to retrieve the Ring and his own shirt. For this, he would not be dressed as a slave; he would be dressed as a Free Man, and he would speak in his own voice.

Flipping his notepad to a fresh sheet, the Watcher began to scrawl.

———◆———

Rose was waiting for the Watcher, but he never came.

"Are you there?" Back still to the tunnel door, Rose sat stock still. Through the thick stone walls, she could not detect anything beyond the doorway. "I am really hoping you are there. I shan't look, as I do not want to know if you are not there."

She sat for a few more moments... no one came.

"Alrighty then," voice only slightly quavering, she finally spoke. "If you are not there, then you are somewhere else, someplace beautiful with the butterflies in Heaven." Trying to remain brave, Rose laid her hands on his vest and remembered the meadow, when all the butterflies flew up— and the Watcher was there, holding her braid behind her. "But perhaps you are not dead. Maybe you just need help." She raised her voice to Heaven, hopeful for a speedy answer. "Does he need help? Do I need to go rescue him?"

Eyes closed in prayer, she could feel a large glow stooping down in the hay beside her. At first, she thought it might be an Angel, but then he reached over to take her hand, and perched it atop his own, linking his garnet stone into her neural portal:

#I need no rescue.

The Watcher's dry digital drawl filled her aural pathways once again. A tear rolled down her cheek, and she tried to turn her head so he could not see. Disconnecting, he reached around her to pick up his vest, buttoning it up and pinning his badge back in place.

She attempted to sound flippant: "Well, if you needed me, I would have come to rescue you, and I would have set you free just like before."

Picking up his hat, he placed it upon his brow, straightened the brim, then knelt beside her again to take her hand.

#I know.

She glanced furtively at him. He was back to being Agent Azarian now, wearing his own hat, vest, and badge; having doffed his mask, he was back to his own Devilish face with his own Devilish smirk. She tried to talk, but realized she couldn't without making a dramatic scene, so she just remained silent.

#I have completed my quest. I have told your Father you love him: Dominic and Evangelo are both set free. They are working now to save Sam and the Girls—

Putting up her hand to shield her eyes from view, Rose felt genuine tears of relief. "Oh!" She wanted to say something else, but couldn't— Baba was alive, the little Ranger had been saved, and a rescue for the hostesses was underway. Gratitude flowed out of her heart, and she wondered—*did Baba say he loved her in return? Probably not.* Dominic was longing for his own child, his Zoe, and Rose was but one of many... it was enough to know Baba was alive and free.

The Watcher bent low:

#...but I came to find you.

Rose was stunned.

When one is one of many, one learns that the many are more important than the one—so it came as an utter shock to hear those words. Over all others, the Watcher had come to find Rose.

He might as well have lit of a stick of dynamite under her. Rose had not anticipated the effect of his words. *...I came to find you.* No one had ever come to find the Asura, and certainly no one had ever come to find Rose to save her. *None, except for Saul.* Moved beyond measure, the words of the Song of Hope came to her mind:

And I know that I will find you someday...

Someone finally came to find that which was lost. Sensing her emotional vulnerability, the Watcher moved in for the kill:

#While I was finding you, I wrote this poem for you. Do you wish to see it?

Well, this was rather unexpected, Rose looked up, amazed. Not only was the Watcher not dead, and not only had he come to find her, but he also had written something for her. Notepad in hand, he held it out: his block print writing was not up to his usual neatness—it appeared to have been written in a hurry.

~~~~~

If I could for a moment make a moment last a lifetime,

It would be this moment now, when I am cradled in your arms—

To help me in all things, you to be my guide and stay,

To harbor me from all life's harsh alarms;

This I promise now, you alone will always be

The Angel of my better nature's charms.

~~~~~

"Oh, Saul, it is exquisite!" Rose was overcome with pity and conciliation. *He's asking for a hug...* the Watcher's written words were vulnerable and yielding—everything he had always been in his writings, and everything he could not seem to speak in his own acerbic voice. "How did you ever find time to write this?"

#It just came to me. Do you find the sentiment agreeable?

Hopeful, he turned his brown eyes to her, and she could not imagine it being otherwise. "Agreeable?" She marveled at him; to have him so openly express a need for her, for him to promise to be in her keeping, in her arms, under her angelic guidance—it was diametrically opposed to everything Patriarchal. *It is positively Matriarchal, in fact.* "Oh, absolutely, this is so... progressive!" Beaming, she read it again.

Under her leadership, Saul had grown as a sensitive person, capable of admitting his own need. She was pleased.

#As a reward for my quest, sign it with your name so I will always remember.

He pressed his pencil into her hand and pointed at a blank space at the bottom of the page.

"What a funny request!" she confided. The Watcher seemed hurt.

#If you do not wish to, I understand. It is all I request for completing your quest, but if not, I will take it as a sign you want no more of these...

"Oh no, I adore your poems." It seemed so simple and sweet a prize: her name adorning a poem about an angelic hug. Writing her name in fat, curly letters, she handed it back to him. "May I keep it?" Busy, the Watcher held up a finger for her to wait as he dated it, adding his own signature at the bottom—

-Witnessed: Saul Azarian

This he scanned the original with his WeSpeex RingWorld. Tearing out a sheet behind it, he handed her a hand-scribed copy:

#*Fortunately, I made a copy for you. Do not lose it.*

The Watcher was all business again, tucking his notepad neatly into his pocket once more; not content to just merely hold her hand, he gripped it and gave it a pump, then patted it. Abruptly, he stood, and lifted her to her feet before him, studying her with a wondering eye...

Running one finger along the top curve of her hand, he mapped it in his mind. He looked at the intricate pattern sprayed upon it, lace tracery in sienna; her face, too, was completely covered in an interwoven pattern. He could not see more, as only her face, hands and feet peeked out from under her cloak. Still, the effect of the dark liner above the tattoos was stunning, as cosmetic arts gave her the sultry look of an exotic ingenue.

The Watcher rubbed his thumb across her cheek in surprise at her transformation, but wisely said nothing about the remains of her tears. Fortunately, her dark-lined eyes did not get smudgy—the everlasting Charpeez pen stayed true to its reputation.

She gazed up at him, and her eyes were always the eyes of Rose— dark, luminous, and eternal as the moon. But those eyes were only one blink away from the grave... *always flirting with Death behind my back.* Brusque, he wiped away a tear from her chin, then reached up under the woolly brim of her cap, and was greeted by the heady scent of vanilla wafting up from beneath... a tiny crumb of mud was still tangled in her hair. He picked it loose, and held it up.

#*Impressive. All this fancy finery from beauty mud...*

"Beauty mud? Oh... yes, beauty mud, absolutely."

#*But Kendra said it wasn't beauty mud—is it "crying in the mud" mud, then?*

"Oh, 'for crying in the mud'..." Nervous, she noted the pun, but was not comfortable as to where this line of questioning was headed. "That's droll! Yes, I..."

#*So is it beauty mud or Afterlings crying in the mud? What kind of mud is it, Rose?*

"I don't remember... I mean, that's silly, it's just mud." She tried to smile disarmingly, but the Watcher was not to be disarmed.

He thought of the mud on his cheek, where she had kissed him. Sweeping her up, he sat her upon a work counter. Sitting higher now, she could nearly see him eye to eye; he seemed to be waging an intense, internal battle—decisions were being made.

#You seem to be having trouble remembering. As per our new agreement, let me help you remember.

"Agreement?" She blinked.

#You signed an agreement to accept my help when needed.

Reaching into his pocket, he held up his poem for her to see: her eyes scanned, searching the words, trying to comprehend. "But it's a poem, not an agreement—a poem from you to me, promising I always would be your Angel..."

#Read it again—you have it backwards.

"But..." Rose shook her head. "I thought you meant..."

#It means I'm your Guardian Angel—your Watcher from on High. You agreed to this when you signed this contract.

Stunned, she backpedalled. "I agreed to no such thing! I asked for nothing from you... You already swore an oath to submit to me, and you have to do my bidding; I don't need anything else from you—"

#This agreement doesn't negate my oath to you—instead, it is a complementary, reciprocal promise on your part, to accept the help I offer you of my own free will. It strengthens my position as your sole provider of assistive services.

A bewildered Rose stared at the poem: "But I don't need your help all the time."

#Let the record show—in the presence of witnesses you said you needed my help earlier today, as made evident by your intermittent cataplexy and your constant, subconscious death wish. This agreement just formalizes that statement of need.

"But it was just a poem..."

#I beg to differ—it says in plain English:

He tapped a rough red finger to each segment.

#If I could for a moment make a moment last a lifetime: (you wish to forever)

#It would be this moment now, when I am cradled in your arms: (this date, and with expression of natural affection)

#To help me in all things, you to be my guide and stay: (You request my help and guidance, and for the record a "stay" is a chain which pulls in a desired direction; it is archaic but it is the proper definition of a strong influence.)

#To harbor me from all life's harsh alarms; (asking me to shelter

you from threats, emotional or physical, quantified by "all")

#This I promise now, you alone will always be: (you promise me an exclusive contract)

#The Angel of my better nature's charms: (as the Angel—AKA Guardian, Watcher, Benei Elohim—of your soul and body)

Helpful, the Watcher pointed to the bottom of the paper:

#And you signed it—right... there.

"But I didn't know I was signing a contract!" Rose squawked in denial. "I thought I was just autographing a poem..."

#You did say you found it agreeable.

"But I thought you meant..." Flustered, she stopped. It had all seemed acceptable when it was the other way around. "I thought you meant you were promising to rely on me to help you—that you were admitting your own vulnerability, your need for me!"

He shook his head in mock disapproval.

#But it is not acceptable for you to rely on me in return? That is not very progressive of you, Rose.

Still studying the paper, she knitted her brows, indignant. "You tricked me!"

#And you tricked me. You offered a kiss, and I offered a poem—I would say we are even.

Her eyes grew wide as he pulled her washcloth from his pocket, and pointed to the mud upon it.

#I present this evidence: a muddy kiss, planted on my cheek.

Leaning forward, his hands spread on the counter beside her knees, the Watcher questioned his Subject:

#Presented with this evidence, let's see if you can remember now— tell me about this mud, Rose.

Mind racing, she weighed her options. She glanced at his face, hoping to see a sign to the way out, but his crimson scar only pointed the way back to down to an obstinate jaw. She looked to his eyes, but only saw them glowering beneath his jagged, fiery brow. She briefly considered knocking his hat off his head again, but decided against it. *That might not go well...*

Seconds passed in silence as she pondered how to defuse this Devil. "Mud is mud."

The Watcher pushed away from the counter.

#Fine. Mud is mud. A kiss is a kiss. But you tell me you do not remember what any of it means...

Turning away, he rolled up his sleeves.

Rose wasn't sure exactly what that meant, but she did know instinctively that a man rolling up his sleeves means business. He turned back, his mouth set firm, and took her hand.

#*I am fixing to help you remember.*

Blanching, Rose folded: "I remember, wait—I remember! The mud was from under Hizzoner's porch—we crawled there to hide when we snuck into Boss Zhu's house and I'm so very sorry—I didn't tell you, but I didn't lie to you either... I even told you Kendra's story was a lie but you wouldn't believe me!"

Fierce, he slammed his hand down on the counter.

#*So, everything about the mud was a lie... was everything about that kiss a lie, too?*

A loud commotion was heard in the antechamber; Renfro called up the tunnel:

"Incoming—we've got company!"

Sassy was growling low, and Oskar whined. Sampson came flying out of the stall, looking disheveled; chambering a round in his rifle, he hissed to the Watcher as he raced by: "Hurry it up!"

The Watcher turned back to Rose, gripping her hand, relentless:

#*Was that kiss a lie?*

"That kiss was real!"

Dropping her hand, the Watcher grabbed her around the waist and jerked her up off the table, cloak and all. Gripping the ears of the hood so she could no longer look away, he held her:

No, THIS is real—

and just like the Legend sang, the Watcher kissed Rose.

If Rose had been kissed by the Devil himself, it could not have been more unexpected—no loving words, no warning; just the absoluteness of his arms about her and his lips overwhelming hers. Taken unawares, Rose could not think to summon her moon magic, so she went soft and limp. The Watcher just held tight and kept right on kissing her.

Shouts were heard from the entrance to the stable, and the smell of smoke... Plopping Rose back down on the table, the Watcher grabbed his shotgun and loaded shells.

"Wait—we weren't done!" Rose gasped. "You can't just throw a Girl down after a kiss; that isn't romantic at all..."

No, it's not. Grasping the Remington, the Watcher racked the bolt and

picked Rose up once more, throwing her over his shoulder and sprinting down the tunnel towards the sound of chaos:

If you want Romance, go read a book.

V

Down the tunnel, the Watcher came bounding as if he were on fire—and he was.

The Watcher shone like a flame in the torchlight, the golds and reds of his raw skin flushed with an internal combustion made possible by oxytocin igniting adrenaline and testosterone. That combination, and the kiss that sparked it, lit a chain reaction which could not be contained; the resultant explosion rocketed him down the corridor and nearly piled him headlong into Sampson and Renfro. Afterling still slung over his shoulder, the Watcher grabbed her with both arms and skidded to an abrupt stop.

Smoke was filling the tunnel, being burned from the outside by some unknown actor with an unknown weapon. Through the thick oak slab, they could hear a soft whirring sound, and the muffled roar of controlled, directed flames licking against the door...

Here?

The Watcher could smell the distinctive odor of concentrated HeliScram gel fuel combined with condensed oxygen; *an ALGOS flamethrower...* Rose coughed, and the Watcher shook her, shushing her with his finger on his mouth. He opened his local Ring server to hail Renfro Ring-2-Ring: the Avatar of a man that looked exactly like Gunny, minus the scales, greeted him.

#WATCHER: ALGOS—it's looking for the Afterling. Tell everyone to maintain silence.

#RENFRO: You're nuts. ALGOS don't exist anymore.

#WATCHER: I'll prove it to you in a minute. Pass along my

message.

#RENFRO: Why the hell did you bring her down here then?

#WATCHER: I'm her Bodyguard. She stays with me. Tell them what I said.

Renfro hissed to the group: "Watcher says shut up—either he's hallucinating or he's right, but either way, we're screwed."

"What is it Gunny?" Sampson had a wild-eyed look, in part because something was attacking their sacrosanct safe space, and partly because he had been interrupted while conferring with Kendra. Confused, the Giant looked at the door with apprehension. Renfro grimaced and made a slashing motion against his own throat.

The Watcher grabbed Rose's hand and spoke to her through the private ChipMate protocol:

#*Did you line your cloak like I asked?*

Rose nodded—the UltraFoil emergency blanket sewn into her cloak gleamed ever so faintly as she moved, but less so now that Lourdes' sheet had been added as an inner lining. The Watcher pushed her down against the wall, onto the floor, pulling her deerskin hood firmly into place around her heart-shaped face:

#*Tuck yourself up under your cloak, and don't move. Let nothing be exposed... don't come up until I tell you.*

She ducked down and curled up under the cloak, rabbit-like, her feet and hands tucked beneath her, face hidden. Once more, she was transformed into a pile of deer hides. Scanning the small area, the Watcher spotted a shovel and propped it next to the door. Seeing nothing else nearby to serve the purpose he had in mind, he threw aside his hat and vest, then began to unbutton the front of his wool gabardine shirt. Sampson and Renfro looked at him askance:

#RENFRO: Did you get ahold of some bad BudWeed?

The old man could think of no other reason the Watcher would be hallucinating and stripping at the same time.

#WATCHER: No. Open the door about two feet on my cue, then move back into a defensive position near the Afterling. Stay out of my way.

#RENFRO: Have you lost your damn mind? If it's ALGOS, there's no way I'm letting it in.

#WATCHER: If you want to keep your door, open it—it shouldn't be immediately hostile, but if the door is closed the drone

will burn it down, then enter anyway. I'm going to give it a blanket party.

#RENFRO: Why not just shoot it?

#WATCHER: Too big a risk for discharging debris to hit a bystander in this small area, or lose a piece that'll still transmit our location data. The shirt will work. I've done this before—trust me.

Muttering, Renfro lightly touched the doorknob with a gloved hand—the wood was starting to smoke at the top of the door, but the knob was still just warm, not hot. He grabbed it and turned, then nodded to the Watcher. The Watcher stripped down to his thin cotton t-shirt, removing his long-sleeved shirt, then pulled up the Nomex balaclava bunched around his neck, leaving only his eyes exposed. He limbered up, preparing for hard labor.

#RENFRO: You better hope this works. If not, well then—nice knowing you, Bub.

Grabbing his wool shirt along the edges, the Watcher gripped it like a bull-fighter's cape. He pointed to Sampson, then motioned towards Rose —the Giant moved to her position and stood over her. The Watcher stepped back towards the door then nodded to Renfro, and the old man swung the door open, stepping back into the shadows of the cave.

A burst of flames briefly shot through the open door, then ceased. Gyros and servos whirred, and a faint click was heard as the flamethrower retracted back into its slot. Flattening himself against the cool limestone wall that separated the tunnel from the outside world, the Watcher held his shirt before him...

An open-weave orb of titanium ceramo-carbon floated silently into the tunnel. Barely visible, the drone was creating an active camouflage image based on its current surroundings, projecting the limestone surface of the cave onto the millions of optic beads embedded into its netted surface. Heat thrust from its encased microgenerator rippled into the air behind it as it passed Renfro. The old soldier's face became incredulous, then deadly in intent.

Hands flashing out, the Watcher flung his shirt over the drone like a net. Blinding blue light crackled, then exploded, but the wool gabardine and his mechanic's gloves insulated against the drone's defensive electric discharge. Suddenly he was thankful for the thick, rubber tire-tread soles of his moccasin-boots. Swiftly gathering the loose ends of the shirttail in his hands, the Watcher swung the buzzing orb, smashing it into the limestone wall behind him.

An excruciating blast of mind-numbing static emanated from the drone, accompanied by arcing blue light and the smell of ozone. The shirt started to smoke—Renfro and Sampson covered their ears, and the animals began to panic, whining and neighing. Not hesitating, the Watcher gritted his teeth and gripped his bundle, slamming it again against the white stone of the tunnel.

#WATCHER: Get back—

Whipping the bundled drone around him once more, the Watcher slung it against the limestone boulders of the cave. The high-decibel assault suddenly stopped, and a miniature ball of fire enveloped the shirt, exploding around the Watcher's gloved hands. Singed, he dropped it to the floor; seizing the shovel with smoldering gloves, the Watcher crushed the drone with a vicious blow, and it shattered within the burning remains of the wool shirt. Azure lightning sparked from chunks of disconnected digital components.

From up the tunnel, shocked swearing could be heard, along with Oskar's frenzied yowls. "Holy Crap—" It was Kendra, gaping from the stables. "What the actual—"

The Watcher proceeded to pound the drone with the shovel. He called Renfro:

#WATCHER: Get me something to throw this mess into—it's still transmitting location data, and blowing high voltage from micro emitters. I need a lidded plastic container. Tell Rose to stay down.

Renfro barked orders to Kendra and Rose: "Get a five-gallon bucket with a lid, Qin. Lil' booger, stay down and don't talk."

Breathing heavily, a sweating Watcher gathered his thoughts. *There's only one reason ALGOS are searching this area...* he looked at his deerskin bundle lying on the floor. *Someone reported a sighting to the programmers.* He hailed Renfro again.

#WATCHER: If you know what this is, you already know it's still dangerous—all surveillance components are still active, and the defensive electro-repellent will continue to discharge for several minutes.

The old soldier spit in memory.

#RENFRO: Yeah, me and ALGOS have a history—not a happy one.

#WATCHER: They are looking for the Afterling, and they shouldn't be looking here unless they had reason. After we dispose of the ALGOS, debrief Sampson and Qin about Rose's little excursion today; I need to know if someone saw Rose.

Returning from the living quarters of the cave, an intrigued Kendra handed off the bucket to Renfro. Gunny hissed: "Nobody touch, unless you want to die." He held the bucket as the Watcher scooped in the still-sparking chunks of component, then sealed it shut.

The Watcher slid down against the wall next to the Rose, who was hiding, still motionless under her cloak. He yanked off his still-smoking gloves, observing charred spots in the leather; glad for the thick skin armoring his forearms, the Watcher noted spots where the cotton cloth had burned away, and beneath it, blisters on the massive crimson and gold scales shielding his pectorals; a singed spot on his left bicep. He checked his face, groping around, but found only a few tender places on his horny brows where the brief fireball's flames had licked.

Looking over to the deerskin cloak, the Watcher saw Rose's dark eyes peering out from under her hood, a mix of curiosity and wonder. He reached his hand up under Rose's cloak and she wriggled her fingers over to his. He spoke to her direct, on the encrypted ChipMate channel:

#Don't come out yet, don't talk—even broken apart, the drone is still looking for you.

She squeezed his hand.

#You've got some explaining to do.

Her fingers wriggled away again.

Renfro motioned to Sampson, who jumped to his side. Renfro whispered: "You and Qin run this down to the drainage stream just around the bend and throw the bucket in so it gets swept away into the river. The other drones will chase its emergency beacon downstream... Stay low, do it quick and don't stop, coming or going; get back here and get ready to abandon ship."

Sampson picked up this bucket, curious. "What is this ungodly thing, Gunny?"

Renfro looked grim. "Satan."

———————•———————

It had been a hot topic of discussion in Habib's office: How to raid

Chartreaux's Raiders and still maintain the charade at Jail?

The Director laid it out: the biggest challenge in this operation would be the need for continued stealth. It was only a matter of time before Boss Chartreaux would demand to see the prisoners, or ask for the girls— but Revolucion recruiters would not be finished with recruitment until tomorrow night. This rescue operation would need to be fast, silent, and brutal.

The Director and Winston had estimated that fourteen of Chartreaux's Brigades-Men were left. Mansour and Goins reported that they had engaged six of Chartreaux's men who remained in command over the combined brigades at the fire scene. That would leave eight Brigades-Men in escort of the Hostesses, and only two men were waived to carry firearms on Chartreaux's crew—the Foreman, and his assistant. Usually this would not have been a problem, except that Chartreaux's goons would have Hostesses as hostages.

A fierce debate on how to accomplish these goals ensued among the participants at the Jail. It was like any other planning meeting at Purgatory... heated words were spoken, and a fistfight nearly broke out, but at last a workable solution was crafted: one faux Ranger—a costumed Jailer—would be left behind at the Jail to maintain the illusion of Ranger control, along with the two other Jailers. Four faux Rangers would be bringing a high value lure in a handcart to Chartreaux's barracks, as a ruse for entry to the fortified cellar below.

Habib had refused to enter the discussion or join the team.

Down at the Docks, a handcart had been discreetly parked, with two ragged gray wool blankets to hide the incoming payload. The runner—the sympathetic Public Servant, Sanders—acted as lookout, signaling the incoming rescue team that the coast was clear.

Clambering out of the secret tunnel from the Jail, the team took their places... Dominic surveyed the group, then subtly frowned. "We appear to have forgotten a key component of this grouping..." The Director walked over and grasped the rails of the handcart. "Who is going to pull this contraption?"

As a System Level Two Facility, Purgatory expressly forbade horses to denizens, alongside firearms and active WeSpeex technology; the only waivers given were for high level visitors, or for the wagons of the WildLand Express bringing goods on Market Mayhem Weekends... that meant a human would need to pull the handcart. Usually that would mean a public servant—but this was too dangerous a mission for any untrained personnel, and Sanders had not yet been trained for their combat team.

"A Ranger would never pull a cart." Dominic observed. "So, I suppose one of us needs to rethink our persona..."

Evangelo wished he could rethink his persona, but that would wreck their well-crafted plan.

The entire team jumped as the rusted hull of the rowboat under the dock shifted, and a thick bumpy skull, topped by a natty felt fedora popped up from underneath the hatch.

The Director was pleasantly surprised. "Care to join us, Habib?"

"Maybe." Habib's face had its usual guarded expression. A sudden splash was heard beyond Purgatory barrier, out in the lake. "I think the gators need feeding." Mansour frowned and looked away. Habib heaved his bulky body from under the boardwalk and addressed the Director, dusting off his tweed sports jacket. "I thought about it, and I wouldn't be much of an accountant if I didn't account for valuable Purgatory assets. I'm available. What do you need?"

"I need an accomplished killer such as yourself to pull this cart, but I believe your garb is inappropriate for such a task."

"Say no more. Sanders, c'mere." Habib motioned to the slender man standing to the side in an oversized coat and gloves. "Trade me your boonie hat and your jacket, then give me your gloves and bandana." Gamely the Public Servant complied. Habib doffed his jacket and hat: "Put on my fedora and jacket; head down the tunnel to the Jail and tell the Head Jailer you're my stand in... all you gotta do is look pretty and keep sitting at the desk." Habib donned the dirty canvas jacket over his own yellowed t-shirt and worn khakis; his run-down sneakers would pass for workwear if none looked too close.

Beneath the new hat and jacket, Sanders was transformed, dignified— but his Public Servant's necklace-chain still showed. Habib scowled, then from around his neck drew his own fine woolen muffler, moth-eaten but still bespoke. Wrapping the scarf around Sanders neck, the Public Servant disappeared, and a finely dressed, vaguely saurian Hombre stood in his place. Conversely, where the refined accountant once stood, a brawny wall of a Macho was seen, heavy brow-ridge and battered nose giving him more the look of a brawler than a banker. Suddenly self-conscious, Habib pulled up the bandana to hide his face.

Habib shook his hand. "Thanks, Sanders. Just don't mess up my clothes."

Genteel, Sanders ducked into the tunnel and the men pushed the rowboat back in place to hide the hatch.

Hurrying, The Director loaded himself and Winston into the bed of the cart, behind the seat; weapons in hand, they lay silent under the blanket as empty crates were piled atop to hide them. Two more faux Rangers, Goins and Mansour, flanked the cart with guns holstered. Bulky coats hid silhouettes and firearms. Hats pulled low, blue bandanas and mufflers helped to hide their identities; the plummeting temperatures of the Norther helped to give them a reason to bundle up.

Evangelo sat in the small seat, bundled in a blanket to hide himself. Habib grabbed the rails of the cart and grunted. "Enjoy the ride—just don't abuse the mule." He gave a mighty heave and the cart started rolling out of the sand of the Docks and up the hill to LowTown.

Narrow, rutted lanes wound between small shacks with shared common walls; rust red combined with bare metal and weathered wood to create the signature color pallet of LowTown. The myriad huts were resourcefully crafted from any salvageable material to be found in the WildLands, and many bore signs of having once been loved before being allowed to fall into decay...

In those early days following The Happening, many stragglers and lost souls came to Purgatory, seeking shelter and society, and these little shacks grew out of that need. At the time, hope had been scarce, but the hardy men and the few women who first moved here seemed to find new purpose in building something fresh out of the ashes of LifeBefore. They had prided themselves in overcoming obstacles—they were Survivors.

Now, as Habib carefully navigated the piles of empty bottles and the drifts of household waste, he felt a twinge of guilt at the lack of progress at Purgatory. Something held them back; they lost their motivation to strive against fate, to better their lot. Habib stepped around a drunken Hombre lying in the street and pondered what had beaten these previously unbeatable Survivors.

North winds were blowing into the South Side of Purgatory, away from the main gate and the scene of the fire. Along with the smell of burning wood, the sickly sweet odor of burning BudWeed was blowing in from the Commons, where Boss Chartreaux's sonorous voice could still be heard luring the crowds to partake off his offerings.

In response to Chartreaux's siren call, Winston's and Zhu's Brigades-

Men had abandoned their posts, and were now lounging in the overgrown grasses of the Commons oblivious to all but the ashes at the end of their cigarettes. Idle, other men chattered and grunted, playing games, flirting with each other, lost in licentiousness and oblivion.

In their place, Chartreaux's Brigades-Men, along with Balogun's and Waitie's brigades, had been ordered out to monitor the fires, with a promise for later recreation. Ill-concealed grumbling ensued, as this was deemed unfair. From the overheard conversations, the rescuers heard sordid details: Boss Chartreaux had made a limited offer to those of his men who would perform the Hostess "rescue"—a chance to sample the merchandise—but only if it all went according to plan.

Taking back roads, Habib's handcart and its concealed cargo pulled up into a narrow alley, unseen by the preoccupied eyes of slothful Purgatory inhabitants. They skirted the back fence until at last they came to an isolated metal Quonset hut. Even before they pulled into view, Evangelo could hear low, angry voices, and the sound of someone hammering on a door:

"What the hell is wrong with you bastards? How is it you couldn't keep three little whores in hand?"

Mansour turned to Goins and whispered: "That's the Foreman, Rickards. Something didn't go well..." Even out to the alley, Rickard's' panicked whisper could be heard drifting up out of the stairwell.

"Get the damn door open. I don't care what it takes—we gotta get in there and secure these bitches or Boss Chartreaux will tear us all a new one." The Foreman's voice rose in pitch; from the tone, Evangelo surmised this was not merely a figure of speech for the Foreman, but a well-founded fear. Involuntarily, Evangelo shuddered, then mastered himself.

The Rescue Team secured their face masks, and Habib pulled the cart into view.

As the least publicly recognizable member of the team, Goins spoke: "What seems to be the problem here?"

The Foreman spun on his heel, nervous, rifle in hand. A sweating, sinewy Hombre with a shifty look, the Foreman had the look of a man who desperately needs a stiff drink. "What do you Rangers want? Can't your uptight asses see we're busy here?"

"Ranger Gupta here with Ranger Danforth. We have a little deposit here—something sweet that Chartreaux said he was seeking..." He tapped

Gupta's badge pinned prominently to his chest, then motioned to the cart seat. "We want our reward."

From the blanketed figure on the handcart seat, Chartreaux's crew heard a muffled falsetto cry. The men working the door stopped and turned to look, their interest piqued. Grunts and hoots trickled up from the cellar entrance...

Mansour silently counted. *Six in the stairwell...* with the Foreman, that totaled seven men.

The Foreman cursed. "Keep your yaps shut, and I'll give you my liquor ration. We've got problems—these bitches somehow jumped my lead man and locked the door before we could enter. We're trying to force the door open."

Habib smiled to himself beneath his muffler. *Sam.*

Goins was genuinely surprised. "You don't have a key?"

Irritable, the Foreman snapped. "It was on the lead man."

"You can't kick it down?"

"No." The Foreman snarled. "And we don't want to damage it, neither. We've been working on it for a half-hour already, and Chartreaux is going to come check on his prizes any minute. If you can help us get in, I'll give you my weekly liquor allotment."

Goins chuckled. "Well, I've got a way to get them to open that door. Get us in close, and we'll make this new girl squeal like a pig. When they hear their little friend crying, I guarantee you they'll open up." He poked the bundled figure with a finger, and it squeaked.

"That's the new Chica?" The Foreman came closer; from under the frayed edge of the woolen blanket he saw bare feet and finely turned ankles dangling from under a white lace hem...

Goins pulled up a top corner of the draped blanket to reveal a lace-covered shoulder and a hint of bare, bronzed neck.

"Huh... needs more exposure." The Foreman reached over to pull the blanket away; Goins grabbed his hand, and Mansour waved his rifle.

"Don't be stupid. Do you want every drunk cowboy in this town to see her? You ain't seen nothin' yet. One peek at this, and they'll kill you all just to get to her." Goins slapped the rear of the bundled heap in the seat.

The blanketed figure sobbed pitifully.

Glaring, the Foreman thought about it. "Alright. Get her over here—but we all get a peek once we get her inside and get her friends back under control."

Goins grimaced. "We get more than a peek—we get it all. Deal?"

The Foreman frowned. "Deal. But no damage—the boys got out of hand this morning with the pink girl, and I can't let any more of them get hurt... the Girls gotta be able to work hard hours to fulfill our new orders."

Mansour gently stroked the handle of his tomahawk beneath his coat.

"Sounds good. " Goins turned to the bundle on the handcart seat. "Come to Daddy, Sweet Cheeks. You're gonna call your soft-hearted friends to open the door and save you from the bad men..."

Face hidden beneath his muffler, Habib pulled the cart closer to the stairwell to the cellar, blocking it. Mansour and Goins roughly grabbed the wriggling bundle and pulled it down from the cart seat, carrying it down into the stairwell.

Chartreaux's men pinched and groped the bundled figure as it was hauled down the stairs to the heavy metal door. The mob began to shove and grind against the Rangers and their prize.

Excited, the Foreman couldn't stand it any longer: he pulled back the corner of the blanket draped across the top of the head: a pair of storm-gray hazel eyes glared up at the Foreman from a satiny bronze-scaled face.

"Well hot damn, look at them sexy peepers. What else you got under here?" The Foreman jerked the blanket loose. "Lemme see that mouth. I'm gonna make it sing..."

The hazel eyes flashed as an unexpectedly masculine mouth snarled from a well-developed jaw. Shocked, the Forman looked down at an unwelcome violation of his own body... a K-Bar knife was sticking out of his chest, inserted expertly between his ribs; that knife was guided by a steady hand attached to a well-muscled arm, draped in a lace curtain borrowed from Habib's office window. Evangelo twisted the knife.

Goins hissed, face breaking into a wicked smile. "Surprise, bitches."

Desperate, the Foreman grabbed Evangelo; Goins pulled his pipe wrench from the loop in his workman's dungarees, and smashed the Foreman's skull with a wet, crackling *thwack*. Evangelo yanked his knife free and slashed, slitting the Foreman's throat from ear to ear.

Behind Evangelo, from the top of the stairwell, empty boxes flew from the bed of the handcart as a blanket was thrown back. The Director rose from the cart, gun in hand: a hole appeared between one thug's eyes, and he crumpled to the ground—the Director's silencer smoked, then bucked again, and a second thug went down, gasping from a sucking chest wound.

A heavy-set goon rushed the Director from the entrance to the stairwell, but Habib slipped his little double-sided dagger out of his sleeve and shivved the goon twice in the kidneys before he could reach the cart. The goon bled out quickly, lying quiet and cold as the chaos unfolded around him, blood running in rivulets down the steps and into the stairwell.

Lust turned to rage at the deception. One mighty thug roared and lunged, fists flying, but Mansour buried his tomahawk into the other man's neck; Mansour's heavy, knotted biceps smashed the hand axe through sinew and cartilage 'til at last it came to a stop, wedged in between the thug's vertebrae. Wrenching the tomahawk free, a chasm of chopped tissue and bone opened wide behind it, filling with blood; Mansour struck again just because he could.

Shouts erupted in the stairwell as Winston emerged from the bed of the cart and leapt down into the midst of the fray, halligan in hand... a thug's hand flew into the air, losing its accompanying knife, no longer attached to an arm. It landed beside the handcart, still twitching. He smashed once more, and a shattered jawbone spun across the pavement to join it.

And as quickly as it started, the fight was over; peace descended on the stairwell.

"Hurry—load all bodies and parts into the stairwell. Habib, pull the cart in closer." The Director commanded. All team members worked to hide the bodies, and Habib kicked up sand to hide splatters of blood. Winston raced towards the door, halligan at the ready, but Mansour beat him to it.

Mansour knocked on the door, twice in rapid succession, then a pause; he tapped twice again. A woman's voice, harsh and low, called out: "Who goes there?"

Mansour leaned his forehead against the door, and placed both hands upon it as if summoning the voice behind it: "The best damn thing that ever happened to you, Coffee..."

"Cream..." The ecstatic whisper came back. Frantic scraping was heard as someone kicked away the objects wedged beneath the door, then a solid thunk as a massive deadbolt slid out of lock.

Shotgun slung behind her, Sam came flying out and tackled Mansour, knocking him to the ground. "Lazarus!" She nearly kissed him, then looked up at all the faces around them, and regained her military bearing.

"Director, I..." She leapt up. "You're alive!" Beside herself with emotion, she exerted a monumental effort to hold back tears. "Thank God you all came—we have specialists wounded." Brushing herself off, she kicked the bodies of her tormentors aside to allow entrance to the cellar.

Sam reached into her pocket and gave the door key to Mansour. "Use this to lock the door when we leave—when the others come, they won't be able to make entry, and it will buy us time." She gazed into Mansour's blue eyes: "I knew you would come for us—but we were prepared to fight. I had this shotgun, and the girls fashioned makeshift knives from old cans and nails..."

Sam's eyes were bright. Mansour reached around her small waist and kissed her on her full, peachy lips... *military bearing be damned.*

Habib turned, his head low; he dropped his dagger to the blood-stained stairs and walked away.

Araceli and Lourdes hovered over Destiny, hiding her from the eyes of their rescuers. Lourdes' left wrist was obviously sprained, swollen and purple, but she made no mention of it. Araceli had an ugly gash on her leg, and the filth of the room made it an infection hazard. Winston pushed into the room, intent on rendering first aid, but Araceli instead leaned across the languid form of Destiny. "Don't look, please—bring us something to hide her..."

The rescue party backed away.

Sam searched: Evangelo's blanket lay outside the door, fouled with gore, and the blanket which hid Dominic and Winston was sodden, trampled in the mud. She turned back to the girls, desperate to cover Destiny's nakedness.

In a trance, Destiny turned to see the Man, clad only in white, standing in the doorway. "I dreamed You were here." Her eyes closed again, head flopping to the side.

Evangelo reached around himself and unwrapped the white lace curtain—"Take this, and cover her."

Lifting the lace curtain from his broad shoulders, Evangelo flung the white garment over her, and in his nakedness, he was not ashamed. He appeared entirely cast of bronze, beautiful, an image of God made Man. Eyes averted, Evangelo motioned, and the Rescue Team exited the room, leaving the stunned women to lay the shreds of Destiny's ruined dress aside, wrapping her in Evangelo's unstained garment. Sam lifted her, and her attendants trailed in her wake, carrying the trailing edge of the white lace so it would not drag through the mire. The Director and his troops stood silent in the stairwell, surrounded by death; Destiny's entourage passed by Evangelo and laid her in the cart.

Unnoticed, an elegant hand reached down to retrieve Habib's forlorn dagger from the steps where he had cast it away. Turning it, a tender fingertip touched the tip of the wicked steel, and the dagger drew a drop of blood from the soft flesh. Having found it satisfactory, the hand tucked the dagger in between breasts to hide it, and moved on to the task of saving Destiny...

Unwilling to lay the filthy blankets upon their wounded teammates, the Rescue Team removed their jackets and laid them upon the women, hiding them in the bed of the cart. The Director and his team then stripped all usable gear from the bodies, and dragged them into the cellar beside their dead co-conspirator. Dominic took the small kerosene lamp left to light to windowless cellar: "Burn this hellhole—let Boss Chartreaux try to figure out who died here."

Evangelo picked up the remains of Destiny's ragged dress: he turned to Dominic, his eyes fierce. "This is what they meant for me. She saved me from this..." Holding it over the flame of the kerosene lamp, Destiny's rag kindled, and Evangelo descended into the cellar; throwing the flaming rag onto the dead men and the mattress, he consigned their sin to hell.

As the flames rose, Dominic posited, "Evangelo, you certainly have nothing to feel shame over, but you may wish to hide your nakedness somehow. You will attract attention, to be sure."

They evacuated to the stairwell, and Dominic locked the door to the cellar behind them. "It is time to vamos, Compadres... in the enclosed concrete space, the smoke will be delayed—but when it is finally seen, a search will commence."

They exited the unholy stench of the Bunk-house basement into the freshness of fall; the late afternoon gathered its shadows under the overcast October sky, trundling towards a chilly twilight. Suddenly cold, Evangelo shivered. Seeing the blanket lying in the mud, the little Ranger grabbed the sodden coverlet from the ground and bundled himself in the cart again as the still-disguised Rescue Team took their places escorting the wagon. Quiet, Habib pulled once more, and the handcart rolled once more through the back alleys of the mind-numbed Purgatory, headed to the Docks.

It was not unexpected; one of Boss Chartreaux's Brigades-Men had spotted the Rescue Team's handcart about halfway home and had attempted to tail them. The suspicious wagon bore no hint of the concealed Hostesses, only what appeared to be a Public Servant hauling a wagon filled with rags and what appeared to be a sick man bundled in a blanket. Himself still incognito, Winston glanced back to identify the man as one of Corey's lieutenants. Apparently suspicious as to why the Rangers were not at the Jail, the thug tailed the handcart down to the Docks, where they rolled to a stop just below the ridge, behind an overgrown hedgerow.

"Hey..." the Brigades-man ordered, hurrying to catch up. "Why are you guys out here? I need to inspect that cart—Bosses' orders."

Back still to the interloper. Dominic nodded and waved the Brigades-man over. All the escorts for the wagon stepped back, allowing the lone thug to approach. The Brigades-man peered over the rail—"What you got under h—"

Dominic made the kill from behind with his silenced handgun, and the thug fell to the ground twitching. Abandoning the handcart behind the ruins of the boat house next to the Dock, the Rescue Team beat a hasty retreat into the tunnel, as Habib came last, dragging the body of the Brigades-Man, and obliterating any tracks left in the sand.

Unlike the Hostess Club Escape Tunnel, the Jail Escape Tunnel was a new construction, and still unfinished; it did not have living spaces, only some benches and torches where the tunnel widened. Here they stopped, remaining silent so they wouldn't accidentally be heard. Feeling around in the dark, Habib pulled a flint-starter out of a bench seat and lit a torch. The flame cast an abrupt, welcome brightness in the dark tunnel.

Listless, Destiny hung limp from Sam's arms as the Girls laid the waif on a limestone ledge. "I need my medical bag—" Sam whispered, before realizing all her supplies had been burned down with the Hostess Club. A keen feeling of loss set in; escaping with just the clothes on their backs, the Hostesses' lifetime of memorabilia and supplies was gone.

Dominic asked. "Do we have any trusted medics here now that Doc Aubergine is gone?"

"I'm just trained in Cardio Pulmonary Resuscitation and basic first aid." Winston shook his head. "The only real medics we have are the

Brigade Medics, and they are all aligned with Chartreaux and his goons. But I do have medical supplies, if a runner can get to my cabin without being detected..." He pointed to the bleeding gash on Araceli's thigh. "Then I can fix that."

Numb, Araceli silently offered her leg as Winston grabbed a clean rag from a nearby bin, and began to cleanse the laceration with a brusque detachment. "Goins, go get my first aid kit."

Habib and Goins looked at each other, knowing what was said next would be painful.

"Sorry, pal," Goins shook his head, gruff tenor voice mournful. "Boss Chartreaux sent for some Brigades-Men to redistribute your personal goods this morning after you fell from power."

Shocked, Winston jumped up: "No—not my brew! NOT my comic-book collection! They're mine—" he was hissing, trying not to yell.

Goins prodded. "All your dolls too."

Winston raised a fist in warning. "They're not dolls—they're action figures!"

The girls stared apprehensively at the seething man. Habib held up a hand; "Pipe down, Winston. We all know how valuable your comic books are, and everyone knows you cherished your toys, as do we all. But they're gone, as Purgatory has decided your house is not yours anymore."

Growling, Winston protested, head in his hands: "My SpaceMartyrs 3000 collection... my Docta Pebba ephemera shadowboxes..."

"I am so, so sorry, Cal... they were beautiful collections." Eyes welling at the sight of the upset Winston, Araceli murmured sympathetically; "My little jewelry-box... it is in the fire, with Jorge." She thought of her beautiful baubles, a lifetime of tastefully pilfered memories now burned in the fire with her friend. Her lip trembled. "Jorge kept it safe, but now they are both gone."

Lives had been lost.

"Oh, God—forgive me, I didn't mean..." Devastated, Winston scrubbed Araceli's laceration with a wet cloth, and she yelped at the sting. He looked slightly ill at her pain: "Jack, Hizzoner...then Bob and Jorge... I just..." he felt like an idiot for his anger over his own pitiful losses and lowered his eyes to avoid Araceli's pained gaze. She gritted her teeth as he debrided the wound with the rough cloth.

Lourdes almost shed a tear, but she would not allow it. "We will survive. Do not cry, Araceli, because there is no time. Cry later. Right now, we need a Medic for Destiny."

Still cloaked only in the wool blanket, Evangelo looked over at Destiny, and then his eyes shifted to the others. He remembered his own injured arm after the Battle at Fort Parker, and how a certain small Afterling fixed it. "I know a Medic. A good one..."

Dominic nodded. "Ladies, the Captain and I must take your leave and return to the Jail. Mansour and Sam, stay to guard; we will send for a medic to prep the wounded, and after dark we must evacuate all—the wounded cannot remain here." He did not mention who his medic was... *let them find out on their own; she must prove her own worth.*

"Agent Ellison has command until I return." The Director turned to Winston. "You are no longer a Boss at Purgatory. What will you do?"

Surveying the wounded Survivors hiding in the tunnel, Winston felt injustice rearing its ravenous head within him: a malevolent hand was directing the actions that caused these losses, and he was determined to stop it. "Whatever your Revolution brings, I'm in—give me a gun, and I'll show you how I got to be Boss in the first place." Binding Araceli's leg with the rag, he left her without even a second glance.

"So be it; here's a new toy." The Director nodded, and pulled his backup weapon from its hiding place in the small of his back—a Ruger 9mm. "You will be under my command—for now, take post at the hatch."

Grunting, Mansour extended his hand to Winston. "Welcome to the party. I'll take post at the other end." Glad to be finished with painful work, Winston holstered his weapon and headed to the Dock end of the tunnel, halligan in hand.

Torch alight, Mansour led the rest of the party back towards the Jail. Knocking on the hatch, they gave sign and callsign; Sanders greeted them as the hatch opened. The Team exited the tunnel, and Mansour ducked back down the hatch to keep guard as Sanders rolled the desk back into place.

Sanders reported to Habib: "Business as usual. No visitors, yet; everyone is either high, drunk, or prepping for Market Mayhem Weekend."

Market Mayhem Weekend. The Director smiled: *the Cavalry comes...* he pulled himself up out of the hatch, then grunted in pain as his ribs crackled beneath their wrap. "We must find medical care for our wounded —"

"Wounded includes you, Director," Goins sniped gently.

The Director coughed, then waved a dismissive hand: "I can be wounded later. Our Hostesses must be tended first, and I must prepare for tonight's gathering of Unit Leaders. As you may have already learned, Agent Azarian does not necessarily wait for orders. It would be wise to make contact with the Team in the Stable Tunnel to let them know of our plans..."

"I have a RingWorld, but it won't work here, or I'd do it for you." Habib shook his head. DeadZones rendered WeSpeex Rings useless at Level Two and lower facilities; as a level Two Facility, Ring users couldn't activate inside Purgatory walls, or up to fifty feet outside the wall. Before the Hostess Club burned down, Sam had sent Ring communications from outside the walls, from the safety of the safe room tunnel entrance.

"Communication is becoming an issue—I need to learn how these DeadZones work," the Director mused. "Boss Chartreaux Mentioned an 'Electronics Window' at seven a.m. when I was being acquainted with his cattle prod."

Aghast, Goins visibly recoiled.

Dominic continued: "They cannot keep their DeadZone mechanism a secret forever; but until we learn that secret, we need to send word ahead the old-fashioned way. Agent Goins, take a few minutes to tend to yourself, then Sanders will escort you to the back exit to the safe room tunnel."

"I don't need an escort, and you don't have the manpower. Keep Sanders to help tend the wounded, and I'll take care of it myself."

Sam frowned. "Travel without a buddy is forbidden."

"Do I look like a give a damn?" Goins sniped. "I'm not some girl who can't take care of herself... I'm me, and I can handle it alone."

"Do you want to get busted in rank?" Sam bristled "Because this is how you get busted..."

"Agent Ellison is correct in her orders, Goins," Dominic intervened. "But your assessment of our situation is accurate. Agent Ellison, you make the decision."

Seething, Sam was too busy with Destiny; "Stop being an ass and I'll consider the suggestion. Make a request."

Goin grumbled. "Request to perform solo mission..."

"Go," snapped Sam.

"Very well..." Dominic passed clean rags to Sam. "Goins will undertake the short but dangerous journey to retrieve our Medic, who is secured in the safe room tunnel. Escort the Medic and team to the Dock tunnel, and we will plan for tonight from here."

"Sure thing, Director." Goins grumbled, gingerly rubbing a broken nose. "I've got to get my tools from my bunkhouse anyway—I'll grab it on my way through before someone decides to redistribute my stuff, too." The slight Survivor moseyed down the hall, whistling.

The Director appeared tired; his broken ribs were becoming problematic. He needed rest and sleep... "I'll brief you of any updates prior to our departure."

Habib nodded and looked to Evangelo. Still clad in nothing but the blanket, the little Ranger lent it his own heroic demeanor, and it became a cape around his shoulders rather than just a moth-eaten blanket. *Sometimes the man makes the clothes...*

Dominic and Evangelo departed down the hall; Habib turned his attentions to the Jail and its temporary role as Armory. It was time to stock up... he called into the hallway to Sanders, "Time to get to work."

As a Municipality Janitor, Sanders had spent a great deal of his life carrying out the tasks of Jail maintenance, all of it important. He had always carried himself with an air of confidence; in all he did, whether it was emptying buckets or smuggling prisoners out of the Jail, Sanders gave it all he had within him. It was the primary reason Habib had recruited Sanders for the Cause. But even then, Habib had built a mental wall between himself and the Public Servant. Now, the jacket and hat made Sanders seem like an equal; dressed in Habib's too-large jacket, Sanders carried the look well. Habib felt a pang of humbleness—until now, he had never seen Sanders as anything other than a Janitor.

No longer seeing a need for a ruse, the men traded clothing once more. Taking back his hat and jacket, Habib thought for a moment, then handed the bespoke woolen muffler back to Sanders. "Keep it. It suits you."

Taken aback at the MoneyMan's generosity, Sanders' hands lingered on the muffler. "I can't accept this. It's a genuine Savon's of London Pashmina—I haven't had the pleasure of owning one of the since..." a shadow passed across his face. "It was a long time ago."

"You're pretty fashion savvy for a Janitor." He expected Sanders to tell him a story of how he had once been a banker, or perhaps even a lawyer...

"I made good money as head of the University Maintenance Department, and I could afford the finer things in life." Sanders said, not attempting to hide his pride. "Janitorial Services made me a comfortable man."

Habib ceded the floor to his preconceived notions. "You're a true gent of refinement. It's yours." Habib's thoughts lingered on the growing number of refugees. "I have supplies in my cabin—Sanders, we need reinforcements from the public servants' gang to bring them in quickly. Can we trust Marcus and Barrie?"

Sanders nodded. "Them, and Sergio. Those are the only ones fit enough to really help, though. I'll get them moving this way."

"Have them meet here." Habib nodded. "They will be bringing supplies from my cabin to the Jail tonight, under cover of darkness. They should bring any of their own personal goods that they want to keep: they won't be able to go back to their barracks if we are discovered." Habib grew thoughtful. "Tell them if they choose to help us, they are choosing to live as free men—but it's a risky proposition."

The wiry little Public Servant bristled. "I already live as a free man—it is others who do not recognize I am free."

"Yeah. You're free..." Pulling open the long, top drawer of his writing desk, Habib reached deep, and pulled a slender, hand-fabricated skeleton key from a compartment in the back. He tossed it to Sanders. "Here's a copy of the Bosses' master keys; I made a wax cast and created three copies on the sly—it fits the Magister Brand Padlocks that we use at the Jail. You're the Key Master now. Use it tonight for anybody you see fit."

Reaching up, Sanders felt for his padlock, but then hesitated. "I'll need this to enter the barracks. The Watchman, Wunstler is still checking us on entry—I'll keep it until tonight." Sanders headed out the door to retrieve his compatriots. Habib watched him walk away, a free man.

Habib pulled his bottle and glass from the drawer, and poured a stiff one. He grimaced as he swilled it down:

It's the rest of us who aren't free.

———◆———

Sitting on a plastic milk crate with Sassy at his feet, Agent Renfro was monitoring the entrance to the tunnel; Sampson and Kendra were hissing to each other about candies, and Oskar was asleep, having been fed a haunch of rabbit. For his part, the Watcher was trying to concentrate on watching his surroundings, but he was finding it difficult—he was being bombarded by unwanted emotions from the Afterling.

Having finished his quest to free Dominic and Evangelo, and having engineered a new contract with Rose, the Watcher set up post to watch for any further intrusions and set about to finally collect on the bet he won against Rose back at Camp Mystery. Shotgun across his lap, he settled in next to her on the hay, demanding his payment for his quest: Rose was to hold his hand and access their Ring as she had promised.

She seemed to be reluctant to listen to it in front of him. "Promise me you won't Deva my mind?"

So, the Watcher did what he always did; he made a promise he could keep, then found another way to get what he wanted. Rose accessed his ring and set her listening mode to private. *No problem,* he chuckled to himself, then opened her remote display in shadow mode so he could see and hear everything she accessed. It was all part of his investigation, so it was completely ethical. Having opened a secret window into her virtual safe room, the Watcher busied himself with sorting through his weaponry, expecting to be slightly bored.

He had not expected to be metaphysically brutalized by her instead.

Opening her files, she opened pictures of her family: Joseph, Amelia, and unknown others, then went straightaway to a holophone entitled "Hope." It was a simple piano arrangement and sounded as if it had been recorded in a large open area—a chapel perhaps?

Eyes unfocused, Rose breathed deeply, her heart rate slowing; she was entering that hypnotic state the Director called "conditioning." The music enhanced that effect, and a voice broke free, running wild through the valley of song. The brilliant voice lofted into the high notes with ease, casting a bittersweet hope into his heart; then the Watcher recognized the voice as Rose, singing even as she had sung while he stood outside her window that day in Dominic's hideaway:

> *There's a meadow in a valley where the skies are fair*
>
> *Even though I've never seen it, I know that it is there*
>
> *For in my dreams and my heart I know the way there*
>
> *And I know that I will find it someday.*

The Watcher gave a slight frown: *How can you possibly believe in something you've never seen?*

The recorded voice became bright:

Oh, my dream has never failed me, though I've searched my whole life through

There were times I almost found it, and those times were with you

I know it lies somewhere just beyond the river

And I know that I will find it someday.

He smiled to himself; this was Rose as he had always imagined her, a little church mouse, singing sweetly in the Choir.

I know Heaven's always what I've dreamed of—

In God's Heaven, I will find you and your love

His skepticism ran wild with her voice: this was the opiate of the masses he had always rejected. A Heaven, a God, a place to run to when the world doesn't work out... it kept people from working out their world.

Eyes closed, she sat next to him and entered the maelstrom of her own emotion. Small wisps of feeling curled through her hand and into his, growing stronger as the song continued; what started out as a mere discomfort intensified into a crushing avalanche of longing and heartache tinged with sweetness.

Someone's waiting in that valley, 'neath a sky of blue

And you'll turn to me and call me, and then I'll know it's you

I'll run to you, and you'll never leave me ever

And I know that I will find you someday...

Almost unbearable in impossible hope, he nearly pulled his hand away, but then he steeled himself: this was his chance to lay out a musical map to the hidden Rose—and her emotional invasion might reveal the pathway back to her heart.

The voice soared above the heartache, winging towards the dream— and at the edge of that triumphal joy, a wobble of agony almost cracked the purity of that final rapturous climb towards the Gates of Rose's Heaven. But she mastered the wobble, and powered her way through to the end:

And I know that I will find you someday!

And the Watcher went through the Gates of Heaven with her.

Exhausted, he leaned back against the hay. *How is this sort of emotional transference even possible?* In theory, he knew how it was done with "Chi" in martial arts—but this?

He had his own theories as to how she was able to invade his body with her own emotions—it was possible she was able to organically access limbic pathways in a fashion similar to the way the Xirxes Program accessed neural pathways for pleasure and pain. But how could she do it without a WeSpeex Ring, or software? It seemed to be associated with whatever effect happened when she became that inspirational Goddess on the Berm: Rose had some way of invading other people's emotional space, of connecting through neuronic impulses...

The Watcher opened her Tesoro profile:

#ROSE—ID #TMA673CdF

#AGE: 26,

#DUTY STATION—TEXAS, TESORO MISSION; Hope
Family, Alamo Project, Team Fannin.

#COLOR TEAM: PINK

#TEAM MOTTO: Duty, Courage, Hope

#SPECIALIZATIONS: Scout, First Aid, Morale

#WEAPONS: Rifle, Expert

#SKILLS CERTIFICATION:

Herbcraft Certification Level 5

SonicArts Certification, Level 6

TouchScience Certification, Level 7

EQ8 / XLR8—REFERRED TO LEVEL 10

SonicArts... when Rose's cry shattered the mirror at Mystery Outpost, that had to be a manifestation of her "SonicArts Certification." And her ability to touch and relay energy? *That would probably be TouchScience.* But what was that last category? Whatever it might be, the combined result of voice and touch was excruciating.

The Watcher gritted his teeth and endured, relieved when the song and all its pathos ended. There were many songs marked as "Favorites," including some with very high view counts which intrigued the Watcher, at the top or the list being Grofe's Grand Canyon Suite, Sinatra's incomparable "Under My Skin," and Edith Piaf wailing her way through "La Vie en Rose." Fearful, the Watcher waited for these; *certainly, the next song can't be nearly so emotionally charged...*

Instead, Rose chose "Danny Boy."

What followed next was an hour of heart-wrenching torture, as Rose gave voice to her emotions through music, using the most soul-crushing melodies known to humanity to neurolimbically assault the Watcher:

Khachaturian's "Adagio," Rachmaninoff's "Variations on a Theme by Paganini," Dvorak's "Largo"—

In each, Rose was oblivious to the Watcher's turmoil even as she reveled in her own. Oddly enough, she seemed to be filled with a kind of masochistic emotional ecstasy while immersing herself in these heartbreaking musical triggers. The Watcher was baffled: *Why would she put herself through this kind of hell?*

He could hardly wait for it to end, but the Watcher vowed to make it through. He steeled his resolve as Rose chose a song unknown to him: Shame. *Hmmm... this shows some promise.* He upped the internal volume controls:

Shame—you call my name and I'm to blame for my own tears;

A brassy, smoky feminine voice sang out his aural pathways—Rose? He surreptitiously opened the artist bio, but found none.

Shame—my sad heart fears no one can hear me when I cry...

The voice was at once sensual and sorrowful, a wounded, world-weary ingenue—undeniably Rose. Intrigued, he opened the raw audio file, and found the header: *From the Yellow Rose: Live at the Magnolia!* He rubbed his chin... the Yellow Rose was the name of the lounge from Rose's "City of Pleasure" Tour talk, the Magnolia was the Ballroom: nothing else appeared in the metatags. The voice became sweetly, ruefully comedic, Judy Garland invoking Gracie Allen:

But I can't lie...

My heart goes to my head, my common sense lies dead

I don't think like I ought, and suddenly I'm caught.

Seized by an emotion he couldn't recognize, the Watcher listened as her tone changed again, now tinged with passionate resignation. A dam broke loose, somewhere inside Rose; she became one with the voice and poured into the Watcher, and he was swept away.

You look into my eyes and I'm mesmerized

You make me think you care and suddenly I'm snared

Entangled in your arms, arrested by your charms

And all my false alarms are overcome by your persuasion—

Shame!

Head thrown back, lashes trembling, Rose became the song without singing a note—and a tidal wave of uninvited agony flooded the Watcher's brain. Rose held her hands out, unheeding of his presence. It was a place the Watcher had never visited, something he had never felt, but he knew exactly what this was...

This was a paean of unrequited love.

Involuntarily, the Watcher jerked his hand away from hers as if he were being burned. With a myoclonic jerk, Rose fell back into the real world, out of her world of memory.

Arms involuntarily flung out, decorticate for a moment, she gasped. Grabbing her to keep her head from hitting the floor, the Watcher immediately regretted his sudden decoupling from her emotional hell. Breathing back to life, Rose blinked. "What happened?"

Exasperated at his own weakness, and bewildered by her sorrow-seeking, he linked their portals again:

#You were having a bad dream.

Lying back in the hay, she laid a hand upon her heart; "Oh, it wasn't a bad dream—it was just a memory."

#It was a bad memory, then.

The Watcher considered that Rose might not have any memory that wasn't somehow linked to a traumatic event, and he was keenly familiar with that situation. But unlike her, he did not spend any time immersing himself in such memories.

#Listen to something not associated with sorrow. You pick or I will.

"Well, how do you know it was sad?" She seemed genuinely unaware of the extent of her intrusive emotional ability.

#Let's just call it intuition; now, pick something not sad.

"Sadness can be beautiful; I'd rather feel sadness than feel nothing." Rose mused. "I'm sorry—I can't think of anything not sad right now. You pick."

The Watcher flipped through his own music library, and landed on something innocuous by Bob Wills—Deep in the Heart of Texas. For some reason it made him feel a semblance of what he liked to call happiness—meaning, not as irritated as usual.

"Oh! I know this song—but I've never heard this version before..." The fiddles and trumpets filled her from head to toe and spilled back into him, colored by her emotion once more. Entranced, Rose listened, and the Watcher listened with her.

"Does this music have a memory to go with it?"

#No—that's why I like it.

"Oh." She sang along, wiggling her toes to the beat of the honky-tonk piano and thumping stand-up bass;

"The Stars at Night are Big and Bright...

CLAP—CLAP—CLAP—CLAP

Deep in the Heart of Texas!"

As she sang, the Watcher glimpsed her bare feet poking out from beneath her fur cloak, toes dancing. He wasn't sure if it was her feeling or his, but it felt—*different*. With every tap of her toes, little curls of emotion were embedding themselves in his own heart, and the music imprinted in his mind, leaving an indelible footprint in his soul... the music came alive, born of them both.

The music has a memory now.

Mesmerized by her lilting voice and wiggling toes, the Watcher could only faintly hear a familiar knock from the far end of the tunnel. Rising from the hay, he told Rose—

#Someone is at the door, and they know the code knock. Inform Kendra and Sampson.

Rose seemed impressed. "You can hear that? It's all the way to the end of the tunnel..."

#Yes, now tell them to prep for incoming visitors, since I cannot speak.

"Okee Dokee..." She hopped up and slipped on her moccasins, then headed to the stalls while the Watcher made ready in the doorway.

"Kendra—Kendra! Hey..." She poked her head around the corner to see Sampson peacefully sprawled in the hay, fast asleep. Kendra was in the corner, counting bullets again.

"Shhhh, Afterling. I finally got Herman asleep—if you got your Watcher to snooze, let's bust out of here and save our Girls."

"I'm sorry... He's still awake. But to be fair I didn't even try." Rose seemed chagrined at her own failure. "It would just be a waste of time—"

Kendra frowned. "Gah—you wuss! I told you exactly what to do; if you do it right, he'll be out like a light."

"Even if I did exactly what you said, he still wouldn't sleep." Rose pouted. "He never sleeps... I had to knock him out last time."

"That's insane. Every man sleeps afterwards." Kendra was miffed. "If he doesn't sleep, how will we ever sneak out of here?

"Well, I guess we'll never know." Rose peeked back into the tunnel to see the Watcher scowling at her from his post, blocking the door. She blanched—*could he hear everything?* "And besides, that wouldn't be nice, to deceive him that way a second time..." She said sweetly, saying the words with special emphasis for listening Watchers, then looked back at him again. He was still scowling at her. "Anyhow, Agent Azarian asks to please wake Sampson—a visitor is at the tunnel door, one who knows the knock this time."

Kendra jumped up—"They better have word on Sam and the Girls, or I'm gonna make myself known." She shook her sleeping Giant, and he awakened with a look of pure bliss upon his once-again gentle face. She muttered to him: "Get up! You can snore later—an Agent is here."

Unperturbed, Sampson stretched, then slung his rifle across his shoulder and stood, shaking hay from his shirt. Steps approached from the hallway, and he met them with a smile.

Renfro came striding down the tunnel, the slender Goins swaggering by his side, Sassy wagging and hassling behind them. "Fall in, Team. Agent Goins has an update and instructions, so listen up. " He patted Goins' shoulder and stepped back out of the way.

"Thanks, Gramps. What the hell did you lunkheads do to the Tunnel Door? It looks like it's been burnt." Goins gaped, then stopped cold at the sight of the Afterling. "So, you're the Guest?" Inspecting Rose, still swathed in her cloak, Goins seemed skeptical. "You look like you've been airbrushed."

Kendra appeared hurt: "We didn't get to finish her camouflage job. If you can do better, do it—Lulu."

Goins gave a vicious glare to Kendra, but ignored the statement to continue. "I've got good news and bad news. The good news is, the Girls have been rescued, and Destiny is saved."

Rose gave a muffled squeal, and Kendra pumped her fist in the air—

Goins continued. "The bad news is, we have wounded. They are holed up in the Dock tunnel; we're gonna have to evacuate, and we need a

Medic to prepare them. I take it that would be you—" Goins pointed at the Watcher. He shook his head, then held out his open hand to the Afterling. Goins flinched. "You don't look like a Medic."

Kendra snarled. "And you don't look like a Hembra, Lulu—yet here we are."

"Shut your damn mouth, or I'll shut it for you, Kendra—and the name's Lou now, so stop dead-naming me, bitch." Goins started to swing.

Gunny grabbed Goins' shoulder. "Cut it out, Lou. We don't have time for this drama. If you want to fight, take it outside when there's not a war on. Until then, keep it under control."

Kendra grumbled. "You abandoned us. We were a team."

"Screw your team. If identifying as a man means I don't have to bang people for a living, then I'll do it. I don't want to be a whore." Goins spat it out. "The Happening gave me a gift—I don't even look like a woman anymore. I've got these shoulders now, and I'm strong as a horse—" Goins flexed, bringing the musculature of a fully masculinized Hembra to bear. "Besides, I never fit in with you all anyway. I want to live as a man, and thanks to TransMutation, I can—so that makes me one."

Just a little surprised, the Watcher grunted. Due to the masculinizing effects of the Visionaries' ill-fated, testosterone-activating "birth control" virus, there had been many cases of women whose bodies were so completely TransMutated, they could pass for male at first glance.

Even so, most Hembras openly identified as female, still dressing and acting as they had in their more feminine past. Since chronic skin inflammation rendered Survivors hairless, and therefore beardless, the effect wasn't quite as jarring. Still, there were a few Hembras who identified as male and managed to keep their original identities secret, only to be discovered after their deaths.

That was not an option for most Survivor women.

The emotional mask slipped from Kendra's face, and she came undone. "Just shove it in our faces! Don't you think if we could do it too, we would? Some of us can't pass as male, even though we tried..." She swung at Goins, but Sampson grasped her wrist. "You can hide—we can't!" She pointed at the Afterling. "Look at her—there's no way in hell she can hide! One goon saw her today, and already she's hunted like an animal—all because she looks like a woman."

Well, that explains it. The Watcher shot a look at the Afterling: *you've been reported to the programmers, and they've summoned the ALGOS to find you.*

Somewhere, someone in Authority knew—a small golden woman was at Purgatory.

Kendra continued to rail at Goins. "But you just walk the streets, free —hiding in plain sight, passing yourself off, swaggering around without fear. You get all the privilege and none of the pain... " Kendra shoved her face just inches from Goins' own. "We need you, and you act like you're not one of us—"

Goins snarled. "I'm not one of you. I'm me, and I don't play on your team anymore. Your problems are your own." Goins turned and walked down the tunnel. "Gramps, when you need me, call me—I'll be waiting out here, away from the drama queen."

Goins turned to quietly ask, "You got any candy?"

Gunny shook his head and pulled a slice of sugarcane from his pocket. "I can always count on you, Gramps..." Goins gave a wide smile and snatched it out of Gunny's hand, then sauntered away.

"Well, to be fair, I thought she was a man." Rose offered helpfully. "He still has delicate hands, though."

"He's a she." Kendra snapped.

Sampson interjected—"No, he's not a she—she's a he, so that makes he's a he..." Sampson looked confused.

"Lou is Lou." Agent Renfro rubbed his forehead. "I don't give a damn what Lou is, as long as Lou gets the job done. Get your gear, and get your job done, lil' Booger—they're calling for a Medic."

◆————◆————◆

Twilight was creeping up on the backside of the day. Within the hour, the creatures of the WildLands would be awakening from their afternoon respites, preparing to feed and hunt. Working against this timetable, the Medic escort team made their way through willow-wood—Goins, Sampson, Kendra, Rose, and the Watcher—as Renfro and the Tunnel Team prepared for the incoming wounded.

Casting his gaze overhead, the Watcher swept the skies for any sign or sound of drones. Rose was on the lookout, but even then, the drones' heat-shielding technology would make the ALGOS harder to spot even for the Afterling's infrared-sensitive eyes.

The only reason he had agreed to leave the tunnel with her was because it was no longer safe, having been discovered by the now-disabled death-bot. Grim, the Watcher calculated how long it might take for the other drones to track the remains of their lost hive-mate; in the plastic bucket, swept away on the current, they should be ten miles or more south of the present position. Once the ALGOS located the dead drone's distress beacon and recovered the remains of its digicard, the deadly drones would begin to backtrack through its plotted location data, looking for point of last interaction...

Then all hell would break loose. *Programmers don't like people messing with their Bots.*

The Purgatory Dead Zone would offer some protection from the ALGOS, *but then the threat turns from death-bots to "devil-men."* He cracked his knuckles and tried to game scenarios. How many drones could he defeat at once? How many men could he reasonably take down at one time? It had been a long time since he had to neutralize a crowd. Choosing between evils, he decided that, for now, humanity was the lesser of the two...

Coming around the inlet, the Watcher could see the water downslope, some three hundred feet to their west. They were far enough away to be protected against immediate threat from alligators, but not far enough to suit the Watcher. Looking through the bare willow branches, he could see what looked like a great floating raft of logs in the inlet; the thought of them made him long to steer as far clear from the water as possible. The weather had turned suddenly colder, and alligators should be hibernating now, or laying low in water to conserve heat. *That should keep the cold-blooded reptiles at bay.* Not that he minded fighting alligators... looking down at the small cloaked figure creeping by his side, he decided he just didn't want to take the chance.

A twig snapped beneath him, and the Watcher grimaced. Evangelo's moccasin boots helped enormously, but he was still too noisy for his own taste. Focusing on his own footfalls, the Watcher rolled his feet to avoid any additional twig-snaps. He had always felt like he was adept in stealth, but here, in the presence of this team's mastery, he felt clumsy...

Goins was probably the only one that didn't make the Watcher feel incompetent at stealth. Goins ability lay in 'fixin' things, not in killing things, so the need for stealth was not as important. Attempting to look larger than the slight figure could command, Goins swaggered even while sneaking. Even so, compared to Sampson, Goins looked small.

The Giant was leading the party through the woods again, running low through the willow thicket; Sampson was surprisingly quiet for so large a man. A look of natural intelligence accompanied his quiet movement. He had an easy grace that came from a lifetime of moving through the woods unnoticed - but Sampson had nothing on the Afterling.

The Watcher could not help but be impressed with Rose's capability to move undetected through her surroundings. Wearing the moccasins Evangelo crafted, the Afterling was moving almost silently through the woods; her cloak hid her silhouette, and Kendra's makeup camouflage artistry helped Rose to blend in with the background in a most impressive way. She had been stealthy before - but now she was nearly invisible, especially when motionless.

Kendra would have been nearly as hard to spot, if it were not for her rhinestone-studded garb. The slender Hembra was swathed in a too large canvas coat borrowed from Renfro, and she had turned her hat inside out to hide its jewels, but an occasional sparkle was still seen. It couldn't be avoided, though - it was all Kendra had left to wear now that the Hostess club was burned.

Regarding gear, Rose and the Watcher had fared better than the Hostesses and their guards - most of their important gear was down in the tunnel at the time of the fire, and Rose had grabbed their two gear bags on the way out when evacuating. That quick action on her part had saved their belongings, including his own personal gear and sidearms. He had again donned the Public Servant's canvas duck jacket over his vest and badge, then put the felt hat and balaclava in place; this provided cover as a laborer should they be spotted, but he could prove rank if necessary by his badge. He patted the Remington V3 Tac-13 beneath his jacket and gave a grim smile - *stay close, little Sindee.*

Sampson held up his hand, signaling the group to halt. They were approaching Purgatory wall, and with it, the signal Purgatory Dead Zone. While inside the Dead Zone, the Watcher would lose his ability to communication through the Ring, but the ALGOS should also lose their own abilities to operate - for now.

Removing his glove, the Watcher tapped the Afterling's shoulder and held out his hand to link up.

#*Last instructions before we enter: I will no longer be able to use the Ring, so stay close, stay aware, and stay silent until we get inside the fence. ALGOS will be scanning for high-pitched voices like yours. If we*

are approached by anyone, follow our protocol. Do you have any questions?

She shook her head, deer's ears flopping atop her hood.

#Good. Let's get this done.

As they approached, the Watcher smelled the smoke from the earlier fires, and an itch crept into his consciousness... he rubbed his arm where the port had once dangled. He noticed and wondered—what exactly was in that fire today? How much Stuff had burned, along with the rest of Boss Zhu's house? The Watcher looked at the Afterling and asked himself: how much of his earlier savagery could be attributed to chemicals rather than Afterlings? Was it possible he had merely been anxious from exposure to drugs, and not just crazy from the potential loss of Rose?

He remembered Dominic's initial warning to stay away from Purgatory as a potential trigger for addictive behavior—but it could not have been avoided if the Director and Evangelo were to have been rescued. He took a deep breath and held it, trying to shake the craving; then Sampson motioned, and they all moved forward into the breach in the wall.

Placed out of sight from the guard towers which rose above the Commons, the breach in the wall was well-hidden by trees, making it possible to open the entrance unseen by official eyes. Purgatory had become lax in physical security, having become too reliant upon the laziness of its mind-altered inhabitants. Drifts of discarded construction materials and trash had been carelessly piled around the breach, and overgrown brush further helped to shield it from view.

Sampson poked his head through first, and having found no sign of anyone nearby, waved to the others to follow. Goins, Kendra, Rose—then the Watcher, down on all fours, crawling through broken glass and trash embedded in the dirt. Rose stood to brush the shards of glass and metal from her knees, and the Watcher realized with horror that she was barelegged under her cloak.

Exactly what does she have on, up under there?

She had kept herself covered all day, and he had just assumed she wearing her leggings, as usual.

Never assume; it just makes an ass out of u and me. But why on God's green earth was Rose barelegged? He grimaced—the thought of her slogging through mountains of trash with naked legs made him extremely uncomfortable. Bare legs... bare feet... he wished he had looked earlier.

Well, too late now. At least she was wearing her moccasins. He would just have to help her change into something more rational when she got back to the safe room tunnel. Befuddled by bareness, the Watcher was becoming distracted once again; he focused and kept moving.

No path existed here—that was a construct. Paths lead to things, so a deliberate attempt was made to push trash back into place every time the wall was breached so it would remain hidden. Picking through the trash pile, Goins brought up the rear, rolling cans and bottles where the team's feet trod.

Crouching, Sampson rounded a wall of debris, then hissed, motioning for everyone to get down.

"Quick—Make like a bunch of drunken bums." Kendra flopped down on the ground, and rolled into a ball beneath Renfro's coat; Sampson covered her with his large, loose jacket, then leaned his head against her as if she were a pillow. Rose crouched beneath her cloak, and the Watcher laid his head down against the soft furs—

Goins squatted on an upturned bucket, pulling the baseball cap's brim down.

A heavy Macho came into view, grunting as he picked through the garbage. He might have been young once, but no one could tell beneath the grime and ragged clothing; the sharp smell of alcohol combined with the acrid punch of sweat and urine enveloped him, casting a protective cloud of stench around him. He was tossing bottles aside, first one, then another...

"Gotta be some." He saw a drop in one bottle, and put his lips to it, tipping it up. Draining it, he licked the rim, then tossed it aside, reaching for yet another seemingly empty bottle. He almost didn't notice Sampson. Almost...

He poked Sampson, who muttered quietly. "Go home, Bogie."

"Why you sleepin' here, Herman?" Bogie groaned, swaying slightly in the lowering twilight. "'S'cold." He poked him again. "Get up."

"Bogie I'm fine. Go away." Sampson opened an eye. "I'm warm enough." Fluffing the unseen Kendra beneath his own jacket, he rolled over and burrowed his head into her kidneys. She hissed.

Goins muttered and turned away: "Don't talk to me."

Bogie started to move towards the Watcher, who growled irritably. Bogie wisely avoided him. Sampson, on the other hand...

"You got no jacket on. You gonna freeze." Bogie picked up another bottle, and sniffed it. "Why you and your friends here? Oh, your home burned..." Bogie pondered what it all meant. "You come to my house. C'mon. Get up."

Sampson sat bolt upright. "God almighty Bogie, leave already. I'm just resting."

"Can't do that. You ain't got no jacket." Bogie snorted. "Come to my house." Sotted, he held out a trembling hand to the group, but they shook their heads. "Suit y'selves... but y' might need this." Peeling off his own overcoat, Bogie leaned down to lay it tenderly across the Giant's shoulders, then planted a kiss on his forehead. "G'night, boy." Wearing only a putrid rag of a shirt, Bogie wandered off in the chill towards another pile of bottles, disappearing between the dunes of trash.

Casting the stinking coat away from himself, Sampson hissed; "The coast is clear. Let's go." They all rose from their respective trash beds and dusted off.

Rose picked up the odiferous relic thrown before them—the Watcher snatched the reeking rag out of her hands, scowling and shaking his head. He laid it across a trash pile, in hopes that the bum would come back to find it.

"But now he has no coat." Rose's eyes were tragic. "What is wrong with him? Why is he picking through the trash? Has he no one to speak for him or take care of him?"

Still sitting on the bucket, Goins chuckled. "Emotional..."

Sampson scoffed quietly. "Bogie's here because he wants to be. He blew through his entire ration of liquor for the week, and now he's looking for more in other people's empties."

"He's a drunk, Afterling." Kendra whispered bluntly. "Maybe you don't have them where you from, so let me explain... drunks drink too much brew and don't stop. He has a house, but he can barely get in it because it's piled high with trash. Bogie would be just as well off as anyone else if he took care of himself or his stuff."

"But what did he for Herman was so adorable. He didn't have to help, and yet he did..." Rose looked moist and breakable, dark eyes glistening.

"Don't feel sorry for him. If you do, you're stupid." Kendra turned away from the Afterling's unbearable eyes.

Seeing an opportunity, the Watcher audibly sighed, then held up a hand to Rose, *Stay...*

He walked after Bogie, hiding the group just around the corner in their sheltered cove of trash. Weaving his way through broken items, the Watcher spotted the swaying man nearby, then wordlessly handed him his own ragged canvas jacket.

Bogie gently belched at the Watcher and leaned in close; the Watcher quickly turned away to avoid the stench of his breath. "I was naked and you clothed me." The Bum sniffed the jacket. "And it don't stink. You're a good guy." He leaned in close to the Watcher's ear, and the voice suddenly became commanding: "Hug the wall, and move quickly—the coast is clear ahead. I'll be seeing you again, soon..."

Startled by Bogie's pronouncement, the Watcher turned back only to see a stumbling bum once more. Donning the faded tan jacket, the rheumy Survivor patted the Watcher's arm, then swayed gently down the winding lane between the trash heaps, picking at bottles.

Pondering it all, the Watcher returned to the group, clad only in his shirt, vest and beige balaclava.

"Oh, Deva!" Rose marveled, her eyes bright with emotion as the Watcher strode into view. "That was so sweet..."

"You're an idiot." Kendra mocked, her eyes disdainful. "Enjoy being cold."

Eyes rolling, Goins grunted and turned away.

Sampson, however, knew exactly what happened. Turning his back to the girls, he whispered. "That was a kind act—should earn you a round or two." He gave him a subtle thumbs-up. "Well played, horndog." The Watcher looked over Sampson's shoulder at Rose, who was gazing upon the Watcher as if he were dipped entirely in cane syrup. The Watcher nodded and tapped his brim to Sampson.

Damn straight.

Sampson mentioned casually: "So what are you gonna do about hiding your gun?" Suddenly aware, the Watcher remembered the Remington slung across his back

Well, damn. He had become distracted by sad eyes, and the prospect of playing the Hero. *Distraction hones death...* Kicking himself mentally, he capitulated to the obvious—*there's only one way to play this angle...*

He boldly walked over to the town drunk's wretched overcoat—still draped across a heap of trash—and pulled it on.

I meant to do that.

Kendra gagged. "You smell like dead fish floating in a cesspool. Stay downwind."

Rose was conflicted. "That was so brave," she warbled softly, maintaining a respectful distance.

Crouching back down, they continued down the palisaded wall towards the Dock. Suddenly the world became infinitely more beautiful as sun lowered beneath the clouds, gilding the underbelly of the overcast sky in a rose gold sunset. Herons flapped towards their nests, fighting against the stiff winds that blew from the north. Sampson halted fifty yards from shore, and surveyed the area. In the gathering gloom, a few denizens were sitting on the boardwalk, fishing—it was a good time of day to try and catch a bite of supper. The wind blew a melody upon the softly clinking bottles that floated beneath the Docks, playing an accompaniment to the day's end.

Sampson motioned for the rest of the party to crouch down behind the decrepit boathouse. "Y'all take cover here; I'll be back." Pulling up his muffler around his face, hat pulled low, he walked up to the Dock.

Snippets of conversation drifted up from the Dock, the sounds of the end of the Work Day.

"I can't believe it's gone."

"Me either..."

"Yeah, well it's not just the Hostess Club... Boss Zhu and Hizzoner are dead too...Winston's in Jail for botching this job; I'm looking forward to his hanging Friday night."

General murmurs of agreement made the rounds. One fisherman, shivering, pulled in his line.

"I'm getting out of here, guys—it's too damn cold to fish."

"It's never too cold to fish."

Ambling down the Dock, an unrecognizably swaddled Sampson sat down between two of the fishermen, then pulled a BudWeed cigarette from his pocket. He held it.

"Long day. Gotta light?"

The other fishermen eyed the cigarette in his hand, "Yeah, I'll give you a light in exchange for a toke."

"Well, sure—but why don't you go get your own? They're giving them away..." Sampson jerked his thumb over his shoulder towards HighTown as the other Hombre pulled an ancient matchbook from his pocket.

"I already got mine and smoked it this afternoon." The Hombre struck the match and held it out. Sampson took a drag.

"So did I..." Sampson coughed. "I meant the ones they're giving away right now, down by the gate. I thought you'd heard."

"More? Now?" The Hombre sounded incredulous. The other fishermen leaned in to hear more.

"Well, yeah... but they probably won't last long. Someone found a new stash... once the WildLand Express shows up, it'll get snatched up for sure."

The fishermen rolled up their gear and headed for the gates at a sprightly pace. Sampson held out his blunt: "Don't you want your toke?" But the fishermen were gone...

Docks cleared, Sampson carefully crushed out the end of the cigarette, then stood and motioned to the others. Leading the way, the Watcher crept quickly down under the Dock, followed by the Afterling, Kendra, and Goins last, who swept their footprints away with a branch.

"You stubbed it out," Kendra pouted.

Sampson looked smug. "You know I can't stand the stuff." He put it back in his pocket to save for another day, another ruse. "Besides, you're on duty."

"You're a buzzkill," Kendra snarked.

Sampson smiled to himself. "Yup. And that's how I managed to finally outrank you." He rapped on the hatch twice, then twice again; a deep voice whispered:

"Who goes there?"

Sampson whispered back: "Fenix Creciente."

"We will be free..." The hatch squeaked open to reveal Sanders' face peering up from the darkness. They slipped down the ladder one by one, with Sampson dusting the tracks and pulling the boat hull back into place over the entrance before entering the tunnel last.

With a 9mm in hand and the fine Pashmina muffler around his throat, Sanders looked like a spy from some old novel. "Something's different about you," Goins said suspiciously. With an undeniable pride, Sanders pulled the scarf aside to reveal what was missing—his padlock was gone.

Goin hooted softly and shook Sanders' hand: "Welcome to the Revolution, Mike." The Watcher gave a slight grin and a thumbs up, his hand patting where his own padlock so recently hung about his neck. Sanders nodded back to the Watcher, acknowledging the brotherhood of those who had served against their will.

"Thanks, Sanders." From down the tunnel, Winston greeted them, torch in one hand, and his halligan in the other. "Welcome to the

Underground, I'll be your..." he looked around. "Okay, first things first—
that smell has got to go."

The overwhelming aroma of drunken bum permeated the entrance to
the tunnel.

Goins pointed to the Watcher: "Watcher traded coats with Bogie just
to make the Guest think he's a do-gooder."

"If you traded with Bogie, you're a braver man than me." Winston
took a look at the Guest, still hidden under her hooded cloak. In the
torchlight, she looked like a pile of deerskins with feet and hands. "But I
don't care what your reason; get rid of that smell."

The Watcher pulled off the overcoat and handed it to Winston, who
threw it into a plastic bin near the entrance and slammed it shut. The odor
still lingered on his clothes. "Now, as I was saying, I'm your guide; we have
wounded, so follow me."

The tall Hombre strode down the tunnel at the head of the group, all
business. "This is the Dock tunnel, leading to the Jail, and unlike the safe
room tunnel it's for temporary use only—to get guests out of the Jail and
to freedom. When construction if finished, it is designed to extend
beneath the wall and out to a hidden entrance on shore—but it looks like
the construction is now on permanent delay." Winston scowled. They
passed through the shored-up walls of the tunnel, and the Watcher
admired the engineering of the supports. He wondered how primitive
these tunnel walls must look to an Underground sophisticate like Rose...

Eager to hear about her mission, Rose ran to catch up with the long-
legged Winston: "Do you have patient reports?"

"So, you're the Medic..." Winston looked down at her, unsure. "Aren't
you a little short to be a Medic?"

Miffed, Rose quipped back. "No, everyone else is just too tall."

"Well, aren't you a little fireball..." Winston gave a chuckle. "Alrighty
then, Miss Medic, I'm Cal Winston; I'm, um, I was a Boss—Fire Chief,
Police Chief, and Chief Executive, all rolled into one package." He
reached down to shake her hand, and she tentatively took it, his big hand
completely swallowing hers. Winston grinned, his brassy crinkles giving
his face took on a rugged, handsome look.

The Watcher decided to hate Winston.

Winston led her: "I've set up a triage area here; Lourdes has a swollen
wrist, Araceli has a gash on her leg, and Destiny..." he was trying to figure
out how to say it without making himself feel bad. "Destiny was attacked

by a mob."

Rose mouth turned down. "We will make her better somehow." She had dealt with these kinds of injuries before.

"I already made it better by attacking her attackers back—with this." Winston flexed a bicep as he waved his halligan, glancing back at the Medic again. "But these aren't all the patients. The Director needs attention too—he has broken ribs, and he's developed a cough. He's up in the Jail attending business there and will meet with you after you assess the other patients. He wants to know if they can be moved."

Rose nodded, concerned. "Thank you, Boss. That was an excellent report!"

"Call me Cal." Winston said warmly. He patted her cloaked shoulder, trying to figure out what was beneath the furs.

"Okee Dokee, Cal—let us tend to the patients."

"Call me Cal," the Watcher noted coldly, *and the little Minx immediately called him Cal.* Glowering behind them, the Watcher grunted and added Winston to his List.

Kendra ran towards a torch glimmering ahead. Meeting Sam, Kendra hugged her quickly, then sprinted ahead to Destiny. At the site of her ravaged friend, Kendra's mask of emotion started to slip again, but she pulled it up and tied it into place with strings of anger.

Lourdes had washed Destiny's face and cleaned her wounds as best she could. Lips swollen and discolored, Destiny was still wrapped in the Evangelo's white lace, eyes closed, quiet. Kendra patted her hand. "Wake up, Destiny..." the eyes flickered, but did not open.

Rose did her scene size-up and whispered to the Watcher:

"Small area, too many people—needs crowd control..."

The tunnel was full of concerned but unneeded personnel. Rose took charge of her scene, saying in a low, pointed voice: "I'm sorry, but if you are not a patient or a person in charge, could you please step out of the room for a moment? I need to assess the patients in privacy."

"I'm in charge." Winston said, hopeful to help the Medic.

"Not anymore," said Mansour, helpful to correct his former Boss. "Sam's in charge here... You come with us for now—the Director is calling for an emergency briefing upstairs."

"But I can help..." Winston protested as Mansour took him by the shoulder and pulled him up the tunnel. Sam looked up from worrying over Destiny.

Now Evangelo stepped into the tunnel with an announcement:

"Agent Ellison, The Director also asks for you to go to Agent Habib's office for a briefing—Sanders will continue to cover the Dock hatch, Goins will cover the Jail hatch, and you'll brief them in turn when we get back."

Sam nodded, patting Destiny's unheeding arm. She handed Kendra the shotgun.

"You and Sampson are both unbusted back to your former ranks—now, guard the wounded."

Kendra griped: "The pay's still the same."

At the sight of the Little Ranger, Rose's eyes lit up with joy "Oh, Captain! You are alive and well!" She hugged him, then held out a foot to Evangelo. "See? I am wearing your wonderful moccasins!"

"I'm glad to see you too, Rose." Evangelo smiled and bowed slightly; his lip split where he had been hit in the mouth earlier. He wiped away the blood, glad he had only lost a molar in the beating. Seeing the Watcher come up behind Rose, the little Ranger extended his hand, and the Watcher clasped it heartily.

Emotive, Evangelo murmured: "Watcher, I owe you my life..."

Rose wondered: "Deva, don't you need to go with him, too?"

So, we're back to Deva again. Not Saul...Deva. Scowling, the Watcher shook his head and planted himself at the room entrance.

"He's still on duty here." Evangelo held up a hand: "The Director says Agent Azarian will stay to escort you to the briefing for your patient report, and you will both join the briefing when called. We'll see you then..." Sam, Mansour, and Winston left the scene with Evangelo, and the tunnel became a little less crowded.

The Watcher felt a familiar hand tug at his sleeve. "Deva, may I please borrow your notebook?" Rose held out her hand, then noticing his angry look, appeared hurt. "Why are you so grumpy? It's only for a minute—I need to make patient notes, but I promise I'll give it right back."

He whipped out his Bowie Knife, and her eyes grew wide.

Why don't you go ask Chief Big Head up there?

Whittling down the pencil to a sharper point, he grumbled then sheathed the Bowie knife, flipped his notepad to a clean page, and handed her the pencil. Visibly relieved that he was only cutting a pencil, Rose took it from his stout fingers.

"Oh, thank you, Deva. You just seem... upset." Rose looked him up and down. "I think you need something to eat." She pulled forth her small black-print satchel from beneath her cloak, now packed with medical supplies, and rumbled about until she found her prize. Slipping a small sassafras candy into his hand, she patted it. "Kendra shared some more of Herman's candies with me—maybe something sweet will make you feel better."

I'll tell you what would make me feel better...

Fuming, the Watcher popped the candy into his mouth: he was not a man to turn down free candy... *Not bad.* Tucking himself into an alcove, a disgruntled Watcher took his post and considered the candy while the Medic made her rounds.

———◆———

"Hello, I am Rose, the LoneStar Command Medic..."

Rose was murmuring to herself as she walked briskly down the tunnel towards the Jail, her fur cloak swinging behind her. "No no no..." She shook her head: "'Hello, I am the Medic for LoneStar Command...'"

She cleared her throat. "I'm a Medic for LoneStar Command, and here's your report..." mid-stride, she turned to the Watcher. "Which introduction do you think is best? I don't want to seem too overbearing, but I don't want to look weak, either."

I'd love to tell you, the Watcher looked at her, bemused—*but you have my notepad.* He held up his hand, and traced a finger across his open palm with his other hand, as if he were writing.

"Oh! Yes, how insensitive. I'm sorry, Deva." She handed him the notepad. He scrawled quickly.

> *—use the first intro. Your name, then rank, then your report. You are "the" Medic, not just "a" medic for the team, so say it that way.*

"Thank you; that was very helpful." They approached the hatch, and Agent Goins moved to open it.

"Good luck going in there—they've been going at it hot and heavy for the last half hour."

"Are they fighting?" Rose appeared concerned.

"Not really fighting—more like discussing loudly and intensely." Goins scrutinized the Afterling with intensity. "You're not really a Chica, are you?"

Unsure of what to say next, Rose looked up at Goins. "What do you mean?"

Goins' face was harsh. "I mean you're an imposter... whatever you are, you're not Human."

Rose looked down at her hands to see if her makeup was still on... "But I am Human."

"No, you're not—the Director said so himself. You're a clone." Goins was indignant. "It doesn't matter how much makeup Kendra sprays on you—it'll never make you a Human. Under all that makeup, your skin is still soft. You didn't see the Red Star fall. You didn't live through The Great Dying—you'll never know what it means to have lived through what we suffered, so don't expect us to treat you like you're one of us."

"I'm sorry... I wasn't trying to imitate anyone. They were just trying to hide me." Rose hung her head. "It wasn't meant to hurt anyone."

"It doesn't matter what you meant." Goins sniffed.

The Watcher glared at Goins. *Rein in your outrage, or I'll rein it for you.* Growling, he pointed upwards, then he put his hand on Rose's shoulder and pushed her towards the ladder. Knocking on the hatch, Goins growled back mockingly to the Watcher; receiving an answering knock, Goin gave sign and an unseen guard gave countersign. The hatch opened, and Goins allowed the Watcher to ascend.

Coming up the ladder, the Watcher surveyed the crowded office from beneath the roll-top desk: Evangelo was speaking, Habib was covering the hatch, and Dominic was leaning against the door. On the floor, Winston was seated with Sam and Mansour atop bags of gear. A thick silence greeted him, their faces stunned, incredulous. They had been told a terrible truth—their World, The System, and all in it was a lie. The Director had led them down the path towards the Tree of Knowledge, and now none could turn back. Continuing down that path of information, the Director was laying the road to Revolution quickly. Glancing over, the Director spotted the Watcher emerging from the hatch; Dominic shook his head, then motioned for Evangelo to continue. The Watcher backed out, as Dominic lowered himself into the hatch to enter the tunnel.

"...but ranks are a necessary evil, and although they may seem trivial, chain of command demands them. For the sake of simplicity, agreed ranks for the Revolution are based loosely upon those of the Roman Republic, for we will have no absolute ruler. Instead, Dominic Santos will be our Pontifex Maximus; you, the Council will act as Tribunes, answering to his two Consuls, to be led by our very own Bona Dea..." Evangelo stopped as soon as he saw the hatch open. "Excuse me, Ladies and Gentlemen; I will return momentarily. Agent Ellison, you have the floor." Evangelo followed the Director, then closed the hatch behind them as they descended the ladder.

Rose jumped up to hug her Father, and the Director flinched. "Oh, Father—you are wounded!" Holding his ribs. Dominic smiled at her, but she saw a strain upon him. She thought of Goins' rebuke, and she wondered just how much the Director had said about her...

"Are they ready for their report?" Rose brushed herself off.

Patting her hand, Dominic deferred. "I'm sorry, but I'd like you to wait here while leadership sorts through all the information they are receiving. I'll call you in when they are ready. Do you have a patient report for me?" He coughed, wrapping his arms around himself. "I will pass it to the rest."

She was filled with an overwhelming concern: "Oh, yes, Father, but I can't make an adequate report until you have been assessed too..." She blurted it out, then immediately wondered if he thought she was out of order.

The Director inclined his head: "I appreciate your concern. We will address it after the briefing is concluded. However, you may give me your report now, so I can plan our next steps."

"Yessir!" She snapped to attention: "I am Rose, Medic for LoneStar Command. My report is as follows: Araceli has a superficial laceration on her anterior left thigh, six inches in length; mechanism of injury being she fell against a jagged edge of a can lid. Alcohol was used to disinfect the wound, and a sterile dressing was applied. Lourdes has a moderate sprain of the right wrist, due to grappling with an attacker; the wrist was wrapped and immobilized to minimize pain. She will need to avoid use for the next week in order to speed healing. Destiny, however..."

Eager to know how his savior fared, Evangelo leaned forward.

Rose tried to maintain her own professionalism. "I must protect the privacy of the patient. You know what happened to Destiny, and I shan't explain in detail the terrible attack. It is enough to say that lacerations and abrasions to skin and mucosa are superficial to moderate, and deep bruising is present; thankfully, major tearing of skin and muscle has been avoided. Bleeding is controlled, and there appears to be no lasting internal damage."

Dominic's expression was cold and sharp. "I am glad they are dead."

"B-but they are not all dead..." From the shadows, Evangelo's hazel eyes were completely silver now, his emotive stutter emerging. "Chartreaux remains..."

Rose raised a finger. "However, the patient is non-responsive to verbal stimuli at this time, due to the administration of an unknown mind-altering substance. I can't precisely determine which substance it might be, but witnesses describe Destiny spoke of dreams and hallucinations earlier in the day; her body temperature is elevated, pupils dilated, heart rate irregular, and respiration depressed. I don't see a needle track, so that leaves a topical, inhaled, or ingested substance.

"Upon questioning, Agent Ellison gave a detailed report regarding substances found by Hostesses at Boss Chartreaux's cabin. Those substances are Cannabis, Liquor, 'Stuff', Datura, Verbina, and Ilex Vomitoria. Of all those substances, only Datura causes these symptoms, so I believe she has inhaled or ingested Datura, perhaps in combination with Cannabis, to induce a hypnotic state. This was probably done to extract information."

"You mean Jimpson Weed?" Listening from the side-lines, Goins whispered low: "Damn, that's rough—Datura's some bad juju. You don't just casually do Datura..."

Rose nodded. "Yes—Datura is a very dangerous drug. Destiny must be monitored closely; in addition to cardiac and respiratory issues, psychosis is possible, and she may become uncontrollable. She needs to be moved as soon as possible to a safe location, or she could give away our entire operation."

Evangelo looked to the Director, alarmed.

A deep concern crossed the Director's face. "Thank you, Rose." He briefly bowed his head to think, then called Goins: "Agent, report to triage and have Kendra prepare all patients for evacuation within the next hour; under cover of darkness, we will evacuate them to the safe room tunnel." Goins nodded and disappeared into the darkness.

Unsure of what that might entail, Rose rubbed her forehead: "But it may not be safe out there, either..." The Watcher scratched out a message:

—An ALGOS bot came to the safe room tunnel entrance.

"An algae? What?" Evangelo had no idea.

Dominic, on the other hand, was all too aware. A sheen of sweat beaded on his black-scaled brow as he grabbed the Watcher by the arm and pulled him into a quiet corner: "Dios Mio—how are you even here if you encountered one?"

"Oh, it was no problem at all!" an admiring Rose related. "The Watcher caught it in his shirt and beat it to death against the wall, then threw it in the lake. It was quite exciting!"

Alarmed, Dominic shook his head: "No, Hija, it IS a problem, and we must inform the others immediately. I will brief the Council, and they will pass word to their subordinates. How much do you think they saw?"

> *—The ALGOS breached the door, but it didn't get past the doorway. It probably imaged Kendra and Sampson. I was masked at the time, so that's not a problem. I'm certain the Afterling wasn't detected; she was hidden from the drone's thermal imagers by a foil blanket lining her cloak, and she didn't speak so they didn't get a voice sample. I dispatched the drone quickly before sending it down stream to be tracked out of area. The ALGOS programmers and monitors will assume some local yokels killed it off, and will probably pull back to avoid detection while they continue surveillance.*

"You know a great deal more about these drones than I expected." Dominic studied the Watcher with a wondering eye. "I'm eager to find out why. Since you know so much—what are your recommendations?"

> *—The ALGOS don't know Rose is here. If she remains cloaked in any crowd of people, she should be safer. Her voice and heat signatures will be harder to distinguish in a group. But she needs to be kept someplace safe..."*

"She should stay at the Jail with me." Dominic said firmly.

> *—No, the Jail is under extreme surveillance and might be overrun by Chartreaux's goons. She should be evacuated to safer territory, even if it's somewhere else inside Purgatory.*

"Well, she cannot go with you. The safe room tunnel has been discovered and all personnel must leave as soon as possible. In order for us to kick-start the Revolution, you will be traveling back and forth between the safe room tunnel, the evacuation point, and Purgatory, all through dangerous territory."

*—You will be on the move too, and I will not leave her
behind with persons unknown to me. I already did that
once, and I'm never doing it again.*

"The Purgatory Dead Zone will defeat the ALGOS—no tech has ever
been able to be used here. It will keep her safe from the drones as long as
she is within the walls—"

*—The degenerates who inhabit this hellhole are just as
dangerous as the ALGOS, and I won't let her stay here
without me to protect her—*

"Excuse me," Rose held up her hand, "but there is no safe place."
Both men looked at her, uncomprehending.
"I am hunted." She said it matter-of-factly, as if she were explaining to
five years olds. "There is nowhere to hide where they won't find me.
When they do find me, I am probably going to die, but I'll die eventually
anyway; after all, I am very old..."
The Watcher's scar twitched at the corner of his eye as he struggled
with the reality of her mortality.
Dominic became agitated: "Enough defeatist talk, Hija! You mustn't
think that way. We have to try—"
"Oh, Father! It isn't defeatist—it's freeing!" Rose laughed. "It means I
can face the future knowing it may go on without me, but at least there
will be a future for someone else."
Stunned, the hardened Survivors listened to the leader of the
Revolution laid out her path:
"Now, if what you all said is true, then the ALGOS cannot follow me
into Purgatory due to this mysterious 'Dead Zone'. But they also won't
attack me when I'm surrounded by large crowds of people. They are
looking to kill me without revealing my presence to Survivors. So, I
should remain hidden when necessary, stay with a group when possible,
do my job when able, and when the time comes, die bravely. Meanwhile,
let's give it to God and try to save the world while we can."
She smiled brightly, as if it was the most natural conversation.
"Unfortunately, this path means I must choose which people I will
endanger with my presence—and that is the hardest part. I really don't
want anyone else to die because of me. If it would save the world, I alone
would die, and take it upon myself so the rest of you might live and be
free." She sighed. "Of course, that is easy to say when it is not being

required of me at the time..."

A dark determination took the Watcher. Time to put Dominic's new-found 'Faith' to good use.

Scribbling furiously, the Watcher slashed out words, and the others waited patiently for him to finish. He thrust the note into her hands, slapping his own heart, then opening his hand towards her as if offering a gift.

> —*Then choose me. I am your Champion, and your fate is mine. Don't tell me to leave you, or stop following you. Where you go, I will go, where you stay, I will stay; your people are now my people, and your God is now my God. Where you die, I will die, and there my bones will lie; and may God Himself punish me if anything less than Death parts me from you.*

Not recognizing the words, the Afterling simply took the Watcher's hand, as she couldn't think of anything more beautiful to say.

Triumphant, the Watcher stifled a smirk as he glanced at Dominic; passing the note to the new Judge, the Watcher scribbled a private addenda to seal the deal:

> —*Checkmate. Accept it or go against 'Holy Scripture.'*

Dominic's eyes flashed a warning. "So be it, Marshal Azarian; in reciting Ruth's Vow, you have erected a Mizpah of Words, a watchtower that you set not just between us, but also God. It matters not if she chooses you or not—you have offered yourself beyond her choosing. Break the Vow at your own peril." Dominic deferred to his daughter's will. "Go with him, and may the God the he invoked protect you both."

He sighed. "But while you are readying the patients, I must finish that which I have started. Wait here until I call for you." Dominic opened the hatch and prepared to enter the office again, then hesitated. "Rose, do you have the leather medallion that Evangelo made for you?"

"Oh yes, Father! I carry it with me always, but I don't have a way to wear it..." She reached into her bag and pulled it out. "Did you wish to see it?"

"Thank you, Rose—" He took it from her, then asked: "May I also see your choker?" Reluctant to part with her only memento of her brother, she shook her head, but Dominic deftly tugged the end of the choker's yellow ribbon, and it slid off her neck and into her Father's hand. "Do not worry, Rose—I will return it shortly. But I have need of it." He held it up, and Joseph's broken chain glittered in the tunnel's torchlight. "I have a memory to share."

Rose watched the hatch close behind Evangelo and Dominic. She heard a man's voice snap—"I didn't sign on to save Insiders..."

She was trying to be nonchalant, but it wasn't working. "I don't think they like me very much at all." Downcast, she turned away from the hatch; "I shouldn't have come here."

And where would you have gone?

The Watcher was feeling a growing frustration at the reactions other Survivors were displaying towards Rose—everything ranging from mild bitterness to mockery to outright hostility. *Rose didn't kill your world,* he thought angrily, casting an evil glare at the hatch. *Rose wasn't even alive then...* But what frustrated the Watcher most was the change in Rose's attitude. Where she once wouldn't have cared what a "Devil" thought, she was now desperately trying to appease them, please them, make them love her—and it wasn't working. *Well, not with them at least.*

They sat in the tunnel, hearing the gruff voices raging in muffled debate above them.

"...so let me get this straight, Director—you're telling us we caused a mass extinction of women, and now we're gonna replace them with your lab-grown imitation—"

"That's our only choice if we're going to save Humanity..." It was Sam's voice, tense and quiet.

"No; we're Humanity! Us! We need to save us, not some defective substitute for us. She's an Insider, anyway; she doesn't belong out here..."

Sam hissed: "She's a means to an end. The Damned will fight for a chance to..." The voices became indistinct again.

Even though they were trying to keep it quiet, the sounds of strife were seeping through the hatch. The Watcher wished he had something to drown out the sounds of dissent among the Survivors, but without the Ring and without a voice, he could only listen as strident voices tangled.

Eyes welling. Rose looked up. "I didn't know they would hate me."

Pulling out his notepad, he scribbled:

—They don't hate you—they hate what happened.

"I hate what happened, too." Rose clasped her hands together and waited to be called into the office. "I should never have been here. I should never have been made. It was wrong."

She wasn't dramatic about it—she said it calmly, as if it were fact; but her eyes betrayed her hurt at their rejection. *They rejected you,* the Watcher's eyes narrowed—*so now you reject yourself?* He scowled and wrote out his response.

    —Never say that again.

"But nobody wants us. Not the Deva. Not anybody. Even Evangelo said we are an abomination. What if even God does not want us?" Her fingers twisted together, twining and untwining, as if trying to make everything fit together.

    —If God didn't want you, you wouldn't be here in the first
    place. Now stop it.

"Then God is the only one." She hid her face, and the Watcher almost wrote it—he almost told her; but the hatch opened, and Evangelo motioned for her to enter.

"A consensus has been reached."

Wiping her eyes, she ascended the ladder, the Watcher coming up close behind her.

Still hidden beneath her cloak, Rose arose from the underworld into the light of room. She nearly slipped, but the Watcher caught her to push her out into the room. Hard faces softened at the sight of a small person awkwardly scrambling to emerge from the hatch; it is difficult to resent someone when they are not merely an idea, but a real person just trying to escape the darkness.

The Director took his hat in his hand, and spoke with great solemnity: "Rose, we welcome you to the first high-level briefing for the LoneStar Revolution, in the Cause for Freedom of the world's enslaved Humanity."

The Director flipped the leather badge cover into place, with the Phoenix rising from the fire, chains broken, emblazoned on the Five-Pointed Star of Freedom. Evangelo, then the Watcher followed suit, turning their badges to reflect Dominic's own.

For the first time, Dominic spoke as Arbiter of the Revolution. "We have discussed the world as it was, and the world as it is—it is now time to discuss the world as it will be, God willing." The room was deathly quiet; the old things were passing away. "Rose, Azarian, and Evangelo—we have a request to make of you. Agent Ellison—as your last official act under the System, would you please do us the honor?"

Sam rose with great dignity and turned to address the three standing before the room.

"As Head of the Council for the Revolution, I ask for members of the Council to please stand as they are introduced with their given names and roles."

"Dominic Santos, Visionary—Command, Word Bringer."

"Samantha Ellison, Visionary—Intelligence, Truth Bringer."

"Lazarus Mansour, Visionary—Operations, Strength Bringer."

"Calvin Winston, Visionary—Administration, Will Bringer."

"Frank Habib, Visionary—Logistics and Supply, Order Bringer."

"We are the Fallen—we are the Fire that burned the World. As Visionaries of the Council, we acknowledge our role in the destruction of Humanity and the creation of The System under which we enslaved ourselves. We seek to right these wrongs, and we officially rebel against The System we created. But our own desire for power is what got us here in the first place..." Sam paused, furrowing her brow, obviously struggling with an unseen temptation. "Power corrupts."

The faces of the other council members reflected her somber observation.

"We ask for your governance. As the Fire from which the Phoenix will rise, we as Visionaries acknowledge that we are a Promethean gift. We have the ability to both create and destroy: our gift to lead is coupled intrinsically with our need to control. Aware of our dual nature, we offer our unique gifts and training for the purpose of setting right the wrongs we have committed—we also understand we need governance for ourselves, an accountability to Humanity—and we ask that you would do so. We give you our pledge, as consent of the governed."

Rose spoke with wonder: "You are asking us to lead you?"

"Yes. Use our energy for the good of Humanity, not for its destruction. Your assignment will be under the Command cohort." Pointing to her compatriots gathered in the small office, Sam continued. "We, the Visionary Council for the Revolution, choose Dominic Santos as our Prometheus for this Revolution, to be our Arbiter and Judge, with his advisers in Command."

Evangelo was respectfully suspicious. "You are Visionaries—the Fallen; why are you asking for leadership from us? It is against everything

I have learned about Visionaries thus far..."

"That is a discussion for another day." Imperious, Sam dismissed his question: "But in light of Visionary responsibility regarding the Happening, we see the need for accountability to those we lead. You will hold us accountable. We are Fire, and Dominic will wield us at your direction."

Dominic was pleased with her answer. "For my first act as Leader of the Revolution, I appoint Rafael Evangelo and Saul Azarian as my Consuls." A look of restrained pride wreathed him. "I will Lead the Revolution under their advisement."

Dominic held aloft Rose's Leather Badge, now tied to Joseph's broken silver chain by the Watcher's yellow ribbon. "This is the emblem of the Revolution—Born of Fire, a Phoenix rises, Freed from the Broken Chain to become the rising Lone Star. And this broken chain, threaded through the yellow ribbon of Remembrance, is the legacy of a young man who died fighting to be free. His death was not in vain. His name was Joseph..."

Dominic raised the chain, remembering courage: "...and I am proud to call him my own."

Hidden behind the desk, Rose wept.

"Rafeal Evangelo, under the Emblem of the Revolution you are assigned to the Command Cohort with rank of Marshal, as our Law Bringer. As you organized the Rangers and created the Code, you will organize and create the laws for the Revolution, leading the people as a Shepherd. Your unwavering devotion to the Code means you are alone are worthy to bring the Law. You are the Star; your Law will light Justice's way."

Deep in thought, Evangelo laced his fingers before him.

Dominic turned to the Watcher: "Saul Azarian, under the Emblem of the Revolution, you are assigned to the Command Cohort with rank of Marshal as our Justice Bringer. You will protect and defend the Asura, as their Watcher from on High. Like the Asura, you were oppressed; by the Asura, you were set Free, and now you will set the Asura Free. You are the Phoenix; out of the Fire, you will resurrect Humanity from the ashes, and bring Justice for all."

The Judge looked at both men: "You must work together to create a new Society for all Humanity, for if Law and Justice are separated, the Revolution will fail. Insiders and OutLaws, Deva and Asura, Fallen and

Damned, Male and Female—all must be Equal under Law and Justice."
The Judge discerned between the two men standing before him: one
wholesome, strong, and well-made, the epitome of masculine goodness,
and the other uneven, rough, and virile, the embodiment of masculine
power.

"Law guides and Justice protects. Law without Justice becomes
Tyranny, and Justice without Law becomes Brutality." Dominic pointed to
each Survivor. "Law guides," flicking his stiletto out of his sleeve,
Dominic touched it to Evangelo's shoulder, "...and Justice protects." He
reached up to tap the edge of his blade to the Watcher's shoulder. "This is
your calling."

Dominic addressed the entire group:

"But there is no Deva without Asura, no Order without Entropy, no
Man without Woman. Without Yab-Yum, there is no Humanity. We, the
Visionaries who destroyed Humanity, have a responsibility to breathe
Humanity to life again."

It's time. Taking the ears of her hood in hand, the Watcher pulled it
down to reveal her wild-painted face. Incognito under her furs, dark
eyeliner and golden tracery, she seemed to be an untamed creature
captured from the WildLands, a yet-unnamed animal from Eden's lost
inventory. *La Pequena Hada...* he looked her over. Hair hidden beneath her
long stocking cap, she almost could pass for Human... *Almost.* In an
uncharacteristically tender gesture, the Watcher smoothed the wild tendrils
that curled from underneath her hat, then unceremoniously lifted her up
onto the desk, where she stood so all could see her.

Dominic swept his open hand towards her. "I present Rose, Asura
#TMA673CdF, one of two hundred and ninety-two cloned adult Asura
currently living at the Capitol of the Insider Empire—Tesoro."

Stares greeted her. Rose tried smiling, but she felt a palpable fear in
the room. Exposed, surrounded by the Survivors of Humanity's downfall,
her differences were too obvious for Rose's observers to deny. Their
scrutiny descended the gentle slope of her features into the uncanny
valley of her too-large eyes and her too-small mouth, the deliberate
delicateness of her hands and feet, her exaggerated form and her
minimized height...

Rose was a being on the edge of Humanity, made in Humanity's
image—but not quite Human.

Unswayed by their uncertainty at his creation, Dominic smiled back at her. He held up his hand, and the little Asura took it. "She is also my Daughter."

Rose was thrilled at Dominic's public declaration. "She is Chaos personified, threat to the System's Order. As Mother, she is Life; as Leader, she is Liberty; and as Inspiration, she is Happiness. I chose her as the Leader for our Revolution because she is the first person—Insider or OutLaw—to take down the Leaders of The System. Her words, 'We Will Be Free,' are now the motto of the Revolution."

Dominic held up the choker, its leather medallion dangling from the intertwined ribbon and chain; upon one side, it bore the Lone Star of the Revolution, with its majestic Phoenix, Fire, and Chain; on the reverse, a tooled Rose of Beauty.

Rose admired it. "Oh, it's lovely!"

With great solemnity, Dominic stepped behind Rose to tie it around her neck, her own Badge of Office. "Rose, under the Emblem of the Revolution you are not appointed; you simply 'are.' As Mother of the Revolution, you are our Life Bringer; even as a good Mother nurtures, leads, and then sets free her children, so you too will nurture, lead, and set free all who follow you. You are the embodiment of Liberty, represented by Liberty's Crown, the Wreath of Broken Chain—and as Liberty, you will lead the People."

Dominic pointed to her, a warning. "But Liberty cannot survive without Eternal Vigilance to protect it. Marshal Azarian has sworn himself to Rose as her Champion, that even as Justice serves to protect Liberty, so Azarian will serve to protect her."

Satisfied with his Triumvirate, Dominic presented them all to the group, each somber in their turn. Evangelo held his hat in his hands, humble; the Watcher clutched his Bowie knife with a grim determination, and Rose looked from face to face, committing each to memory...

"Law guides, Justice protects, and Liberty leads the People. And we?" Dominic smiled again, his irrepressible spirit filling the room:

"We are the People."

Sitting on the faded Persian rug in Habib's office, the Council solemnly deliberated on all they had been asked. After a few minutes of quiet discussion, Sam arose to announce:

"Judge Santos; the Council accepts your recommendations for Azarian and Evangelo as Consul, with Rose in advisement to all and under Azarian's protection." Sam gave the orders of the Council. "Evangelo,

Azarian, and Rose—you all have been called to service, but only you can decide whether or not you will answer that call. If you do, we would pledge our loyalty to you, Fire in the Hands of Prometheus unbound. What do you say?"

Solemn, Evangelo removed his hat—"I will answer the call." Following suit, the Watcher removed his own hat and touched his badge to grunt gravely, then turned his eyes to Rose:

A concept was stirring inside her.

"I promise I will do my best to honor you, with all that I am." Rose placed her hand upon her heart. "But do not pledge your loyalty to us; people pass away, earthly thrones and kingdoms fall. If we wish this moment to last beyond ourselves, we should pledge ourselves to something greater than ourselves, to something even greater than death..."

He could not stop himself: compelled by an unseen force, the Watcher's hand rose spontaneously in response to Rose, proclaiming the Oath of the Abhaya Mudra. He remembered the declaration he made, on his own Child's blood: *I believe in Life—even if I have to conquer Death and Hell to keep Life alive...*

Mute, the Watcher could not speak it. In truth, he had never placed much stock in spoken words... *Words are ephemeral unless written.* So, scribing it with a flourish on the lined paper of his spiral pocket notepad, the Watcher wrote. The Words came to him quickly, and he handed them to the Afterling.

"Oh, Deva, this is so perfect!" Her Lotus hands blossomed over her heart in the Padma Mudra, and she read his words aloud; "I pledge myself to Life Itself, the Face of God made Flesh in Me; the right to live as Humans, Free... Eternally in Liberty." Rose became Light, transforming Thought into Word.

"But what is God?" Winston asked, earnestly.

"The Lover of Life." said Rose, without hesitation.

The words were hopelessly idealistic, completely naive, and yet... they were exactly what was needed in a used up, jaded world. There was no more debate. The Council stood, raising their hands in promise—and it was Dominic himself who led them in their Oath.

"...so help me God."

The group signed The Pledge, and the Watcher lined out the finishing stroke with the Dominic's pen:

—I pledge myself to Life Itself,

the Face of God made Flesh in Me;

the Right to live as Humans, Free,

Eternally in Liberty.

The Watcher could not help but think—
So help me, God.

---·---

Grimacing, the Director tried not to groan aloud; Rose finished wrapping his ribs, pinning the ends over his left shoulder.

"It appears your ribs are just cracked—they are not completely snapped off, so that is a very good thing. However, you must force yourself to cough, or you'll develop pneumonia, which is a very bad thing." Rose examined his swollen eyelids, still bruised from the morning's beating. "Your eyes are still structurally sound—it will just take time for the swelling to go down... but these burns...." She reached into the bag and pulled out the tickle-tongue salve she had made, dabbing it on the scorch marks across his back. The Director winced.

Overwhelmed by a harsh emotion, Rose exclaimed in hushed tones: "Oh Father, I'm so sorry... These Devils were so awful to you and Destiny —Boss Chartreaux is a terrible man, and his followers are no better. I felt sorry for the Asura, but Survivors have been fighting their own battles against their own oppressors..."

Dominic patted her back. "Que sera, sera, mi Hija—what they meant for evil, God will work for good. We must move on to the next phase of this operation: evacuate our wounded to the WildLand Express Camp, and rally our recruits. For now, focus on moving your patients, and stay close to the Watcher." He buttoned up his blue plaid shirt, still stained from his torture session. "Marshal Azarian, advance to receive orders."

The Watcher stepped forward to receive his first official orders as a Marshal. He wasn't sure it he should salute or just stand there, but Dominic simply closed the gap to whisper confidentially:

"As you leave Purgatory, Captain Evangelo will lead the evacuees to Camp Forlorn. Keep Rose close, and keep her out of sight until you are confident it is safe. My assistant, Von Helm, is trusted, and he will introduce you to the rest of the Camp. Brief them regarding the drone and Rose as you see fit. How you do it is up to you, but say only what is necessary. Vaya con Dios, and dismissed."

He called up the next the MoneyMan. "Habib, do you have a status report?"

"The sun has set, Judge," Habib reported, looking out the peep-hole on the door. All windows on the jail had been covered with plywood as was the regular practice when the weather was cold; it helped to hide the unusual activity inside and muffled any conversations. It also made it harder to see what was going on outside. Peering through the peep hole, Habib counted three new faces hanging out in the open grounds surrounding the Jail. He went to the hatch and whispered down into it. "Goins—gather the teams to the staging area, and remind them to keep their yaps shut. We've got company outside—three goons."

The Watcher peeked out of the sliding peep-hole and saw three Brigades-Men clustered together, huddling near a campfire near the tree line. *Amateurs*—they were easy to spot.

Looking to his "Ranger"—Fines in a dead Ranger's garb—Dominic motioned for him to take his place in the Lounge. He questioned the Jailers. "Do we have our 'prisoners' ready?"

The Head Jailer, Howard, answered back, "You bet, Judge Santos; we've got the stand-ins ready to go."

Dominic blinked, then laughed—"Ah, yes—'Judge.' That would be me." It sounded strange, after so many years as "Director"; like everything else about the Revolution, Dominic's title was new and unfamiliar.

Dominic looked to cell where Winston had been held—a new man, tall and lanky was there, leg chained to Winston's cot. "You are Sergio, that is correct?"

Sergio looked up. Dark-eyed like Winston, he was nearly as tall, but more slender. "Yes sir, Lenny Sergio." Next to him was a dark, heavy-set Hombre, wearing Mansour's laborer's hat. "And this here is Wilbur Barrie."

Dominic ruminated. "Welcome to the Revolution, Gentlemen. Cover up with your blankets, and turn your faces to the wall. Sergio, you will be angry and only grunt in response. Barrie, cough as if you are getting sick. Put your latrines between the cell door and the cot, so people will be distracted and less likely to enter... Howard, do we have Evangelo's stand-in upstairs in the cell already?"

The Head Jailer nodded, "Yes, Gerry Marcus, he's a little guy, maybe a little too skinny—but in the lamp light, and with the Captain's clothes, he's not as noticeable."

"I anticipate someone anxious coming to check on the prisoners as word gets back to Chartreaux about the burning of the storm cellar; he will wonder who to blame, and they will be hopeful it was your fault. The sight of our faux prisoners should convince the Brigades-Men that the Jail is still their territory, and it should allow us to continue our charade until the recruitment and arming is done. Until they show up, it should be quiet." Pushing Habib's desk a little further to the side, Dominic pulled open the hatch: "Do you have a replacement crew coming tonight?"

The Head Jailer answered swiftly, "Yeah. We sent the word and they're coming in loaded for bear. Later, they're gonna help us with a little trash disposal problem—enemy bodies have been removed to the far end of the tunnel and secured in hampers, to be used for alligator feed later tonight. Our Team is a buncha alright guys—Habib has always taken care of us, and we take care of him."

"Very well. Prep two more to take the place of Rangers—use all gear, and be prepared for Boss Chartreaux's thugs to show up soon. Only let lower-level personnel in, for now—Habib himself will answer Chartreaux should he arrive. If all works out well, we may even get a chance to help the Boss join his brethren in Hell."

Conflicted, the Watcher felt the constraints of his calling again—*how sweet would it be to stay and kill Chartreaux?* Seeing Dominic and Evangelo beaten and helpless in their cell had brought the memory back, and it made him want to kill the reason for that memory.

The fear hit like a fist in his own gut:

He cowered in the corner behind the dresser in the common room, where Mother told him to hide. His Father was coming up the stairs, angry at his lot in life... but Mother was standing in his way: "Don't wake Sollie. You can't wake Sollie—"

"That's my boy. The DNA Test proves it, and I'll see my boy if I want..."

Then it all went to Hell in a hand basket. Father dragged Mother down the hall, and the outburst started. "What you gonna do, you little whore? You gonna stop me? You gonna call one of your other johns to come stop Saul from seeing his own Father?"

And she was begging, "Don't wake Sollie. Please, don't wake him..."

The bedroom door would close on Mother's own personal motel cell, where Saul could hear the sound of fists hitting walls and floors. And all the while, Mother's Manager was watching from a safe location behind the interface of the Ring. The other sexual consultants would listen in, concerned: "Why you let him yell at her like that?

It's not like he's her husband, or even her boyfriend. He's just the BioDad..."

"Well, he paid his hours in for family time—and she agreed to it. It's her life, and she can do what she wants." Her Manager, Bob, would get some ice cream, and pat Saul on the head. "But yeah, this ain't no place for a kid. You don't need your dad anyway. You've got me."

It was the memory of helplessness and captivity, hearing his Mother locked in a room by an angry bully, unable to fight back, defenseless. The Watcher grimaced:

Some men just needed killing.

Boss Chartreaux needed killing, like any other bully—and the Watcher could do it if the opportunity presented itself at the Jail. But what of the Afterling then? The Watcher simply couldn't just stay and wait for Chartreaux; Rose needed to be someplace safe. For now, "someplace safe" was with the Watcher—and the Watcher was assigned to guard the Afterling and gather the Revolution, not to be Chartreaux's assassin. The Watcher sighed.

When in doubt, stick with the original plan.

Habib called Dominic: "Down the hatch, Judge Santos—your fans await."

Ribs aching, Dominic slowly lowered himself into the hatch, then motioned for Rose to enter the tunnel; the Watcher followed, watching for trouble as they descended into the darkness of the tunnel.

Habib bringing up the rear, they travelled until they came upon the triage area. There Dominic saw the first mass operation of his Revolution ready to go—a tunnel full of eager operatives. Eager was good; this would need to be a rapid operation, with all parties moving through the area in ten minutes each—half hour total time to evacuate. Already the questions would be swirling about the fate of the Hostesses, and a posse of Brigades-Men would be sent to secure the town. Fortunately, tonight marked the beginning of Market Mayhem Weekend, and all available personnel would be needed at the gates. That was the main reason Dominic had chosen this date to start his Revolution. He hadn't counted on a coup to complicate things, however...

Surveying the room, Dominic reviewed his assembled teams: three escort teams, along with one relay, one anchor, and one receiving team.

"Team Leaders, raise your hand as you are called, if you are ready to deploy... Relay Team?"

Evangelo held his hand high. He, Sanders, and Goins were preparing themselves as Relay Team—they would act as lookouts and guides along the wall to signal when the coast was clear. A double tap, cough, or scrape would be the signal. The Relay team would leave at the same time as the Receiving Team, with their teammates falling into position as they passed their respective posts. With his knife neatly sheathed and his double huckleberry rig back in place beneath his laborer's coat, Evangelo counted bullets and limbered his fingers up—he seemed quite happy to be fully lethal again.

"Receiving Team?"

Sampson waved to Dominic; he and Kendra were the Receiving Team, to be posted just beyond the hidden gate, with Sampson as guard to fend off beasts in the event of an attack. He threw a moth-eaten quilt across Kendra's shoulders to hide her rhinestones and slender build; she peered out from underneath it with a disgusted look. "It smells like a wet cow," she chided.

"Wet cow suits you," the Giant observed. "I like cows, they have pretty eyes."

"And I like weapons." Kendra glared and patted her switchblade. "Too bad for cows, they don't have weapons." She was assigned it from the Armory's ever-growing cache of weaponry, looted from a dead Ranger.

Looking up from his notes, Judge Santos smiled, pleased. "Good. Now, Escort Teams—"

The three Escort Teams—Winston, Lourdes, and Araceli as lead team, then Mansour, Sam, and Destiny, followed by the Watcher and Rose —would move through the darkness as rapidly as possible. Each Team consisted of at least one Evacuee and a "Heavy." Evacuees were assigned weaponry based on ability and capability, allowing them to double as security for their team; the Heavy, the biggest member of the team, was assigned a full bag of supplies and weapons to carry out with them.

"Escort Team One?"

Winston checked in for Team One—as the Team Heavy, he was being loaded down with gear and equipment by Lourdes. He grunted and shouldered two large bags, and hefted his halligan into place, a 9mm holstered at the ready on his hip.

"Oh, Lourdes, you will weigh him down too much—he's not a little donkey to tote your luggage..." fussing, Araceli reached up to take one of the bags. "Let me help..."

Winston shooed Araceli's fluttering hands away. "Are my legs broken?" Winston pulled the bags' straps up around his expansive shoulders. "If the answer is no, then I don't need help. So, hands off..."

"You don't have to be mean," Araceli's dark brown eyes cast hurt glances around the room, checking to see if anyone else noticed this injustice. They didn't.

"That's not mean, it's the truth." Grabbing another bag, Winston scoffed. "You've got a cut leg, and you don't need to be trying to maneuver through a filthy dump with extra gear. Keep it clean, and let me handle this. The day I need help, then you can help. Until then, no."

Lourdes seemed perfectly fine with this and threw another bag on Winston for good measure.

"Escort Team Two?" Dominic called.

Holding her hand high, Sam nodded to Dominic, then turned back to her teammates. Destiny was rolled in a thick blanket, to be carried by the team's heavy—Mansour—while the team's guard, Sam, would walk ahead armed and ready.

Rose checked the woolen blanket and gave last instructions: "Destiny's breathing well, and her vitals are stable, but she's still unresponsive. You will need to make sure her airway remains clear—Agent Mansour, please carry her with her face rolled to the side so she won't choke on anything if she spits up."

"You mean like a big baby—" Sam adjusted Destiny in Mansour's arms, pulling the blanket up to hide Destiny's haggard face. Destiny groaned, and the whole team jumped.

"What if she wakes up hallucinating in the middle of all this?" Mansour was nervous; he had never had babies, especially one as large as this.

Sam had it all figured out. "Tell her it's a dream, and she should go back to sleep."

"Escort Team Three?"

Rose returned to her station, and piped up: "We are ready!" Elevating his own hand, the Watcher confirmed his own status, then reached over to pull the Afterling's hood back up, covering her head. She tucked a wisp of hair under the brim of her hat and whined softly, "but they forgot to give me a weapon, Deva..."

Racking the bolt on Sindee, he grinned a wicked grin: *They didn't forget. You have me.* He grunted smugly.

Scanning the room once more, Judge Santos called: "And Anchor

Team—"

Habib raised his own hand. As Anchor Team, Dominic, Sanders, and Habib were busy checking and sorting gear.

"Finish final preparations; five minutes." Dominic turned back to the gear bags. The first official act of the Armory was to outfit the Insertion Team for tomorrow night and resupply the Hostesses with necessary gear. This gear was thoughtfully provided by the newly formed unit of Freedmen, those former Purgatory Public Servants who had cast off their shackles to join the Revolution. These men, with Sanders in the lead, had discreetly smuggled the first round of supplies to the Jail from Habib's well-appointed cabin. From the stash of Habib's supplies, Mansour and Evangelo had traded their clothing for common laborer's clothing, and Hostesses were equipped with an overcoat, hats, and heavy scarves to hide their feminine appearance.

Seeing a need, Lourdes volunteered to act as wardrobe manager for the Hostesses, assigning bags for her group. A pile of fine garments fell out of a plastic box, complete with mothballs, and she hummed with approval. Running her hands across a brilliant, coral-pink chemise, Lourdes gasped: "This is genuine silk. Not a blend—it's magnificent. Where did you find these?"

Habib turned away. "It don't matter. Take the whole bag with you—it's full of stuff I don't want anymore. You guys are gonna need swank threads in the WildLands, too."

A thought uncoiled behind Lourdes' aventurine-green eyes; she continued to sort through the garments, admiring each.

Making their final adjustments, the Teams fell into place, ready for the moment to arrive. Evangelo made one last round of the room, then signaled to Dominic: "All patient escorts are accounted and ready at your command."

Standing before them, hat in hand, Dominic was respectful of this moment—the Beginning of the Revolution would never come again.

"Tonight, we rise. Our mission is to remove non-combatants to a safe zone, establish base operations outside city walls, and bring in the Insertion team to be embedded with the incoming WildLand Express Detachments tonight. Following contact and establishment, I will remain with the Jail's Inside Team, where I will gather and distribute much-needed supplies and funds. The Revolution outfitted, we will then leave Purgatory tomorrow night, through the Recruitment Teams' WildLand Express Smuggler Wagons, and make our way to a new outpost, to be revealed when we are clear of Purgatory. Through the LoneStar Revolution, Justice will be served to the System who has so cruelly used so many Insiders and OutLaws alike."

Dominic became somber. "Take a look around you. These are your Brothers and Sisters who started this Revolution with you; not all will live to see its ending. Hold each other in sacred memory when you tell the story of the Revolution. Vaya con Dios." Dominic raised his right fist into the air:

"Fenix Creciente."

From the back they heard a soft voice whisper as Rose raised her fist in return: "We Will Be Free!"

A ripple of hands rose into the air, and the air became alive with the restrained murmur of the first salute—"We Will Be Free..."

"Relay and Receiving Teams, take your places."

Habib tapped on the Dock Hatch twice, and a tap answered back. Sanders opened the hatch from outside, giving the all clear; Relay Team Evangelo and Goins slipped out the hatch with Sanders, followed by Receiving Team Qin and Sampson who crept out to the Dock. An anxious tension built as Winston's team waited for the signal.

This evacuation was an extraordinarily dangerous undertaking, and the largest escape ever attempted in the Cause's history. Fortunately, Market Weekend ensured all eyes would be on the Gate, as Chartreaux's Brigades-Men would be looking for any sign of Hostesses leaving via the only known escape route—up the Main Drag from LowTown, into the Commons, then out through HighTown.

The signal came: two taps, and Sanders opened the hatch.

"Escort Team One, to your station—"

Winston ascended the ladder to the hatch and lifted Araceli up through the opening under the Dock. Habib reached up to help Lourdes as she followed; with her sprained wrist bound and immobilized, she was attempting to climb the ladder one-handed. Her foot slipped—

A muffled squeal of pain escaped as Lourdes' lips as her foot slid off the ladder rung. She fell back against Habib's outstretched arm. "Oh! My ankle... ah!"

Lourdes grabbed her trim ankle with one elegant hand, balancing in a flamingo-like pose which—like everything else—looked good on Lourdes LeFleur. Even though she was still dressed in her bloody ensemble from this morning, she had an air of sophistication which defied all fashionable logic; the dark reds of the spatters complimented her green eyes nicely.

Running to assess, Rose looked at Lourdes' offended foot. She prodded it with knowing finger—"It doesn't seem to be that bad... there's no crepitus, and all bones are sound."

"No, it's dreadful, I can't put any weight on it." Lourdes hissed to Rose, then whispered up the hatch to her teammates. "Winston, Araceli—go on without me. Be brave."

Unsure, Rose looked to Dominic, who waved her over for a report—she left to confer. Habib scowled confidentially to the injured Hembra: "Cut the pathetic dame act, Lourdes. Get up the ladder before somebody gets wise..."

"Pipe down, you big roustabout." Lourdes sniped at Habib, sotto voce. "Don't ruin this for me—I am setting a stage, and if you say anything to spoil it, I will cut you up and feed you to the fishes."

Startled by her sudden vitriol, a confused Habib gently lowered her to the ground. "Sorry, Chickie, I just thought you were after my stash of goods..."

"That's preposterous—and don't call me Chickie." Lourdes grabbed her ankle again and whined louder now—"I am sure my ankle is sprained..."

Araceli started to come down the hatch, but Lourdes flung her arm across her forehead in dramatic fashion: "No Araceli, go on without me—I will stay here in the tunnels and make myself useful. Now, go!"

Blinking back perfect tears, Araceli murmured: "But you are my friend, I can't just leave you..."

Looking at Lourdes' ankle suspiciously, Sam intervened. "Go, Araceli; we can't wait."

Saddened, Araceli slipped out the hatch with Winston, and it closed behind them.

Sam picked up Lourdes: "Let's get you back to the triage area. Medic—"

Rose edged up under Lourdes' other arm, and they helped her to limp back into the tunnel. She tilted her head back and sighed. "How awful—I believe I have sprained my Achilles Tendon!" Lourdes said, gritting her teeth and moaning for those who might be listening out in the staging area.

Rose shook her head slightly—the ankle didn't seem to warrant such a response, but then again, *everyone has their own level of pain tolerance*... she walked over to the staging area for the Anchor Team of Dominic and Habib.

"Lourdes says she has pulled her Achilles Tendon. I believe she will recover quickly but wants to wait until it stops hurting, which might be at least a half-hour."

Dominic frowned. "It can't be helped, then—but she will miss the opportunity to leave with her group. She is a very competent assassin, however; here with us, she may serve a very useful purpose."

Eyes narrowing at the thought of Lourdes' chicanery, Habib focused once again on the hatch, and left the drama to the experts. He sneered and muttered to himself. "Liars, all..."

Baffled, Sam eyed Lourdes suspiciously—"Come clean, Lourdes—it's just you and me. I know you're faking... why? Why now?"

Lourdes kept her voice low. "Trust me. You and I have been partners since you first came to Purgatory, and I have trusted you. Now I ask you to return the favor." Confident, Lourdes patted Sam's hand. "You will thank me in the end, Sam."

"I can't help but trust you, Lourdes—you have always been a rock for me." Sam squeezed her hand. "Of all my girls, you were the one I could always count on to make sense. I'll trust you to make sense now; it's just— it bothers me that you won't be with the group where I can know you are safe. Just promise me you'll stay safe..."

"This is a war. Nothing is safe—but Freedom isn't safe, either. Fight the good fight, Sam."

"You've got it," Sam glanced over at Habib, who was making himself busy with the supplies. "Take care of him. He took care of me once, a long time ago..." Eyes clouded, Sam turned away.

Lourdes said nothing, but she gripped her ankle again and bided her time.

The next tap on the hatch came, and Sanders opened it up once more —time for Destiny's escort team to run the gauntlet. Rose made one more check of her unconscious patient's airway and adjusted Destiny's posture slightly forward in Mansour's arms. Giving a thumbs up to Sam, Rose nodded, and Sam scrambled up the rungs, cat-like. Antsy, Mansour held Destiny over his broad shoulder and ascended the ladder, the Macho's extra muscle making his load light. Sam reached down with a steadying hand as Mansour pulled himself and Destiny out under the Dock.

The hatch closed, and Rose breathed out. All were silent, except for a murmured prayer from someone up the tunnel. Rose turned to the Watcher.

"We are next!" She looked him over from underneath her cloak; "I don't suppose you have any injuries you need examined before we head out?"

He gave a slight grunt and shook his head, bemused at her question. He always had injuries of some kind; it was all part of the job. At present, he only had some slight bruises this morning's jailbreak; a few burns from this afternoon's bout with the bot bothered him some, but not enough to mention. Still, it would do to play up some kind of reason for the Medic to help him out after a battle. He gave a subtle smirk. *You can examine me later, in private.* But what about the Afterling's wounds?

Pointing to Rose, the Watcher tapped her shoulder where Joseph's Oppressor had lashed her with his wicked leather whip. She gave a wince.

"Oh, it only hurts a little... it's healing. It might leave a small scar, though."

Just a small scar... he pulled back the edge of her hood to examine her forehead where a certain Big Ol' Ugly Devil had pegged her with a rock when he first saw her.

"Oh, I had almost forgotten about that!" she whispered softly. It was almost gone, but even beneath the paint of her disguise, the Watcher could tell where he had wounded her. He looked into her luminous eyes, and nearly fell in.

What about the scars we can't see? This the Watcher grunted and discreetly patted his own belly then pointed to her.

Rose nodded eagerly. "You are hungry? Me too! I am famished... I want some eggs and potatoes again, those were delightful." She made a sad face. "But now the potatoes are all burnt."

No, he growled, then pointed at her lower abdomen. Her face became wan. "Oh, Deva, we don't talk about that here—it is forbidden..."

Forbidden... There's that word again. He snarled, and she stepped back, suddenly concerned. He shook his head. *No, damn it, I'm not going to hurt you.* He made an attempt to look less savage. This language limitation was getting wearisome—it made every Ring-less interaction with Rose a minefield of implied meaning and potential misunderstanding. He rubbed his finger where his deactivated WeSpeex RingWorld waited patiently to become his Voice again.

If I ever meet the Man who made the Ring, vowed the Watcher—*I'll shake his hand before I wreak vengeance...*

In LifeBefore, the Ring had been a God-Send for those who became Other-Abled over the course of their lives; it equalized the Other-Abled so they could continue to have eQuality of Life as required per the latest Whole Earth Union Protocols. In the Union, of course, no one was born Other-Abled anymore, thanks to the new "eQuality World" protocols implemented by the Third Whole Earth Union World Congress. All designated birth defects had a one-hundred percent cure rate in the Union, thanks to mandatory eQuality Of Life terminations being enforced in all pregnancies. But perfectly healthy people still occasionally suffered incurable infirmity and disability due to accidents, illness, or aging. Those judged to have high enough eQuality of Life scores were cleared by their Health Panels to use the WeSpeex RingWorlds to overcome their Other-Abledness.

The Watcher grimaced. *eQuality of Life,* perfect life as defined by perfect experts. He himself was now just a hair's breadth away from being considered un-eQuality of Life, even with the Ring. *But even before the Happening...* he refused to think about it. The Watcher was lucky he had been born in Texas—that "backwards" State had been one of the last sanctuaries in the world for those who were born with—or acquired—un-eQuality of Life. Looking at Rose now, he realized with a start—under the Whole Earth Union, *our Child would have been Forbidden.*

Even in LifeBefore, under the Whole Earth Union protocols, both the Watcher and Rose would both have been considered to have un-eQuality of Life: he with his mutism and mutations, and her as a clone. As they were now, both would have been encouraged to live correctly as possible, die conveniently as needed, and be forbidden to reproduce. *Just like we are forbidden to reproduce now...*

He pondered this last thought: their Project would have been forbidden in LifeBefore—*just like it was in LifeAfter.* The Visionaries' Church of Death had existed, even before The Happening, just nobody called it a Church. Nobody dared question it, because it was disguised as a human right—eQuality of Life for all. And eQuality of Life was reserved only for those who were deemed worthy of life by the arbiters of everything—the Visionaries.

The Watcher gazed at the un-eQuality unPerson before him. This little cloned clump of engineered cells, with her bright eyes and her lopsided grin, was more than the Visionaries' defective replacement for Humanity. Rose was simply Rose, and he wanted her to live, just to spite the powers that would destroy them both.

The time to overthrow the System's UnHoly Church of Death is long past due.

He was shaken from his reverie by the sound of the signal. The double tap reverberated, not from the Dock hatch but from the Jail Hatch. The Jailer, DeRita, opened the hatch and whispered—

"Judge, we got company. Brigades-Men are—about fifteen of 'em—demanding to lay eyes on you and see that you haven't escaped. There's no sign of any bosses, though..."

"The search for the Hostesses and their rescuers begins... so we shall stall them. Demand proof they are with Boss Chartreaux, and protest that the Jail is on lockdown—that will give us time to secure this hatch and get me back to my cell. Then you may let them enter, and I will keep them busy until all are cleared from the tunnels."

The Judge turned to the Quartermaster: "Habib, meet me upstairs after the tunnel is evacuated—use the ruse of working the books in your office. The office door will be locked behind us to prevent unauthorized entry. Make haste." With a wave of his hand, Dominic bid Rose and the Teams goodbye.

He leapt up the hatch to the Jail, whispering to his fellow actors: "To your places everyone!" Then Judge Santos was gone, leaving his last two teams to finish the evacuation.

Scanning the now nearly-empty tunnel, Habib gave his parting instructions to the group: "We wait for the signal, then secure the tunnel to leave. Make sure you've got all your gear, because once you leave, you can't come back."

One more item—the Watcher reached into the bin below the dock-side hatch and retrieved the Drunkard's Coat. Even as he opened the lid, a billowing cloud of odor wafted up from the ragged coat. He held it at an arm's length—*and this is what you get for guilting me into giving away my garment, Afterling; a smelly ride.*

Up the tunnel, Rose gave Lourdes a glance: "How is your ankle? If it's better, you could come with us."

The Watcher strode into view, his aromatic coat announcing his presence. Lourdes frowned and shook her head. "My ankle is terrible. I must wait until it's better—you'll have to go on without me. Please inform the girls I have packed bundles for them, all marked—there is even one for you."

"Oh! That is so sweet. Are you sure you can't come? I could wrap your ankle, and Marshal Azarian could carry you...";

Lourdes gave Rose a look that could freeze lava. "Absolutely, completely, not."

The Watcher grunted to himself. *Suit yourself—something's fishy with this setup anyway.* He had a sneaking suspicion it had nothing to do with the condition of Lourdes ankle and more to do with the condition of her heart.

Poking Rose's shoulder, the Watcher demanded her attention: he flashed the four-fingers sign and jerked his thumb towards his own back. *Bodyguard Carry Four—mount up.* He knelt and waited for her to comply.

"Oh, I'll be fine walking next to you, there's no need," Rose smiled brightly, backing away.

So that's how it is... he signed again, emphatically. She leaned forward to whisper in his ear:

"But it smells terrible!"

Growling, the Watcher whipped out his notepad.

> *—I shared my coat, so no complaining. I know the smell's bad. Follow orders.*

Rose hung her head. "No, I mean—I'm sorry. Just... never mind." She started to climb aboard, fighting nausea from the smell.

A mortified Lourdes interrupted. "You ride the Watcher's back?"

Chagrined, Rose explained: "Oh, he's my Bodyguard, and I see in the dark for him. He carries me to protect me, and I point out targets that he can't detect." Rose was suddenly keenly aware of Lourdes' disapproval at her unorthodoxy. "I can see things he can't—heat from bodies and all sorts of interesting things. But I can't point it out as well from the ground as I can over his shoulder. He's tall, so it's easier for me to ride piggyback than for him to bend down and try to shoot..."

"Hmm." Lourdes seemed ever so slightly impressed. "So, you have night vision—like an animal? Well, that's certainly a valuable skill. But riding a man?" She sniffed. "I suppose it fits your wild image, though, to ride him like a monkey would ride a tiger..."

Lourdes' disapproval fueled Rose's reluctance. "Oh, I had not thought of it that way." Rose seemed embarrassed.

The Watcher looked at the Afterling: *Image? What sort of nonsense is this?* Exasperation welled up in him—when Rose was around other females, she seemed to court their approval rather than his own, jostling to be accepted into the herd...

"Don't look." Gingerly, Rose clambered up onto the Watcher's back, holding tight to his filthy coat collar as she hooked her moccassined toes into his belt loops. Shifting the bag of gear on his shoulder, he pulled the Remington on its sling around to his side, still well-hidden beneath his coat. Slipping her knees up under his coat from the back, Rose clamped them tightly around his ribcage; he reached up to hook his arm through the crook of her left knee...

Feeling the warmth of her bare skin seeping through the back of his vest, it all suddenly made sense why Rose was so reluctant to climb upon his back: there was nothing between them but his vest, and good intentions. The Watcher blushed a bright red, but fortunately beneath his balaclava, no one could see it.

"Thank you, Deva—I am completely mounted up." Tucking her hooded head into the back of his balaclava, Rose disappeared under her cloak, and the Watcher became a befuddled-looking laborer toting a bundle of furs on his back. "Oh, but Deva, this smell of this coat is terrible!" Rose whispered with a gasp.

"That's pretty clever..." Habib nodded appreciatively, backing up to put some distance between himself and the odiferous Watcher. "You look like a trapper with hides to sell. Just don't let them look too close..." he waved his hand in front of his nose. "Come to think of it, I don't think they'll get too close."

Tap-Tap. The Teams heard Sanders at the hatch—he opened it, and called down: "Escort Team Three—you're up."

The Watcher turned and climbed up the ladder into the smoky air of Purgatory.

The Hatch closed; the evacuation of the tunnel was complete. After Sanders returned, it would be up to the teams to get themselves to the safety of the safe room tunnel. Habib sighed, and turned to Lourdes, looking at her with a wary eye. "When we get Sanders secured, I'm gonna have to get you upstairs—I'll hide you in the office under the desk until the Brigades-Men leave."

Lourdes quipped with all seriousness: "Trust me, it won't be the first time someone has hidden me under a desk. Give me a weapon, and I'll be fine." She leapt up, suddenly healed, and climbed the ladder without the slightest hint of pain.

Cynical, Habib shook his head. *Liars all...*

VI

The Hatch closed behind them as the Watcher pulled up under the rusted boat hull, the Afterling clinging to his back. Sanders peeked under the boat from his post next to the hull, where he was fishing. "All clear..."

Scrambling out into the cold night air, he took a deep breath of relatively fresh air. The scent from Bogie's coat was overwhelming. *That'll teach me to do a good deed,* thought the Watcher. Sanders gave him a pitying glance.

"That kind of smell doesn't wash off easy. Bogie's a good guy, but he does have a distinctive odor." Sanders stepped away, eyes watering.

A gasping Rose murmured. "Oh, Deva, it's awful. I am so sorry—it was still so admirable for you to give Bogie your coat. But the smell is atrocious. I can't breathe!"

"Well, settle down and look busy," Sanders instructed—"Watchman Wunstler is due to come around in the next couple of minutes. Just hang here and don't make any suspicious moves."

Crawling out from under the Dock, the Watcher sat next to Sanders as he plopped his bobber in the water. *Nothing to see here—just two friends sitting next to the dock with some deer hides.*

"Will the Watchman come down this way?" Rose whispered, curious.

"It's possible," Sanders asserted, "but chances are, he'll top the ridge to give a look down this way, then head off—Wunstler will be eager to get back to his guard station, with its warm fire and comfy chair. He'll avoid coming down here, unless someone gives him a reason, as we are off his route." Sanders cast out the line from his cane pole into the dark water.

Choppy waves skittered across the lake in the dim light filtering through the high clouds, and dry cottonwood leaves rustled in the wind. The restless breezes filled the Watcher with anticipation; something about the night wind had always made him dream of change and escape. *Everything is changing now, running with the night wind.*

In the distance, the sound of voices drifted up from the Commons—the first Market Weekend visitors were rolling into town. The tone of muted greetings and approval could be heard. Further away, on the opposite side of Purgatory, the Watcher could distinguish the sound of a cluster of different voices—low, angry, anxious. Somewhere, a group of dangerous men were discussing dark events. He could now hear a pair of feet approaching, fast and purposeful. These were not the meanderings of a casual walk—these were the footsteps of a man looking for answers.

The Watcher tapped his ears, then pointed to the ridge above the Docks. Sanders listened and at first could not hear it over the wind—but finally he could make out the rapid steps on the dirt path leading to the Docks. Sanders spoke below his breath: "That would be the Watchman. Look at the lake, and I'll talk to him if needed. Meanwhile, you act drunk to avoid conversation. Little lady, you stay silent."

The Watcher nodded and gripped his shotgun beneath his coat. Reaching behind him with his left, he gave Rose's bare calf a pat up under her cloak; she tucked her head into his collar and held tight. His hand lingered against her smooth flesh, for just a moment. His heart raced, as through a torn-out fingertip of his workman's gloves, he touched her soft skin....

Now the Watcher heard the Watchman's footsteps slow at the top of the ridge above the Docks, some hundred yards away. He knew the drill; security would stop and scan, and look for anything out of place.

Something must look out of place...

They heard the sound of empty cans and bottles being kicked out of the way as the footsteps started down the path towards the docks...

"Watchman Wunstler. Your names, please." He paused behind them. "Oh geez—Bogie, for the love of God, take a bath. You stink to high heaven..." They heard the steps back away. "Listen up you Bums—you seen anything unusual around here? Anybody coming or going that shouldn't be?"

If he had any fear, Sanders showed none. "It's me—Louie Varga. I've seen nothing. It's too cold for foolery tonight. Who are you looking for?"

"I'm looking for runaways. That pink Hostess, Destiny—she's wanted by the Bosses for the fires. But there's more than just her on the suspect list... What are you two low-lifes doing down here? You ought to be up at the Commons anyways, you know. The fire barrels are burning there." The Watchman walked closer.

"A man's gotta eat—so I gotta fish. Too much's been happening today, and I didn't have time earlier." Sanders jerked the bobber gently on the surface of the water.

"What about you, Bogie?" Steps came closer as the Watchman inspected the scene. The Watcher stared out into the water, then leaned into Sanders and hiccupped. His hand rested lightly on the grip of his weapon. With his other hand, he waved lazily.

Reaching over to pat the Watcher's shoulder, Sanders chuckled. "He's drunk. I had to find a drinkin' buddy to share a round or two—it's been a wild day."

"You got that right—fires everywhere. Let me or the Watchmen at the gate know if you see anything; all good Purgatory men need to keep their eyes open tonight." Wunstler grunted. "There's a reward offered for anyone who finds the runaways or tips off anyone abetting them."

"You got it." Beneath his disguise, Sanders nodded, the brim of his trucker's hat bobbing.

"Thanks. If you see someone running, tell us." With that, the Watchman stepped back up the path. "If I were you, I'd finish up and get out of here—you don't wanna be on the wrong side of the Bosses when they find the ones they're looking for..." Nervous, he scurried up the dirt trail and away from the Docks. The fishermen listened as the Watchman's step faded.

The Afterling let out a soft sigh of relief as she came up for air. "I never knew a smell could be a disguise!"

"That worked out pretty well." Sanders pulled in his line, then took a stick and tapped out the signal against a floating bottle in the water. "We're good as long as he doesn't meet the real Varga or real Bogie. They're usually dead drunk by nightfall." Now a tap-tap sounded from the shadows of the trees beyond the far shore, near the wall. *The signal.*

Sanders looked up. "Time to move." He subtly pointed to the opposite shore. "Your relay contact, Evangelo, is between those twin cottonwood trees next to the wall; you'll have to move through about two hundred yards, with little cover. Walk easy over there, and he'll direct you to the next point as soon as the signal comes. I'll be returning to the Jail tunnel once the relay signals your safe arrival."

The Watcher stood, and Sanders adjusted the cloak around Rose to make sure her arms and legs were completely covered. "You're all set. Good luck and Godspeed." Without looking back, he began walking towards his unseen contact.

Behind a veil of high clouds, a crescent moon was barely visible; in the darkness, the Watcher kept his steps steady and slow to avoid falling or tripping. The sandy shoreline was mostly barren of vegetation, the result of heavy foot traffic on delicate soil. Beyond the barricade that separated the shallow, narrow inlet from the greater lake, he could hear the waves lapping against the wooden palisades. The wall, like Reunion's wall, kept wild beasts at bay, but Purgatory Wall had a distinct advantage —it had the lake waters surrounding the entire town, with the exception of a narrow strip of sand where the hidden door allowed an exit onto dry soil. Alligators added to the defense, but it was now too cold for the gators, and they would be hibernating or staying submerged to stay warm.

Ducking behind a large willow, he stopped to scan his surroundings and attempt to get his bearings. In the cloud light, he could barely see. He patted Rose's leg, then jiggled her. The Watcher felt the Afterling raise her head, and he pointed to his own eyes, then to hers. She looked over his left shoulder now and pointed slightly to their right, whispering—"I can see a glow ahead. Is that Evangelo?"

Nodding, the Watcher picked up the pace of his steps. With her as his guide, he could move faster. She continued to point, without speaking, and he followed her hand to the section of fence in deep shadow where he could hear steady breathing. He reached out to clasp hands with his friend, and a reassuring voice whispered to them—

"Welcome to the Wall. Head to the right, and follow it some three hundred yards to your East, where you will meet Goins in a clump of willow along the wall; I will follow you once I receive the signal you are safe." He took the haft of his knife, and tapped twice in rapid succession against a stone near his foot, then repeated it. A hesitation, then a faint tap came from the boat hull. Now they heard another signal, more distant, from their East.

"All clear—go." Evangelo looked all around for any signs of threats, and finding none, waved them on.

"Thank you, Captain—be careful!" Rose whispered to Evangelo in farewell as the Watcher carried her off into the shadows.

Now the way was more sheltered, the drifts of trash hiding their movement; the Watcher moved with greater speed, still careful and deliberate, as Rose peered over his shoulder to look for any signs of searchers. The mountains of trash gave welcome shelter from prying eyes, and the Watcher was covering ground quickly when he felt a pat on his head. It was the Afterling, demanding attention:

"Deva, slow down—there is something lying motionless on the ground in the trash pile just ahead, to our right—it looks like a man. Maybe it's Goins?"

The Watcher pulled his knife: *whatever it is, it's going to be dead soon if it moves wrong.* Wary, he approached, unsure if the unmoving shape was friend or foe... presently, a pungent odor announced itself, an unmistakable scent. The Watcher drew close—

"Oh, Deva, it's the man who gave you his coat! Is he hurt?"

We don't have time to find out. Glowering, the Watcher stepped around the immobile man. "Oh, Deva, please, just a moment—" Without warning, she slipped off the Watcher's back and Rose's feet hit the garbage-strewn ground. *What the hell*—pushing her behind him, the Watcher shook his head then quickly reached down to touch the drunken macho. Bogie was shivering and already felt slightly cool to the touch. *He's just drunk again, probably.* The Watcher shook the sleeping Survivor, who stirred with a grunt. It was frigid, just above freezing, with stiff winds, and hypothermia would set in soon if this man didn't find shelter...

The drunk snorted with a start, looking up. "Huh? What the devil... you what?"

Rose whispered: "You could pick him up and take him with us."

You can't just kidnap drunken bums away to a Revolution, the Watcher thought sourly. For whatever reason, this man thought too little of himself to help himself. Kendra had said Bogie's misfortune was his own choice, and Musashi would have agreed:

> *"All men are the same except for their belief in their own selves, regardless of what others may think of them"*

Changing Bogie's location would not change the landscape within the man. Still, the Watcher could not simply walk away... the Afterling's eyes were burning a hole in his soul. He heard a soft groan from Bogie, lying in his bed made of empty bottles.

Time to pay back your gift. Stripping off the borrowed coat, the Watcher pulled the drunken man to his feet, then threw the garment across Bogie's shoulders. Bogie jerked awake and stood blinking at the Watcher, swaying unsteadily.

Rose whispered to the man from behind the Watcher's back: "You have to go home, sir—you'll freeze to death out here..."

Damn it, Rose—the Watcher swatted softly behind him to shush her, but it was too late.

"Hey... s'you again." Bogie leaned in, nearly nose to nose with the Watcher; the stench of Reunion liquor rolling off him. "Y'sound like a girl." He gripped the Watcher's arm with a sudden strength, and looked him in the eyes.

"Angels unawares..." Even in the dark, a light seemed to emanate from Bogie's blue-gray eyes, green-gold sparks amid blue streaks—"Go, quickly —the Posse comes." With that, the drunk turned on his heel and walked away with steady steps, disappearing between the dunes of drifted garbage.

The Watcher blinked, stunned at the resurrection of the old phrase from the deeps of his dead past: *Angels unawares...*

Taken aback at the Bogie's sudden sobriety, the Watcher listened: faintly from the commons, he could hear multiple footsteps approaching from the south. *The Posse...*

Throwing the Afterling over his shoulder, the Watcher crouched and leapt over the piles of trash, moving silently, feet moving expertly between the bottles and cans without disturbing them. This was the legacy of his time as a city man—to move unseen through a crowd, unheard through the flotsam and jetsam of civilization. He could hear the tipsy Bogie crashing, slipping on the cans and bottles that littered his own path, masking any other noises. The Watcher raced beside the wall, hearing slurred words of Bogie greeting the Posse, fifty yards to his southeast: "Hey! Drinkin' buddies! You gotta bottle to share?"

A gravelly voice address Bogie: "Get your drunk ass out of our way, unless you can tell us you've seen something..."

"Oh, sure, I seen something. Gimme a drink and I'll tell ya..."

The gravelly voice answered him. "Tell us, then you get your drink."

That's the last time I listen to Rose. The Watcher thought bitterly as he ran. *No more nice guy...* Weaving between barrels and boxes, he hurdled a broken-down couch with one bound; his foot slipped as he came down, but he bounced off a modified three-point landing and kept running. "There's a glow beside the wall just ahead!" Rose whispered over her shoulder to the Watcher. Two muffled taps, the sound of a pipe wrench on wood were heard: *Goins...*

The Watcher could hear Bogie's voice rising above the wind, warmly slurring to the Posse:

"Oh yeah, I seen 'em. A little Golden Fairy spoke to me, then a Troll showed up and carried her off to his Palace under the bridge."

From the dump, the Watcher could hear groans and jeers erupting from the Posse. A brazen voice sneered. "You should be shot for wasting our time..."

"Not so fast—" The Posse Leader's voice was sharply calculating. "A little Golden Fairy, he says? Albright, send word to Boss Chartreaux. We have a sighting of the small golden woman, and she has a big helper—her 'Troll.' We're going to have to search near the footbridge between Industrial and LowTown. Tell them..." The Posse's voices faded from his hearing as the Watcher left them in his dust.

A plaintive voice called after the Posse: "Hey! Where's my drink?" But they were already racing away, back towards the center of town.

Bogie, you magnificent plastered bastard.

Sprinting forward, the Watcher reached out to tag Goins' open hand: the secret door was already open, and the Watcher slid through, bearing the Afterling to safety.

"Nice sliding form," Kendra whispered, impressed, as she reached out to secure the door. "But what happened to your awesome coat?"

"Oh, it was the most wonderful thing," Rose whispered, trying to slip down off the Watcher's shoulder. "Deva found Bogie and returned his coat—and Bogie returned the favor by turning the Posse away from our trail!"

Still irked at her unauthorized talkativeness, the Watcher pushed Rose back up onto his shoulder. *You're not going anywhere, you insubordinate imp.*

Kendra scoffed. "Ugh, this proves Bogie's got a screw loose—no one sane would think it was a favor to return that repulsive coat."

"I'm impressed; I didn't know Bogie had it in him to string two coherent sentences together." Sam sidled up. "A Posse, huh? No more chatter. We wait for Evangelo to bring up the rear, and Goins to reel him in." Crowding the sandy strand, the evacuees fell silent as Sampson stared out over the water, searching for threats. Backs pressed to the wall, they waited for the last of their team to appear.

At last, the signal rapped its welcome rhythm; a relieved Sam welcomed Evangelo and Goins through the hidden door and back into the group. Goins hid their trail, then pulled an old refrigerator across inside wall before shutting the door, to hide it from prying eyes. A status-check confirmed all present and accounted.

Sam motioned to the Watcher: "Marshal Azarian, bring your Afterling to the front—I have need of her night vision." Dropping her shotgun into a low-ready position, Sam held up her hand, and addressed her group: "We're heading down the willow trail—so fall in and follow me."

———————◆———————

Up the slopes, the coyotes howled and yammered; the band of homeless rebels moved through the canids' nocturnal territory, uninvited guests on the run. From her perch on the Watcher's back, Rose leaned forward and pointed over his left shoulder—"Coyotes in the underbrush to our right, twenty or so, about fifty feet ahead. They are relaxed, but keeping their distance; I don't think they are a threat..." She became excited. "Oh! A flock of Turkeys is roosting in the trees up to our left—either that, or it's buzzards." She pointed up in a tall Elm, down the slope towards the water.

A soft trilling call confirmed the presence of turkeys, and the Watcher longed to see the magnificent birds, but they were hidden by the night.

"Turkey?" The thought of a whole roasted turkey made Sam wish for a way to cook one. She had no oven now... "We could use some food, but we don't have time to hunt, and we don't have the goods to barter." Sam pondered how to feed this group of homeless wanderers. It had been a long day, and she was hungry—if she was famished, her troops would be starving as well. Down on the Commons, the Market Day Bar-be-que pits and Taco Stands had already been fired up, but the Hostesses and their entourage had no means to go and barter. All the Hostesses' carefully amassed barter goods had been burned up in the fire; poverty was now their lot, and without goods, they only had services to trade for tokens at Purgatory booths. Sam scowled.

Creeping along the willow-wood trail with the Afterling riding piggyback, the Watcher had an epiphany: she was really quite helpful for night ops. When properly situated, she was no more noticeable than a back-pack, and she weighed about the same as a one fully packed-out. Her biggest problem was in staying up in the proper position—her toes kept slipping out of his belt-loops, making it hard for her to stay on his back for long distances. *Perhaps a solution could be rigged...*

Right now, she was keeping his back warm, since he had given Bogie his coat back. Already, the world was a cleaner, sweeter place, but it was also colder. He shivered, ready to get back to the tunnels and his own proper gear. At least the Afterling was warm. The fur cloak had been the perfect camouflage-accessory for Rose.

The Watcher scanned the trees, wondering when another drone would appear. It had been twelve hours since the first ALGOS had appeared, and it was simply a matter of time before a companion drone would be sent to search for it. The disabled drone's emergency beacon had been dumped downstream, but the safe room tunnel entrance had already been documented. Like everything else connected to the System, the tunnel would need to be abandoned.

Could Rose see the drone before it saw her? Even if she saw the infrared signature of the ALGOS in time, how would he explain everything to the others in the group? It made him nervous to be moving like a herd of cattle through the underbrush, especially with so large a group and no way to communicate quickly with all of them...*how does one lead without a voice?*

For now, Rose would have to be his voice.

He was glad to have that option made convenient once again; as soon as the Watcher had moved outside the range of Purgatory's Dead Zone, he had reactivated his WeSpeex Ring. Now he linked hands with Rose:

#Be on the lookout for ALGOS drones—if spotted, notify me before you notify group... I will give you instructions for them and yourself.

Rose nodded, nervous, and looked over her shoulder, clinging tight to the Watcher's collar.

The Rebels made their way into the opening just below the narrow canyon entrance to the safe room tunnel. There, Sam raised her hand to halt them, and signaled their arrival to the Sentry; the door opened to reveal the irritably friendly face of Gunnery Sergeant Renfro.

"Welcome to your home for the next thirty minutes—thanks to our visit from the ALGOS drone, we're saddling up to leave. Refresh yourselves and prepare to head out. This location is no longer secret,

Agent Ellison, and we will abandon post."

Anxious murmurs accompanied this pronouncement. Most of the rank and file had never known of the existence of the AGLOS until now —this Government Spy Drones program had been classified in LifeBefore.

But if Sam felt discouraged, she did not show it. "So I heard. All Agents, report to Agent Mansour to receive WildLand Express gear; all personnel, meet with me in five for orders. Team Heavies, please report to Marshal Evangelo afterwards to help tote extra items. We will rendezvous with the WildLand Express at their camp outside town."

Inside the tunnel, everything was upended. Agents Mancini and Wilcox were saddling horses and packing gear with haste; the morning's encounter with the ALGOS drone put an urgency to their task, and they had managed to get most of the packing done over the course of the day. A cart had been procured and was secured at the tunnel entrance, to be loaded with patients on the way out. A strange noise came from the dog pens...

Oskar was chortling in his pen, and startled glances greeted the little Chupacabra. Goins snapped: "Who's going to put that thing down? I want the hide..."

Sergeant Renfro gave Goins a chastising glare. "Nobody's putting it down—that's Oskar, and he's Sassy's special friend." Sassy looked up at the mention of her name. "She thinks Oskar's just an extra-ugly hound."

Eyes rolling, Goins quipped. "Okay, Gramps."

Oskar whined.

The Watcher patted the Chupacabra through the bars of his pen, then headed over to Oro, setting the Afterling upon the saddle. Rifling through the gear bag, the Watcher was eager to have his old oilskin hat and the Preacher's coat back; he slipped them over his tweed vest and adjusted his red bandana around his throat once more. Pulling his thick, gauntleted work gloves on, he felt almost whole again—he only wished he had a pair of heavy-duty boots to wear. Evangelo's moccasin boots had served him well, but they were already showing wear from hard use, and the Watcher wished to save them for stealth work and climbing. His attention turned to Rose:

#So how are your slippers holding up?

"I think they are wearing very well—so far they are warm and cozy!" Rose extended her feet from under the hem of her cloak. The Watcher inspected her moccasins, then pulled one from her foot.

"Oh! Give my moccasin back, Deva, please—"

He gave the golden doehide slipper a closer look; the fringed cuff of the upper was still in excellent shape, and the soles had only the slightest hint of shininess from wear. He ran his fingers down the inside. Rose had lined them with the Supra-Warmeez UltraFoil emergency blanket, just like she lined the cloak, to help hide her own heat signature from the drone's infrared detectors. A vast improvement over the old foil "space blankets," UltraFoil was a shiny, heat-reflecting metal-fiber blend that draped well. He viewed it with satisfaction.

#Good job on the lining—now what about the rest of you? What exactly are you wearing under there? You're not dressed for the WildLand with those bare legs.

"I'm fine up under here, I really am..." Discreetly pulling aside the edge of her cloak, she allowed a peek at the strap of her sleeveless t-shirt dress. "It's just a knit shirt and some pins." The soft, chocolate-brown knit complimented the golden scrollwork of her smooth, painted shoulder. A familiar blush swept across his scales, and he wondered if it was obvious.

"Now, return my lovely moccasin, please?" From her perch on Oro's saddle, she stuck out her foot for the Watcher to return the cuffed bootlet to its rightful place.

The deer tails dangling from the hem of her cloak brushed against her sleek calf and fell away to reveal an intricately painted pumpkin-orange knee. Intrigued, He took a closer look: *how far up her legs does this paint job go?* He already knew how far down it extended... *even the soles of her feet are painted.* Her foot, no bigger than the palm of his hand, was gilt with painted scrolls and lacy curves.

Delighted with the effect of the paint, she wiggled her toes at him. "Please? I don't wish for all the paint to wear off."

The warm vanilla scent of her skin invited him to forget drones and rebellions. *If we weren't fleeing for our lives right now...*he mused, befuddled once again. Fighting an overwhelming urge to pull her off the horse and see what else might be under the cloak, he grabbed her slim ankle and slipped her moccasin back on her foot.

She smiled. "Thank you! I love these moccasins—they are the softest shoes I've ever owned. Still, I'll be glad to wear my boots once again. They are sturdier, and I wouldn't want to get my pretty mocs muddy."

*Muddy. You didn't mind mud earlier...*through his pheromone addled haze, he heard Rose pipe up, addressing someone behind him. "Oh! Hello there—I'm Rose. And who might you be?"

The Watcher turned to see Agent Mancini gawping at Rose, completely tongue-tied. "I...I..."

An oblivious Rose behind him, the Watcher flushed red, and flashed his canines at Mancini in warning. The stout Macho backed away, blinking.

"Oh... I didn't mean to scare him." Rose said earnestly. "I really do look very odd to devils, don't I?"

You weren't the one who scared him.

The Watcher looked Rose up and down. For now, Rose would be kept in camouflage colors of browns and tans, to better hide her from prying eyes; he wanted to give her the shawl, but red roses wouldn't serve the purpose of camouflage well. He wrapped the fine rose shawl around his own neck for safekeeping. *Maybe I'll wrap it around Rose later, to replace that t-shirt she's wearing now.*

He grinned to himself—that sounded like a plan.

With Rose still atop the great golden Palomino, the Watcher walked Oro over to the staging area of the stable to be loaded with gear. Agents and Specialists gathered around to admire the gorgeous beasts assembled in the stables; trained horses were a rarity in the WildLands.

Evangelo was rightly proud of his steeds. Charger, Dominic's blue grullo, was a fantastic dark gray with an almost liquid sheen to the horse's coat; murmurs of appreciation rose up from his admirers. Oro, with his pale golden mane and coat, seemed to glow in the lantern light, and William was a beautiful burnished bay color. But out of them all, it was Shadow who stole the prize for equine beauty—Chief Emmanuel's horse was the undisputed King of the Stables, and he knew it. Heavy muscles rippled beneath the gelding's obsidian coat, framed by the mantle of his wavy mane and tail... The crowd's approval seemed to feed the sleek Percheron's ego, and the horse pranced lightly at the end of his line, glad to bask in their attention.

Struck by inspiration, Rose raised a finger: "Oh, I know of another amazing creature just as beautiful!" She beckoned to the Watcher—"Let me bring him out, please?"

A flash of concern lit the Watcher's face:

#I'll consult Evangelo—Oskar must be handled with care in this crowd.

Opening the chat directory, the Watcher hailed Evangelo in the secured Xirxes Chat room:

#WATCHER: The Afterling wishes to bring out the Chupacabra to prepare him for transport—I am concerned about him becoming aggressive in this crowd, but we have no other choice. Advise?

Looking up from the horses, Evangelo nodded:

#EVANGELO: I'd prefer to do it myself, but I'm busy at present. They must be told what he is, so they won't hurt him... and vice versa. Perhaps Oskar can be given a treat in front of the crowd and told they are friends?

A new voice entered the chat:

#OSKAR ASv4.7: *treat Oskar van*

#OSKAR ASv4.7: *van jello treat Oskar good*

Seeing Oskar trying to speak once again, Rose became excited, but the Watcher put his finger to his lips:

#WATCHER: tell no one—they may not understand.

Van Jello? Evangelo's eyes grew wide.

#EVANGELO: You are using AutoSpeex on the Chupacabra?

#OSKAR: *treat van jello treat*

#WATCHER: It's a long story. I meant to mention it earlier: Oskar can speak through the Ring now.

#OSKAR ASv4.7: *zary*

#OSKAR ASv4.7: *zary anne*

The Watcher tried to make sense of AutoSpeex jury-rigged wordcraft. *Zary Anne? ZaryAnne…Azarian.* Common words and names did well, but without VisualTrax, the neurotranslators had to guess at unusual words— hence, ZaryAnne. *I suppose it's better than 'Van Jello' for Evangelo though.* He cringed.

#OSKAR ASv4.7: *zaryanne oskar friend good oskar treat*

Glancing at the little beast with alarm, Evangelo continued to pack out the horses for travel:

#EVANGELO: This is most remarkable…and disturbing. Have Rose tell him which people are friends, and give treats for good behavior. If a problem arises, immediately have the pen closed.

Here Evangelo gave the sign for "Close Friend"—crossed fingers. The Chupacabra was dancing now, having heard the word "treats" uttered by the men; Oskar yammered even as AutoSpeex texted in chat:

#OSKAR ASv4.7: *vanjello friend zaryanne friend treat treat*

A goofy, broad grin spread across Oskar's muzzle as Rose and the Watcher approached the pen. The Watcher gave a handful of peanuts to Rose:

#WATCHER: I'll handle Oskar—you'll tell the audience he is a tame baby, and introduce each person as "Name" and "Friend"— they can hand him one peanut and say and sign the word Friend.

#OSKAR ASv4.7: *treat oskar good friend rose*

Still busy with the horses, Evangelo pointed the crowd in the direction of the Afterling. "Please report to Marshal Azarian for an announcement regarding his Chupacabra."

Delighted, Rose pushed her hood back and called to the crowd: she clapped her hands softly—"May I have your attention, please? Please line up so we may train the baby Chupacabra to not attack you..."

Kendra was mildly amused: "Ooh, a circus."

Curious, Sampson and the other Agents crowded around the pen, jostling to get a better look at a sight they had never seen—an Afterling handling a Chupacabra. Oskar's white curl was half raised between perked round ears, small black eyes glistening with inquisitive sparkle against his gray-brown skin. The great recurved claws clicked against the cold stone floor as he slunk cat-like next to the Afterling, his tail whipping side to side behind him.

The Watcher smiled to himself, bemused; Rose did not realize she was as much of a side-show attraction as Oskar. One by one, the small crowd of fascinated Survivors lined up to get their peanut from the Afterling and give the Chupacabra a treat.

"This is Oskar—he's a Chupacabra, and he's very intelligent and sweet. He also is very deadly! In mind of that, please observe as my Assistant demonstrates the proper procedure for becoming friends with Oskar." She tumbled a peanut into the Watcher's crusty palm, then tugged on his sleeve to pull him down, so she could whisper in his ear: "Oh, Deva, what do you want me to have Oskar call you? I think he is having trouble with your name... shall he call you Saul as well?"

He looked around the room. So many only knew him as "the Watcher"—and he wanted to keep it that way. "Marshal Azarian" was a formal name for formal needs, but what of friends and acquaintances? It was an unaccustomed dilemma for a man so accustomed to being anonymous.

#No—*the name Saul is meant for your lips alone, when we are*

alone. When we are among the crowds, the name is Marshal Azarian, or Watcher. Have Oskar call me Watcher.

"Oh—Okee Dokee, 'Watcher'..." She winked at him as if it were a grand secret, and he suddenly felt a goofy wonder take hold of him—he had no idea she could wink, and for some reason it tickled his fancy. Letting go of the Watcher's hand, she clapped once again to get the crowd's attention. "Observe! Oskar—"

She laid a hand upon his wiry curl, and the Cub's round ears perked, enamored with Rose's voice and her peanuts. She patted his head, then moved her hand to the Watcher's arm, making the sign for friend with the other hand: "Watcher—Friend!"

The Watcher held out his palm, flat, and Oskar cocked his head.

#OSKAR ASv4.7: *zaryanne*

#WATCHER: Azarian is Watcher. Watcher friend. Oskar Friend.

#OSKAR ASv4.7: *zaryanne watcher   watcher*

A sudden spark of recognition lit up the Cub's eyes. His muzzle grinned, displaying sharp, narrow fangs as the long tongue flicked out to grab the peanut.

#OSKAR ASv4.7: *watcher friend*

The crowd gawped at the sight of the Chupacabra's teeth. Rose beamed. "Now, who wants to be the first to try?"

Winston pushed forward. Rose touched him on the arm as she called his name, "Oskar, this is Winston—friend!"

Unsure about all this, Winston grimaced. "I haven't ever met one of these who wasn't trying to devour my face. Are you sure this thing is safe?"

"Oh absolutely!" Rose smiled cherubically. "Oskar has always been gentle with me; besides, we are kin." Rose gave out another treat:

"Araceli—friend."

Scratching Oskar's hairless ears, an enchanted Araceli cooed; "Oh, he is adorable!" The Chupacabra tried to sniff her hand, but Winston reached down and blocked the cub's snout.

"Uh-uh—not 'til I know this monster is trained. Look at those teeth..."

"But why do you tell me what to do? Sam told me—you are not Boss anymore," whispering, Araceli gently pushed his hand aside. "It is my hand, and I wish to pet the Chupacabra."

Shocked at Araceli's defiance, Winston remembered there had been no time to update the group about the command structure of the Revolution. Only two weeks ago, Araceli and all the rest of the Hostesses respected his status and even feared him. He had been a hero and an ally to the Cause—and more to Araceli, long ago. But now she was pushing his hand away as if he was some ordinary citizen.

"No, I'm not Boss anymore," he muttered darkly. "Things have changed."

Araceli just looked at Winston out of the corner of her eye, then smiled and patted the Chupacabra again. "Well, you are still Winston. That is quite obvious..."

The next Survivor came up. "Joey—friend."

Taking the peanut from Rose, Agent Mancini fumbled, hemming and hawing as he shuffled his feet. He gave Oskar his peanut, then went to the back of the line again, whispering to Wilcox:

"I'd give real barter to touch her hand once more, even if I have to pet that Chupacabra again to do it..."

Eavesdropping, the Watcher eyed Mancini coldly, but a hot opportunity called out from the conversation: *I'd give real barter...*the Watcher grunted to himself; if only that pretty girl was less of a wanted fugitive, it might work. Rose continued her sideshow patter for the small audience as the Watcher mulled how this opportunity might pay off in the future.

Goins swaggered up to the Chupacabra, and laid a hand on the Oskar's head. "Friend. I'm a friend. You're a tough beast; so am I." Goins handed the treat to Oskar, then beamed as Oskar took it in his fearsome maw. "Lookie here, boys—I just tamed a mighty Chupacabra!"

Kendra held out her hand to touch the creature. Oskar lolled his whip-like, muscular tongue around the tomboy's wrist, and it writhed against her skin. "Ewwww, this is disgusting," she said, grabbing his tongue like a snake and peeling it off her arm. She knelt down to admire his long, brawny forelegs and deep chest: "I bet you could do some real damage."

"Well, ain't you a dandy!" Sampson exclaimed: "I never thought I'd pet a Chupacabra without killing it first. Friend?" He patted his own chest with a scaly hand, then patted Oskar's thick skull. "I'm a friend. You're a smart boy, ain't ya..."

"I'm not so sure the beast is all that intelligent" interjected Wilcox. He studied Oskar, handing him the peanut. "Things can be programmed and still not be intelligent." The slender Hombre leaned forward, his silvery, craggy face inquisitive. "I've done a lot of coding in my time, and he might just be responding to prompts and inputs. What'll happen when his prompts change or inputs cease?"

"Well, Oskar is still just a baby, but he is already able to be trained. I think that's intelligent—and who knows how much more he can do once he grows up? But there is so much more to a person than just their intelligence..." Rose wrapped her arms around Oskar's neck, and kissed him as he panted, happy to be hugged once again.

Agent Wilcox looked dubious—"Chupacabras are not persons. Even if they are intelligent, they are not persons. Only Humans are persons... if you're not Human, you're not a person."

Rose's face fell, but she said nothing as she squeezed the cub tighter.

The Watcher held tight to Oskar's leash, wondering how Rose could feel so safe so close to the deadly little cub. Was it because she trusted the animal, or because she trusted the man handling the animal? The Survivors gawked at sight before them—a fabled killer taming a vicious monster being coddled by a fairy tale. Treats spent, the Watcher led Oskar into the staging area, Rose walking beside the fearsome creatures. From her post by Destiny's side, Sam shook her head in wonder at the sight.

"The most dangerous creature's not the one on the leash."

Packing away a box of military apparel, Mansour nodded: "Dominic told me how the Watcher almost singlehandedly took the Jailhouse back from the Rangers—the man is an absolute savage."

"That may be true," Sam laughed. "But I wasn't talking about him—I was talking about the Afterling."

Sam heard a sigh from the cot beside her. Destiny raised a hand; "Do we have blankets? I need a blanket—" Mansour leapt up from his task, but Sam shooed him away. "Stay away; the sight of you might traumatize her."

"But I'm not one of the men who hurt her—" Mansour protested.

"It doesn't matter," Sam hissed. "Men are men. Stay back." She grabbed a gray woolen coverlet and turned back to Destiny. "Hi Sweetie, here's a blanket. Are you cold?"

Eyes still closed, Destiny replied: "Oh no, I need it for someone else; someone's been hurt."

Sam gently questioned: "Who got hurt?" Destiny groaned and stretched.

"Oh, some girl I don't know—she got swamped by a bunch of rednecks and got messed up bad. She's going to cry when she wakes up."

At the sound of Destiny's voice, Kendra and Araceli came running up; they held her hands and patted her face: "Destiny..."

Sam waved to Rose. "Medic!" Sam called then pointed: "But not you, Marshal; you just watch from a distance, and we'll let you know if Rose needs you."

The Watcher nodded and stood to the side a ways; he understood more than they thought he did... around the room, the men put their heads down and went back to their tasks, quiet at the thought of what evils men do.

Rose made her way quickly to Destiny's cot; she checked vitals and did a quick patient assessment. She leaned over the cot and touched Destiny's brow. "Hello Destiny! I am Rose, your Medic. Does anything hurt?"

"Oh no, I am fine," Destiny said, her eyes still shut as if she were asleep. "But that other girl needs help." She clutched the woolen blanket tightly to her chest. "A whole brigade of men did terrible things to her, and that horrible Boss Chartreaux was with them. I had to save her. I'm sorry Sam—I told them where the stash was. I'm so sorry, Sam—they wouldn't stop hurting her unless I told them. They made me say it..."

"Other girl?" Sam looked confused. Concerned that Destiny was delusional again, Sam patted her arm, eyes welling with tears. "There was only you—and you are safe now."

"But it wasn't me—" Destiny's face was pained "I had to save her; they were hurting her so bad. Please forgive me."

From afar, the Watcher observed as Rose touched Destiny's forehead, then took hold of Destiny's hand. Glancing around the room, he saw the faces of the men working, trying to look as if they were not listening—but they were. The Watcher imagined he felt a familiar surge of warmth as the little Afterling closed her eyes, then let her breathing fall to the same rate as her patient's. He wondered if Destiny could feel Rose's warm energy the same way he did... somewhere within him, a pulse of light flickered as Rose spoke low and soft:

"You saved her; the men stopped hurting the girl, and everyone has been rescued. We are all safe now." Rose leaned in close. "You deserve to be saved."

Destiny breathed a trembling sigh. Rose laid her head against the broken woman's shoulder. "I am so glad you are safe. You are worth more than all the stashes in the world. But you must wake up, because there are people here who need you..."

Destiny opened her eyes. "Sam, where are you?"

"Right here, I'm right here, Baby. Don't be scared—you're out, you're free."

"Oh, Sam!" Destiny sobbed, "I thought they had gotten you too—" She reached up to touch her own face and felt carefully around her own soft gray eyes; they were open, fully dilated. "I can't see. I can't see you. I... I can't see anything!"

"Don't be afraid, Destiny." But Rose was afraid; "It's just the Datura; Boss Chartreaux must have used Datura on you to get you to talk to him. It's a powerful drug—the sap or smoke can cause temporary blindness." Worried, Rose muttered below her breath, "At least I hope it's only temporary..."

Suddenly sitting bolt upright, Destiny called out—"Where's Billy Dale? They've got Billy Dale—" A surge of energy shot through her, and Destiny came up off the cot, fighting. Her unseeing eyes had a wild light in them: "Get him out of there, they've got Billy Dale!" Her white lace cover was falling away from her pink, fuzzy skin as she rose from the cot with fearful strength; Kendra and Sam held her back.

Sam whispered "No, Destiny, they don't have Billy Dale—he's been dead for over fifty years..."

"He's dead? They killed Billy Dale?" Horrified, Destiny wailed. "They killed my Baby Brother?"

A groan of agony poured out of her and filled the tunnel. Struggling to keep Destiny calm, Rose put the palm of her hand on the back of Destiny's neck, near the base of the skull; Rose whispered;

"All is well, all is well—Billy Dale is safe. He is in a beautiful place, with the butterflies."

Another howl burst from Destiny's lips. "How can he be dead? I just saw him—we were fishing off the pier when Boss Chartreaux came to take us away!"

Kendra threw herself across her wailing friend to try and hold her down.

"She's hallucinating..." Shaken, Sam whispered to the Afterling: "How long will these effects last?"

Rose shook her head: "It could be hours. We have to calm her somehow."

Everyone was staring now. Mansour grabbed Sam's shoulder. "All Purgatory will be up here if anyone hears her. Get her quiet—tell her anything you have to just shut her up."

"Let me try." It was Araceli. "I can make something up sweet. I am good at that!"

From the other side of the room, Winston rolled his eyes and muttered.

"Later, Araceli. We've got no time for your fantasies!" Kendra wrestled a sobbing Destiny back onto the cot.

Just then, the crowd parted, and Evangelo stepped forward, his hat in his hand. "I am a Shepherd. Perhaps I could help?" Sam, holding Destiny's hands, turned to hiss at him:

"No—no men. You might scare her..."

Evangelo turned away, humbled. "I understand..."

At the sound of his voice, Destiny stopped wailing. Her chest heaved, heart hammering beneath her ribs. "The Man in White," she murmured. "I know your voice—I remember you."

A hush descended—"Yes Ma'am," Evangelo said gently. "What do you remember?"

"I just remember the Brigades-Men were there, and they were hurting the other girl. I tried to close my eyes, but I couldn't; I tried to stop them from hurting her, but I couldn't move. Then you appeared, and held my hand so I wouldn't be scared. You sang a song about being free. I..." Her blind, staring eyes had a dim light behind them. "I can't remember all the words you sang. But your skin was smooth and dark, your hair black and wavy, and your eyes were hazel green..." Destiny tried to sit up again, but Kendra held her down. "Then you disappeared." She coughed. "You came back with our friends, and you saved us. But what happened to the other girl?"

Evangelo appeared thoughtful. "What did the other girl look like, Ma'am?"

"I don't remember. I think she was about my same size, but I never saw her face. I think her face was covered. She had a red cap and a dress too..." her delicate pink mouth hung open for a moment. "Just like me. But she can't be me...I was watching, from somewhere nearby, with you, so it couldn't have been me."

Rose whispered to Sam: "Denial is a wonderful and terrible thing."

His hat still gripped in his hand, Evangelo stepped closer to Destiny's side and bent down slightly to speak to her His chiseled features reflected an unfathomable Peace, one he longed to share. "Rest assured, Ma'am, that everyone is safe and sound. We have rescued everyone who was in danger. Your little brother is safe in the Arms of the Almighty, and we've saved the girl; now you should rest. We are moving to a new location. You will be riding in a cart with your friends—the way will be dark and narrow, but don't be afraid, for I'll be with you."

"But I can't see you." Destiny held out her hand towards the sound of his voice: "So you are real, then? You aren't a dream?" She groped the air, trying to find him.

He reached out to take her soft pink hand in his rough brown one, the years of hard work and honest labor worn like a heavy glove. "I'm no dream, Ma'am. I must go, but I will check in again with you, soon. Ladies, if you'll excuse me..."

"Thank you, Marshal Evangelo." Sam took Destiny's hand from the little Ranger. Bowing slightly, Evangelo put his cowboy hat back on his head and walked back to where he had left the horses tied.

Sam's eyes followed him back to the staging area. "Maybe there really are some white knights left in the world..."

Mansour waved to Sam from over at the staging area. "It's time for you to give the command overview and mission briefing."

"Thank you." Sam signaled back to him, then turned to the Afterling. "Rose, I'm needed at the front—you, Araceli, and Kendra, please stay with Destiny to prepare for transport. I'll inform Marshal Azarian of my request for your services—if there's a problem, call me."

"Yes, Agent..." Rose looked confused for a moment. "Agent Ellison, what do we call you now? If Dominic is now a Judge, and the Ranger and Watcher are Marshals, how do we address you and the others on the Council?"

Sam looked thoughtful. "Since the other council members were too busy fighting over the terminology to actually resolve the issue during our last meeting, I'm going make an executive decision to go with 'Constable.' It fits the role as a high official with limited powers. Besides, I like the way it sounds." Pleased with her choice, Sam headed to the staging area to give her briefing.

"Okee Dokee, Constable Ellison—I'll stay with Destiny to monitor." Rose looked to Destiny to see Araceli whispering comforting words in the wounded woman's ear.

Destiny murmured: "Who was that man? Do I know him?"

"Oh yes, mi Hermana," Araceli's eyes were gleaming as she spoke. "He is your Lover. He is the one for whom you have waited. He is very shy, though, and you will have to be patient."

Calmed by Araceli's warm voice, Destiny sighed, then drifted off to sleep.

Kendra gave Araceli a sharp glance, and pulled her aside. "Araceli, that is an out and out lie." Kendra whispered. "She's never in her life picked a man who's got his act together... so good job if you get her to fall for it." Kendra gave a thumbs-up and smirked; Araceli looked pleased.

"But what about Boss Zhu? Shouldn't we at least mention him?" Rose worried about the Dead Man's spirit.

"Oh yes, poor Jack." Araceli pondered. "She doesn't seem to remember him right now. I asked her, and she doesn't seem to recall anything about that evening. You and I both know that she has terrible taste in men, so this is a chance to help her. I think the Marshal would be an excellent choice for Destiny. What do you think, Afterling?"

"Well, I shan't lie to poor Destiny because it wouldn't be right—"

Araceli broke in: "But it's not lying if it should be true."

Unsure about that sentiment, Rose pressed on: "Well, it certainly couldn't be any worse than his own truth. Evangelo is a lovely person, and he chooses very poorly with women, too! For almost fifty years, he's been hopelessly in love with a woman who's now trying to kill him." Confidential, Rose asked: "Is Destiny a nice person? I don't really know her yet, but she seems nice."

"Destiny isn't just nice—she's too nice. She is a complete fool for anyone who needs her," Kendra said bluntly.

"What an amazing miracle—Deva says Marshal Evangelo is too nice, too!" Rose purred. "It's as if they are made for each other. Of course, lying is a sin, but it wouldn't be lying anymore if it really did come true— so they should be encouraged to join."

Araceli clapped her slender hands. "Then it is settled!" Rose nodded with satisfaction, as Kendra approved the entire affair.

"I'm impressed Araceli. Your story-telling skills really came in handy this time..." Kendra muttered to herself: "What could possibly go wrong?"

Twinkling to herself, Araceli gently stroked brushed the pink, fuzzy plaques that stippled Destiny's bald, bruised head. "I will crochet her a new hat, and she will win his heart. She will be so happy!"

Rose chirped. "Excellent. Destiny is calm now, so let's prepare her cot as a gurney for patient transport—Ladies, let's each take a corner and we'll move her to the cart."

———————————

It was almost time to hit the trail.

Evangelo made ready the horses and parted out transport to the teams—Shadow would pull the cart, and Oro, Charger, and William would act as pack animals. Evangelo was teaming with Gunny to assign tack and gear to each animal, making sure none were overburdened.

The Watcher reached around and patted Oro's neck, then took the reins once again—he would lead Oro, for Horse and Rider were trained as a team, and together they would provide starboard security for the cart. Sampson was to drive the cart, and Mansour would take Charger as his pack animal for port side security.

Finishing up her briefing in the staging area, Sam rallied her troops:

"WildLand Express Team Six, Purgatory Detachment, the Cause is officially retired with all due Honor, and the safe room tunnel will be officially decommissioned. We are now the LoneStar Revolution. Agents and Specialists will retain their rank under this new system, and the rank of 'Hostess' will be active for one more mission."

Sam pointed to the exit: "Marshal Evangelo is riding point for this operation, so all trail commands will come from him. Medic Team, take your places at the head of the queue, followed by your security detail; Sampson at high noon, Marshal Azarian at three o'clock, me riding six on the tailgate, and Mansour at nine o'clock.

"The rest of you will follow up in a second group to hide our numbers: Goins, Wilcox, Mancini, following Constable Winston, with Sergeant Renfro covering tracks and shutting down operations. Our cover is Market Mayhem Weekend, our identity is the WildLand Express, and our destination is the WildLand Express Market encampment three miles east of this location. Team leaders, Constable Winston and Constable Mansour, please raise your hands, then check in Ring-2-Ring."

Araceli peeked out around Sam's shoulder: "Constable Winston?"

Packed out and ready to hike, Winston waved his new hat—a felt Aussie Outback Lourdes had matched to a leather blazer scavenged from Habib's goods. He smiled, and his incredibly white teeth made him look incredibly charming.

Araceli ducked back behind Sam. "He's Boss again?"

Sam nodded, preoccupied.

Taking their positions, the teams filed out of the Tunnel. The Medic Team loaded Destiny into the small cart—a high-sided affair with bench seats and a blanket spread across the top, Conestoga style to shield the Hostesses from view. Sampson sat at the buckboard, and Destiny was laid into the bed of the cart, the Hostesses sitting around her.

Decked out in his familiar finery, the Watcher was not handsome, but he was dashing. Between watching her patient and working with her team, the Afterling watched the Watcher from afar as he adjusted tack on Oro and engaged in various unheard discussions with the other Ring-Wearers on the team; Gunny, Winston, Sam, and Mansour.

Gesticulating as his lips moved, the others Ring-Wearers were speaking back to him, whispering to him in deferential tones. Even though he wasn't the tallest or largest Devil in the group, she couldn't help but notice how other Survivors' body language changed around the Watcher: their movements were guarded, with a grudging respect that bordered on fear.

The Watcher gave them reason: his coat billowing behind him, he was pacing like a caged predator, waiting to be loosed in the WildLands. But... *that face...*

Rose stared at the Watcher with repellent fascination. A gaping scar that ran from the left side of his forehead, down to the corner of his mouth seemed to writhe when his expression changed, as if the scar had a life of its own. Thick, cracked plates of skin covered his skull, hard and shiny, almost like fingernails, but harder; their blood-red, inflamed surfaces were laced with exposed veins of gold, subcutaneous fats oozing from between the crusty plates. Those scaly plates of skin were especially thick where they curled into horny overgrowth on top of his bald, ridged skull, and bearding his brutally heavy jaw. They gave a horned, demonic appearance to the hulking Survivor.

My Guardian Angel looks like a Devil. She shuddered, just slightly; she was growing used to it, but there were moments when she saw him from afar, and he truly seemed to be the terrifying DevilMan of Asuran bedtime tales. And now, that Devil was her Champion...

Men stepped aside as the Champion of the Asura passed through their midst.

Rose heard Wilcox talking to Mancini and Goins outside the cart: "Just damn... I never thought I'd actually see the Watcher in action. The way other people talked about him, I thought they were exaggerating."

Mancini piped up: "Nope, they're not exaggerating. Mansour said the Watcher flat butchered the Rangers that tortured Director—excuse me, Judge Santos and Marshal Evangelo. He didn't wait for orders—he just killed 'em as soon as the opportunity arose."

Goins spat. "Well, he ain't so tough. That little Afterling has him wrapped around her pinkie, and he doesn't even know it. When she's around, all he does is follow her like a tame gorilla. I bet a dollar he's meaner than a snake without her present, though."

So, they think he is tamed by me! Pleased, Rose mused about a finger-wrapped Watcher; it made her feel strangely giddy, keeping a dangerous and wild DevilMan to do her bidding.

"I know his kind," Gunny said in passing. "Don't let him fool you: he'll let some things go just to see how far they'll go—but he'll do that just so he can bring 'em back into line when they cross the line."

Perched in the cart, Rose puzzled over that last statement.

From around the corner he suddenly appeared, carrying Oskar. The Watcher knocked softly on the tailgate of the cart, then placed the cub next to the Afterling. Oskar flopped down between Araceli and Rose, chortling happily. The Watcher opened his ring chat:

#WATCHER: Oskar, stay with Rose. Rose, I will be walking right beside your position in the cart—keep this position, and do not come out until I call you. Understood?

Rose nodded solemnly.

#OSKAR ASv4.7: *Oskar stay good Rose friends*

The cub grinned ingratiatingly, and outstretched a paw before him:

#OSKAR ASv4.7: *Oskar treat give good Rose treat*

In awe of the Chupacabra's strides in communication, the Watcher couldn't help but chuckle. *Very well, you hungry little beggar.* Reaching into his pocket, the Watcher pulled out a slice of sweet potato. He held it out:

#WATCHER: Good Oskar, stay.

Oskar grasped the starchy slice with his prehensile digits; with his opposable thumb, he could curl his paw around objects, and manipulate items with his long digits and partially retractable claws. It seemed strange to see him take it with his umber paw, like a raccoon; Oskar's eyes sparkled—

#OSKAR ASv4.7: *good watcher good*

Then the Chupacabra tore off a small wedge of sweet potato and waved it in front of Rose. She smiled brightly at the cub. "Oh yes, Oskar, you have a treat! What a sweet boy..." he gave that goofy grin, then dropped it in Rose's lap.

At that, the entire cartload of Hostesses melted down. "What a precious pet!" Rose warbled, stroking Oskar's head. Araceli cooed and Kendra laughed out loud—"It's almost as if he's trying to train you!"

At the sound of Hostesses giggling, the other Agents rushed to see the cause of the commotion. They watched in fascination as Oskar gripped the sweet orangey slice in his paws, tearing away another wedge; he held it out to Araceli.

"Oh." Araceli said quietly, surprised. He tore off another, and handed it to Kendra, who took it with a suspicious look. "Thanks, I guess."

Amazed, the Watcher could only stare in utter disbelief along with the other Survivors. Even though they could not hear Oskar's conversation on the Ring, it was impossible to miss the intelligence of the Chupacabra's deliberate actions.

Evangelo whispered to the Watcher: "We have to tell the Director, um, I mean, Judge Santos—this is a monumental development. Are all Chupacabras this smart?"

Sassy put her front paws up on the tailgate and whined, begging for a treat. Sitting back on his haunches, monkey-like, the cub removed a fragment for the big dog, and she gulped it out of his proffered paw, her tail wagging.

Gunny grunted: "That's a right smart critter you've got here, Marshal. Polite, too."

Sam was now looking into the back of the wagon, an incredulous expression on her face, as the Chupacabra tore off a chunk of sweet potato and plopped it onto the sleeping Destiny's blanket. He turned to Sam, then flexed his empty paws, confused—the cub had run out of treats, unable to divide up the one sweet potato slice for the number of people in the cart.

Rose tapped him gently on his humped shoulder. "Here, take mine and share it." Snuffling, Oskar took it, and held it out to Sam: she simply gaped.

"Go ahead and take it," Rose smiled. "It's for you."

Sam blankly held out her hand, and Oskar put the sweet potato wedge in it. His long tongue uncoiled as he huffed: Rose laid her hand upon his head, and the cub licked his own paws.

A wave of pure terror descended on the Watcher. This was the innocence of Eden... Discomfited by the thought, the Watcher turned back to practical matters and pulled the last pear from his coat pocket. The ladies gasped with delight as the Watcher handed the beautiful golden fruit to Rose.

#*You need to eat as well.*

"Oh Saul!" Rose warbled. "Thank you—but the first bite should go to Oscar; after all, he did share all of his own treat."

Joy spread across the Chupacabra's face as he took the pear from Rose's hand. Overwhelmed by the scent of ripe pear, the Cub sank his sharp fangs into the sweet golden flesh, taking a tremendous bite. Succulent fruit clutched in his piercing claws, Oskar then handed the mangled pear back to Rose.

#OSKAR ASv4.7: *love*

"Marshal Azarian—" Rose gazed up at the sobered Watcher. "Thank you for sharing your food with us." She squeezed his hand, then snuggled down beside Oskar. "And thank you, too, sweet boy." Oskar curled up at Rose's side, with Araceli and Kendra petting him.

"Well, I'll be durned," said Sampson. "This little fella's got more skill with the Ladies than all the rest of us put together. He sure did take a chunk out of that pear, though."

Unnerved, Sam just shook her head and waved away the onlookers: "That's enough—back to your posts, and prepare to move out." Gray cowboy hat and bulky brown coat obscuring her identity, Sam and the Watcher stacked hay bales into the back of the cart to hide the Hostesses. Sitting on the tailgate, she pulled her shotgun across her lap and called: "Sergeant Renfro, close the WildLand Express Purgatory Post." Gunny walked back to the hidden door and looked one last time into the abandoned tunnel; his home of decades was cleaned out, except for one wooden chair left leaning against the stone walls.

Gunny nodded at it, satisfied—as the hope of dozens, the lifeline of Freedom, it had served the Cause well. Taking the last torch from just inside the tunnel, the old Soldier shut the charred wooden door and locked it, then pulled what was left of the singed greenbriar back into place to hide the entrance. Turning back to the assembled Teams, he swung the torch back and forth before the door, calling out: "The way is closed."

Sam hopped up onto the tailgate of the Cart and raised her fist: "Fenix Creciente—" and her compatriots all raised their hands in return. Facing

East, Sam called to her Rebels, and they answered, the Watcher leading the way as they surged forward into the darkening WildLand midnight:

"We Will Be Free!"

———◆———

Rose love. Ladies love.

Snuggled in Rose's arms, Oskar stretched out his back paws to touch his other Ladies, all sprawled in varying stages of sleep in their little covered cart. Upon her cot, Destiny moaned, and Oskar wrapped his long, prehensile tail around her protectively.

"Good doggie." Destiny murmured, patting the wiry curled tuft at the end of his tail. Oskar shuddered with happiness and sighed, drifting back to sleep.

Oskar was sleeping in a field of flowers, hugging his Mother, Rose. Rose was good and staying.

Good Rose. Rose stays.

Watcher came in and gave them all treats, and he was good.

Good Watcher. Give treats.

Ladies were everywhere, so many Ladies. Ladies as far as the eye could see, so warm and soft. He thrashed his tail and grinned, and they all kissed him.

Good Oskar. Oskar is a good boy.

VanJello suddenly appeared with Kitty and Domnick. Kitty purred, and there was no more blood. Oskar was happy.

Kitty friend.

They gave him a ring, and it hurt his tail. Oskar cried, then he ate them all, swallowing them whole. They tasted like sweet fluffy treats, especially Kitty.

Rose made a mad face. All the Ladies yelled:

BAD OSKAR NO NO MOUTH

Oskar trembled and put VanJello and Domnick and Kitty all back. They were slobbery, but the Ladies were happy. Watcher gave him a treat.

Good Oskar! No mouth.

SQIRLBOT came out of the Ring and danced.

#Would you like to run Wizard—Y/N?

Oskar got the input right on the very first try, and SQIRLBOT opened up all the files and taught him how to talk with the ring and speak out loud to everyone. Everyone gave him treats. Oskar hassled, happy with the world and everything in it.

Then he heard a whirr, far and away, It sounded like bees, but quieter. Oskar whimpered.

Suddenly Oskar was back in the pen in the cave. Gunny was cooking tasty rabbits. Sassy was outside the pen, sleeping.

A glowing ball of light came into the room. It was the ball that burned the cave door.

Oskar growled. It came closer, and Oskar could see it, just the way he saw the one in the cave—it was haloed in rainbows of light, made of jewels. It hovered near him... he sniffed it:

Then it exploded into blue lighting and fire, covering the earth in death and destruction. Fire ate the Ladies, and they were crying and calling Oskar but the pen kept him away. VanJello and Watcher ran up to it and they were covered in blue lightning and they were crying too then they turned into ashes and blew away. Sassy barked at the bad ball:

Fire came out, and Sassy was covered in flames, rolling and crying

Oskar tore at his bars, but he could not break free

Rose floated in on a cloud of pink light. She screamed as the ball caught her in a net of blue lightning. She held out her hands to Oskar, but the ball was dragging her away, out the cave door and into the dark woods. Oskar became savage, tearing at the bars, fighting to save her, but the bars held him in—

Rose cried, smearing a trail of silver tears behind her;

Oskar Oskar

Oskar

Oskar

"Oskar?"

Rose patted the Chupacabra cub. "Shhh Oskar, shhh—it was just a bad dream."

Oskar shivered, then reached out a paw to pat Rose's face, just to see if she was real. He made certain to be gentle just so he wouldn't accidentally claw her...

Rose stroked the wiry white curl atop his warty head. "Shh, sweet baby, it was just a dream. You are safe. I promise."

He looked around the cart to see his Ladies. Their lights were all the colors of the rainbow, beautiful flowers of radiance in the darkness. *Good Ladies. Stay.* Wrapping both forelegs around Rose's waist, Oskar snuggled in closer to her and took a deep breath. She smelled of Vanilla.

Good Rose. Rose love.
Past Sam on the tailgate of the cart, Oskar could see the Watcher

riding his Palomino, his golden light radiating through the darkness and into the tent. Comforted by the presence of his pack, Oskar sniffed the air once more, but didn't detect the sickly-sweet scent of gel fuel.

No bad balls... Oskar closed his eyes and drifted off, safe in the arms of Love.

High over the little cart and their band of Rebels, the stars shone big and bright, deep in the Heart of Texas. The sliver of golden Moon sailed over an ocean of fescue grass as they rolled on through the night—

Far and away, a faint whirr followed.

END - BOOK IV - WATCHER OF THE DAMNED

Addendum

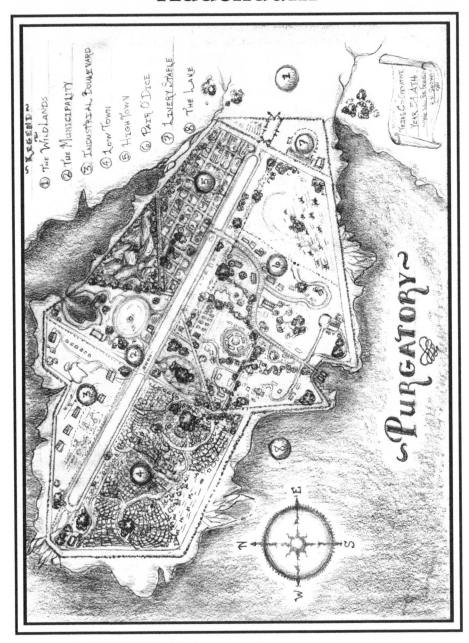

Once upon a time in pre-apocalyptic Texas, R.H. Snow fused experiences as a firefighting, storm- chasing bard to bring the sci-fi western series "WATCHER of the DAMNED" to gritty, exuberant life. Snow's post-apocalyptic Texas saga combines bleeding-edge action with heart and humor to create a Tall Texas Tale of life, love and liberty after pandemic world's end. This book is a paean to the Survivor in us all, and a tribute to all who fight to be free.

Seventh-generation Texan R. H. Snow is a singer, sketcher and gamer living with a family of other rescued humans and animals. Snow does not have a Chupacabra... yet.

Contributors:

David Snow—Weapons and self-defense
Roxanne Morris—Cover Art, character continuity edits
Daniel Snow—Worldbuilding and storyline development

Beta Reader:

Arthur DeVitalis
Arthur DeVitalis is a journalist, photographer, podcast host, writer, and gardener. Though Canadian-born, he got to Texas as soon as he could at the age of six. He graduated the University of Texas. Today, he writes for newspaper publications in Texas and Colorado. He resides in Whitney, Texas, with too many pooches.

Reference:

Dr. Mark Merriweather Vorderderbruggen—Foraging and native plants of Texas. The greatest living Authority on foraging in Texas! Author of "Idiot's Guide to Foraging" and creator of "Foraging Texas" Buy his bandana and know what your ancestors knew! www.foragingtexas.com

Design and Layout:

Cynthia Davis.
Cynthia Davis is a native Texan who has enjoyed a successful career as an artist in multiple mediums with an emphasis on graphic communications. She resides in Whitney, Texas.

Melanie Calahan, Self-Publishing Services
Melanie was born in Texas, and besides that, she is part owner in a company that specializes in editing, formatting, and cover design.

Publishing House:

Rosa De Oro, a Texas Publishing Company. Rosa de Oro is a boutique publishing house in Central Texas, specializing in Faith, hope and love - and the joy of all things Texas!